Books by
A. Claire Everward

The First

Oracle's Hunt
Oracle's Diplomacy

Blackwell: A Tangled Web

A. CLAIRE EVERWARD

ORACLE'S HUNT

BOOK ONE
IN THE ORACLE SERIES

Author & Listor

First published in 2017 by Author & Sister
www.authorandsister.net

Print ISBN 978-965-92584-0-6
eBook ISBN 978-965-92584-1-3

This one I wanted

Chapter One

The fire was scorching hot even this far away and even though it had started in the underground level of the low building, where it was still raging with unrelenting ferocity. Someone had wanted to make sure there would be no evidence, United States Federal Investigative Division Agent Donovan Pierce thought, contemplating the scene before him. Still, this wouldn't stop him. He'd worked with less in the past. He would find something, he always did. And this particular incident would warrant all kinds of resources. Unlimited, in fact. No one would take the destruction of the data storage facility for the major defense and security agencies worldwide lightly. After all, he was here, wasn't he? They didn't call him in unless a high-profile incident was involved.

He watched the firefighters try to approach the flames again. And fail, again. The order was given, and the robotic firecraft moved in through the dark sky above, hovered high over the blaze and sprayed down high-expansion fire-suppressing foam, which, sensing the heat of the fire below, hardened to create a shell that suffocated the flames within moments.

A good thing, in theory. Except that the reason the firefighters had attempted to avoid using it in the first place was that it would be hell to work with later. Digging through it would take time and effort, and Donovan wondered how much of the already scant evidence he had hoped to find would be destroyed by the foam itself.

From the corner of his eye, he saw his techs prepare their equipment. He turned to watch them working efficiently under the artificial peripheral lights that would be their only visual support on this heavily clouded night. The medical examiner's van stood beside them, and nearby the rest of his lead investigative team stood watching the crime scene with interest, talking among themselves. Other than them and the firefighters, no one else was here. The data center's backup security teams—and Donovan was still wondering how whoever had destroyed the place had managed to do this without their being alerted in time—had hermetically closed the area, and his people would not be disturbed. Not even representatives of the agencies that had a stake in this data center were here. At this point, he was given priority.

His eyes narrowed. This would be an interesting one. And there would be pressure, lots of it, from above. But then with his investigations there always was.

An official-looking sedan came to a halt beside the medical examiner's van. Donovan frowned when his boss got out of the car and looked at the scene with nothing short of horror. It had been a long time since he'd seen USFID director Leland White at the site of an investigation.

A lot of pressure indeed.

The sun had already broken through the clouds when his people were finally cleared to go to work, and it had begun to set again before they could move freely inside the building, or what was left of it. Nothing survived inside, it was all destroyed beyond recognition. Even the heart of the place, large enclosures especially designed to protect the data storage units within them, was almost entirely gone. And these enclosures were made of composite materials used for space and military applications, tested and retested to withstand extreme conditions. This wasn't a regular fire, Donovan thought as he absently stroked the twisted protective coating of the exterior walls with a gloved hand. It was potent enough to deliberately destroy materials meant not to be destroyed.

The way things were looking, there wouldn't be much evidence here, just as he'd expected. Already his techs informed him that the damage was too widespread, obviously intentionally so, to pinpoint exactly which data storage unit the perpetrators had been interested in. Which meant that whoever did this had wanted to make sure no one would be able to figure out what data they might have been after, not even from what agency.

Donovan frowned and scrutinized the destruction around him. Something, he needed something to get the ball rolling. Maybe the security footage he had already requested from the USOMP, the federal office in charge of maintaining and protecting this highly confidential data here in the United States, would shed some light on what happened. Apparently there had been very little human-based security on site, nothing remotely enough to stop whoever did this, as the bodies already being autopsied by USFID's medical examiner attested to. The data center, he had learned so far, was fully automated and was supervised from a designated monitoring station at the USOMP building not too far from here, in Washington, DC.

According to the supervisor there, the first sign of trouble had been that the security signal, including all its camera and sensor subcarriers, stopped abruptly. Which took everyone by surprise since the security system was supposed to be infallible and the signal could not malfunction, nor could it be cut or jammed, for the simple reason that no one was supposed to be able to track and lock on to it in the first place. Except that one of the three certainly seemed to have happened. The security guards on site could not be contacted, and by the time the backup security teams got there, the data center was already in flames and the perpetrators were gone. Which raised the next question—how could whoever did this get in, take what they wanted, and cause such widespread damage so quickly?

Funny thing was, his break in this investigation just might come from an oversight by the USOMP itself in setting up the security for this place, something it took some prodding by Donovan until the supervisor at the USOMP finally realized. Apparently the security system was replaced a little more than a year earlier, and a part of the old system, a number of cameras in the corners of the underground data storage level's ceiling, wasn't removed because of time constraints and because it didn't interfere with the new system. Even when the new system was upgraded, just a few months later, the old cameras remained where they were, always active. An added security measure, if superfluous, the supervisor had said, one that they had stopped watching since the new security system's visual components were so much more advanced.

Except, not so superfluous after all, as it turned out. Whoever had broken into the data center didn't know that these older cameras were still active and sending data to the USOMP mainframe, and so their signal, which was not the same as the new system's security signal, was apparently not targeted and remained undisturbed until the full force of the explosion hit. Which meant that at least some of them might have been operating when the break-in was still in progress.

Just then, Ben Lawson, one of his investigators, approached him with a small screen. "Sir, we just got that output from the USOMP. Not much, just one camera, but it might give us something."

Donovan took the screen from him and ran the footage, his people squinting at it around him. The video was a little jumpy, but it was clear enough. It showed two figures entering from the data storage level's only door just under the camera, both clad from head to toe in one-piece body suits. Their faces were completely covered, other than the eyes that had reflective covers over them, preventing recognition. Donovan watched intently while they moved in, certain, it seemed, that they were not being watched. One proceeded to take small devices from a bag he was holding and to place a device on top of each of the enclosures that held data storage units in them, each of which was assigned to a different agency— whatever these devices were, Donovan didn't have to look again at the ruins around him to know that none of them had survived the initial explosion. The fully-clad figure then walked beyond camera range, back in the direction both figures had originally entered from.

At the same time, the second figure walked without hesitation up to a specific unit, connected a small screen to one of the connection points in the composite grid protecting it, and proceeded to watch the series of frames that appeared in sequence on the screen. A preprogrammed hacking medium, Donovan wagered. Seconds later data began to run on the screen, and several moments after that small, scattered flashes appeared in it. Exactly two minutes after the video began, the figure disconnected the screen and followed the other perpetrator out. Forty-five seconds later the place erupted in a blinding flare and the footage was cut off.

"How do I go back in this? I want to see the screen that person's holding up close," Donovan said, and one of his techs adjusted the footage and replayed it. It zoomed in at a higher contrast, and Donovan could now see the data that the perpetrator had apparently downloaded, but it was all encrypted, so that nothing was intelligible. And then those flashes began to appear. Donovan touched the screen and slowed down the footage, and saw that each small flash was data being automatically deciphered, to show a word. It was only one word, always the same word that lit up whenever it appeared, one word that was the target of those who had made such an effort to procure this information, destroying everything on the way.

Just one word.

Oracle.

Chapter Two

"Damn," someone behind her grumbled in frustration. "Damn it, we're going to lose them."

Lara heard him, but disregarded both the words and the sentiment behind them, not allowing either to affect her. No, they won't be lost. Not today.

"Stand by," she said into the nearly invisible microphone of her headset. On the screen to the left, Captain Alexander Carr nodded once and remained quiet.

The silence in International Diplomacy, Security and Defense's dark Mission Command was increasingly deafening as the minutes ticked by. The officer who had moments earlier expressed his frustration shifted uneasily, prodding the security agent beside him to put a hand on his arm, not to calm but to silence him.

Oracle was working.

The eyes of the woman behind it never left the satellite, drone and ground feeds that raced in split views on the wall screen that stretched to both her sides. Oracle missed nothing and analyzed everything, filling the gaps where there were any, and there were.

For anyone else, it would be impossible to deduce from the flow of information anything useful enough to act efficiently under the circumstances.

Not for Oracle.

Breaking her silence, Lara spoke quietly into the headset mic. Her words were carried through individual earpieces to the military and civilian men and women seated behind her, where they would not disturb the mission.

"Move," was the only order Oracle relayed. In the center view, the satellite registered movement that was enhanced through real-time footage from the helmet cams of the soldiers on the ground, displayed in smaller views around the main satellite and drone views Lara had before her. It was how Oracle itself organized the split screen and chose the views, communicating changes and enhancements directly to the IDSD Missions mainframe. The system operators seated on both ends of the screen were ready to provide backup at all times, but until their assistance was called for, they would remain idle, staying out of the way.

Once Oracle stepped in, no one else interfered.

On the screen, the small troop moved according to Oracle's precise guidance, carrying its injured. In a fine dance of life and death, every step they took, covert and hushed, brought them dangerously close to their pursuers, who swarmed the area around them like angry wasps. Yet it did so at just the right timing, the right vector, for those Oracle was there to guide to stay out of the pursuers' reach.

The silence in Mission Command was tense, the only sound Oracle's occasional order, uttered quietly, succinctly, with confidence. Even as distance began to open between soldiers and pursuers, the silence held. Not until Oracle issued the command that had two stealth vertical takeoff and landing transports uncloak and drop to the ground to pick up the soldiers, then swoop back up, leaving their angry pursuers behind shouting and waving their weapons, did the cheers erupt behind Lara.

But not her, not yet. Only when the transports landed safely on the aircraft carrier, and Captain Carr confirmed that the soldiers were safe on board and that the casualties were in good shape and there were no fatalities, only then did Oracle power down, and Lara took off her headset and stepped back, let out a long breath, and shifted her focus back here, now.

She turned around. She never really knew what was going on around her when she did her job. Unless someone disturbed her, but that was, without fail, immediately dealt with by the IDSD security agents stationed in here precisely for this purpose. Looking around her now she saw the relief, heard the congratulatory exchange, but her own thoughts were still with the men whose safety she had just secured.

She turned back when Vice Admiral Francis A. Scholes, her direct boss, came up behind her and put his hand on her shoulder.

"Rare save. Good work, Lara," he said.

Lara acknowledged the compliment with a nod and allowed him to lead her to the door of Mission Command, everyone stopping to look, regarding her with respect, awe at times, even those who had seen her do this many times before. There were murmurs of congratulations, but she didn't heed these, never did. The soldiers she had just pulled away from the edge, they were the ones who should be congratulated, they were the ones who had held on, faced the real danger and survived, not her. Not even Oracle.

When they exited to the bright light of IDSD Missions' vast war room, she squinted, rubbed her tired eyes, and forced herself to focus. Before them stood an anxious Aiden, her aide, and Celia, the vice admiral's aide.

"Sir, ma'am." Celia spoke with some urgency. "Admiral Helios is in your office, sir. He's waiting for you, for both of you."

"Now?" Scholes said with evident surprise and a slight furrow of his brow. He would be concerned about her, Lara knew. Always was after missions, especially those such as this last one that had come her way unexpectedly, demanding her attention, near misses that didn't end up as such only because Oracle intervened at the last moment, but that consequently required every resource it had.

Still, even as he spoke, Scholes guided her toward his office, Celia and Aiden in tow. As the head of

IDSD in the United States, Admiral James Helios would be well aware of what was going on up here, and if he asked to see Lara now—more than that, if he took the trouble to come here from his own office at the IDSD Diplomacy building—there had to be a good reason.

Admiral Helios acknowledged them with a nod, his expression somber, and gestured for both aides to remain outside and close the door. In the office with him were two other men. One was Carl Ericsson, head of IDSD Security, and the other, a distinguished-looking man with graying hair and scrutinizing eyes, was introduced to Lara and Scholes as Paul Evans, the incoming director of the US Global Intelligence Agency.

"Director," Helios said, "I'd like you to meet my second-in-command and the head of IDSD Missions, Vice Admiral Frank Scholes, and this"—he turned to the woman who was the reason for this impromptu meeting—"is Lara Holsworth."

Evans looked at Lara with unveiled curiosity and extended a hand. "It's a pleasure to finally meet you in person, Ms. Holsworth," he said, and repeated with a nod, "Lara," when she corrected him.

Helios dived right in, focusing his attention on Lara and Scholes. "Last night, the alliance's US-based data center was broken into and destroyed. The only data storage unit targeted was IDSD's."

Scholes turned to Evans, who filled them in. He

then looked at Ericsson. "We on this?"

"As assisting only."

Scholes was about to protest when Evans intervened. "All agencies with a stake in the data center would only be assisting here, Admiral. I've got USFID investigating this, specifically SIRT, their unit that handles major investigations at this level, and its agent in charge, Donovan Pierce. He's the best. I've worked with him in the past."

Scholes turned to Helios, a frown on his face. He wasn't convinced. It was the IDSD unit that was the target, and yet they weren't the ones leading the investigation. And as if that wasn't enough, they were letting US Global Intelligence, the agency in charge of the USOMP that had been tasked with keeping the data center safe and yet allowed its destruction to happen in the first place, call the shots. "Jim? What's going on?"

Helios let out a heavy sigh. "Whoever did this appears to have been looking specifically for information about Oracle." He addressed Lara. "And we have a reason to believe they found something."

All eyes were now on Lara. She nodded slightly, composed, although a thousand and one scenarios were chasing through her mind.

"The thing is," Evans said, "they had to have been planning it for a while, and they're obviously clever. We don't know yet if they specifically hacked the IDSD unit because they knew what they were looking for—Oracle—is here, or if they hacked it only because IDSD is the crossroads for all international missions, in which case they have no real idea which agency this code name belongs to. On the off chance that they don't know who Oracle operates under, having the investigation be run by someone other than IDSD just might throw them off. Hell, we don't know if they even know for sure what Oracle is."

"And if they do? And know it's ours?" Scholes still wasn't convinced.

"That's why USFID-SIRT is on this. They're good and they're impartial, and Agent Pierce really is the best. The guy is relentless, he'll find them. And finding them is a priority here." Evans turned to Lara. "You will, of course, be updated at all times, and you have an open line directly to me."

"I'd like to speak to the investigator, this Agent Pierce," was her quiet response.

The others exchanged a look. "We would rather you didn't involve yourself in this, Lara," Helios said. "At this point we must maintain a strict separation between you and this investigation, and, to the extent possible, between you and Oracle, for your safety."

"I want to hear from him personally what he has found so far."

Scholes intervened. None of them knew Lara as well as he did, had for five years now, five years and countless missions he'd been through with her since she'd joined IDSD Missions. He understood that she needed to actually see the man on whom her and Oracle's safety would now depend, speak to him, lock on her only tangible connection to the investigation. Once she did this, if she felt she could trust him, trust his work, it might be easier for her to step aside and stay out of it. He hoped.

"Actually, I'd like to do that myself. Lara can be there while I speak to him," he said with finality.

Neither Evans nor Ericsson liked this unnecessary exposure, in their opinion, but Helios nodded, trusting his second-in-command. "Very well."

Donovan raised his head from the screen, on which yet another secure database turned up nothing about the only lead he had for now, Oracle, as a shadow fell across his desk. Director Leland White stood there, looking perturbed.

"And there we go," he said.

Donovan waited.

White sighed. "I just received a call from IDSD's missions arm here in the United States. They want to talk to us. To you, actually."

Donovan said nothing.

"Yes, I know." Exasperation seeped into White's voice. "But we knew they'd butt in. And since it's their data storage unit that was hacked, they are likely to be the target in this."

Donovan didn't confirm. As far as he was concerned, the investigation had barely begun, and he didn't know yet who the target was. Or anything else, for that matter. In his experience, investigations tended to have surprises hiding in the most unlikely places.

"Vice Admiral Scholes's aide says he would like a briefing about everything we've got so far. US Global Intelligence confirms we should comply."

"Vice admiral?"

White nodded emphatically. "Second-in-command of IDSD here and the head of IDSD Missions."

"A bit high, isn't it?"

"You should be used to it by now."

True, Donovan had to admit. But usually those ranks settled for bothering White, and this left him to do his job without interference, which was the way he liked it.

"Come on, let's get it over with," White said wearily. It had been a long day, and the days ahead would be full of pressure as he would do his best to keep it away from his best investigator. He was really looking forward to heading home.

The floor they were on, the one reserved for the SIRT unit in the USFID main building, was empty at this hour. Donovan had even sent home the investigators working with him on the data center break-in, not long after they'd returned from the crime scene. He preferred to have them back fresh the next day, especially since they'd been on duty since the middle of the previous night. He now transferred the call from the director's office to the main screen on the floor instead of to the one in his own office, and as

Scholes's aide transferred the call to his office at her end, the vice admiral appeared on the screen.

Donovan saw before him a black giant, close to sixty, he guessed, who looked too big even for the massive desk he was sitting behind. His rugged face was as stern as the intelligent eyes that bore into them through the screen. But Donovan saw the vice admiral only for the split second it took him to register the woman behind him. She was standing, leaning on the window sill, between photos that, he supposed, belonged to the owner of the office. Well dressed, he noticed. Good body, he couldn't help but see. Her hair pulled back. Seemingly relaxed, looking down, her arms folded across her chest. As the vice admiral began to speak she raised her head, and her eyes fell on Donovan's. And stayed there.

He knew *he* was mesmerized but he thought, it seemed to him at least, that she had a similar reaction to him, too. And then a veil fell over her eyes, and he could no longer read anything in them. He felt himself do the same as instinct kicked in and all the defenses he had so carefully built over the years came up. But behind them, behind this facade that would enable him to get through the videoconference until he could get away, get away and think, he could still feel it.

Her effect on him.

The vice admiral's booming voice broke through Donovan's thoughts. Dispensing with the formalities, he came to the point. "Director White, Special Agent in Charge Pierce, I assure you IDSD has no wish to interfere with your investigation. However, considering our involvement, we would appreciate it if you could walk us through what you have so far."

Smooth, Donovan thought. Rather appeasing, in fact, from a man who was in a position to walk all over them, if he wanted to. And, he noted, the vice admiral never bothered to introduce the woman behind him.

"Of course, Admiral," he said, and proceeded to walk them through every detail of the crime scene, from the moment the break-in was first discovered by the USOMP. The vice admiral never took his eyes off the screen, listening to every word and asking the occasional question. The woman simply stood there, her head lowered again, until Donovan brought up the photos taken at the scene, but he had a feeling she'd heard every word he said.

"How did you know it was IDSD's unit that was hacked?" the vice admiral asked.

Donovan explained and showed them the footage the USOMP's security camera had taken, carefully watching their reaction when he zoomed in on the encrypted data the perpetrators took, and on the single word that flashed throughout it.

Both remained impassive.

"This is all we have for now," White said. "But we have of course only begun to investigate. We'll update you when we have anything new."

The vice admiral nodded. "Director White, I am

well aware of USFID's excellent capabilities, as well as of your unprecedented record, Agent Pierce," he addressed Donovan. "I have every confidence in your ability to find whoever is behind this."

"Sir," Donovan interjected. He wasn't ready to end this interview just yet. "Could you tell me what Oracle is?"

The slightest hesitation. "I'm afraid I can't help you there."

"I've run a check on it, but I haven't been able to find anything, not even a mention of it. In fact, if I wouldn't know any better I would think it doesn't exist." Donovan paused. No reaction. "Either that," he continued, "or it's got the best security I've ever seen around it."

"But surely, Agent Pierce, an investigator of your caliber should be able to proceed even if you do not know what this . . . Oracle you said? . . . is. We would gladly provide you with any help you might need in tracking the perpetrators through their connection to IDSD, assuming there is such a connection, and I know for certain that all our peer agencies would be happy to do the same."

Any help except information about Oracle, apparently, Donovan thought.

"In fact," the vice admiral continued with practiced equanimity, "I will provide you with a liaison for this investigation, to facilitate your dealings with IDSD."

"And you?" Donovan asked, shifting his gaze to

the woman, who'd said nothing throughout the conversation, and who had lowered her eyes yet again. She seemed calm, no fidgeting, no reaction at all.

She raised her head and met his eyes, confirming again that she was, in fact, listening quite intently. "I'm sorry, Agent Pierce. I can't help you."

He nodded slightly. "Will you be the one working with us on this investigation?"

He thought he saw curiosity appear in her eyes. And something else, something he couldn't quite put his finger on. "No, I'm afraid that's not what I do," was all she said after a pause.

So what do you do? Donovan wondered as he let White and the vice admiral end the conversation amicably and, he thought, very diplomatically.

As soon as IDSD signed off Donovan turned to look at White, his eyebrows raised.

"Yes," White said before he managed to say anything. "Right? What was that all about? That's all they wanted? You provided all of this to their head of security—Ericsson, was it?—earlier, didn't you?"

"Including the photos and the footage." Which might explain why they had managed to remain impassive when viewing the footage. Would they have had time to watch and decrypt it? Why would they ask to hear it all again from him? And why the hell would they withhold information relevant to an investigation designed to help them?

"I have to say though, I'm not sure I wouldn't

have done the same if it were my agency that was attacked that way. Check us out, keep close to see what we've got. You think the other agencies won't do the same, even those that know us? You know what that data center was." White waved a hand. "But don't worry, I'll keep them away from you. You do your job, I'll do mine."

"Except for the liaison."

"Hey, you might as well get more information out of him than he'll want to give. You're good at that." White sighed and turned to leave. "Right, I vote to call it a day. Go home, Donovan. Before tomorrow."

"In a bit," Donovan replied, his mind on the call. And on that woman who wasn't introduced.

At IDSD Missions, Scholes turned to look at Lara. And waited. She was thinking, he knew. Processing. Finally, she moved her gaze from the dark screen to him. She looked tired. She'd kept up the adrenaline that always came with missions Oracle was involved in longer that she should have, to get through the meeting with Helios and the videoconference, but her exhaustion was finally showing. And now this, the data center break-in, its connection to Oracle, wouldn't let her alone. He was worried, the implications of all he'd heard so far already beginning to sink in. *Was* someone after Oracle? Could anyone actually get through it to the woman behind it? And what would they do? What did they want?

He didn't say any of this aloud. He needed to consider the situation and its potential implications, and he didn't want to do that in front of Lara, not now. But his face must have betrayed his concern—and the thoughts he was already having, of placing her under increased protection.

"Don't even think about it," she said. "I'm going home. To my home. It's secure enough."

He raised his eyebrows.

"Yes, I know how you think, Frank. We've been there before. And we don't know what's going on yet. Nor do whoever did this necessarily know what Oracle is, you saw the data they took." They both did, with Ericsson and Evans, after decrypting it—it was after all IDSD's encryption. "They're not likely to make the connection, not from that data."

But what if they had somehow gotten other information before? What was it that had led them to search for Oracle, of all things, in the first place? Still, Scholes didn't push the point. There would be no arguing with her, he still had too little to rely on for that. "I'll let it go," he said. "For now. But we'll be watching you more closely from now on."

He wasn't surprised at her sigh of irritation. Yes, she knew they would. And she hated that. Off work, she liked to be left alone. "Come on," he said and stood up to guide her out of his office. He gestured, and Aiden came forward hurriedly. "Make sure Ms. Holsworth goes home," he ordered before the aide even came to a stop.

Lara began to protest but he stood his ground. "You've been here for days, Lara. Go home, get some rest. It will all wait."

Once in the elevator that would take them from the top floor of IDSD Missions to the main lobby of the building, Lara allowed herself to lean back against the wall and close her eyes. She felt tired and tense, but then that was what it was usually like when Oracle was called in. Even in preplanned, far more gradual missions like the one that was completed earlier that day, successful as they were, she ended up exhausted, her mind having to constantly be alert, often being called to work at maximum capacity for days on end. And tense, always incredibly tense, as if her body was unable to unwind from the effort. But days like this, in which an unscheduled incident came in, a mission gone wrong that called on Oracle to help before it even had time to switch gears from a too-recently completed mission, took every resource she had left. Normally after a hectic day she would go to the pool and swim as many laps as it would take for her to feel better. But not tonight. She was too tired. The past days, this day, had taken everything she had.

And now this, the data center break-in. She tried to take her mind off it, at least for now. It needed a good looking at, and she was spent. She couldn't even begin to find the energy to think clearly anymore. Good. Maybe she could sleep. She had to sleep. When was the last time she had slept?

The elevator doors opened, and Aiden Jenor, Lara's loyal aide ever since she first came to IDSD, walked her to her car, which stood in its marked spot in the adjoining parking lot that was never even close to being empty.

"Go home," she told him as she was getting in, and frowned when he shook his head.

"I'll just wrap up some things first, ma'am."

"Go home, that's an order," she insisted. "You've been here as long as I have."

Yes, he thought as the car exited its spot and sped away. Except I actually got some sleep during that time while you spent all of it saving them in there. But he would obey the order, leave now and be there when she arrived the next day to wrap up the final details and debriefing of that day's missions and prepare to deal with whatever else came along.

Too tired to drive and smart enough to know this, Lara let the autonomous drive take over. It would select the route with the least traffic—not a problem at this hour—and would bring her quickly to the address preprogrammed into it as her home.

She watched the IDSD complex go by, then dark fields under heavy sky, thick woods in the distance, then into the city and to the Washington, DC, suburb she now lived in. She wasn't used to it yet, to these streets with their elegant two-story homes with lush gardens surrounding them, trees proud with age, a testimony to the longtime existence of this quiet neighborhood. Homes here had seen quite a few generations grow old. This was a place of families, traditions, love.

But not for her. She had known this place for many years, but had only lived here herself for a few weeks. And even these she spent working, her hectic job mandating that. As it did at times, it had taken her to Brussels, where IDSD had its headquarters, and the days since she had returned had been a tangle of missions that kept her for the most part away from here.

The car drove through silent streets, allowing her a look at the dark homes of neighbors she hadn't met yet. Finally, it stopped at the curb, and the door swung open. She got out and stood looking at the house, her house, lit now only by the front lawn lights the security system had turned on. Not quite home, not yet. Too new for that, new to her. Not her choice, either, not directly, anyway. Donna's choice, really. In fact, the way the house looked was Donna's doing, too, inside and out. At least that. Lara had had no inclination to take care of it herself, and Donna had a way of knowing what she needed.

She took out her briefcase and left the car at the curb, making a mental note to have it programmed to enter the garage by itself or at least go up the driveway. She walked up to the front door, and as she did the home security system recognized her and the door opened, letting her in and locking again behind her.

Inside, she walked through the short entry hall into the living room and crossed left to the stairs to the second floor, never stopping. The lights followed her, and in the absence of a vocal order from her they switched on at the default half-dim as she approached them, then off again as she walked on. Upstairs she ordered the bedroom lights to low dim, then touched the wall safe to open it and placed inside the laptop she took out of her briefcase, along with her IDSD ID. She closed the safe, left the briefcase where she had dropped it on the carpet, stripped and crawled into bed. She was asleep the instant her head hit the pillow, her sleep so deep not even the thoughts, the endless analysis that would normally churn through her mind after a mission, nor the knowledge that someone was now targeting Oracle, got through.

Donovan pushed his desk screen away in distaste and stood up. He stretched to remove the kinks from his neck, toned muscles flexing under the tailored shirt he was wearing. Nothing. Dead end. It was as if Oracle simply did not exist.

The restructuring some years earlier had brought together under a single umbrella, USFID, all powers and resources of what used to be the investigative departments of the different arms of the US military. And since he was the agent in charge of the Serious Incident Response Team, the extradepartmental team that handled all investigations involving more than one department, non-USFID or non-US agencies, and, in general, high-profile cases with a potential for sensitive entanglement, he was used to having access to wherever he wanted and getting whatever information he needed. On the rare occasion that clearance higher than his was required, White's authorization as USFID's director took care of it. And here he was, unable to retrieve anything, anything at all, about Oracle. Yet the short conversation with IDSD earlier had left him convinced that, whatever it was, it did in fact exist.

He wanted to know. He probably could, he had to admit, find whoever had broken into the data center without that knowledge, but having it would in all likelihood make things easier. It would certainly move them along faster.

And he just really wanted to know. He couldn't remember a case where one name, one code name, brought only silence from every person he talked to at every agency—and he'd contacted the ranks of officials that should have had access to such information—and drew a blank at every database, every query, every source he turned to. And the fact was that this word was all he had to work with for now. The techs would only begin to analyze the evidence collected in the morning, and they would still need to decrypt the data stolen by the perpetrators, what they could see in the break-in footage. This last thought made him frown. Normally he would simply ask, but it didn't look as if IDSD would be too happy to provide him with the decryption. Still, that didn't mean he wasn't going to try for it himself.

He walked out of his office and crossed the silent floor to the windows overlooking USFID Plaza and the Anacostia River beyond it, and stood staring at the darkness outside. He had meant to get out of here earlier, start fresh the next day, but the videoconference with IDSD had only raised more questions, and he had decided to stay, use the silence around him to organize his thoughts, see what he did and didn't have, and plan a course of action.

At least that was what he told himself. The fact was that he needed to regain his balance and this was the best place for him to do so. His job, that professional side of him that was always so focused, never failed him. He had worked hard to make it the center of his life, and it was the only thing he trusted he could always fall back on. Everything else came second. His personal life was carefully controlled, meticulously delimited, deliberately kept in check, and he never allowed himself to deviate from the lines he himself had set. Not that this was a problem. Nothing, or perhaps he should say no one, had ever held his interest long enough to endanger the boundaries he had so carefully laid around him. No one. No woman.

His mind went back to the videoconference. To *that* woman. Tried to figure it out. Figure himself out. Tried to tell himself he was obviously supposed to stay away from her, deal only with the liaison. Tried to remind himself that once the investigation was over, he wouldn't have to deal with IDSD at all.

Tried.

Up in the dark sky, a shooting star momentarily visible through a lull in the high clouds caught his attention. He followed its path, then turned away from the windows and left, grabbing his jacket from his office on the way to the elevator. He picked up his car in the mostly deserted parking lot and drove through empty streets, which served to settle him further.

As he arrived home he slowed down. The lights were on, though dimmed low, on the second floor of the house next to his. His brow furrowed. He'd known his new neighbor had moved in. The Howards, who had lived there long before he himself moved next door to them just a few years earlier, had moved out over a month before. Closer to two, he reminded himself. Donna, their granddaughter, had come up the week after with a flurry of helpers, including her ever-faithful spouse, Patty, and had pretty much taken the place apart. In what little he'd seen when he was home, she had had the house refurbished inside and out, sanded back to its original color and its windows and doors replaced with ones with a dark color that blended in nicely with the cozy work she had done inside. The kitchen and bathrooms had also been replaced in their entirety, and the wood and stone coating of the walls and floor and all carpeting renewed. It had taken her less than three weeks, which made him think she'd been intent on doing that for a while. She'd even gone so far as to hire a landscaper, who had replanted the entire yard around the house.

Giving him a proud tour of the renovated and refurnished house, Donna had enthusiastically told him that she was preparing it for her best friend, who was away for work or something of the sort, she hadn't volunteered any additional information. But the house in its present form raised his curiosity. Unlike the colorful and sparky decorator, the interior she had designed for her friend was warm, cozy, with gentle colors that spoke, it seemed to him, of someone who valued quiet. At least that's what the investigator in him told him. He'd meant to ask Donna more about her friend, he'd regretted having the Howards gone and the prospect of someone new disturbing the peace he'd managed to create around him did not appeal to him. But just then the movers had arrived, and Donna had run off to order them around. She didn't seem to need any help, with the small army she had around her, so he'd escaped to work.

That had been a couple of weeks earlier. He knew his new neighbor was called Lara, Donna had told him that much, but he had no last name for her, and there wasn't one on the door. He also knew that by now she had returned from wherever it was she had been to. But he hadn't seen her yet. A few times he'd seen a small woman, wiry and energetic, drive up in a small, tidy car, take out groceries and bring in the dry cleaning. A housekeeper was the logical conclusion.

Nothing except that, no sign of his neighbor. Until now, until the light in what he knew, knowing the house, was the window of the master bedroom. Still, his curiosity would not be satisfied that night. It was well past one o'clock in the morning. Not a time to call on a neighbor, even if she might still be awake.

He left his car outside his garage, as he always did, and went inside. The house was silent, giving him just what he wanted, the solitude he so carefully nurtured. It suited him just fine, and he wasn't about to allow anything to change it.

Certainly not a split second of . . . whatever it was earlier that night.

He pushed the thought away. It was easy to do that, with the practice he'd had. Focus on an investigation, find something else to think about.

Still, sleep took a while.

Chapter Three

The first rays of early autumn sunlight found Lara showered and refreshed, and holding a cup of her favorite coffee blend, in the middle of her new back yard. She contemplated it absently. Green dominated still, although the red, yellow and orange of the cold season were already showing. This is only the beginning, spring would bring with it a burst of lively colors, Donna had said. That too, the impeccably organized garden to the back and sides of the house, and the generous lawn at the front, was her best friend's doing. In the weeks Lara had been in Brussels, Donna had prepared this house, packed her apartment, moved her here and then unpacked, placing everything in its perfect place, of course. Lara had no idea how she had managed that in so little time, but then, that was Donna. She threw a look back at the house. She wasn't used to it yet, to this place, as her new home, but it had potential. And it was a house that had seen much kindness in its past, and that, she supposed, had to count for something.

A bird chirped close by, and she closed her eyes

and listened. The cool breeze, the fragrant air, the silence, even the feel of the warm coffee mug between her palms, soothed her. It was rare for her to feel such peace. Had been for too long now. But she had resigned herself to that. Too much had happened, too much for it to be fixed. For her to be fixed. But she had long resigned herself to that, too. She took a deep breath and returned her mind to the breeze, the air, the silence. It was good, this quiet moment. After all, she had a busy day ahead of her.

The thought brought back the data center break-in, and she contemplated the implications it could have for everyone involved.

And for her.

Dawn found Donovan walking out to his back yard. He liked that, going outside first thing in the morning to the start of a new day. It was calming, too often the only quiet moment in his day. He breathed in the clean air, that seam between summer and winter at its best. Gentle wind ruffled the leaves of the trees bordering his property and separating it from the park on its right and the Howards'—or what used to be the Howards'—property on its left. Their granddaughter had low shrubs planted among the trees, and these already boasted warm autumn colors, which she had said her friend would like. He walked over, the lively color drawing him.

And froze.

From where he stood, he had a clear view of the house next door. Its patio doors were open, and, even at this early hour, his new neighbor was standing outside.

The woman in Vice Admiral Scholes's office.

She was standing in the middle of her back yard, her eyes closed, her hands around a mug, it looked like, something hot, he thought, on this cool morning. He was able to have a better look at her now, and saw that his impression hadn't been mistaken. In fact, it was much clearer now that she was here, so real, before him. Unlike in the previous night, this morning she was rather more informally dressed in jeans, black boots that hugged her calves, a white blouse with the top button open, and a tailored black jacket. Her hair was down this time, not pulled back like it was then, but laying in soft waves against fair skin. A deep brown color, he saw, the sunlight playing with soft auburn hues. He mused at what was going through his mind, and realized the investigator in him was hanging on to details to protect the man.

At least, it was trying to. He wanted to move, leave, think. But all he could do was stay, watch, react. He finally managed to convince himself to take a step back when she opened her eyes, saw him, and he saw those intriguing hazel eyes that had mesmerized him that first time he had seen her—he thought he saw golden flecks dancing in them now—focus, surprised, then contemplate him.

Neither moved for an endless moment.

"You're *that* Donovan," she finally said.

"And you're Lara," he managed. "You didn't introduce yourself yesterday," he added, then realized
it wouldn't have made a difference, he still wouldn't
have made the connection.

And then silence.

"I have to..." she began, and pointed toward the
house.

"No, yes, me too. The investigation." He cursed
his clumsiness. He was always the one who rattled
people's equilibrium, and with women he never had
to work hard. And here she was, just by being there
she...

As if on cue, they both turned and walked away
from each other.

Minutes later he came out of the front door of
his house, in time to see a sleek dark red convertible
slide away from the curb in front of hers, accelerate
gracefully, and speed away. He stared at it, then
shook off whatever had come over him and got into
his car.

This couldn't be. But then, she should have figured
it out. Donna had said her neighbor's name was
Donovan. How many guys with that name were
there? How did she not make the connection?

She forced herself to stop fretting over it. She'd
been busy and tired, exhausted more like it, and her
neighbors in this new place she had moved to hadn't

been on her mind, not at all. And in the videoconference the previous evening, she hadn't really focused
on his name. It wasn't his name that had caught her
attention.

She had no idea what to do with this. Nor did
she want to think about what to do with this, not a
bit. The night before it had seemed easy. She hadn't
expected to ever have anything to do with Agent
Pierce—Agent *Donovan* Pierce, she thought ruefully
—again. After all, she had a direct line to anyone else
she chose to speak to if she wanted to know anything
about the investigation, which she was supposed to
stay away from anyway. As far as she was concerned,
she would never have to see him again.

Except he was her next-door neighbor. Her next-
door neighbor who just happened to be the lead
investigator in a case that had everything to do with
her. And she just happened to be keeping a key part
of his investigation from him.

No, she had no idea what to do here.

Okay. Okay, she thought. I don't have time for
this. There are more important things to deal with.
Safer things, a small voice whispered in her mind,
but she forced herself to disregard it and turned her
thoughts to the day ahead.

By the time she walked into her office, her mind
was focused on the tasks that required her attention.
The designated system identified her as soon as she
stepped in the door, and all wall screens activated,

the IDSD Missions symbol on them giving her the settling sense of anticipation, of things to be done, to be prepared for, that she needed now.

Aiden walked in and placed a cup of coffee on her desk. Her preferred blend, the same one she drank at home. "Anything you need from me, ma'am?" he asked.

As she did at least once every day, Lara sighed. She'd been trying to get rid of the "ma'am" since the first day he'd been assigned to her, and had so far been unsuccessful. It was his way and that was that. Even the fact that she was a civilian didn't help. She outranked him and was his direct boss, and that was how he was trained to address her. Both by the IDSD military and by his parents, he'd explained to her long ago.

"I'd like an update on the injured in yesterday's unscheduled JSOC mission," she said. "Do we have anything yet?"

"Only that they've been flown to the alliance military hospital in Brussels, and are still being treated and debriefed. I'll get an update."

"Good. JSOC will be sending the mission data, their original plan and its execution until Oracle was called in, I want to see what happened there." IDSD didn't even have to request it, the US Joint Special Operations Command had worked with Oracle before and had notified Lara directly that they would be sending her all info. This was standard procedure when a mission went wrong and required Oracle's unplanned intervention. It was a learning opportunity, and a chance to make changes that could be implemented next time, to perhaps avoid a mission going wrong, or at least tag similar missions to be brought earlier to Oracle's attention. The later a mission called for it to intervene, the riskier things were for the people involved, those who just might not be saved next time.

"In the meantime," Lara continued, "I'll be doing the Joint European Command post-mission analysis, see if I can wrap it up. Do I have anything else today?"

"Yes ma'am, a three o'clock meeting here on the Somalia mission. You should receive the preliminary African Independent Territory files on it sometime before that."

"I'd better get started, then." She picked up the coffee and turned her attention to the wall screens. Aiden turned to leave.

"Aiden, the data center break-in."

He turned back. He knew about it, of course. As her aide, he was privy to much of the confidential information she received.

"Did Vice Admiral Scholes assign USFID a liaison already?" she asked.

"Yes, last night. Nathan."

She nodded. Good. "I'd like to see him when he comes in."

He "ma'amed" her again and left. Behind him, the door to her inner office slid closed as she prepared to view the data, visuals and audios of the Joint European Command mission, which she had helped plan and Oracle had overseen the execution of just before the JSOC one had come in.

But the door opened again almost immediately, and she turned back to see Frank Scholes walk in. He sat down heavily on the soft recliner standing in the far corner, and it screamed in protest under the huge man's weight. He tried to find a comfortable way to stretch out his legs, clad in impeccably pressed uniform pants, then gave up, as he had countless times before.

"You should replace this thing, you know. Something bigger, I think. I'm sure I can get requisitions to find something that would fit. Hell, I'll go buy you something myself."

"This one fits me just fine," she said, as she always did, and would have smiled, as she always did, if not for the worry she saw on his face. "What's wrong, Frank?"

He squinted at her. "That Agent Pierce is still looking for Oracle."

She sat back in her chair.

"After you and I talked to him yesterday, he did some pretty intensive digging."

She didn't need to ask if he found anything. She already knew he wouldn't. "This worries you."

He leaned forward. "Lara, someone broke into one of the five most protected data centers in the world, knew to go to *our* data storage unit, and knew to look for information about Oracle. And now an agent on our own side is creating new traces of Oracle by doing this search. Yes, I'm worried."

"I thought Evans was going to instruct USFID's director to stop that line of investigation."

"Evans is the one who updated me about this. He only talked to Director White early this morning, after he was alerted to what Pierce was doing." He shook his head in distaste. "Of all things, this is what he had to lock on."

"Tell Nathan to give him whatever else he needs for his investigation, and he won't have a reason to go after Oracle."

"Unless he thinks he does. Or just wants to. Wouldn't you be curious, all things considered?"

She would. And no, she wouldn't let it go either if she were in Donovan Pierce's shoes. "Frank, worst case..."

"No, don't even think about it! I want you out of this!" He pointed an admonishing finger at her. "Keep out of this investigation and keep away from Agent Pierce. That's an order."

She tilted her head slightly. He never gave her orders, he knew better. It had been one of the conditions they'd agreed on when he recruited her to IDSD, as a civilian who could, in theory, walk away whenever she wanted.

Which was before she became what she was and the responsibility became too great—impossible, in fact—to walk away from.

He was ordering her now, which meant he really was worried about her. So she wasn't sure how he would take what she was about to tell him. "Yes, well, that might be a bit of a problem," she finally said. "The keeping away from Agent Pierce part."

He glared.

"He lives next door to me."

His jaw dropped.

"I moved, remember? When I came back from Brussels?"

He nodded. IDSD Security was required to approve the address.

"Well, apparently Agent Donovan Pierce lives in the house next to mine."

"How the hell did they miss that?"

"They probably didn't. Security would have seen a nice, safe neighborhood with a next-door neighbor who is basically a law enforcement officer. That's a good thing. In theory."

"The irony," he said, and let out a sigh of exasperation.

Lara didn't need him to tell her what he was thinking. He'd been bugging her to move into an IDSD secure complex, or any secure residential complex of any military or agency of her choosing, for that matter. They would all welcome her, he assured her again and again. But she consistently refused. So, as was the standard procedure for officials of her rank and security clearance, any place she lived in had to be cleared by IDSD's security division. And they would have loved the fact that a field-trained USFID agent was living right next door to her. Except, it just happened to be this one.

"Frank." She stood up, came around the desk, and sat on it. "I won't get involved in the investigation, and I will keep away from Agent Donovan Pierce."

And she would. Or at least, she would do her best to. The question, they both knew, was if the investigation and Pierce would stay away from her.

"But I want updates," she added.

He nodded his consent, although he didn't look entirely convinced. Or less worried.

As soon as the vice admiral left her office, Lara turned to her laptop, which she had placed on her desk. She accessed USFID's human resources management system and brought up Donovan Pierce's file. While the mainframe that controlled her office was registered as IDSD's, the laptop was untraceable, thanks to the security measures installed on it. Her accessing his file would not even be recorded.

His photo was the first thing that came up, his physical features listed beside it. Thirty-six, interestingly young for his position at USFID. But then, at a few months over thirty-one, the same could be said about her. Six feet two. Dark brown hair, nearly black. Thick, she remembered, and cut short. Stylish and kempt, but then she wasn't surprised. It fit with what she had seen earlier that morning, the way he was dressed, although he seemed casual about it. It came naturally, she thought, and wondered why her analytic thought processes even bothered to go that far. Blue-gray eyes, more blue than gray in the early morning light, she remembered that too. Her gaze moved to the photo. Even now his eyes seemed to bore into hers, even from this, a mere photo on a screen. But this way she could at least study him in leisure. The handsome face. Serious, something in him that would not accept defying. Something that would warn people not to come too close.

She switched to the federal service tab and had a look at his USFID record. His appraisals. Good. They confirmed what she thought, what she'd seen so far in his work. She noted his impressive field background, then skimmed over the no less impressive data in his military service tab. Which explained the confidence in his stance, the evident strength in him, she couldn't help but recall. Her eyes went to the other tabs and stopped on the personal data tab. She contemplated it thoughtfully.

And then closed his file without opening it.

Chapter Four

Donovan fumed. He stood before White's desk, his eyes narrowed.

White sighed. "I know, I'm sorry, but this time there's nothing I can do."

And that was something USFID's director was rarely forced to say.

Donovan couldn't believe it. He was called here as soon as White arrived, to be told that under US Global Intelligence's orders, backed by the one authority no one in the United States could say no to, he was to suspend all inquiries regarding Oracle. Otherwise, he was allowed to proceed with the investigation as he wished, and US Global Intelligence and IDSD would provide him with all the help he would need, at his request, as would, of course, all the other agencies whose data had been stored in the data center destroyed.

Anything he needed, except Oracle. Now where had he heard that before?

He strode out of White's office. This day was getting better and better. As he stepped off the elevator on the floor designated for USFID-SIRT, heads came up to look at him, but no one dared ask. Approaching his office, he saw Ben, whom he had designated to head the team assisting him in the investigation, standing beside the door, chatting with a short, heavyset, middle-aged man wearing a spotless IDSD uniform and a bright smile. The eyes that now turned to Donovan, though, were focused and intelligent.

He introduced himself as the IDSD interagency liaison for the investigation, Lieutenant Commander Nathan Walker. As he and Ben followed Donovan into his office and sat down, Nathan, as he insisted they call him, acknowledged that he had seen the investigation materials provided to IDSD the night before and that he would gladly help in any way he could.

"Yes," Donovan said in a matter-of-fact tone, settling behind his desk and smiling lightly. "I was assured by Vice Admiral Scholes and by Ms. Lara..." He faltered, as if trying to recall her name. Beside the liaison, Ben hid a smile.

"Holsworth?" Nathan helped.

Gotcha. "Yes, Ms. Lara Holsworth. I didn't catch what she does at IDSD. I understand Vice Admiral Scholes is the head of IDSD Missions, and Ms. Holsworth is...?"

"Vice Admiral Scholes is, in addition, the second-in-command of IDSD in the United States, and our assistance in your investigation, which is, of course, of a high importance, will therefore be overseen directly by him," Nathan said smoothly.

"And Ms. Holsworth?" Ben prodded, following the line Donovan started and feigning entering the information he was hearing in the investigation log he was holding, something that usually prompted people to be more helpful than they meant to.

"Ms. Holsworth just happened to be in the vice admiral's office at the time of your conversation. She is assigned elsewhere." Nathan's tone was pleasant, but there was a finality to his words.

Donovan motioned his investigator to let it go. He needed the lieutenant commander's cooperation, and alienating him would be a mistake. "I see," he said in a no less amiable tone. "Be that as it may, I was assured of IDSD's assistance."

"Yes, of course. That is why I'm here. I thought we might get things going, see what you need from me," the seasoned liaison reiterated.

And he was indeed forthcoming. He answered every question either Donovan or Ben had and made sure to note down the information they asked him to obtain. While USFID had access to all US-related sources, which included also access to certain levels of information from other territories in which the United States could exercise extraterritorial jurisdiction, IDSD did not fall under its jurisdiction in any way—in fact, it fell under no country's jurisdiction —and Donovan's access to it was highly limited. Which meant that the liaison's assistance was indispensable. And here, at least, IDSD seemed entirely genuine in its intention to advance the investigation by all means possible.

To Donovan's question, Nathan answered that like all other government entities that had partnered to construct the five secure data centers that were scattered worldwide, all with identical information stored in them, IDSD kept in the data storage unit assigned to it in each data center the plans for its facilities, complexes and bases, information about personnel at all ranks, including and exclusively personnel in sensitive positions, and highly confidential details about diplomatic and military operations and missions as well as about its diverse joint ventures with fellow agencies within the alliance. While some of these were also stored in the databases kept by IDSD in its various branches, there was certain information, Nathan emphasized, that was stored exclusively in the data centers due to its sensitivity. He was unable to provide much information about the destroyed data center itself, its structure and its security, but Donovan didn't need him to. US Global Intelligence was already arranging for the USOMP to provide him with that.

Nathan had fallen silent, and seemed to be deep in thought. The subject at hand was, clearly, close to his heart. "You need to understand," he said after a lengthy silence, "that other than the obvious for a formal body engaged in both diplomatic and military missions, IDSD's added sensitivity comes from the fact that as the only truly international entity, it has made possible unprecedented cooperation between regimes, and between military and diplomatic forces worldwide. And perhaps for the first time in human history there are solid indications, a true chance, that this cooperation could one day lead to the resolution of armed conflicts and a major shift to peaceful global synergy that would advance the eradication of that which ails humanity—poverty, ignorance and human rights abuse—and would allow it to invest its resources in progress."

He barely paused for a breath. "But there are still those who would do all they can to prevent this, both inside and outside the alliance of peaceful nations, an alliance your own country is an important part of. No matter how much humanity advances, there will always be those who value hate, destruction and ego over tolerance and progress."

Donovan listened without irony. In the past, what the liaison was saying would sound like a fantasy, nothing more than a dream. But the fact was that it was now a real possibility. After the accelerated spread of regional terrorism in the presence of a line of hesitant leaderships in what was until then the world's stronghold of freedom and democracy, alongside failures that had brought down with resonating finality the major economies and had sent the world into unprecedented uncertainty and dissent, and the wars that were then waged by too many who thought they could now rear their heads and take over their weaker peers on the way to cruel domination, the entire world had been plagued by violence, intolerance, hopelessness and distrust.

And that was when the Internationals rose— people worldwide who decided they would break away from their respective nationalities and create a new one, millions who had succeeded in convincing the International Court to announce a new citizenship, an international one. The way the world was conducting itself, as fragments whose sharp sides were aimed at one another, was simply not working, the Internationals had asserted. They would, they vowed, treat humanity as one, and find a way to unite it. No matter how long it took, they would convince all nations to work together toward a better future for everyone.

People ridiculed them, nations dismissed them, but the Internationals persisted. And they turned out to be as pragmatic as they were patient. Before long they had a governing council, boasted an efficient diplomatic corps and a highly-specialized military force, both under IDSD, and it wasn't long before they were mediating disputes worldwide. They were increasingly being heeded to and successfully bringing nations together, gradually and sturdily forming a global alliance. Their people had their own passports, and were soon accepted by all allied countries, and could live everywhere. The word International now had a whole new meaning. That had been several decades earlier, and there were now many who had already been born Internationals.

Except that those who chose to remain outside the alliance were increasingly worried they would disappear or be rendered powerless, or simply wanted their way to prevail. And they deemed the continued strengthening of the Internationals, their plans for global unity coming to life, to be a major hindrance. Donovan could see how the theft of information from IDSD's unit in the data center would worry all the allies, and not only the Internationals and IDSD.

"Fact is, the information stolen could be used to foil ongoing efforts to resolve disputes in unstable regions and to empower those living under authoritarian rule, who want to join the alliance." Nathan stopped and let out a short laugh. "Damn, I really don't mean to sound so formal. It's the job, you know. Look, some of the places we operate in aren't easy, to say the least, and getting people to have enough confidence in us to allow us, all of us, all the allies, to help them—and they do need our help— takes time and is a constant touch and go. Imagine if whoever broke into the data center misuse what they took, in effect intervening in what we do. And there are too many ways they could do that. Hell, IDSD and the alliance's reliability could be shaken. Perhaps irreparably so. And just think about it, what if this information is used to seek out and harm people critical to our activities? Think where this could lead. IDSD is no different than any other agency in this sense. We too have key personnel who are integral to what we do, and some of these people, whether they're in the field or not, must remain hidden. We've got to ensure their safety."

Donovan contemplated this. "Why did whoever they are choose to attack the data center here, in the United States? Why not one of the others?"

"Well, for one, only two are common knowledge, if you can call it that. The data center just outside Washington, DC, and the IDSD-based data center in Brussels. The other three serve as critical backups, and as such their locations are not easily known. As for why the United States and not Belgium . . ." He shrugged. "Our intelligence division assumes this might be because while Brussels is the home of our main diplomatic activity, the United States is where our main missions activity is."

And so, assuming IDSD was in fact the target in the data center break-in, and IDSD was assuming that, Nathan confirmed, whoever did it was probably after something that had to do with IDSD Missions, and they must be found before they proceeded with whatever it was they were planning to do with the information they stole.

"The thing is," Donovan said, thinking aloud, "it stands to reason that whoever carried out this specific attack was an independent group, not closely, if at all, affiliated with any of the rogue regimes that might oppose your work. A country as such would not likely pull something like this off—something that would most certainly lead to the unforgiving retaliation of the full force of the allies, especially the United States on whose soil the data center was attacked—without taking more than was actually taken. And for anyone who actually wants a war, there are easier and more obvious ways to start one. No, whoever did this was, I'm thinking, an unaffiliated group. And likely a highly sophisticated one that wants to remain hidden until it accomplishes its goals."

Which again raised the question of what those goals were. And the likelihood that this was an independent group bothered Donovan. It meant that its identity and goals would be more difficult to identify, especially since they were obviously intelligence-wary and didn't tend to brag about their actions, otherwise something would have been picked up by the allies' intelligence agencies during the time it must have taken to plan the break-in. And an independent group with the kind of capabilities that allowed it to break into and destroy one of the most secure data centers in the world, meant they had to have substantial resources, money and minds alike.

"There have been attacks on IDSD before, and on Internationals, just like there have been attacks on other nations' forces, diplomats, or citizens. But there has never been an incident such as this one," Nathan said. "We've already begun looking for possible perpetrators, but from what we can see so far, the existing organizations or militant groups that oppose the alliance or even only IDSD or the

Internationals aren't capable of pulling off something like this. And in any case, like you say, Agent Pierce, it doesn't stand to reason that they would go to the lengths of planning such a break-in. They have far easier ways to accomplish what they want."

"Not to mention noisier ones," Donovan added. And the fact was that the data center break-in and destruction was a substantial achievement, and yet whoever pulled it off did not advertise it, but rather was keeping it quiet. Which meant, Donovan said, that the break-in itself, an obvious and quite significant embarrassment to the allies, and to the United States in particular, since it took place on its turf, was not the goal. Which, considering the data stolen, pointed to the conclusion that whoever did this was not finished yet and wanted something IDSD had. Badly.

Nathan's gaze wavered, his eyes moving away from Donovan's for a moment. A split second only, but it was enough.

IDSD already knew that. And it obviously knew exactly what whoever broke into the data center was after. Oracle came to Donovan's mind. Anger flared, although he kept it carefully hidden. He didn't like anyone getting in the way of his investigation, and it seemed that for Oracle, whatever it was, that was what even IDSD itself, the target of the attack, was doing. And Donovan had certainly never encountered an incident where his own peers, US agencies that had an interest in having his investigation proceed

fast and without a hitch, stonewalled him so relentlessly on any one piece of information he tried to
obtain. What the hell was more important than finding whoever broke into the data center on US soil
and then destroyed it with such vengeance? And why
were the allies cooperating with IDSD on this?

"Right," he said with assumed calmness. "Well,
my people are also looking at militant groups and
past incidents, both through our own resources and
through the other agencies that had a stake in the
data center. What I need from you are specific
IDSD-related incidents that could be linked in some
way to this one. Theft of information at high encryption levels, high-profile data. Attacks on your
databases, cyber ones but also physical attacks that
would require a certain level of sophistication or
ones in which a highly potent fire or explosion was
involved. And, of course, the perpetrating groups.

"Or better yet, attacks where the perpetrators involved are unknown or"—he thought for a moment
—"see if you can find discrepancies. Unexplained
data glitches. Sensitive personnel with high-clearance
levels who died inexplicably, so that perhaps their
death was a disguised killing and they might have
disclosed to their killers sensitive information before
their death. That sort of thing. And not necessarily at
IDSD here, something might have taken place at
one of your other locations." He stood up. "That's
fishing a bit, I suppose, but once we know more
about what the break-in involved, I'll be able to

provide more focusing parameters."

The lieutenant commander acknowledged that he had understood, and promised to start sending information as soon as IDSD's intelligence and security divisions provided it.

As soon as the liaison entered the elevator, Donovan turned to Ben. At least there was one mystery he could solve right now.

"Get me everything you can find about Lara Holsworth. Start with her service file." He began to walk away and then, in an afterthought, turned back. "And don't summarize it. I want to see it all."

"But she's IDSD. And she's an International, isn't she?"

Donovan raised his eyebrows.

"Right," Ben said and went to work.

After only a few minutes he came to Donovan's office, looking perplexed. "I can't."

"Can't what, Ben? Get into her IDSD file? Try US Global Intelligence's database for all foreign officials. Hack it for all I care."

"No, I mean I can't even get the system to admit she has a file. I can't find anything about her."

Donovan stared. "What the hell are you talking about?"

"It's a zero-access name. So any information about it is only stored..."

"In the data centers. Like the one whose break-in we're investigating."

Ben nodded.

After the investigator left, Donovan considered for a while. He then ran a search for the license plate of the car he saw his neighbor leave in that morning. It was registered to IDSD. This made him pause. To the best of his knowledge, even IDSD didn't assign luxury convertibles to its staff. He then checked the house, but at this point he already knew he wouldn't find anything useful.

The house was listed as having been owned by the Howards until seven weeks earlier. It was then listed as having been sold and being under private ownership. And that was it. He thought a bit, then checked who the bills and any other formal mail were addressed to, expecting to find IDSD again. He was right. Except that this time, the address provided was that of IDSD's legal division in the United States. He shook his head. Another mystery. And this one he definitely wasn't about to let go of.

He had to know who she was.

Somewhere deep inside him a voice whispered that this had nothing to do with the investigation, that he didn't need to find answers to the questions he had about Lara Holsworth.

Except that he did. The same irritatingly persistent voice tried to ask him why, but he pushed it away.

He thought about calling the Howards to catch up, see how they were, maybe find what they knew about their granddaughter's friend. Then dismissed this, wondering why he was even considering going to such lengths. Tried hard to convince himself he was simply intrigued about his new neighbor who, on the one hand, was just a very real woman who lived in an elegant house that was decorated for her in quiet colors by her very colorful best friend, and who liked to enjoy the peace of her back yard with a cup of whatever it was that had been in that mug she was holding in the morning, and on the other hand, he, the senior investigator for the top investigative authority in the United States, couldn't find one bit of information about her. And, he reasoned, gladly finding a connection between his personal curiosity and his professional capacity, if she wasn't a part of this investigation, why was she in the vice admiral's office the night before? Why had she been privy to his findings from the data center break-in? Thinking about this only brought the discrepancies about her to light more sharply. He considered the Howards again. He didn't expect to learn anything substantial, but it would be a start.

Movement at his office door caught his attention. Reilly and Sidney, his two best techs, hovered excitedly, with Ben behind them.

"We know what burned down the data center," they said in unison.

"And we know how the bad guys found the security signal," Sidney said, and Reilly added quickly, "But the USOMP helped with that."

The floor assigned to Donovan's teams in the imposing USFID building was silent again, though not entirely empty. It wasn't nearly as late as the night before, and several of his investigators were busy wrapping up a previous case of his, which he'd all but completed when he was pulled to this one, and working on other open interagency investigations USFID-SIRT was in charge of. Donovan himself was sitting in his office, contemplating what he knew so far about the data center break-in, which was more than he had at the same time the day before. Not enough yet to reach a critical mass of information, which would allow him to begin to solve this case, but enough to bring in more of his past experience. He was also reviewing what the intelligence community knew about groups of the types he'd discussed with the IDSD liaison, unaffiliated groups that might have procured the type of expertise required to attack the data center and that had an interest in intra- or inter-nation disputes or some other reason to want the allies or specifically IDSD hurt. He was looking for the extraordinary, but so far was finding only the all too ordinary.

An incoming message took his eyes off the notes he was jotting down and to the desk screen. IDSD, Lieutenant Commander Nathan Walker. Donovan absently accessed the secure message, which included an orderly preliminary linked list of the information he had asked for. He began skimming through it— Ben's team would later canvass every bit of this data and provide him with the key points—but then stopped and returned to the top, then went through the list again, slowly this time.

Every single document, photo or footage was automatically tagged by every person who had seen it. This was standard procedure, all the more so where confidential data was involved. Normally tags would be hidden, unless whoever was viewing the data wanted to see them. But USFID's business was investigations, and so everyone who had clearance to see the data was automatically presented with the tags on the screen. Donovan had clearance.

And he could see each of the names of the people who had seen the data he had requested for his investigation, before he did.

The first two names were, logically, the heads of IDSD Intelligence and IDSD Security, the divisions that had prepared the information. The third was Vice Admiral Francis A. Scholes, head of IDSD Missions. The fifth was Lieutenant Commander Nathan Walker, IDSD-USFID liaison, as the last reviewer before the information was sent out.

The fourth was Lara Holsworth. No title, no rank, no position. Just Lara Holsworth.

Donovan fought a sudden urge to shoot someone.

He left his office a short while later. He couldn't focus, and thought he'd better get out of there before one of his people got in his way. He wasn't one to take his anger out on anyone, certainly not his own teams. He considered blowing off some steam in the training facility on the other side of USFID Plaza, but instead found himself getting into his car and heading home. Pulling into his driveway, he noticed the lights were on next door, on the ground floor. He started toward his own front door, then stopped and cursed under his breath. He skirted his house to the back and crossed to her back yard, then strode to the open patio doors. Unannounced and uncaring, he walked in.

She was sitting on a couch, sideways so that she was facing him. Her legs were comfortably tucked under her, and she was studying a small screen she was holding, her other hand toying absently with a glass of red wine. He had fully intended to stride in, but instead it took him a moment to realize he'd stopped at the open doors. She was just sitting there, relaxed, her dark hair down on her shoulders, the soft, white sweater she was wearing open at the neck. She was breathtaking wasn't the thought that passed through his mind but the feeling that pierced his entire body.

His anger flared, more powerful than before, his unwelcome reaction to her fueling it. She looked up and saw him, and her only visible reaction was a slight narrowing of her eyes.

"What the hell do you think you're doing?" he asked, not bothering to hide his rage.

She tilted her head slightly in question.

"You're interfering with my investigation."

"How so?" Her tone was infuriatingly indifferent.

"You have access to it, to what I'm doing, don't you? Today you saw the information I requested from IDSD before I did."

"I am IDSD."

"You're not part of my investigation."

"You run the investigation, you don't run IDSD. Or me, for that matter." She had no idea what made her react this way. And in principle, he was right. In fact, he should never have known she was being updated about his investigation. Nathan was a good liaison, but perhaps he was too cooperative.

Donovan was furious. He was also finding it hard to control himself, which made him even angrier. He was used to being the one in control, and yet this woman was looking at him calmly, not even a little intimidated by his anger, completely impervious to his role in this high-profile investigation that had as its focus the organization she worked for. And he could swear he saw a glitter of something, amusement he thought, in her eyes as she watched him.

"Stay away from my investigation," he said, his tone unmistakable, and turned to leave.

"Oh, by the way."

Her quiet voice had Donovan turn back to her. She was looking, maddeningly calm, not at him but at the wine in her glass, swirling it lightly, the light bouncing off the reddish liquid reflected in those entrancing hazel eyes.

"The next time you decide to try to run a check on me"—she met his eyes with ice that matched his —"don't."

He hoped he hid his surprise as well as he thought he did. How the hell did she know? Saying nothing, he walked away.

Behind him, the ice in Lara's eyes gave way to a worrying frown. From her own inquiries and from what she'd seen so far, he was relentless. And apparently the best.

She needed him to be.

Chapter Five

The old woman sighed and tried to think how she would go about doing this. Her frail form, hunched over a cane, began to bend down in a strenuous effort to retrieve the purse she had dropped. But she barely had a chance to move before someone picked it up and handed it to her, steadying her with his other hand. She looked up and smiled at the nice man who had helped her. "Why, thank you, young man."

"You're welcome," he said with a kind smile.

Nice accent, she thought. Not too pronounced, but she was curious about that sort of thing, so she noticed. Not local, no. She tried to place it as she wobbled off, content with the knowledge that there were still such nice young men around. British? No, that did not fit. South African? She knew someone from South Africa once. No, not that, either. She continued to contemplate this, then forgot all about it when she met her friend down the street, at the entrance to a small mall.

The man watched her leave, then turned away, the smile disappearing, coldness taking its place in his eyes. Appearance is everything, he thought as he walked toward an unobtrusive one-story warehouse. Whitewashed, the high fence around it new, the narrow strip of concrete between the structure and the fence cleanly swept. Appearance, he thought again as he crossed it and stepped through the door, is certainly everything.

The heavy door closed and locked behind him. Had it not been him, an automatic security system would have electrocuted him as soon as he touched it. But then, had it not been him, he never would have made it past the seemingly innocent fence. This warehouse, the former supply center for a robotics company, was now the temporary base of operations of his group. It was disguised as a pharmaceutical research lab, which ensured that it being off-limits to anyone who was not supposed to be there would not seem odd. He snickered to himself. How easy it was to hide his activity under the claim of the secrecy medical research required, even in this day and age, when a lack of transparency was frowned upon for security reasons.

He passed through an inner door and scrutinized his surroundings. Behind thick soundproof, bulletproof glass ahead, the room that took up most of the floor was packed with guns. Most of his men were there, too. Training. Preparing. The others were maintaining the vehicles in the parking area to his left. To his right stood the tracking and jamming technology, idle now until it was called to serve him again. But what interested him most was this, the sight immediately before him. The hacker and the massive computing capability at his fingertips.

Working to decipher the data he and his men had stolen.

"It's a bit too clever, I have to say," Bill Reese, the supervisor in charge of the data center's automated function and security at the USOMP, was saying. He shook his head, looking dejected. "This system was my pride and joy, and these guys reduced it to..." He tried in vain to find a word, then gave up. Donovan chalked it up to the fact that the man looked as if he hadn't slept since the break-in. Which was most likely the case.

They were standing in the data center's monitoring station, now ominously silent. Normally, Reese had explained, this room would be humming with incessant activity. "In the past weeks we even had reps here from the other data centers, and last week we were told our security system has been selected for implementation in all four of them. Now it won't even be implemented in this one, when it's rebuilt. I mean, look at us," he said, throwing his hands up in despair.

Donovan knew where the sentiment was coming from. After the break-in, US Global Intelligence, the USOMP's parent agency, clamped down on it, taking all data security protocols apart—all of them, not only the data center's—to ensure no other sensitive information was at risk. Which was why even he had to wait until now to get the access he needed for his investigation. And getting to the monitoring station on this floor, into the USOMP building, in fact, he'd had to go through a number of stern agents who were not about to trust anyone anytime soon.

He couldn't blame them. This incident, which had, as if matters weren't already bad enough, finally leaked out, put quite a dent in the confidence in the ability of the United States to protect both its and its allies' most sensitive data, and already there was talk about whether it should be the one to control the fifth data center, when it would be rebuilt. Which was why the pressure on USFID to solve this had now increased, in the hope that what the investigation found would take the hook out of the United States, or at least distribute the blame. And a quick resolution in itself would decisively show both the country's enemies and its allies that no one could get away with attacking it. But then again, that was why he was here, receiving unlimited access to the most sensitive information about the data center—and the USOMP's failure to protect it— even in the midst of a massive security shutdown.

He contemplated the idle equipment around him. "My techs tell me whoever did this took advantage of repairs." Sidney and Reilly had explained it, but he wanted to hear it again directly from Reese.

"Well, not exactly repairs, not technically. See,

this security system was entirely new, we had designed it especially for the data center. There is nothing like it. We originally installed it about . . . well, more than a year ago now. And the transition to it, from the previous system, was flawless. But after working with it for a while we decided to make some adjustments we'd made note of in the duration, and, while we're at it, upgrade. Upgrades are always done, you see, always something new, learned, improved. Especially with a new system like this one. But the work on it caused some hitches, and between these, the upgrade and the original adjustments we'd meant to do, we had signal disruptions between the mainframe here and the security system at the data center. It was just for a few weeks, not much longer, and we had the manned on-site security at the data center enhanced during that time. We were being careful, we . . ." His voice trailed off, and Donovan saw in his expression the renewed realization that careful had not been enough.

"See," Reese continued in a subdued voice, "what we think happened is that these people, whoever they are, had managed to identify not the data center security signal itself but the disruptions in it. They then locked on to these disruptions and piggybacked on our repair warning signal back here, and into the mainframe on which the security system works . . . worked, and then they rode the security signal back to the data center. Then they just waited, undetected. They now had both ends of the signal and a clear path between the heart of the data center's monitoring functions and its on-site security, and could jam the signal pretty much at will. They even managed to make it look like it was a malfunction."

He rubbed his eyes in despair. "Stupid, stupid mistake. I should have kept the old security system working alongside the new one during the first year, then all I would have had to do was take the new system entirely offline, make all the changes and simulation-test it, then bring it back online at once, without any disruption, just like we did when we originally made the replacement. Then these guys never would have had a duration of disrupted signals to lock on to. And even if not, even if they'd already been watching the data center and had managed to lock on our taking the system offline and then re-activating it, since it would have been a flawless signal it would have given us a good chance of seeing discrepancies caused by their actions and catching them. As it was, we didn't notice their disruptions among the ones we were causing. God, spend years creating a full-proof, self-sustaining data center and then its security system—our security system—of all things, is used to breach it."

Donovan didn't give a damn about the USOMP's mistakes. He needed one from the bad guys. "So they piggybacked on the warning repair signal. Can we use this to trace them?"

Reese shook his head. "Dead end by now. Traced

it back to a loop. In and out without anyone knowing. I wouldn't expect any different from whoever pulled this one on me."

The man's self-pity was wearing on Donovan. "If they were in the mainframe all this time, why use it just to break in? Why not simply hack into the data center?"

"Impossible. You see, the reason the data centers were designed as they were was to allow absolute data security and exclusive access by its owners. The alliance wanted something both tangible and that cannot be hacked—why do you think we didn't just use clouds? The idea was to create an impenetrable disaster-day thing, and since now we can cram huge amounts of data into relatively small maintenance-efficient structures in terms of fringe services— cooling and power and whatnot, you get it—the data centers idea was viable. And they're secure . . . I mean, were supposed to be . . ."

He must have seen the growing impatience on Donovan's face, because he stopped his flow of words and sighed, then got back to the point. "The mainframe isn't connected to the actual data, and neither are any of the security system's components. That's the way it's done in all these data centers. The only way the data itself can be accessed is either by connecting to the data storage unit itself, at the data center, and only the unit owners can do that— well, in theory at least—or remotely, via an undisclosed designated system, with a different system and encryption for each unit owner. And again, only the data owners can do that and have the access system and the encryption. So that, as in our case, to get into the IDSD unit in the data center these guys would have had to physically be at IDSD in order to access the designated system used to get into the data remotely, or to break into the data center and connect to the unit directly, which they did."

"And to do that," Donovan said, "all they had to do was halt the monitoring functions from inside the mainframe and then cut the security signal, virtually isolating the data center, quickly and theoretically without anyone being able to identify them."

"And while they were in our mainframe, they could also get all the information they needed about the data center's structure and peripheral security." Reese was looking more dejected by the minute.

Donovan nodded. Reese had already taken him through the data center's blueprints, the same ones the new security system had relied on, and that could of course be found in the monitoring station's mainframe, which was how the perpetrators got them.

That, apparently, had been the easy part. Scanning for, identifying and locking on the security system's signal might have taken a long time, Reese told him, depending on when whoever did this began staking out the data center. They didn't have to know beforehand that changes were being made to the security system—all they had to do was watch remotely and try to identify which of certain types of signals in the area was linked to the data center, and the signal disruptions happened to have given them the opportunity they needed to do that more easily than it would otherwise have been. Had the system not been adjusted, as Reese had explained, the signal would have remained smoothly undetectable, and it would have been longer before they managed to get in, if at all. There was nothing simple about the underlying technology of the security systems, both the new one and the previous one.

But as chance would have it, the security system was interfered with, the disruptions that allowed the security signal to be targeted did occur, and once the perpetrators were in, all they had to do was collect all they needed about the data center's security measures both from the very system built to protect it and from inside the USOMP's mainframe. And then, when the time came for their attack, all they had to do was disable the security system to avoid detection, which also meant disabling all locking mechanisms controlled by it, walk into the data center, as they had, take the data, and leave. It seemed that the bad guys had had luck on their side. Either that, or they were patient and had waited for the opportunity for a very long time. And that worried Donovan, since, more than anything, it attested to how serious these people were.

And then there was the manned security. The fully automated system didn't need people, it ran itself. The guards stationed at the data center were only there as an added measure, and for deterrence, if anyone managed to get near it. Of course, in theory, no one could get anywhere within six miles of the data center without additional security teams being immediately alerted. The same alert that never went off until the building began burning, thanks to the perpetrators who had disabled all security protocols from inside the USOMP's mainframe. And by the time someone noticed that the security system wasn't working and that the data center had been breached, the perpetrators had been in and out, taking what they wanted and killing the on-site guards on the way—this couldn't have been difficult, since these guards knew they were guarding an advanced-technology, high-security building no one was supposed to know the exact location of, let alone get within miles of. Despite their training, they seemed to have been unprepared for the attack.

Donovan's eyes narrowed. Senseless deaths. He hated senseless deaths.

Chapter Six

Lara turned her multitouch and holoplatform com-
bination desk off. She was sitting in her inner office,
the door closed. And while she could see to the outside of where she was sitting, either outside of the
window or outside to the floor her office was on,
no one could see in. Anyone outside could only see
tinted glass, which gave her complete privacy to view
confidential information. And everything that came
through this office was confidential. In fact, quite a
lot of it required the highest possible clearance.

A moment earlier the views on her desk showed
the faces of the special forces soldiers who would be
going on the Somalia mission. They were already en
route there, and would remain off-shore to the east
until it was time to go in, when conditions allowed it.
She leaned her elbows on the surface of the desk that
was now dark and silent, as were all the wall screens
around her, and rested her chin on tented fingers in
contemplation. She didn't only have in her mind the
faces of those who would, sometime in the coming
days, be risking their lives on this mission. She also
had every piece of information ever written in each

of their files, every word they had ever uttered and every smile or frown that had ever crossed their faces in a debriefing or profiling session, etched in her memory for use, if it came to that. If Oracle needed it. The human factor tended to be critical in these missions, and she had to be prepared for it.

But that wasn't all she had. This was a rescue mission. A few weeks earlier, the African Independent Territory, which had succeeded in cutting itself off from the rest of the continent that was still in an unending turmoil, and had been working with the alliance, had launched an unsanctioned intelligence mission in Somalia. It wasn't that they were strictly required to inform the alliance, since they weren't formally a part of it. But because they chose not to inform it, they couldn't benefit from its intelligence capabilities and its help—they never asked, and so no one knew to offer. As it turned out, while the mission had a useful goal, its implementation had been bad. All five men disappeared.

And so those five men, she'd also viewed their files. Knew everything about them. Their lives. Their families. Their kids. The women who loved them. For her, they were as much a part of the mission as their would-be rescuers were.

This time, for the rescue mission, the African Independent Territory had brought the alliance into the loop. None of the allies would play an active role in the mission—the special forces unit was also the African Independent Territory's—but they were asked to watch from afar and to assist in guidance and extrication if anything went wrong. And while the African Independent Territory didn't know about Oracle, the allies had asked IDSD that Oracle will be aware of what was going on, in case its help was needed. Of course, to protect it and hide its existence, Oracle would, if it came to that, provide support not directly to those in the field but to a Joint European Command field liaison who would be passing on its guidance. Oracle never spoke directly to anyone outside the alliance, and even within the alliance, it only spoke to carefully selected designations.

Lara rubbed her eyes. She knew everything that was currently available to know. About the initial mission, about the pending one. About the current situation in Somalia. And when the time came, if it did—no, it would, she was certain of that, knowing what she did—she would receive last minute information about allied forces deployed in the region. She was used to that, to the picture changing fast, faster as a mission approached, was initiated, then progressed until it ultimately reached its crisis point, which was when things went wrong. She would be ready when the time came. So would Oracle. It would have no helmet cams to watch this time, but satellites and high-altitude surveillance drones, these eyes in the sky, they would be Oracle's to choose, call on in this one. Close air support and a stealth transport, too. They would be at its disposal without delay, no questions asked, if it chose to deploy them.

Oracle would be ready to use any means it needed, take any action it needed. As always. As in each and every one of the missions it had been involved in, and in every one of the missions that had a chance of crossing its path in the coming days and weeks, and some of these were already a certainty.

As ready as could be, that is. After all, the whole point was that these missions had too high an uncertainty level. If—when—things went wrong, they tended to go irreparably wrong, and then Oracle was the last chance of bringing those out there back home alive. But Lara never thought about it before a mission.

After the mission, that was another story.

Her phone emitted a cheery jingle, snapping her out of her thoughts. Donna. They hadn't had a chance to meet since Lara returned from Brussels, except for Donna coming over to the house to show her around. Her initial thought was not to answer, just send Donna a message saying she would call her later, but then she reconsidered. Why not talk to her, maybe even meet her? Mission chased mission lately, and then there was the data center thing. A break might be . . .

"I can hear you thinking, you know."

Lara hadn't even realized she had touched the phone, prompting the call to be taken.

"I'm on my way to your place," Donna notified her cheerfully.

"I'm not at my place. I'm at work."

"So? We're going out. Patty is staying with baby Greg, and you and I are going to that new place on New Presidents' Quarter."

"A club," Lara grumbled.

"A nice club, from what I hear. Classy. Music, good food, bit of fun. Come on, you won't even have to change. Okay, you'll have to change. It's a club, for Christ's sake."

Lara laughed despite herself. She didn't have to argue with Donna, Donna did that so well on her own. They'd known each other since they were kids and had been best friends from day one. Donna knew how to get through to her. Especially when she felt that her friend was troubled or tired. That was probably why she chose the club, even though Lara wasn't the clubbing type. Nothing like a complete change of scenery. Some noise, some fun, and a way to get Lara out of the house for an evening.

She gave in. It wasn't as if she was likely to sleep anyway, certainly not well. Sleep didn't come easily around missions, and was rarely peaceful when it did. Spending time with Donna was a good alternative, even if it did involve going out to a place full of more people and probably a whole lot more noise than she would be comfortable with.

It took her just a few minutes to leave her office, and by the time her car was speeding to her new home she was up to enjoying a night out with her best friend.

Donovan rounded the last expanse of trees, and headed toward the familiar path that stretched before him. It would bring him to the street, and to his house. This was one of the main reasons he had chosen this house in the first place, some years earlier. He had still lived at that small apartment the military had made available to him back then, housing for singles, well maintained, comfortable enough, no hassle. He could afford more, a whole lot more, but he simply didn't care. He wasn't there much, so it didn't matter to him. But then things changed, his professional life took a different direction, and he was home more. It was time for something else.

He happened to come by here a couple of times and had noticed this house, right next to the park. It looked empty, although the neighborhood management maintained the yard around it, not allowing it to run down. He liked that, too. He'd driven through the quiet neighborhood, saw residents who didn't look at him with suspicion when he drove by but nodded, said hello, with the confidence of people who had roots there, who trusted this place, their life in it. Eventually he had asked about the house, not really intending anything, and was told the owners had passed, that their son had already bought a place of his own and was considering what to do with this, the house he grew up in. And so Donovan offered to buy it. The man had hesitated to sell to the single young man who turned up out of nowhere, but hearing what Donovan did for a living he understood. Military presence was prominent around there, and these people didn't always get a chance to start a family, settle down, lead the quiet life most others did. He came to like Donovan and appreciated his continued interest in the house. Thought that maybe the family would follow the home. Life did have a way of taking its course, he'd said.

And so Donovan became the house's new owner, but even after he did, and after the place was renovated, ready for him, it was almost a year before he moved in. Throughout that time, if he saw a piece of furniture he liked, an item he fancied, he would buy it. Take it to the house, find a place that suited it. This was also the case if he bought a book. A shirt. New running shoes. He would come here at times, instead of to his apartment, if he wanted some place more solitary, peaceful. Away from the connection to his work. Then he started running only here, in the park beyond this house. Gradually, he was here more than in his apartment. And when the move came, it was no longer a major leap. He'd already made this place his own.

He approached the house. He felt better now, more relaxed, always did after a long run. After his visit to the USOMP he'd come straight home, made it an early day. Relatively early, that is. He needed to clear his mind, and running helped. USFID had an expansive training facility complete with holo-interlaced gyms, weapons training ranges, tactical fitness training venues and multi-purpose simulation halls, but although he used these pretty much on a daily basis, running was the one thing he still did outdoors. It felt more real to him, more satisfying, running with the ground under his feet, dry in the summer or heavy with water or snow in the winter, the sun—or the gray, darkening skies, as was the case that day—peeking through leafy trees, the clean air rushing toward him.

He skirted the house, and passed between his black official USFID-issued car in the driveway and the trees that lined his property, separating it to an extent from the house next door. He continued beyond his garage, on the recently mowed lawn, and was about to turn right toward the back door when he heard the cheerful call.

"Hey, handsome!"

He swerved toward the voice, and a smile crossed his face. He liked Donna. Over the years he'd never seen her as anything but a kind woman, who judged no one and seemed to tolerate everyone. Some people took life's lessons at face value and became better for it, and Donna was a good example.

"You look colorful," he said, which was an understatement.

"Going clubbing and dragging your new neighbor with me kicking and screaming. Once she gets here, that is." Donna gave an exaggerated sigh, then shot him a sly look. "So, I hear you met her. Lara. I can't believe you two work together." Her grin was bright, infectious.

"We don't." His tone unwittingly took an edge that made her eyes widen with interest. He snuck a look around her, at the house next door.

"Yes, she seems to have some objection to you, too," Donna mused. In fact, it was a while since she'd seen in her friend such a powerful objection to anyone. But then, she was finding the irritation that had just now flared in this man's eyes new, too. "I meant, those places you two work in are working together on something, aren't they?"

"You know what she does?" Donovan turned his eyes back to her.

"We never really go there." Donna shrugged. "Someone's got to take that girl outside work, and that's me. So what did you do to her? Or better yet, what did she do to you?" She changed the subject without skipping a breath.

He was about to answer when Lara came outside, smiling. "There you are, Don," she said, and then saw the man standing beside her friend and faltered. She tried hard not to notice how he looked in that USFID T-shirt, and focused on mirroring the ice that enhanced the gray in his eyes at the sight of her.

Donna looked at the two of them alternately, her interest piquing. "So, neighbors." She tried. "Isn't that nice?"

"Spied on any investigations lately?" It came out before Donovan could stop it.

Recovering fast, Lara raised her eyebrows. "No, not really. Oh, except yours, of course. I hear you're making progress. Got the signal question figured out, have you?" Even as she made the hit, her eyes flickered to Donna, subtly warning Donovan that their mutual friend had no concrete knowledge about the investigation.

He understood and switched gears. "I'm beginning to think it might be a good idea to haul you in. See what you really know that you're hiding."

"Mmm. Yes, interesting idea indeed. Except you can't touch me. But then you already know that, don't you?" She was baiting, she knew, despite knowing he wouldn't hesitate to go through walls to get to her if he thought this would help with his investigation, and that the way things were going between them, he just might do so to spite her. Part of her warned, another marveled at the simple fact that she couldn't stop herself.

"Maybe. Maybe not. We'll see about that. In the meantime, however, I do seem to be developing an overwhelming desire to shoot you." His tone was conversational, a friendly smile on his face.

"Well, that would certainly delay your investigation. May I suggest you wait until you resolve it?" She spread her hands, her smile every bit as sweet as his. "I am, dear neighbor, here for the shooting later, any time you want."

Donna gaped. "Okay, enough. Enough, both of you. Truce!"

They both stepped back, realizing they were now toe to toe.

"What on earth is wrong with you two?" Donna looked at both of them in disbelief. They still hadn't taken their eyes off each other's, both clearly still aiming for a fight.

"Enough already! What's going on here? Look at you!" Her voice took on an edge of distress.

Lara heard it and immediately turned to her and put a gentle hand on her arm. "You're right, Don, I'm sorry. Don't worry about it." She spoke soothingly, throwing a subtle look at Donovan, and he gave the slightest nod and joined in.

"It's nothing, Donna. Just work issues," he said.

"Oh, so you don't want to kill each other?"

"You called a truce, remember?" Lara smiled, avoiding answering. Just then her phone beeped. She took a look at it and frowned. "Sorry, I have to take this."

Donovan watched her walk a distance away, noting the sudden alertness in her step.

"I didn't even consider the possibility that the two of you wouldn't get along. I made her come here because I thought it would be good for her. I hoped she would be happy here." Donna looked miserable.

Donovan frowned. "You made her come here? I don't understand."

She looked toward the house, shaking her head. "My grandparents wanted so much to move, you know that. This place was becoming too much for them. Solitary, too. They wanted to go somewhere nice, to that new retirement community all their friends have already moved to. But the difference in the prices . . ."

Donovan knew what she was talking about. He had even considered buying their house himself, so they could go, but then they told him it was already sold.

"Lara bought the house for the price it cost them to move there," Donna said.

It was his turn to gawk. That was one hell of a thing to do. Even with the status of this neighborhood, it still meant she'd paid a substantial premium for the house.

"Yes, exactly. They wouldn't let me do that, and with the baby . . . Lara lived next door to Patty and me, you know. Even before Greg was born she talked about moving out, giving us her apartment so that we could extend ours. She'd thought about getting a new place somewhere, a new apartment, maybe closer to IDSD, and then when this came up, when she bought the house—she wasn't going to live here, you know, she only wanted to help my grandparents and thought that she would rent it out or something, didn't really think about it. But I talked her into actually moving here. Even though it's a house, you know. She was pretty set on an apartment. Not a house. A house would be . . ."

"Lonely," Donovan completed the thought.

She looked at him, then back at the house, and he had that feeling again, of something being hidden from him. He glanced at where Lara was standing with her back to them, still on the phone.

"It's a good place, and it's nice and safe, and I know you, Donovan, you've been such a good neighbor to my grandparents and you're a good guy. I wanted someone to watch out for her."

Once again, her choice of words confounded him. From what he'd seen, Lara Holsworth didn't need anyone to watch out for her.

"She didn't even decide at the end, you know," Donna continued. "I knew she would be away for a few weeks, so I prepared everything, you saw it, and then I just packed and moved her things. Made it a surprise. I thought it would be good for her, the change."

"You're right, it is a good place to live in, that's why I moved here," he said, reacting to the worry that was so clear in her voice.

Donna looked up at him, unhappy.

"I promise I won't actually shoot her," he said, smiling, trying to cheer her up. "Just please don't tell her that."

"She is really an amazing woman." Donna said quietly, her eyes somber. "I wish you knew . . ."

She stopped as Lara came toward them, putting her phone away, her eyes thoughtful. She was a completely different person now, as if she'd slipped into some professional persona. Just like he did when he was on a case, Donovan realized, coming back from where Donna had taken him with her surprising revelations about Lara to who she was for him, and wondered about her again.

"Oh, please don't tell me you're being called in again," Donna said, and Donovan frowned.

"No," Lara answered her, acutely aware of the USFID investigator's presence there. "It was just an update. Come on, let's go before I change my mind," she prodded, using the opportunity to get away from him.

Waiting for Donna to give Donovan a friendly kiss, noting with some irritation how she whispered to him, "Behave!" and trying not to note with more than a little irritation at herself that quick, disarming smile meant for Donna that lit up his blue-gray eyes, she led her friend away.

Donovan's mind was on her as he walked into his living room and found a message in his home system voicemail. Jenny, a woman he'd been with on and off in the past months, had called to tell him she was in the city, if he wanted to hook up. Just the right diversion, he thought as he took out his phone and started saying her name to initiate a call. Then he stopped. Stared at the phone. Flung it at the sofa with a curse and walked away.

Chapter Seven

Sundays tended to be slow and provided a respite, to an extent, unless an investigation demanded his attention. And this particular investigation couldn't wait. But on this Sunday Donovan chose to work here, in his home. The quiet, the solitude, the rustle of trees in the cool autumn wind took away an edge that would be there if he worked in the sprawling, even if mostly empty USFID building, where, as the agent in charge of SIRT, he would be available for unwanted interruptions.

He would go farther away, if he could. If he didn't need to think about work, he would go even farther away. But today he had to balance the need for solitude with the need to think, to focus, to resolve. And this house, on this quiet day, in the autumn peace, would do.

The morning after a sleepless night—and he still wasn't ready to ask himself why—found him sitting at his kitchen nook table with a hot cup of coffee, contemplating his techs' reconstruction of the data center break-in based on what they'd deduced from the forensic evidence collected at the site and what he'd learned at the USOMP. If not for the footage they had from the on-site camera, the data center destruction could well have been mistaken for an accident, so that the theft of data from the IDSD unit would never have been discovered, and that had been the perpetrators' plan, Donovan knew now.

According to Reilly and Sidney, the perpetrators used the fire suppression system against itself, which would likely have been perceived as an internal malfunction. When the two techs broke the footage down into frames and analyzed them, they found that the devices the perpetrators had placed on the individual data storage units had initiated a high-intensity spark that created a plasma gas that, Reilly and Sidney had said, had to have been manipulated to increase its potency. The devices then seemingly communicated with one another, generating within a split second plasma arcs among themselves. The arcs reacted with the inert gas in the fire suppression system and with the electricity in the storage units, as enhancers, causing a devastating explosion and a high-temperature fire that fed on the composite materials enclosing the data storage units as well as on the protective coating on the inside of the data storage level's walls. The devices themselves were completely destroyed in the initial explosion, not leaving a trace, so that if not for the camera footage, their existence would never have been known.

Between that and how they had gotten into the security system and disabled it in the first place, in and out without anyone knowing, as Reese had said, clearly the perpetrators hadn't intended to be discovered. But then there were the dead guards. A mistake? Donovan now knew that the perpetrators probably wouldn't have known about them beforehand. This particular manned security, a secondary, even redundant feature, was not included in the USOMP mainframe's security protocol for the data center, unlike the backup specialist security teams, which the automated system was programmed to both manage and alert if they were required. And Donovan didn't think the perpetrators had been watching the data center in any way other than remotely scanning for the security system signal as they had. The kind of surveillance that would be required to watch the secure perimeter around the building, which was located in an uninhabited area, would have meant risking exposure, and these guys seemed to be too smart—and too technologically savvy—for that.

Still, anyone planning an operation of this sophistication would be prepared for the possibility of human presence, or it would be an oversight. And the perpetrators were obviously armed, so they must have been ready for at least some resistance—they were, after all, aware of the presence, even if offsite, of the backup security teams who could turn up at the data center if they suspected anything was wrong. So, once they did in fact encounter and kill the data center guards, why not dispose of them in the fire, instead of leaving them outside the fire perimeter with bullets in them? Why not make it all look like an accident? He himself could think of a couple of ways to do that.

So maybe these guys didn't care after all if it looked like an accident or not, and only wanted to ensure that no one would know which data storage unit was accessed and what data was stolen, information that could possibly point to their identity, not to mention their intentions. Either that, or they were arrogant enough to think no one could get to them.

The latter possibility worried him more than the former one. A lot more.

He leaned back. These guys were well trained— the data center guards had had designated training and would have been able to respond to an attack, even if they hadn't expected one, and yet there were no indications of any resistance by them at the scene. And the perpetrators had gotten through the outside perimeter six miles away covertly—even with the security system disabled, they had run the risk of the backup security teams' spotters identifying them. And yet they managed to avoid them. They were clearly highly capable technologically speaking, and patient—finding and locking on the security signal, using it to get both into the security system at the data center and the monitoring station mainframe at the USOMP, learning the security layout from inside while laying low, undetected for months, and carefully preparing, attacking, and disappearing again without a trace. Literally so—they had apparently been prepared for the ground conditions around the data center and had concealed their tracks, despite what would have been a hasty escape.

And they were determined. This wasn't something militant groups did, work so long, so hard on a single attack that wasn't even the final target, and then keep quiet, no boasting, no exploiting the windfall of their success.

This thing they were looking for, this Oracle, had to be one hell of a target. It looked too much like it was worth a lot to them. Worth everything to them.

So what the hell was it?

It wasn't the code name for an operation. What his techs told him didn't support that. They hadn't managed to decrypt the data, but they did analyze its underlying patterns, and these didn't conform to the mention of a single unrepeated operation, but rather to multiple instances in which this code name was used. It wasn't a person, either. People could be found using far easier methods, no matter how important or protected they were. No need for the elaborate measures these guys seemed to have taken. It obviously had some sort of connection to them, did something to make them react in the extreme way that they did. So, a weapon? A missile, a drone, or maybe even core technologies—control, communications. Intelligence, perhaps. But then it would have been better for the perpetrators to stay under the radar and steal it in the field, then reverse engineer it. Even some of the narrow AIs used for these applications were accessible in the field if the perpetrators could get their hands on the systems using them, and these guys were certainly resourceful enough to do so. Except what if they couldn't, what if there was no direct access to this AI in the field? And what if it did more than control a single system, a single application, what if its impact was more encompassing, more critical, more damaging perhaps to those who were now after it?

Artificial intelligence. Now that was an interesting thought. Donovan contemplated it for a long time, then played with a memory, something from a past incident he had not given much thought to at the time. Something that connected all too well with his current line of reasoning.

He got up, went over to his living room screen, and made a call. On the screen, a bleary-eyed Sidney appeared, her hair—pink that day, to match the shiny pink oversized pajamas she was wearing—sticking out to all sides. Behind her, the living room of the home she shared with Reilly, her identical twin sister, looked like it had been hit by a disoriented tornado. He tried hard not to smile. He needed her focused, and it looked like that would be difficult to achieve as it was.

Sidney yawned. She had obviously just awoken.

A perpetual early riser himself, not much of a sleeper in fact, Donovan still accepted that some people liked to sleep late on a Sunday. Especially since the sisters had diligently prepared the data center reconstruction for him most of the day and night before.

Sidney yawned again. "Sorry. Morning, sir. Boss. Agent Pierce. Donovan." She went through the range of choices fast, pretty much as she always did, then gave him a bright smile.

"Sorry to wake you, Sidney."

"Party," she reminisced dreamily. "Time?"

So it wasn't just the reconstruction. "Eleven. In the morning. I'll let you get back to sleep as soon as you explain something to me."

Her eyes opened wide.

"AI."

"Wrong twin. Reilly." And she turned her head, and shouted at the top of her lungs, "Reilly!"

Donovan had to make a real effort not to laugh. Which was tough, with those two.

A yellow-haired, bright yellow pajamas-clad Reilly shuffled into the room. So they weren't in sync that day. It was a bet that ran in the SIRT unit, pretty much daily.

"What?" Reilly answered, then saw him on the screen. "Morning, sir. Boss. Agent Pierce. Donovan," she said distractedly, then turned back to her sister. "What?"

"AI," Sidney said profoundly.

Reilly squinted at Donovan. He briefly explained the type of artificial intelligence he had in mind.

"Would it be able to run a field mission?" he then asked.

"No. Well, not completely. Not even close. No."

"Why?"

"These things can do a lot. Organize and analyze data. Run scenarios and probabilities and provide recommendations. The control side of the mission, they can run drones and identify targets or deploy missiles in response to a threat and stuff, yeah, they can do that, be autonomous to an extent. We've got AIs running military aircraft and robotic support for field combat, that too. But they have crucial limits. They can only deduce and decide to a limited extent, and they can only operate within limited uncertainties and even less so in the presence of incomplete information. No matter how advanced we've made them, they still need to be preprogrammed and pretrained, and given boundaries within which they would act."

She had obviously thought the concept through. "We people can reason and guess and use our intuition and be creative, unlimitedly so. We can go the extra mile, out of the box. We can think like only we can, that's the point. We can make split second decisions in the presence of unexpected occurrences based on experience, gut feeling, and a lot of stuff that we've accumulated in our mind. We can see the exception to the rule and act on it."

"And we can feel," Sidney chipped in and received a glare from her sister.

But Donovan was interested. "That's important?"

"Sure." Reilly was still glaring at Sidney, although the words were aimed at Donovan. "We've got machines out there, but we've got people, too. People who walk into danger. People who could be injured, who might have a peer, a friend, injured or dead. Who might find themselves under attack or need to attack targets that are not straightforward, like ones in too close a proximity to a civilian population. A zillion scenarios. The human factor here is significant. A computer still can't understand that, it can't assimilate that fully into its set of considerations and deductions, into a decision what and how to do next. Plus, a computer isn't able to talk to soldiers on the emotional level. It can't . . . talk people down. Or up."

"So artificial intelligence can't replace a person."

"No. Not yet. Not for decades. We've come a long way but an AI that can also truly emulate human capabilities—and be trusted to do so correctly and infallibly—is still a dream, even today. It's still an unscalable wall, very much so. You invariably need humans beside it."

Donovan considered this. "Who?"

"Sorry?"

"What human?"

"Let's see. Running a mission, right? Military? Experienced combat soldiers, someone who actually commanded others in the field would probably be best. Strategists, tacticians. People who can run the show as it happens. Know the available technologies and weapons. Deal with the soldiers, deal with the enemy, deal with uncertainties. Them and more."

"No. Too many." It didn't fit in with the theory he was still constructing in his mind.

"Well, theoretically. . ."

"Theoretically?" Donovan prodded.

"Human-AI interface. Like, really put the human alongside the computer. Link them. The AI brings the, well, AI capabilities, the human brings the human factor, and any other information can be fed in from outside as either of the two needs it. Problem solved."

"That's one hell of a human."

"On more than one level. I mean, the knowledge, the capabilities—the ability to receive multiple types of information from multiple sources at multiple instances within a limited amount of time, the ability to absorb and understand it all, integrate it all, to react fast enough, to understand the AI's side of it in order to be able to intervene if the AI did something that would interfere with the ability of the humans in the field to act. And too many other factors. Oh, and the effort. The emotional strength, the physical durability."

"Physical durability?"

"You try doing that for hours and hours. Alone. And with that responsibility on your shoulders. Geez.

I'd die." She shrugged. "And it still wouldn't be perfect, anyway."

"Why not?"

"Computer limitations. Human limitations. Interface limitations. Uncertainties due to missing data, unknown parameters, incomplete intelligence info. Even a person can only deduce up to a point, deal with uncertainties up to a point. Plus," she said, "no one can see what's not before them, and no one can predict the future."

True, Donovan thought.

"Basically, the optimal mission coordinator would be required to make the optimal decision at the optimal point and to have whoever or whatever is in the field make the optimal move at the optimal time, all in a complex situation and in suboptimal conditions. It can't be done. We've got mission coordinators working in real time in groups with AIs as data, scenario and even field support and it's still not enough," Reilly said.

Donovan frowned. Perhaps not, but what he was thinking of came quite a long way toward that.

"But anyway, what you're asking about, that's a dream. We're not even close. Otherwise, we'd know about it, wouldn't we?"

"Yes," Donovan said thoughtfully. "I suppose we would know about it."

He was about to end the call and let his two brilliant techs go back to sleep when something occurred to him.

"Wait. Everything you just told me, Reilly. You didn't need to think about it. Not much."

"Well, yeah. People talk about it, about advanced AIs. What they could do."

"People?"

"Her kind of people," Sidney said. This time she received not a glare but a quick hug for the pride in her voice.

"Yeah. You know, in conferences, virtual forums, academic and private sector and military research groups. It's a big thing," Reilly explained.

"So it's an existing aspiration. Something that is being seriously discussed out there."

"Right on."

Donovan's eyes narrowed.

He ended the call and made another quick one, this time to confirm something that would support his newfound theory. He then went back to the kitchen nook and sat down. Okay. Say Oracle was a technology. Artificial intelligence, for argument's sake, human-machine link or not. How did the perpetrators learn about it? He himself couldn't find anything about it, couldn't even confirm its existence. So how did they? And how did they know where to look for it? And how the hell did they have the encryption key for the data they stole?

And why weren't they attacking yet? If they had the information they had come for, and if their target was IDSD or Oracle or both, why hadn't they done anything yet? This part worried him most.

Every day that passed since the data center break-in increased the imminence of an attack.

This raised again the question of the perpetrators' silence. The fact was that all the intelligence agencies—and all allies were cooperating in this— had been desperately looking for chatter, and there was none. Not even now, days later. No one was talking about the destruction of the data center, no one was updating partners or peer groups, coordinating plans, nothing. So what did that mean? That they didn't get what they wanted after all? Did they need time to decrypt the data—was it possible they didn't have the full decryption capabilities? But they obviously had enough to know where to go and what data to steal. Which brought Donovan back to the burning question that could be his key to identifying them—how and when did they get that information in the first place?

Still, he had a lead of sorts now, something tangible to focus on. The data center security breach itself, the way it was done, indicated that the perpetrators were already on this almost a year earlier, at least, certainly at the time the data center's new security system was upgraded. So whatever gave them the information they needed to know to search for Oracle and to do so in the data center must have happened before that. The encryption, whenever they had put their hands on it, would have taken a while to break, which could further pinpoint when whatever it was that had alerted them to Oracle had happened. When they gave him the data center reconstruction, Reilly and Sidney had told him that they themselves couldn't decrypt the data seen in the footage immediately. They would need a hell of a lot more time than he had. Which meant that the perpetrators would have needed at least that much time, too. Unless someone had given them the key, which was also a possibility.

He had a lot more information now, but he still needed to put all the pieces together. He needed more. He needed . . .

He sat back, deep in thought, his eyes on the tall windows that dominated this corner of the house. Outside the sun was high up, autumn allowing summer a last peek at the world below. His gaze moved to the open door. Abruptly, he got up and strode out.

Chapter Eight

The house next door was silent, but the patio doors were open wide, and he knew she was home. This time he slowed down as he approached. She was sitting on the same couch he'd seen her sitting on the last time he was there, a patch of sun that had found its way in through the open doors on her. She was deeply absorbed in the screen she was holding, so he had a chance to watch her quietly.

And he did.

A flock of migrating birds screeched high above as they took off from the park, and he glanced up at them, their graceful forms dancing in the sky. When his gaze returned to her, she was watching him.

He approached her slowly. "Truce," he said in a quiet voice, using Donna's way of disarming their recent clash. "Truce, for just a few minutes," he repeated.

She considered him, then gave a small nod. He stepped in and took in his surroundings. The house looked lived in now. She'd made it hers, he saw. A cozy-looking throw in red tones, loosely folded, was draped on the back of a soft cream sofa. A scenic painting of a forested mountain lake under clear blue skies adorned a wall, and one of sparse autumn clouds above a spring winding gently through a wooded meadow caught his eye on another. And the mantel of the fireplace set in a stone accent wall of deep, warm colors, it now had photos lined up on it. He could see one from where he stood, and it struck him. She was much younger in it, smiling happily into the camera, her arm around an equally carefree young Donna. Something that wasn't there anymore, it seemed to him. Something in the eyes of the girl in the photo that was no longer in the eyes of the woman who was right there in the room with him.

He focused. He only had moments, that was his truce. He turned back to the real woman, still sitting on the couch but not relaxed anymore. He read the slight tension in her shoulders. It wasn't there when she'd been watching him before he came in. It appeared just now, when he'd looked toward the photos, and as he stood not far from her. He considered this, then moved physically farther away from her and from the photos that gave a peek into her life to the other side of the sofa, and put his hands on it, leaning. Experimenting.

The tension in her relaxed somewhat. Distance. She wanted distance from him. And she wanted to distance him from what was personal to her. Something Donna had said to him the other day played at the edge of his mind, but he couldn't place his finger on it. He let it go for now, reluctantly, and came straight to the point.

"Let's assume for a moment that you're part of my investigation."

Her eyes narrowed, and he put his hands up, palms out. "Truce, remember?"

She settled back, waited.

"I'm not asking you what you do at IDSD. I'm not asking you why you have access to my investigation. I am asking you to allow me to run through you certain thoughts that I have."

"You were assigned a liaison."

"I'm going above the liaison's head."

Her eyebrows rose slightly and she contemplated him. But she said nothing.

"I need to, let's say, brainstorm with IDSD directly on this, and right now you're the most available. I can approach IDSD through the liaison, use formal channels, but at this point I don't think either of us can afford any more delays."

Lara gestured slightly for him to proceed. She was curious to see where this was going. He obviously wouldn't be here unless he felt he had to. Still, that first time she had seen him, in the videoconference, while it had convinced her that he was sharp and thorough, that he potentially could do what IDSD—and Oracle—needed him to do, it had also made her realize that not much would escape him. He had fished then, wondered about her presence there. She had been careful not to let her guard down then, and since she wasn't ready to trust him yet, she wasn't going to let it down now, either.

Donovan started with the easier question. "Is it possible there was someone inside IDSD working with whoever broke into the data center?"

"No, that wouldn't make sense."

"I assume that's not IDSD pride talking."

"Anyone can be infiltrated," she said dismissively, and he found himself smiling. So, no ego here.

"No," she continued, "the problem in an insider theory is the data taken." She hesitated.

"I was told to stay away from the data stolen, and IDSD hasn't supplied the encryption key my techs need to decipher the frames we have in the footage you've seen. So I get that it's sensitive enough to hide, even now," he said evenly.

She assessed him. He let her. And wanted her to know he did. He waited. Then went with truth and trust. "You were right, I tried to run a check on you. And you must have run a check on me. The difference is you would have succeeded. So you know I'm good at what I do. But I'm running into walls here. Whatever these people want, they're going to do it whether you and I like it or not. We've got to stop them before anyone else gets hurt."

"I know," she said, letting out a long breath. "I know."

Something about the way she said that struck him as worried.

"And," she added after a brief moment of thought,

"you're right, I did check out your professional service file. And if you expect me to trust you, you're going to have to do the same."

"Okay." So she read him as well as he read her. He would have to accept that, although he wasn't even remotely used to it. He came slowly around the sofa and sat down. At a distance, safe not only for her. "Then tell me only what you can."

She nodded.

He went straight for it. "These guys came for one thing. Not IDSD. Oracle."

She said nothing.

"I initially thought Oracle was the code name for an operation. Something done against whoever it was who targeted IDSD's data storage unit. That perhaps these guys are a group that is after whoever is behind that operation."

She remained impassive.

"But the frames we can see in the footage are periodically interrupted. So that, while we cannot read them, my techs think that the pattern in which the data runs and stops, and the way it seems to be organized, indicates that the hacking medium used by the perpetrators was pulling data from different points. Since all the data came from IDSD's unit, a likely conclusion is that it was pulled from different date clusters, or locations, or operations, or all of the above. Not many, looks like maybe three, four, although, since we can't read it, we can't be sure."

He paused. "So then I thought this meant that

Oracle is a weapon. It made sense, something used on different dates, at a number of locations, in different operations. But the problem with this theory is, if there is some weapon that has been used against this group or has been seen by it in the field, why go to the trouble of working for close to a year to break into the data center and destroy it, potentially alerting us to their existence in the process—that's the time since the disruptions began that had allowed them to track down the security signal and the time they spent since then learning the data center security and preparing to jam the signal, as you know. And add to that the time it must have taken before that to obtain IDSD's encryption, and to even know where to go look for information. And to prepare for this entire operation of theirs, let's not forget that. No, if it were just a weapon, like a gun or a drone or a robotic system or whatever, I'd put all the time and knowledge and resources into putting my hands on it out there in the field and reverse engineering it."

She was easily following his logic. He expected nothing less but found he was enjoying the mind behind the intelligent eyes focused on his.

"So, I'm thinking it's not just a weapon. It's something more complex, more elaborate. Something they had to break into a data center for, because it's not out there in the field and is too carefully hidden. Something that can foil their plans and hurt them, but does so remotely. Something that can hit—no, scratch that. Something that can be employed at any date, for any operation, anywhere in the world. Something worth all that trouble. Something like a computer. Or an AI. We do have them, after all, AIs. We've got the best machines in the world working alongside the best military strategists, helping them accelerate data sorting and analysis, setting out for them scenario simulations, hell, we've got narrow AIs controlling most of our weapons and our air, water and ground surveillance, response measures and transport technologies.

"Except that that's not new. These have been in use for a while, and everybody has them, even if at different levels of advancement. And if not, they'll get them, copy or simply purchase the technology in the free market. So no, I'm thinking that's not enough to warrant everything these guys did." He leaned forward. "But an advanced AI that can actually oversee and guide missions, not merely provide mostly dry technical support, that's different. Except that it's impossible, isn't it?"

He watched for a reaction. There was none. He continued. "There have been countless attempts to have AIs run missions in Threat Alert Centers. But human operators are still needed, alongside military strategists and tacticians. They all have to work together, human-machine collaboration is a necessity. There's no way around that, because no matter what the machine can do, there are too many variables and unknowns that call for what only the human mind can provide, our way of thinking which we develop in a lifetime of experiences, our ability to break beyond bounds, and our capacity to constantly evolve and adapt. And the technological factor has to be complemented by human sentience, empathy, the ability to relate to people who are fighting to survive extreme situations at critical mission points." He was thinking aloud now, analyzing what Reilly had said, using his own experience to make it real. "And even then, even when the AIs we do have work with the people alongside them, we fail, have failed so many times over the years, because missions have too many unknowns, too many gaps in data, and nobody, *nobody* can deduce beyond a point. And nobody can deduce ahead more than the calculation of scenario probabilities."

He was good. Too good. Or good enough, Lara thought, to save Oracle.

"Except that I'm an ex-military USFID agent with a job that touches both worlds, you see. And I've seen countless operations through in USFID's Threat Alert Center. Ran quite a few, too. And a while back, we had an operation go wrong. It was doomed. And in that operation, the USFID TAC was online with US Global Intelligence and with the Joint Special Operations Command TAC. And rather interestingly, at a certain point, when we'd reached a dead end, US Global Intelligence contacted someone. And who-ever it was, their TAC took over. And from that moment there was nothing we were needed for, any of us. All we could do was sit there and listen as a computerized voice disentangled the situation. And it did so as if it was nothing, the easiest thing in the world. We'd spent the better part of a day working— TACs, mission coordinators, and all the experts you could want, all experienced field people. Including myself. And we'd lost. Those guys, there was no way they were getting out of there alive. They had no way out. And then I sit there, with a bunch of confused people, as our agents are saved. By a computerized voice that communicated directly with the field and that sounded impossibly capable of doing the work itself. One voice."

Lara remembered that day, that operation. She remembered all of them. Still, she showed no reaction. Hiding Oracle was something she was used to doing.

"I didn't think about it until today," he continued. "I figured it was some TAC we weren't cleared to know about, a bunch of brilliant experts in a dark room and an efficient computer to help them. But looking back, that wasn't what it sounded like. People argue, have opposing opinions, give commands that sound like they came from different people. No, the way that voice sounded . . . it spoke in a single, consistent voice. It was IDSD, wasn't it? You do have a new technology. You've got an AI-human link of some sort, maybe even a full interface. An AI controlling missions with a person working alongside it. Seamless operation. The coveted seamless operation none of us have managed to attain."

He paused again. "I made two calls before I came here. One was to my techs. One of them knows more about computers than anyone I know. A brilliant kid. She tells me it's possible. Just not probable. Hasn't been done yet. Otherwise people would talk about it. But if there's one thing I've learned from this thing with Oracle, it is that even nowadays things can be hidden."

His eyes were intent on hers. "The second call was to a friend at the Pentagon. Seems we don't lose as many people in critical missions as we used to. We don't lose as many missions that in the past were considered dead end. For the past few years, something is turning missions around at the last minute. Something is coming in at critical points in missions and turning them around. Something that for him is only a rumor."

Lara's heart was beating hard, and she was glad he was far enough away for her to hide it.

"That's what they're after, isn't it?" he said. "Our side has something that works against them and they want to stop it. For revenge, to prevent it from standing in their way, whatever. They'll do anything, it's all worthwhile to them just as long as they destroy it. They want it gone."

His last words hit home too hard, and finally he saw it. He'd read no change in her as he talked, but now he saw it. The intake of a breath, the sudden concern in her eyes.

"The way I see it, they could do it in three ways,"

he continued, unrelenting. "They can hit it through cyberspace. But that obviously can't happen. Not only because this thing would be highly protected, but also because with the post-break-in security shutdown even we can barely access our own data. So they can attack the AI physically. But would they know where it is at IDSD? And could they even pull something like this off, attack a secured computer within the IDSD complex here, assuming it's even here, in the United States? That's not the way I'd go unless I was unsophisticated or desperate. They're obviously neither.

"Or, they could kill whoever is behind it. The person it can't operate without. That would set it back. Unless there is more than one person. But my tech doesn't think so. She thinks the optimal would be one person working with the AI, a single seamless connection that would eliminate internal conflicts. So one person. And once that person is dead, it would take time to train another. But a person who is capable of what I'm thinking—that cannot be even remotely easy, finding someone like that. Or, hell, maybe I'm wrong, and there is more than one person behind the AI. But even then, why not just kill them all?"

He frowned. "I don't expect you to confirm or deny. But I need something to find them. So let's assume I'm right."

Lara closed her eyes, all too aware of his ability to read her. She couldn't allow him to see too much.

Oracle had to be protected. She forced herself to calm down, to regain the ability to hide what she wanted to. To think.

When she opened her eyes, they were focused again. She'd decided how far she would go. "You're right," she said. "You won't decipher the data they stole. Not without a hell of a lot of computer power and a lot of time."

"Okay." He let her take her own way, choose how to help him. Her mind was clearly working now, thinking alongside his.

"So how did they?" she continued.

He sat up. "How long would it take to do that, decipher IDSD's encryption?"

"Not our regular encryption. The encryption for the data center. That's the best of all our encryptions. At least, it's supposed to be," she said. "And I don't know." She nodded and continued before he had a chance to speak, "But you need to know, in order to set a range for how long this group, as you say, has been working on the break-in. I understand. I'll make sure you get what you need."

"Good. Thank you." His brow furrowed. "Why can't you just get it yourself?"

"I'm not supposed to go anywhere near your investigation."

"But you're updated."

"Yes."

"And you are able to make sure I talk to whoever I need to."

"To an extent."

He looked at her curiously. She could just as well have lied to him. Or simply denied everything he'd said. It occurred to him that she never had, not once since they'd met.

"Will you be reprimanded for having this conversation with me?" he asked.

A fleeting, amused smile. "Hell yeah."

"Would whoever reprimands you be surprised that you did?"

Lara thought about Frank knowing that the investigator was her neighbor. Knowing what she would never risk, what she could never allow to happen. Knowing that ultimately only she could judge where to help and where not to. "Hell no."

He looked at her in wonder. Who are you, Lara Holsworth?

She settled back, her gaze thoughtful. "They had to have some reference data."

His brow furrowed in question.

"They got the encryption somewhere. Unless they actually got the key, and there's no way they did, they would necessarily have put their hands on sample data with the same encryption, something they could work on, learn the encryption and how to decipher it."

"No data theft of that level has been identified."

"I know." She noted the obvious. "But there had to be one. They had to have something to work on, something to get them started on this encryption."

"And something to point them to IDSD—IDSD in the United States, that is—and to the Oracle technology it has that they want destroyed."

He wasn't baiting her, she knew, just using the only assumption he had that sounded logical. "But there is a time limit here, which you might also be able to use to locate them," she said. "Encryptions change, are replaced for security purposes. The data center encryption included."

He nodded. "You're right, USFID does that too, everybody does. So they had to do this relatively quickly—get the encryption, decipher it, and get what they wanted from the data center before the encryption is replaced—and this does limit the time frame within which the encryption fell into their hands."

"An encryption of this level would be replaced less frequently, but still, yes, if you assume that they did in fact know our replacement frequency, then that, together with how long it might have taken them to learn the encryption, should still give you a limited range to work with. And as you said, they had to have been working on the data center break-in for more than a year. This helps further pinpoint when all this started."

On the table, her phone beeped. As she picked it up its screen came to life and Donovan saw what looked like a short code, although he couldn't make it out from where he was sitting.

"I've got to go in," she said absently, her mind

already elsewhere. She stood up. "I'll pass on what you told me. All of it, if that's okay with you. It'll shorten the way to getting what you need."

"Can you do that in a way that won't get you in trouble for talking to me?"

She wondered that he would even think about it. "I'll survive," she said, but the words were followed by sudden doubt. Will I? She thought this thought that had never before occurred to her. Will Oracle survive whatever was coming? Pushing the thought out of her mind, it had no place, not now, not ever, she turned to walk upstairs, get ready for what experience told her was waiting for her at IDSD in the day, or days, ahead. Then remembered he was there, and turned to see him standing, watching her thoughtfully.

He'd seen enough people called to duty to recognize it. "Until the next truce," he simply said and turned to leave, but then immediately turned back to her with a small, impish smile he hadn't known he had in him, considered asking her after all what she did at IDSD.

"Don't," she said, surprising him by anticipating the question, and for the first time, she laughed. Really laughed. Grinning now, forgetting everything that came before that laugh, he turned and walked away.

Chapter Nine

Donovan was back in his kitchen nook, deep in thought, when the call came in. The head of IDSD Intelligence herself, Ruth Larsen, confirmed that she had spoken with Ms. Holsworth, then discussed with him at length how incidents could be identified that might point to the identity of the data center perpetrators, going back to his conversation with IDSD's liaison, where he had begun to profile the types of groups he thought could be behind it. Finally, she told him she would get back to him as soon as she had anything that could advance his investigation, giving him a feeling that she was, in fact, making this her top priority. Ending the call, Donovan chuckled in appreciation. Lara Holsworth had come through.

He immersed himself back in his work.

And sometime later realized he was staring at his screen, thinking about her. The way she sat on the couch, comfortable in her own home, yet intent on their conversation, her eyes focused, golden flecks set in soft hazel enhanced by the gentle sun peeking through the open patio doors. She was obviously a professional in whatever it was she did—even if he still had no idea what it was, he'd now had a front seat glimpse at the level of intellect she operated on, and her calm confidence indicated to him that she was used to this, used to her mind being looked up to.

But she also had the looks that would draw a man's attention. Yet what he'd seen in her so far told him that she didn't see her looks as what made her who she was, didn't attempt to use them, even if she didn't care to hide them, but just accepted them as they were—the way she dressed, the way she held herself, spoke of understated femininity. And while a woman like that would be used to having the attention of a man, something about her was forbidding, subtly designed to maintain a distance.

Except it wasn't going to work with him, that much he already knew, now, after this morning. He thought of the way her eyes fell on him when she assessed him, the careful distance she kept from him. As the investigator in this case, or as a man? he asked himself, then realized he was hoping it was the latter, and wondered if she even knew her effect on him. He doubted it.

He realized he couldn't get her out of his mind. Angry at himself, at the professional side of him not being able to take over like it always had, at this part of him he had been sure did not exist choosing now to awaken, at the most unlikely, unwanted time, at emotions so out of character he had no idea how to react to them, he transferred his work session to his office via the USFID secure channel that connected his home and SIRT and turned off the screen, leaving it on the table. He grabbed a jacket and his Glock and badge on the way to the front door, and left. That should do it. It had to. He had to take his mind off her. This, she, had no place in the life he had chosen.

With little traffic on the way, he made it to USFID Plaza in no time. The USFID-SIRT floor in the main building was empty, the way he needed it to be. He got some coffee in the kitchenette and settled down to work in his office.

USFID director Leland White thought he would wait with the results of the reconstruction of the data center break-in until Monday, but two calls from officials too high up in the US Administration to be disregarded prompted him to leave the family gathering in the backyard lawn of his home and initiate a call from his study, after making sure to close the door behind him.

Donovan took the call on his wall screen, and White realized immediately where he was. "What in the world are you doing in your office?"

"Investigating," Donovan said, a tad impatient.

"Ah. Do tell."

The communication with the director was a secure one, and Donovan updated him.

"So we're waiting for IDSD."

"They're the only source we can get this information from. It's their encryption, and apparently their Oracle." Donovan raised his eyebrows in mock innocence. "I could have Reilly hack their internal missions database, the one at IDSD here."

"You finally got them to work with you, so don't. And I don't need a diplomatic incident. Not on this. It'll have everybody on my back, so seriously, don't." White knew Donovan was baiting him, but he still hoped to God the man wouldn't hack IDSD just for the heck of it. Donovan didn't like anyone interfering with his investigations.

He contemplated what Donovan had just told him. Something there eluded him. "So you talked to Lara Holsworth. And she cooperated."

"We had a professional discussion about an investigation aimed at assisting IDSD."

A bit enigmatic, White thought. A bit defensive, too. Donovan didn't do defensive. "How?" he asked.

"Mmm?"

"How did you get to her?"

On the screen, Donovan seemed to feign interest in the file he had open on his desk screen. "I told you my neighbors next door left," he said.

"Yes, to that retirement community. They were nice. I liked them."

Donovan raised his eyes to meet his. "Apparently they sold their house to their granddaughter's friend. She moved in. I met her. The day after the data center break-in."

White's jaw dropped.

Donovan nodded.

"Let me get that straight. Because I'm thinking I've lost it here. Your next-door neighbor is Lara Holsworth, our mystery woman from IDSD."

Donovan nodded again.

"Wow. The odds on that." White chuckled. "So how'd you get her to talk to you?"

Donovan took a deep breath.

"No. No, no. Really. No. You didn't hit on her?"

Donovan raised his eyebrows.

"No, of course not. Next-door neighbor is too close for you. And connected to an investigation. No, certainly not. What was I thinking? You wouldn't, I know." White stared at him, thinking, rather frantically he had to admit. "No. I know you. You did something. What did you do?"

Donovan was silent.

"Oh no. Donovan, don't make me come there. It's Sunday, Victoria will kill me. Please. Please don't tell me you did something you shouldn't have, that I'll have IDSD to deal with tomorrow."

"No, you would have already. Apparently she's not the type to run and tell, and she deals with me nicely herself."

White hadn't expected the appreciation in the younger man's voice. Not willing to let the matter go, not in the least, he leaned forward in his chair, saying nothing, his eyes on Donovan's, his eyebrows raised. And waited.

Finally, Donovan let out a breath. "We might have had a couple of minor clashes since the investigation began."

"Couple? Minor? How minor?"

"I told her to stay away from the investigation and threatened to arrest her. And I might have threatened to shoot her."

White forgot to breathe. "No."

Donovan shrugged.

"What did she do?"

"Gave me back as good as she got." A smile played at Donovan's lips.

"Really?" White settled back in his chair, considering this. With a woman who looked like Lara Holsworth did, Donovan was one to either make a move or turn his back in disinterest at the outset. And in an investigative setting, he would conduct himself professionally and with considerable self-control, certainly never mixing work with anything personal. He was doing none of the above. They had known each other for a long time, and White had never seen Donovan this way. Somehow, this woman had gotten to him.

"Don't." The gray in Donovan's eyes had an icy warning in it.

White didn't, ending the conversation at that. He wouldn't push this, not until after the investigation was over. This wasn't the right time. But he would get to it, eventually. That was the one thing he and Donovan had never seen eye to eye on. Relationships.

At forty-eight, Leland White had been married to Victoria, the love of his life as he called her, for over fourteen years, much thanks to Donovan, who had talked him into taking the right step all those years earlier, when White had been a senior agent on a field mission with the special forces team a young Donovan was a part of. Donovan had saved his life on that mission, and had then gone to see him in the hospital and had told him to quit stalling and settle down before he got himself killed. White had done just that, and Donovan hadn't been wrong. The marriage was a happy one, and Victoria and he had two kids. Mark, their oldest, was almost twelve now, and Sean was nine.

Donovan, however, did not take for himself the advice he had given the man who had since become his close friend. He was not, as he called it, husband material, or common-law partner material, which was the way most people went nowadays. He wasn't even boyfriend material. He had no intention of settling down. His flings—they never came close to relationships—were all short-lived, and he nurtured that obsessively almost, not letting any woman in. He never wanted to stay, never wanted one of them to stick around.

He never cared enough.

White knew where that came from. The kind of military history his friend had, had a way of distancing its best from permanent relationships, and his years as a field agent hadn't helped either. Donovan had spent too many years knowing he might not return from his next mission, and bringing someone into that life wasn't something he was inclined to do. He'd been to too many funerals and had seen too many anguished families. Unfortunately, even in the more stable life he led now and this job he was in, in which quite a few of those around him did not hesitate to have families, he'd kept to his old ways, not letting anyone close. What a waste, White thought. Donovan was a good man. He wanted more for him, even if Donovan himself didn't care.

He sighed, left his study and joined his family.

Donovan turned off the wall screen, shaking his head in irritation. He knew where White was going with this. He didn't want to go there. This isn't the time to deal with this, he told himself, and dived back into work. Here in his office it was easier to focus, and he was deeply immersed in reviewing his investigators' work on another investigation when the call came in. Throwing a look at the clock—he wasn't surprised that the caller was spending Sunday night the same way he was—he took it.

Ruth Larsen appeared on the screen. She greeted him, then excused herself and added someone else to the videoconference. Donovan's wall screen split into two views as US Global Intelligence's director, Paul Evans, joined in. Having worked with Evans in the past, Donovan was not at all surprised that he was dealing with this himself. There was no arguing that the man deserved his newly-acquired position.

"Your line of thought, Agent Pierce, has helped us find a lead. A strong one, we believe," Larsen said. "It has to do with an IDSD-led mission in Lake Chad —in Africa—a year and a half, no, almost two years ago."

"You should be getting the file from my office now, Donovan," Evans said just as Donovan's desk screen registered the incoming message. He didn't open the file yet, wanting to hear it from them first. When people talked, they had a tendency to let slip things that didn't appear in organized files they had time to review before archiving them. Or giving them to investigators. Trust in those who had kept information from him wasn't high on his priority list right now.

"About a year prior to that mission," Evans continued, "our intelligence picked up some suspicious money transfers linked to Africa. They went through seemingly legitimate accounts, but we found they were being used to finance arms deals. Additional digging then linked these deals to a new group. NWM, New World Militants. We began looking for them in chatter but found them only when we looked deep underground."

Which meant, Donovan knew, that NWM had taken extreme steps to remain hidden. And there were too many ways in which militant groups could do that. They had been doing it long enough now to learn how the allies' intelligence might find them and constantly devised new ways to conceal themselves.

"We listened for a time. Just listened, so that they wouldn't know we were on to them. We learned they were a group of extremists who understood they were getting nowhere after years of fighting among themselves and having to defend themselves against attacks by African governments trying to rid the continent of them. Their leader, a man named Sayed Elijahn, was born in Chad, and studied in England and then in Belgium. We know he was born into an affluent family, none of them militants themselves but his father and uncle had both made their fortune by dealing with them.

"He must have seen his country and its neighbors torn apart by militants—much like those his family had been working with—during that failed war of the region's governments against them, at the worst time for the already unstable region. Except that the effect of this on this guy seems to have been rather unique.

"The way we profiled him, we believe that while he was in Belgium, in Brussels to be exact, he saw what the Internationals have achieved, and thought why not do the same with the militants—unite all independent militant groups, much like IDSD has united nations all over the world, pardon the crude comparison, and through this gain power, maybe ultimately take over some of the rogue and unstable regimes and destabilize the world again by going against the alliance.

"By the time we found out about him and his New World Militants, he already had quite a few militant groups on his side. He was dealing arms and drugs, and getting funds from some of the wealthier groups that had begun taking interest. We even think a couple of regimes were already backing him. But the thing is, this Elijahn was also buying people. As in engineers. Weapons experts. Hackers. Data whizzes."

Donovan nodded. He got what Evans meant.

"Back then, Elijahn wasn't that powerful yet, but he was getting there, fast. He was using his money and preaching his plan quite cleverly, and eventually he built a base in a strategic, isolated spot near where Lake Chad used to be, in the Chadian territory side of it. By then much of the Lake Chad Basin was already deserted and for him it was perfect. There were no unwanted elements around to bother him —governments no longer had interest in the area, no civilians had remained there, all had long been displaced by drought and war, and any militants around had already joined him—and the place is at the junction of what used to be five major countries, so that whatever infrastructure still existed in the area allowed him convenient access to resources. A land-locked no man's land, easy to protect, lots of empty miles to do with as he pleased with no one minding his business.

"Those weapons we were tracking were going

there, to his base, substantial amounts of them, some serious equipment, too, and that's where he was training his people. Not that many yet, in the hundreds only. Quality over quantity, that was his motto. He amassed smart weapons and smart people, and trained militants at the level we do our soldiers.

"He spent a long time just preparing. And then the chatter changed. He started hinting at a demonstration of his seriousness, his capabilities. And this guy's smart, you see. He didn't go around blowing up things like militants had been doing all along. This guy had a goal in mind and was willing to do what it took to achieve it. See, he decided to show the groups that hadn't joined him yet and anyone else who might stand up to him that he could, and would, become the new international superpower. And so, in that base, at Lake Chad, he prepared his people to destroy IDSD's headquarters in Brussels."

Donovan's brow furrowed.

"At that point, US Global Intelligence came to us," Larsen said. "We alerted all the allies, and together we decided to finish Elijahn before he went any further."

"You attacked," Donovan said.

"Everyone participated in some function or another. IDSD took point."

"So what happened?"

Larsen hesitated. Finally, she spoke. "Toward the end of the mission, a command drone went down. Malfunctioned."

"Okay," Donovan prodded.

"It was designed to automatically self-destruct when it falls. We thought it did." Larsen paused. "The mission was a success. When our forces left, there was nothing left of Elijahn's base, nothing and no one to salvage. But some time later we received a brief signal. The drone was activated."

"It didn't self-destruct."

"No, not when it fell. But if this type of drone is activated in this way, not by its operators and not by its control center, an internal command comes online and any information in the drone is deleted, and a secondary self-destruct device is activated. We have reason to believe this second device worked."

"But?"

"But we cannot be sure no data was downloaded in the interim. If someone succeeded in connecting to the drone before reactivating it, they could theoretically have downloaded part of the data before the self-destruct. Normally we wouldn't think this possible, but in light of recent events, we have no choice but to assume that such a download was somehow successfully done."

"What makes you think this is the incident we're looking for?"

"The encryption basis for this type of a system, a command drone that must not fall into the wrong hands, is similar to the encryption we used in the data centers. The best encryption there is."

Not really, as it turned out, Donovan thought, but said nothing. From what he'd seen these past days, in all agencies, lessons from the break-in were already being implemented. Nobody took the data center incident lightly, and criticism about past mistakes would do no good at this point.

"And," Larsen continued, "the data taken from the data center contained missions that took place at around that time frame, of the Chad mission."

Donovan contemplated this. "You say the encryption of the data in the drone is similar to the data center's encryption, not identical?"

"Not identical, no. When we discovered the drone had been activated, we implemented a safety measure. We didn't . . . it was, perhaps, an oversight, but we didn't replace the encryption at that security level in its entirety. However, we did introduce some changes both in the encryption of field applications and in the data centers encryption, different changes to separate the two this time. As I said, the original encryption was already the best, and we thought the drone data files had all been destroyed, so that this was only a precautionary measure."

"So anyone breaking the original encryption of the data in the drone . . ."

"Would not have to take that far a leap to decrypt the data stolen in the data center break-in."

"There was one word they certainly already had the decryption of," Donovan noted.

"Like I said, we only made limited changes,"

Larsen said. "And if they were targeting something specific..."

"We should now assume they have at least part of the data that was recorded by the drone in the course of the Chad mission," Evans said. "The drone contained both visuals and audios of the field-side of the mission but the visual data would have been the first to go when the drone fell, so they probably got only the audios, and likely only part of them before the drone self-destructed."

"Would the audios lead them to the data center?"

"All we can surmise is that they were enough to lead them to look for something they couldn't find, so they went to the highest-clearance data source. The data center."

"The US-based one."

"The drone was marked as belonging to IDSD-US, so that the mission would have been recognized as originating under IDSD Missions in the United States," Larsen said.

Considering how forthcoming both Larsen and Evans were being, and the fact that thanks to him they now had a strong lead on the identity of the perpetrators, Donovan would have liked to use the opportunity to ask what Oracle's capacity was in that mission, why information about it was in the drone, and what it did that would make the perpetrators focus on it, but he didn't. He didn't give a damn about what he was or was not supposed to look for, but the one thing he understood already was that

Oracle was not to be discussed on such a video-conference, not even over this secure line. Not while the people who were looking for it were still out there. The thing was, if his suspicions about what Oracle was were correct, he not only had a pretty good idea what it did in that Chad mission, he also knew now that it had to be one hell of a system. One that he himself agreed should be protected.

"I'll need to know more about the drone and what was on it." His tone did not leave room for objections, and he didn't care who he was talking to.

Larsen nodded. "I'll make it available to you in the morning."

"And you're assuming the data center break-in is in fact NWM's work. Elijahn."

"We're still looking for other incidents that might fit, but yes," she said. "The file we've sent you provides all the details of the Chad mission, including profiles that we prepared of the group and of Elijahn himself. Photos, too, we have those, although faces can be changed. We have no audio of him, and no biometrics."

"The thing is, Donovan," Evans said, "we never found out if Elijahn was at his base or not when we attacked it. We have no indications from the pre-mission intelligence or the mission visuals that he was there. But we haven't heard anything about him or NWM since, nothing at all, no matter how deep we've looked, so all we could do was assume he was dead and watch to see if he would surface. It looks as if he did. Now all we need to do is find him."

Before he finds your Oracle, Donovan completed the thought.

"Are you sure?" Elijahn asked again, his voice sending everyone in the room into trembling silence.

"Yes," the young man intent on the computer screen said, again.

"Are you sure?"

"Yes. It is still the only explanation." The young man, an experienced hacker, did not allow impatience into his voice. Despite his importance to this job, the man beside him would not hesitate to kill him with his bare hands if he detected disrespect. Respect was big with this guy, but then that's what this was all about. That, the hacker sighed inwardly, was why he was stuck in this moldy warehouse in this country he hated while back home summer still reigned, and his friends were probably having a lot more fun than he was. How the hell did he get into this? Money, he answered himself immediately. An obscene amount of money.

Which did not guarantee he would come out of this alive. He wondered if he could, perhaps, find a way to leave, escape, when Elijahn and his men left to do their thing. Prayed that he could.

"You heard the audios yourself," he said, and cringed visibly when the burly man's eyes flashed dangerously. "The voice was computerized," he continued quickly, "so that has to be it, only something like that could do this. And this," he said, indicating the data taken from the IDSD storage unit, "confirms it. This Oracle was there in the attack on your base and in the other attacks we got from. . ." He cringed again. Only two attacks, just two IDSD-led attacks against militants in which Oracle was involved, in the data they took from the data center. He was supposed to get more, but the encryption programmed into the medium he had prepared to search and download data from the storage unit turned out to be not quite the right one—something he hadn't considered—which had limited his ability to immediately recognize what he was seeing, and of the few attacks he'd had time to get information on in the time frame set for him by Elijahn in his anxiety to get in and out, only two had Oracle mentioned in them.

But what they did get, attack transcripts in which Oracle was mentioned, supported what the hacker had thought. Oracle was an advanced artificial intelligence that was behind the operations that destroyed their base and that had foiled at least two plans of their sister groups, and most likely others. Possibly, probably in fact, many others—the transcripts had a regularity about them, experienced efficiency.

For the hacker, that was the amazing part. When he cracked the original audios from the destruction of their base at Lake Chad, he, like Elijahn, had expected to hear people's voices, the voices of the enemy's commanders speaking with the wretched soldiers who had destroyed all they'd worked for. Instead, there was only one voice. A computer. The hacker had thought it might be a disguise, the transformed voices of the people who would normally run such missions, but the words, the orders, were too consistent. And there were no delays, there was none of the hesitation that he would expect from a group of people discussing, perhaps arguing, a situation, no speech interrupting another. And the voice itself, it was too cool, too sophisticated, too quick— quick thinking, quick deduction, quick logic. That, and the versatile complexity of the orders it gave made him think it was in fact a computerized intelligence.

The notion excited him. People had been dreaming about it for so long, so many had tried to develop artificial intelligence that would go beyond the commercial applications that were all too common nowadays, as in the autodrive of his parents' car— he tried not to think now of their embarrassment at the life he had chosen—or the ones that controlled the service technologies in their home. What everyone wanted was to develop a thinking computer, one that could do a whole lot more than that. He himself had dreamed of it since he was a child, and had spent long hours online, where so many like him never stopped talking about what the future could bring. But so far no one had succeeded. Computers were fast and smart, but still had a long way to go before they could exceed their preprogrammed capabilities, and still did not have, were not close to demonstrating, the flexibility and creativity of the human mind.

But this was military. No, better than that—this was IDSD and its allies working together. And even more, it was the Internationals, and no one pushed for progress more than they did. What if they had succeeded? What if they really had jumped light years ahead and created the artificial intelligence he had seen in the movies of his youth?

He simply had to know. He spent many a night hacking universities, private labs, military research facilities. Searching, hoping to find it. Hoping to find something that would support what he wanted so much to be true, that what he had heard, the thing that had run the attack, was artificial intelligence. That a machine had guided those soldiers who had destroyed the base.

But there was nothing. Nothing he found had come close. Yes, there were some developments out there, major ones he had not known about, but nothing close to what he had hoped. Nothing that would not merely serve as secondary support for the people who ran the show. If it really did exist, his dream come true, it was well hidden.

At the same time, he had also looked for that name, Oracle. Elijahn had been livid after hearing the audios from the drone. He had become obsessed with it, with Oracle, and had ordered his people to find what was behind it, no matter what it took. The hacker had gone to him—when it was safe— and had told him that the voice in the audio files had to be a machine. Elijahn had told him to make sure, to find it. Whatever it was, he wanted it destroyed. And so, like the hacker's peers, the other unfortunate minds working for Elijahn, the hacker had looked for it. But he had not found it, the thing the soldiers in the audios had called Oracle, the thing he wanted so much to be artificial intelligence. Still, he had not lost hope. Something like that, it would have to be a secret. *The* secret. And so he kept searching, kept digging for clues. Until the idea came to him where it must be hidden. And there he had found it. In that data center.

And it had turned out to be everything he had dreamed of. The transcripts he now had, of those two attacks, had him elated as he realized he must have been right. The enemy had created the coveted technology. Oracle existed, and it really was a smart machine, an artificial intelligence like never before seen.

True, the second of the two attack transcripts had him worried. There was a place in it, a short segment, where Oracle had spoken to an injured soldier. And the tone and words of that conversation made him certain that a person, a human, was dictating to the computer what to say, perhaps even using its voice directly to say it himself. But then he realized what it must be. This computer was state of the art, unprecedented, no arguing. But it would still need an operator. Someone who would accompany it, be there to watch it, step in if needed, be the human in the equation. Someone who knew it enough, worked with it enough, to do so seamlessly.

The hacker wanted, needed so much to know more. He had pushed to be near Elijahn, to be the one good enough and trusted enough to be taken along on this job, just so that he could be nearer to it. To the machine. To Oracle. Still, what he wanted would not interest Elijahn. Elijahn wanted Oracle eliminated. And thanks to the hacker's brilliance, his idea to go for the data center and his plan how to get in, they were on their way to finding it.

He sighed in contentment, but then snapped out of his reverie to find Elijahn watching him. The dangerous flash in the man's eyes made him focus. He tried to remember quickly what Elijahn had asked. Yes, the computer.

"It's not just a computer, it's actually artificial intelligence," he corrected and nearly fell off his chair when Elijahn turned on him. "It has to be, to do that. To do what we heard, and the way it did it. They must be light years ahead of everybody else. I'm sure—"

"So you can find it now." Elijahn cut off his panicked ranting.

"Maybe. We would need more information from the data center for that, and you destroyed..." He scrambled away when Elijahn reached for his gun.

"It wouldn't matter, that kind of machine would require some major physical space, and it would be well secured. It would probably take..."

The gun was pointed at him.

"But we don't need it, we don't need the machine, we don't need it!"

Elijahn lowered the gun. Just a little.

"The operator, get the operator." He was talking fast, too fast, had to gain time, had to think. This was over the top, yes, but if Elijahn bought it, it would give him time. Maybe he could run. Damn the money. "Yes, it must be an advanced artificial intelligence but it can't have existed long, these things take time, improving, learning, no matter how good it is it would still require programming and teaching and experience and human intervention... No, it still has to be reliant on an operator, its creator most likely, or someone integral to its creation. Yes. Has to be. I compared the audios from the drone to the transcripts we got from the data center, in one of them you can see the operator interfere." He nodded vigorously. "Yes. Someone is talking to it, guiding it."

"How many?"

"Several at least. To monitor, maintain. But in the middle of an attack, like what they did to our... your base, one person to communicate with it one on one. At the most sophisticated stage, I mean I don't know if they have that, but it would be the artificial intelligence for the attack as a whole, the person for the system oversight and for the human angle. And we only heard the artificial intelligence, so I would bet the person is very experienced in working with it. Has to be, it's as if they are one." He was rambling. Staying alive was a priority now. Elijahn was not a patient man. Smart, the smartest the hacker had ever worked for, but not patient.

"Creator or operator."

"Most likely both."

"And if that person dies?"

"That would set them back. At least."

Elijahn nodded. "Find him."

Chapter Ten

Donovan gazed thoughtfully at the dark screen. The incident that Larsen and Evans had provided had all the right elements. It explained a lot—how the perpetrators had access to just enough of IDSD's highest level encryption, how they had first learned of Oracle and deduced it most likely belonged to IDSD. Why they were going to such lengths to find it.

This last thought raised some serious concerns. NWM was certainly not the first technologically savvy group encountered since the Internationals began their efforts to tilt the scales toward peace and unity and away from the old ways, of wars and division. Much had changed in that time. Technology had advanced significantly, and too many militant groups advanced with it. There were those who still advocated using car bombs or suicide bombers, even though they were finding it harder and harder to reach their targets since the allies were increasingly implementing measures that could easily identify such crude means from afar. But other groups had transitioned to the recruitment of engineers, hackers, programmers, weapons experts—brains, dangerous ones—much like NWM's leader, Elijahn, seemed to have done.

But as the file Donovan had just gone through showed, Elijahn had a rare drive in him. Donovan tried putting himself in the man's shoes. He wasn't just a militant per se. No, he had others around him for that. He saw himself as a leader. He'd been educated among those he later decided to go against, and sought to surpass them. He was extraordinarily ambitious in his desire to unite groups that wanted each to stand out, seeking its own prestige and power, because he wanted to create a global organization that would be strong enough to influence, and eventually control, the world's rogue regimes and their militaries. He wanted to head an international militant force that would be able to stand up to the allies, and shape the world as he thought it should be.

With Elijahn's illusions of grandeur in mind, losing the Chad base the way he did would have put a serious dent in his plans, and in any respect he might have gained until then. So what better way to regain his prestige and manufacture for himself and his domination plan a second chance among groups that did not give second chances, than to go against IDSD that had destroyed his base, and that in his mind was leading the allies in the war against the militant groups, Elijahn's own included? Applying what he had seen from his own world of militants, he would think that hurting IDSD, crippling it, would break down the alliance and instill fear. In his mind, the mind of a warmonger, he would not understand that his acts would do just the opposite, bring the allies around IDSD and the Internationals to protect them, protect what they had achieved and what was giving whole nations so much hope.

But the problem was that while Elijahn's actions would not destroy the alliance, they might unjustifiably make it seem weak and exposed, enough to distance from it those who were just beginning to trust its strength and deciding to stand up to a violent regime or put aside differences with long-time enemies, and try something new, a future that would benefit them. This would be a setback that had to be prevented, for the sake of many.

An attempt by Elijahn to cripple IDSD would take something special. Something clever. Not destroying its headquarters in Brussels, that wouldn't be possible. That plan of his had been foiled once before and, in any case, the allies had taken that option from him when they destroyed his base, killing his people. No, it would have to be something that would require the kind of resources he could assemble quietly, under the radar, and while he was still in hiding. And his ideal target would be something that ran like a thread through IDSD's missions, the missions of the allies and their military forces and defense agencies, the missions that had been hitting those same groups whose support Elijahn needed to regain. Something that would enable him to let these groups know he was alive without fearing their rejection because of his previous defeat. Something the destruction of which would bring anti-militant missions, and perhaps a whole lot more than that, to a standstill.

Donovan was sure that was Oracle, the unique artificial intelligence.

And then there was the matter of revenge. For Elijahn himself, for his dreams, for his aspirations. For his life's work that had been destroyed. And revenge was an all too powerful motive. The man was driven, strategically smart, and patient, and Donovan doubted anything would deter him from his goal. In fact, there was only one thing Donovan thought Elijahn wouldn't readily give, and that was his own life. He would want to live to reap the fruits of his long-awaited success.

Which made it worse. Elijahn was not about to let his plans fail. He was coming after Oracle, no matter what, and he was doing so to win.

The question was what that meant. With what he now knew about Elijahn, the likely perpetrator in all this, Donovan went back to the possibility of a physical attack on the AI. Could Elijahn do that, come after the artificial intelligence itself? Would he think he could, or even risk it, considering that the allies had foiled a major physical attack by him once before? Would he think that the element of surprise was on his side, that it would be easier for him to act because they didn't know that he was alive and had not forsaken his plans? Would he even have the kind of force needed to take on the IDSD complex here in the United States? The answer to that last question, Donovan was ready to wager, was no. That would require means that were not being assembled anywhere around here. Otherwise, intelligence would have picked up on it. And security at IDSD was especially high these days, so something like that couldn't be pulled off anyway, not even by a specialist team. Not even in disguise—identification systems had long ago taken care of that, and again, current security was too tight to allow it.

So if not the physical system—or the cyber connection, which would be not be possible with the AI he had in mind, certainly not now—what then? People again. The people behind Oracle.

The person in the human-AI link or collaboration or whatever it was that IDSD had. Now that, according to Reilly, killing whoever that was, would do the job. Donovan frowned. He wouldn't wait to receive from Larsen the information he'd asked for. He would go get it itself, first thing the next day. It was time he had a face-to-face chat with these people, get the facts straight. All the facts. Before someone else died.

He touched his desk screen, brought up the file Evans had sent him, and went through it again.

Elijahn watched his people. Not many, but enough. The best he had. Or had left. None of them had been at the Chad base, and so they had survived the wrath of his enemies. He could not recruit more people since, could not risk exposing the fact that he was still alive, or where he was hiding. And so they were all he had, them and the locals he had hired. They were all training now. Preparing here, in the soundproof part of the converted warehouse. Final preparations. It was almost time. Soon he would have his revenge, and he would have what he was entitled to.

The hacker working just outside this training area was the same guy who had figured out how to get the data out of the drone. Audio only, true, and partial at that, but it was enough. Enough for Elijahn to hear it, that thing they called Oracle. Enough for him to realize it was responsible for what happened to the magnificent base he had so carefully built, to the people he had so carefully trained, to the contacts he had so carefully created and nurtured. To his dreams, his ambitions, his destiny.

He was not at the base when the attack came. He was at his headquarters. That was where the technologies and experts were, the brain of his group, while the Chad base had been his power. And then it was gone. Nothing, nothing at all was left, not a building standing, not a weapon intact, not a person alive. And he could do nothing.

He had no idea his enemies had found him

already, no idea they had been following his people's communications. His group was substantial by then, with many affiliations, with people, weapons and money moving across the globe. That meant, unavoidably, communicating, and as much as he had worked to hide it, his enemies were ever looking, and discovery at a too early a stage had been a known risk.

And that was precisely why he had the base built as it was. With the best modern security means there were. Multiple traps had been laid around it, from motion detectors and temperature sensors to automated gunfire to mines that could wreak havoc, and the best of all—a controlled electromagnetic disruption that would go off outside the protected perimeter, taking down electronics from the ground up at a sufficient radius to disrupt anything those who would come to harm him might use. Everything was computer-controlled from deep inside the base. And anyone managing to get through, which was, in his mind, impossible, would encounter not only additional security means, but also his warriors, hundreds of them, trained for combat and full of hate. His enemies could send hundreds, thousands, swoop down with jet fighters, drop bombs, and still he would be ready.

But they had only sent dozens. Just that, dozens. Stealthy, they had crept through, not activating any of the security defenses. Not triggering a single system. Not one. As if they had eyes everywhere. As if they knew, at each step, what awaited them and had circumvented it. They had breached the base perimeter, and when finally his people inside realized they were there it was too late. They had spread through the base, moving as if they knew where every person, every weapon, every technology was. Used his own defenses against his people, moving at the last minute so that automated fire found his people and not them, IEDs ripped through his people, not them. Dozens, against his hundreds. It was over so fast nothing could be done.

He had watched it all from his headquarters, through cameras carefully set. Right up until the base disintegrated, his cameras with it.

Not one of theirs was killed. All of his were eliminated. Men he had borrowed, bought, convinced. Trained. Controlled.

He had been shocked, confused, could not begin to understand how this could be. He had spent long years studying them, his enemies—their weapons, their capabilities, their methods and ways. He had based his people's training on that knowledge, planned his base's location, its structure, its defenses on it. And yet when it came down to it, somehow they went through all that he had painstakingly built as though they knew all about it, as though they had been right there in his head when he planned, when he implemented.

He had remained hidden. And for a long time he had only watched and listened. He knew those he had partnered with had turned their backs on him, saying he could not deliver on his promises. Saying he had been weak. Saying the alliance had gotten the better of him. They had thought he had been there, in his base, and had said that he had died in shame. That it was as it should be, in their world failure such as his warranted death. And he knew his enemies, those who had destroyed him, had searched, until finally they too thought that he had died in their attack. But he was alive and hiding where none of them could ever find him, and when it was safe he had gone back himself, one last time, to see it, his ruined base, his lost hope, in anger, in despair.

And that was when he had found the drone. Half-buried in the sand, a distance from what used to be his base. He had taken it back to his headquarters, where he still had his best brains and a few select warriors. No one, not even his former partners, knew where his headquarters was, or that it even existed. And there, his engineers had opened the drone, carefully so, and even then they had almost lost the data. Almost. Enough remained, thanks to the hacker, precious audio segments. It had taken them, the experts he had painstakingly collected, long months to work with these, and he had waited patiently. They could not decipher the audio files fully, but they deciphered enough.

And he heard it. The mechanical voice, giving orders. Guiding the enemy soldiers quietly, quickly, never hesitating, moving from team to team, angle to angle, seeing it all, anticipating it all, as if it was right there inside his base, as if it knew about everything, everyone that had been placed in their way. As Elijahn had listened to the impossible, he had understood. He now had a name for his anger, for his hate, for his revenge.

Oracle.

IDSD, that was who the drone belonged to. The very organization he dreamed of replacing someday had done this to him. He began to plan his revenge and had searched for the nemesis it had set upon him. But he had not been able to find it. Having to stay down, stay dead, made it difficult.

Finally, the same hacker who had helped recover the data from the drone, who had been searching like him, like all his people, had come to him, told him what he thought his nemesis was. The hacker was also the one who had come up with the idea to go to the one place all his enemies' data was in, the one place he could, perhaps, find something, anything, about this Oracle. And he had found it there, in the data center. He found Oracle. Or at least enough to confirm what it was, that it was used by his enemies in other attacks too, attacks that had set back those who had been his partners. And if that was true, if that Oracle had been involved in those two attacks he now knew about, how many other of their plans had it foiled? How many plans of others, others who would join him if he eliminated Oracle?

Luck, it seemed, was finally on his side. If he could destroy Oracle, then expose its existence to his world, he would have all the respect, the power, he deserved. No, not only to his world. To the entire world. Oracle would be made public, IDSD and its wretched allies would lose their advantage and suffer the consequences of their shameful defeat by him, and his victory—and his revenge—would finally be complete.

Yes, mistakes had been made. He should not have left those guards at the data center to be found with bullets in them, even if these could not be traced. He should have stuck with his original plan, to make the fire look like an accident in order to mask the theft. Not given them a reason to look for anyone in connection with the destruction. But success, finally being so close to his revenge, had made him careless, and now IDSD, like everyone else, his hacker and the scout he had sent out had told him, was protecting itself against both physical and cyber access and was looking for whoever had destroyed the data center. Still, that did not matter. They would not know what he had done, what he had been after, or that it was he who had caused the destruction. And this time there would be no intelligence to lead them to him.

He would win. He was alone, but not for long. He would have his revenge, and his place in his world like never before. And they would all fear him.

Movement caught his eyes. On the other side of

the glass, the hacker was waving excitedly. Elijahn left the training area and walked over to him.

"I got it," the hacker said.

In his office at IDSD Missions, Vice Admiral Frank Scholes faced the two heads of intelligence. His, in person, and US Global Intelligence's, on the screen.

"Is that so?" he asked.

"Yes," Larsen said. "Agent Pierce gave us what we needed to identify who broke into the data center, and he managed that even though we stalled him on Oracle. And you know Elijahn, you know what Oracle did to him. He won't stop until he gets what he wants. We believe that if we bring Agent Pierce into the loop, he would understand. He would also be able to anticipate Elijahn's actions better, and we might have a better chance of bringing this to an end faster. And protecting Oracle."

"I have to agree," Evans said.

Scholes nodded. He'd already reached this conclusion himself, having followed the investigation—and Lara—closely. And having run a more in-depth check on the USFID agent, once he learned the man was Lara's neighbor. For his own peace of mind.

"Very well," he began, when the door to his office burst open.

"We've got a security breach," IDSD's head of security said, his face ashen. "Another one."

The beeping sound was insistent and broke into some dream Donovan forgot as soon as he opened his eyes. He fumbled in the darkness and found his USFID phone.

"Agent Pierce, this is Nathan, Lieutenant Commander Walker."

Donovan was instantly awake.

"We have a situation here." The liaison was being carefully vague, Donovan noted, and he suddenly had an idea what this was about. "We would appreciate your coming here, to IDSD Missions."

Donovan sat up, ordered the lights on and looked at the bedside clock. Four in the morning. Rubbing his eyes, he got out of bed and went to the shower.

Chapter Eleven

The security agents at the IDSD gate cleared Donovan through immediately. Security was high here, higher than he remembered from his last visit, and even then it had been substantial. But then with the perpetrators of the data center break-in still at large, it was the way things were everywhere these days. He followed the agents' instructions and drove through the modern complex—artificially lighted in the pre-dawn darkness—to the visitors' parking lot of the. He'd been here before, but never to IDSD Missions. This was the most restricted area in the huge complex.

The security system tagged and identified him as he approached the building's entrance, and the doors slid open before him. A security agent waited for him on the other side, and escorted him to an elevator bank. On the top floor, the agent didn't get out of the elevator but was replaced by Nathan, who was waiting for Donovan just outside the elevator doors.

He walked into the hushed space and looked around him with curiosity. The last time he'd been to IDSD, he was on an official visit with USFID's director in the IDSD Diplomacy building. Where that building spoke of plush comfort, designed to cater both to the diplomatic corps employees who were far away from home for long stretches of time and to IDSD's guests, this floor and, as he could see from the glass elevator on his way up, the entire structure, was a state-of-the-art affair, somber and efficient, and, he would wager, with close to if not unlimited funding.

In the section of the top floor he was in now, a number of people, all uniformed, worked in the open space, even at this hour. In front of him, beyond the open space workstations, the floor was cut across its entire width by what looked like a reinforced opaque glass wall, the wide double doors in its midst closed. A low-hued security light flashed back and forth above the doors. Not at all subtle, this light was meant to be noticed.

This was where Nathan was leading him. When they approached the wall, Donovan heard a soft beep, although he could see no visible sensors, and the doors slid open silently. He was certain this level of security would take them into nothing short of a TAC, as it did at USFID, and was surprised when instead they entered another open space, spanning, he estimated, the greater part of the floor. Here the tension level was higher, and so was the efficiency. The center of the spacious area was divided into a number of partially enclosed workspaces, several of which had what seemed to be designated teams working in them, most uniformed, a few not. Donovan thought he heard a range of languages, though nothing coherent—the place was designed to enclose the voices of each team within its own workspace. He peeked into the nearest one and saw comfortable workstations. He noted that the people inside, a small group engaged in some sort of a discussion around two semi-spherical holoscreens running what looked like floor plans and simulations, were officers from different IDSD military branches, and two were Joint European Command air force officers.

Nathan beckoned him, and led him right, across the width of the floor, and then left, skirting the workspaces and coming to walk along a window wall that encompassed the floor's entire length. As he walked beside the liaison, Donovan took in the entire floor, now extending to his left. Far on the opposite side, beyond the workspaces, he could see a series of transparent walls with doors in them, each leading to a spacious office. Each of these offices had an external space with a small conference table in it, and beyond it a fully tinted glass divide, with a door to an inner office. Some inner offices were open, others closed. Immediately to the right of these offices was a large conference room.

Nathan indicated and he turned his gaze ahead, to a large office with an aide's station in front of it.

"That is Vice Admiral Scholes's office," Nathan said. "You've already met, of course, so to speak, the day of the data center break-in."

Extending to the left of the vice admiral's office and to the right of the conference room on the other side, the walls continued uninterrupted up to a wide, heavy-looking door, with an armed uniformed giant standing before it.

"That's our Mission Command," Nathan said in answer to Donovan's question. "It's the best in the world. And this entire part of the floor is our war room. From here we handle high-risk missions and crisis situations worldwide." He indicated the opposite side of the floor. "That's our war-conference room, or war-con, as some of the aides have gotten used to calling it over the years. It stuck, I guess. And beside it on the left are the criticals."

At Donovan's frown, he explained, "The people who determine the go-no go and to a great extent the success of the missions. Critical Mission Experts Renard, Edwards, and you've met Holsworth."

Donovan halted in surprise, and turned to look again toward the offices on the other side. "Critical mission expert...?" Some things clicked in his mind. More questions followed. He glanced at Nathan. It struck him that the liaison was being unusually forthcoming. In fact, Donovan was not being treated like someone who had been consistently stonewalled in the past days.

"Critical how?" He ventured to see just how forthcoming Nathan would be. They were now standing before the workstation of the vice admiral's aide, but

Donovan's attention was still on the three offices on the other side.

"Ah, well, that's a whole other clearance level. This designation is as such for security purposes. I'm sorry." He raised his palms up in a peace offering as he caught the glare in Donovan's eyes. "It's not my call."

"So you can't tell me what she does here?"

"Ms. Holsworth? Let's just say she . . . manages missions at their critical end. Yes, that's it. Anything more, that would be Vice Admiral Scholes's to say." Nathan turned away quickly, deflecting further questions. "And here we are." He nodded to the aide, and they were immediately ushered in.

Inside, Scholes stood up and greeted Donovan with a firm handshake. "It's good to meet you in person, Agent Pierce. I appreciate your coming here."

Donovan acknowledged with a nod. The big man before him was clearly worried and was not making any attempt to hide it. Neither did the blond, lanky and right now very pale man introduced to him as the head of IDSD Security, Carl Ericsson, or the one he already knew, Evans. Something had certainly happened to change their approach to his investigation. And to him.

"Allow me to get straight to the point." Scholes sat down heavily. Tiredly, Donovan thought. "We had another security breach last night. This time here, at IDSD."

"Obviously, we cannot be accessed from the outside, other than from other IDSD branches or with certain IDSD IDs. So they took one of our people. One of my people," Ericsson said, enraged.

"Carl," Scholes said quietly, and the man nodded, breathed in, and turned to Donovan. When he spoke again, his tone was controlled.

"One of my senior security agents never came on shift last night. We have a strict protocol, and the team we dispatched found him dead at his home, the place ransacked. By then his ID had been used to remotely access our administrative system. Normally we probably wouldn't have known it—it was done cleverly, whoever did this even changed the login time to reflect entry during the agent's last shift—but obviously now we knew to look, and knew what to look for. Anyway, they got in. And they might have managed to get more, but the new security protocol we've been implementing since the break-in restricts all authorizations until this thing is over. Although I'm thinking they got exactly what they wanted."

"Which was?" Donovan prodded.

Ericsson threw a look at Scholes and sighed. "A list of certain people present at IDSD Missions on the date of the raid on the base in Chad, and on two other dates."

"Two missions that their search for Oracle found during the break-in," Donovan guessed.

It was Scholes who responded to that, without

hesitation. "Yes."

"You said certain people."

"People in certain positions, with certain titles, backgrounds—the little that this security agent's authorization level allows to view—and clearance levels. Attendance dates, too, specifically the dates of the missions in question, but not only those. For safety purposes, the safety of these people, we need to assume Elijahn thinks one or more of them are the people he's looking for."

Donovan leaned forward. "So you're certain it's Elijahn."

"We've found no other incidents that fit, certainly not as well," Ericsson said.

"And the fact that one of the dates in question was of the raid on his base does seem to support that." Donovan chuckled mirthlessly. "And you already knew he was after someone here, didn't you? And this data theft, he's trying to identify a specific role here, isn't he?"

Their silence confirmed that he was on the mark. "He wants to find whoever gave the orders on the mission that destroyed his base," he continued. "He really does want revenge." He was thinking aloud now, following what he knew. He wanted them to hear it, deny or confirm. Damned if he was going to let more people die because of further stalling. "And he would want to get his reputation back. Otherwise it would all be for nothing, wouldn't it? He needs something that would get him back on track. But that would mean he thinks whoever he is after is someone who could get him what he needs, after his last failure. Someone who matters enough to you, to all of you. Someone the elimination of whom could hurt all of you in a way that would help him get what he wants."

He paused. They were all looking at him attentively. "Someone—or is it something? I raised an assumption when I spoke to your Lara Holsworth. A far-fetched one, I know, but she didn't deny it. Now I hear that she is a, what was it, critical mission expert? A rather obscure title for someone whose function at IDSD has so far remained hidden from me and who works in your war room. That's usually how it is for people with top clearance, which she obviously has. So I'm guessing she would have the necessary authorization to know exactly what I was talking about."

He shook his head. "That technology, that AI I talked to her about exists, doesn't it? You're not using only people to watch and guide missions here, in, what was it Nathan called it, the best Mission Command in the world, are you? You've managed to attain active computerized mission participation. Maybe even a computerized mission coordinator. Not autonomous, not entirely, so there's a person involved, it's more of an AI-human collaboration of some sort, right? And Elijahn can't get to the AI, so he's looking for the human, for whoever operates it or controls it or works alongside it in missions, or whatever that person does in your little project, and who had used it to destroy his Chad base. And he thinks that by killing that person, he'll cripple your ability to use the AI, probably for a long, long time."

The eyes that bore into Scholes's were not accepting anything but the truth now, and all of it. "That's Oracle. That's what it is, isn't it? A technology, an unprecedented achievement that all of you, IDSD and the allies, are keeping hidden. One of a kind. It is, isn't it? You've got your own little weapon that's getting in the bad guys' way, destroying them, and now this particular bad guy wants revenge on it so badly he's willing to do anything to get to it. And you're so busy keeping it hidden, protecting it, you're getting people killed."

"One of a kind, that's certainly true," Evans said in what Donovan actually thought was incredulity, and Scholes sent a silencing look his way.

"Yes." Scholes addressed Donovan. "And no. Yes, Oracle does exist. But no, it's not a weapon, and it's certainly not here to destroy. It's here to save lives. That's its primary directive."

"That's how all weapons start, and it's always part of their designation, isn't it? Save the lives of the innocent. But they kill on the way," Donovan said evenly.

"Oracle won't kill unless it has to. It is activated only when a critical mission hits a dead end and the good guys—to use your terminology—are about to get caught and killed. And in the past, that's exactly what happened. Since Oracle, it happens a lot less. In fact, there are many things that happen a lot less thanks to it."

"An AI that makes the decision not to kill unless it has to. That can prioritize based on sentient parameters. Or is that the person behind it? Whoever our bad guy is looking for? Man and machine working hand in hand?"

Scholes and Evans exchanged a look.

"Oracle," Scholes continued, not giving a direct answer, wanting to make sure Donovan understood first what Oracle was, "is also used for diplomatic missions gone wrong and for civilian rescues. Under IDSD, it is used by all allies, for varied missions, all critical. We're also increasingly involving it in mission planning, we've learned that doing so decreases the number of missions that go wrong. Less people get hurt. Less people die. We haven't had Oracle for long, but it has already made a hell of a lot of a difference. We're still learning where we can use it and how we can help it achieve its best without . . . burning it out."

Donovan frowned. Scholes really wanted him to understand. It was almost as if this was personal for him.

"Okay, let's say I understand its importance." And he did, if only because of the way Oracle had been protected by everyone, even at the expense of a crucial investigation that they needed solved without delay. He still had no concrete idea what exactly Oracle did at the Chad base raid, but Scholes's description of what that technology was, what it did, what it was achieving, its depiction as something that reached everywhere, had its hands, so to speak, in everything, making a difference like perhaps nothing else could, was only adding to what he had already understood the more his investigation had progressed—that hiding it just might be the right thing to do. Although he wasn't going to tell them that at this point. He still had his investigation. And he still had no idea what he was doing here.

He looked at Scholes thoughtfully. "Why is it so important to you that I know about Oracle—no, that I understand Oracle, now?"

"Oracle isn't just important, Agent Pierce. It is one of a kind, indispensable, and irreplaceable. To all of us." Scholes sounded almost desperate now. He took a deep breath. "As for why now, well, simply said, Elijahn is getting too close. And so you are here because we need you to understand what Oracle is, why it has to be protected. We hope that by telling you about it, you might be able to help us do that more efficiently than we have so far allowed you to."

Donovan raised his eyebrows.

"Yes, I know we've been standing in your way. But please understand we thought that's what we had to do to protect Oracle."

"Fine. So Oracle is important. It must not be

destroyed. But what about the person behind it? That's who Elijahn will get to. That's who he was looking for in this last data theft, remember? Is this person even important to you? Do you want to protect him too, or are you just afraid that if Elijahn will take him out you won't be able to use your precious Oracle?" Donovan was angry. He'd had enough.

Scholes took a mental step back. It would, he realized, be best to just show him. He walked around his desk to his office door. "Please." He indicated that Donovan should follow him. When Donovan didn't budge, he said, "Oracle has been called to a mission that has escalated. If things go the way it looks, it will be required to intervene."

Donovan wanted to argue, but he was curious. He wanted to see this thing that was the focus of everything that had happened. And there was something in the man's eyes that made him stop.

Scholes wasn't just worried. He cared.

Chapter Twelve

Following the vice admiral, Donovan turned back to look at the others, who stayed behind.

"Nathan isn't cleared," Scholes said, "and my head of security still needs to deal with this latest data theft. And Evans, he's been here all night working with Ruth—Larsen, you two have spoken—taking apart the drone data on the Chad raid. We're all, as you can imagine, working on this on our end too."

He led Donovan toward what Nathan had called Mission Command. Only when the armed security agent moved aside did the heavy door slide open. Donovan followed Scholes inside, then slowed down, astonished. IDSD's Mission Command was impressive in every way that mattered, and he had seen enough TACs to compare it with. And right now it was also dark, and very active.

At Scholes's urging, he came to sit beside him, in the front row of the half-packed room. Rows of seats stretched to his left and right, and sloped up all the way to the wall behind him. On them sat mostly uniformed men and women in combat and non-combat roles and of varying ranks. A mix of

IDSD, US military and Joint European Command, he saw. The entire length of the wall before him was covered with a multipurpose holoscreen, and under it stood an operations platform that stretched the length of the screen. Both on its right side and on its left stood stations for system operators, which he assumed were there to help operate Oracle.

Right now the screen was in two-dimensional mode, and was split into multiple smaller ones, displaying different views of a rough sandy terrain. A mission was in progress, or the aftermath of one, it seemed. Whatever it was, there was trouble. A uniformed man whose insignia Donovan couldn't see was standing on the left side of the operations platform, talking to the operator at that end, and an IDSD mission coordinator stood in its middle, speaking to the captain of the warship whose image was on the screen beside his. In the earpiece Scholes had given Donovan, he heard the chatter, bordering on urgency now, as the mission coordinator told the ship's captain to hold the transports, he couldn't get the men to them, and in the background he heard someone shout they were under fire and realized this was coming from the screen, where a helmet cam view appeared, blurry, its wearer running, then stopping, crouching down beside a low wall. As whoever had the helmet cam on turned his head Donovan saw several others around him, combat soldiers in full gear. Under attack, the intermittent sounds of gunfire clearly heard. Beside him, Donovan heard

Scholes say somberly, "Looks like we've got a live one for you, Agent Pierce. Unfortunately, right on time."

On the screen, the action intensified, the soldiers pinned down beside what Donovan could now see was a structure of half-broken walls, no roof. The helmet cam's wearer rose and peeked through a gap in the wall he was near and Donovan saw men, far too many, closing in on them. Not soldiers, it looked like, not in uniforms, although at least some were wearing tactical vests and their guns were certainly heavy duty, and one of them was down on one knee, setting up a portable rocket launcher, Donovan managed to see before the soldier crouched back down. The tension in Mission Command was high, and he heard someone behind him exclaim, the sentiment echoed by others around him. He looked at Scholes, but the vice admiral shook his head and indicated for him to remain silent.

"This has been unraveling for a while," he said quietly. "And as bad as it looks, it's not over yet."

Donovan had seen, had been in enough such situations in his past. It was over all right.

A movement to his left, and a figure moved into view. He sat up, surprised. It was Lara Holsworth. What the hell was she doing here? She obviously belonged, the way she walked over to stand facing the screen, the way both officers running the mission until now moved back, the way Mission Command fell silent in anticipation. She turned her head, and he saw that she had a headset on, a slight one with a mic near her mouth. Her next words had him stand up in surprise.

"Master Sergeant Giles, this is Oracle."

Donovan took a shocked step forward, but a security agent moved in the darkness and positioned himself before him, without saying a word. Donovan stepped back, and Scholes pulled him back down to sit, his expression grim. Donovan turned his eyes back to the woman now standing alone on the operations platform.

On the screen, the soldier she was talking to reacted, his gaze sweeping around, trying to take in the threats surrounding his men. "Oracle? Oracle, we're in a bit of a fix here, can you help us?"

"You'll make it to your kid's birthday tomorrow, Finn," she answered calmly.

On the screen, the master sergeant's eyes focused. "On your command," he said with a calmer voice.

Donovan saw her nod a little. Clever, he thought, even as she spoke quietly.

"Stay down, stand by," Oracle said.

A fast set of commands then uttered expertly, confidently, and all views on the screen shifted, reorganizing. More helmet cam views were added, along with a satellite feed of the soldiers and their immediate surroundings. As Donovan watched, she stepped back and took it all in, for a moment, only a moment, before she began issuing orders, directing the soldiers where to go. The satellite feed showed the movements of their pursuers around them, but then Donovan realized that her orders were coming first as the pursuers moved on the screen. Split seconds before, then seconds, then longer, in effect increasingly anticipating what the pursuers would do. It can't be, he thought. There must be a satellite delay, she must be getting the information on her headset. Except that the satellite feed data was, as indicated on the screen, in sync, while her orders were now being given before the pursuers even moved, putting the soldiers an increasing step ahead of those searching for them.

She led them away from their pursuers, away from the walls that had served as their interim cover, through sand dunes and sporadic low brush, until the helmet cams showed two amphibious transports coming toward them on land. Finn was ordering his people to board them when a bright laser point appeared between the soldiers and the amphibians, then another, both moving toward the transports. Except that a fraction of a second before that an aerial view appeared of two armed enemy drones from above, a satellite view swooping down beside it, and Donovan barely had time to register what he was seeing before the new views showed both drones explode in the air. On the ground, the laser points disappeared. The aerial view hovered while the satellite view distanced itself again, and the screen was once again dominated by ground views in which the soldiers boarded the transports that then proceeded to move back through a barren beach Donovan didn't recognize the location of, and into the water, chatter indicating that they were being met by the ship.

From the moment she stepped in and took over the mission, until the moment the amphibian transports were safely away, and the fighter jets she had directed to swoop down and bomb the site all the way to the beach and along it did just that, then rose up again to provide multiple escorting views of the amphibians from a growing distance above, the amount and complexity of the data and visual feeds she requested and received from whatever sources she was working with and her apparent manipulation of these were staggering, and the orders she issued were precise and unfailing. What he was seeing, he realized, was humanly impossible.

And yet there she was. Oracle. Lara Holsworth. No computer, no artificial intelligence, no weapon, no technology.

Lara.

He realized he was still staring at her when the last satellite view switched off, making way for the IDSD symbol that had already replaced all other views and data, and he heard people talking around him, relief in the air. Lights came up, though dimmed, and he saw Lara take her headset off, then rub the back of her neck to clear the tension away. No one approached her, no one but a young man with an aide's insignia who took the headset from her hand and put a bottle of water in it, which she accepted absently.

Putting his hand on Donovan's arm, Scholes motioned him to remain where he was, then stood up and took a step toward her.

"Oracle," he called out.

She turned around.

And saw Donovan. Her brow furrowed slightly, and then, to his surprise, she nodded slightly, as if resigned. She looked at Scholes, who said something to her, his voice quiet, his hand on her arm. She nodded again and walked away from Donovan, saying nothing. He wanted to follow her, but Scholes stopped him, and he watched as she walked out, the young aide beside her. He thought about the effort, the weariness in her eyes. Considered what it was like for her, what she had just done.

And wondered why it mattered to him so much.

Once she was gone the lights were turned up, and Mission Command gradually emptied around Scholes and him until only the operators remained, both now on the side farthest from them, talking among themselves. Mission Command was going from critical to low alert. Donovan turned to the vice admiral, who met his eyes with quiet somberness.

"Two years ago, it was Lara who stood right here in Mission Command and guided the alliance's soldiers into Elijahn's base. She then directed its annihilation. And as you must have already understood, she had no choice but to do that. It was one of Oracle's most intensive and difficult missions, in more sense than one." Scholes paused. "She told me about the incident you were privy to at USFID's TAC. That was us, we took control of that mission. US Global Intelligence notified us and asked for our help, and Mission Command took over. And that computerized voice you heard was Lara. Her voice is disguised as a computer voice that cannot be decrypted to identify the human voice behind it." His eyes held Donovan's. "There is no artificial intelligence. No person behind a machine. It's all Lara."

Donovan shook his head in disbelief. Even having seen it, it was still hard to believe. "She would need to be able to . . . God, she would have to have a staggering amount of knowledge, of experience. And those capabilities, what she did. It's not . . ."

"She gets all the information she needs. As soon as we understood what she is capable of, we began teaching her everything there was to know. Tactics, operations, training, weapons, aircraft, ships, technologies—anything you can think of. Everything, for every ally and for everyone who is not part of the alliance, at every level. Friends and threats alike. Dry knowledge, given to her by the best. Unless there was anything specific she asked to see or experience, be it a gun or a fighter jet or to observe a special ops unit in training.

"And it was enough. From the very beginning she seemed able to grasp the applied side of things just by connecting to the user. To those out there, in the field. Gradually—and I assure you it wasn't slowly—she accumulated a critical mass of information and began standing on her own, began pushing for knowledge faster than we could give it. And she developed with every mission. It's been five years. That's a lot, for her. Now we mostly just keep her up to date. Anything new—newly commissioned weapons, redeployments, operational forces, anything that could affect the outcome of a mission—it's all sent to her office.

"And when she takes over a mission, whatever information she needs she gets without delay, and she has access to any person or technology in the field and has command override authority. Mission Command is designed so that she can get to anyone and anything and she invariably has priority. You saw our drone take out their two? She did that. Did you see the visual from it, on her right just under the corresponding satellite view? She likes to keep armed autonomous drones high above and to command them directly, use them to watch or to intervene if she wants to. And those fighter jets? The data she got while she was already working the mission would have told her what was in the air in the area at any moment, and she followed that deployment continuously, don't ask me how she absorbs it all. And she used them, she simply gave the command directly from here, she can do that if she needs immediate point action. When she sees or anticipates something is about to happen, something no one else has seen yet, that's what she does. And it works. She is getting better, stronger, more knowledgeable, more capable with every incident."

"She doesn't rely at all on a computer, on some sort of computerized intelligence?" It seemed impossible. That much information, in that capacity and at that speed, with that promptness and preciseness of commands and action, all by a person.

"She doesn't need to. Does it all in that mind of hers. And we've had something to compare her achievements with. Pre-Oracle era. And we still do, she's not on all missions. She's never used if another configuration can do the job."

"To avoid burning her out." This, said earlier by Scholes, now made sense to Donovan.

"Yes." Scholes chuckled softly. "Funny, isn't it? For decades, humanity has dreamed of creating a technological intelligence that will integrate human capabilities with computer strength. Instead, we've got a superbly capable human with unprecedented spatial and temporal abilities who can operate at a level we haven't seen before. And I'm not telling you that AI attempts aren't done. They are. But the fact is that no one, nothing, comes anywhere close to her, to what she can do, and every time we think she has reached her limit, something happens and she shows us something new."

"What she did now, that goes beyond knowledge, it goes beyond experience, too. Take those away and you'd be left with . . ." Donovan stood up and walked up to the platform, faced the screen. He shook his head in disbelief. "How the hell did she do that?"

Scholes got up and came to stand beside him. "Damned if I know. She just does. Point is, she's the only one who can. And you haven't seen the half of it. Where we stop, the best of us, the best people, the best technologies, she takes another step forward and sees beyond it, beyond us all. And no one has any idea how." He shook his head incredulously. "Oracle. The woman who sees beyond."

"What you're describing should be protected. Taken care of and protected. If anyone puts his hands on her . . ." Donovan whirled around, realization dawning on him. "When Elijahn finds Oracle, he finds her. He finds Lara."

Scholes nodded. "Her name was among those he took in this latest data theft."

Donovan's heart skipped a beat. "He'll kill her."

Scholes let a breath out, worry evident on his face. "Do you have any idea how many would want Oracle gone if they knew about her? If this guy makes her existence known, they'll all be after her. And if he kills her himself, he'll get everything he wants from every one of the people in whose way she's ever stood. He'll be their hero."

"How the hell . . . she's out there, she lives right there next door to me, in plain sight! Didn't you think to—"

"Did you manage to find her?" Scholes cut him off.

"No," Donovan had to admit.

"And back there in my office, you just proved to us how well we're hiding her. Even you were sure Oracle was a technology. You never would have thought a person was doing all this. You saw what we do, all of us, you saw how we hide her."

"There seem to be quite a few people who know."

"What, the people you saw in here? Or in the war room outside? The captain? The soldiers she's just saved? These were IDSD and Joint European Command special forces, by the way. She's worked with them in the past. Those who need to be aware of her existence because of their position or what they do, those whose path crosses Oracle's, they know. But every single one of them is aware of her importance, and of the need to keep her existence confidential. Those in the field want themselves and their peers to have a better chance of coming back home safely on their next mission, and they were all either themselves or had friends saved by her. And those who plan, decide, oversee—they are all too aware of the influence she has on missions, on whole operations, and on the work the alliance does. No one takes her existence lightly, and everyone wants her safe."

He sighed. "Five years, the circle of people who know about her grows, and yet the secret is kept.

You know it can be done. We protect her. We began to use the critical mission expert title at IDSD because it helps conceal Lara among others with this title, and it explains her clearance and excludes the need for her code name to be used. We even talk about Oracle like it's a thing, an *it*, not a person. And thanks to the voice we use for her, not everyone who speaks to Oracle knows who she is. Some are still sure it really is an advanced computer, like you yourself thought. We've created a wall around Oracle, and we consistently separate Oracle from Lara." He chuckled bitterly. "And then this damn freak accident happens and a drone fails to self-destruct like it's supposed to, and now we've got Elijahn, of all people, after her."

Donovan took a step toward him. "With everything she does, everything she knows, is she able to protect herself, to physically protect herself?"

Scholes shook his head, but Donovan realized he didn't need the answer. Considering his own training, he would have recognized if she was. "You need to protect her."

The vice admiral sighed. "It's not that simple. For one, Lara has never cooperated with protection. She wants to live her life, and one of her conditions for becoming Oracle was that she would be allowed to live outside the protected IDSD complex. She allows us to approve the place she chooses to live in and to run her home security, but that's it. And if you think about it, that's the best cover Oracle can have.

If she disappears now, with Elijahn watching, with her on his list, he'll know she's behind Oracle. And with both Lara and Oracle disappearing, many others who have no business knowing will know it, too. And then she'll be hunted by more than just Elijahn."

"So no protection at all?"

Scholes smiled.

Donovan nodded. "Cameras?"

"We're piggybacking on municipal and law enforcement cameras. And we have a designated drone, way, way above her house. If needed, we can use our satellites to watch her, too, there's a standing order for that. She would kill me if she knew, by the way. As long as she doesn't ask, she doesn't know. So please don't tell her. And we can track her phone, laptop and car, of course, and that she's aware of."

Impressive, Donovan had to admit. Not enough, though, for him. "But if anything happens, you can't get to her in time."

Scholes looked at him.

Donovan chuckled. "So that's why I'm here."

"That's a part of it. The fact is that with what you now know about Oracle, you'll be able to understand Elijahn better, his motives. This might help you find him faster. But," he continued, "yes, I'm also hoping you'll help me keep an eye on her."

"Help you."

Scholes glanced at the dark screen, shook his

head. "Donovan," he said, surprising the younger man by speaking informally. "I brought Lara here, you know? I did. Even before I fully knew what she could do, before she herself knew. And I haven't regretted it a moment since. The things I've seen her do, the lives she's saved, that woman is a damn miracle. And it takes a toll on her. She goes right into the battlefield with them, she's as much there as they are, sometimes for days on end, and she knows them, she knows everything about them and she puts all of herself into saving them, and you saw, didn't you, you saw her eyes? It takes everything she has. Their lives are in her hands, and every time someone dies, every time one of them doesn't come back home, part of her dies with him. And it's not only them, every time she has to give a kill order, destroy, even though she knows it has to be done, that it would save lives, every single time it breaks something inside her.

"We called her in, you were there in her house, I know, talking to her when we called her in for a mission—that was yesterday, and it was over only a few hours ago, and this one, the one you just saw, it wasn't even hers, it was something that wasn't supposed to go wrong, but it did, and you saw how she just jumped in to help. And on the night of the break-in she was here too, you know? While this damn Elijahn was out there trying to find her so that he could kill her, she was here for four days, most of them she spent in here, in Mission Command, and then a mission she wasn't scheduled for went wrong and she'd intervened in that one too, one of yours, do you know? A US special mission unit ran into trouble, in the last moment it was, and she saved them, they would have been killed if not for her. And she will never stop, don't you see? Even now, when she is being targeted, she won't stop. She knows what she does, and she knows she cannot be replaced." The big man sat down, shook his head.

"You really do care about her." Donovan's voice was quiet.

Scholes looked at him. "Everything Lara does, everything she is, revolves around saving people. To do that she gives everything. It's like she feels them, like she locks on to something beyond, something in them, something in those fine threads connecting each and every one of them to existence itself. I don't know. That's the way she tried to explain it to me once and I can't explain it any other way. Somehow it's enough for her to be able to place them in a context she can look at, see and feel, and then she brings them back home. To do that she would have to open herself up in ways I cannot even begin to understand. I sometimes wonder where she goes, how deep she really goes, to save them. To save us. And the toll it must take on her." He shook his head, worry clear in his eyes. "And she won't let anyone in, you know? No one. Not anymore. She just goes through it all alone."

Donovan frowned. Not anymore? But the vice

admiral wasn't about to elaborate, and Donovan
wasn't about to push. This wasn't the time.

"Help me protect her," Scholes said.

Donovan looked at him.

"I checked you out, Donovan. You're a good man.
And you stop at nothing when you think someone
should be protected, needs to be kept safe. And I also
know that service pistol you're carrying isn't just
for show. They've used you in some of those same
field operations Lara is now untangling, even after
you already joined USFID, before you became too
valuable as an investigator for that. So you know
what that's like."

Donovan's eyes narrowed. Scholes had to have
gone to some lengths to get that.

Scholes stood up, walked to him. "You live in the
house next to hers. When she's not here, she's there,
and I'm not asking you to constantly be with her,
just . . . watch out for her. Please. I would," he said,
"consider it a personal favor."

Donovan never really needed to be asked. "I will,"
he said.

Before leaving IDSD Missions Donovan wanted to
see Lara, but by the time he left Mission Command
with Scholes she was in the conference room with
some of the people he'd seen sitting around him
during the mission. As he followed Nathan out of
the war room, on the way to Ericsson's office where
he would be shown the data stolen in the latest

data theft, he saw Scholes join them. When the vice admiral walked in, Lara turned to him and caught Donovan's eyes through the open door. Her gaze lingered for a moment, perturbed, and then she turned away again.

Back at USFID some hours later, Donovan went straight to White's office. He entered, closed the door behind him, and ordered Sensitive Compartmented Information Mode.

White looked up from his desk screen, then settled back with a smile. "Well. I assume then it was enlightening."

By the time Donovan finished filling him in, White was wide-eyed, speechless, and a smile was far from his mind.

"Right. I see. So I take it we never had this conversation."

"You and I did, no one else. That's the deal with Scholes and Evans."

"I don't blame them. I can't believe we didn't know about this."

"We're not that kind of agency, Leland. We didn't need to know until this happened."

"Still, this would have come up. They must have one hell of a blackout on this."

"They do. Wasn't enough, but not maintaining it to the extent possible will make things worse."

White's interest piqued. "For her."

"For many people."

"The other day you were raging mad because

she was privy to your investigation without you knowing. Then I think you said you threatened to shoot her. Then all of a sudden you go talking to her, voluntarily brainstorming with her. And now you've agreed to watch over her?"

"Doing my job."

"Yes. Right. Of course."

Donovan stood up. "Something you want to say, Leland?"

White's gaze was serious, something soft in it. "I'd be the last person to say anything about this, old friend."

He watched as the younger man walked out of his office. Here's to hoping, he thought.

Chapter Thirteen

Donovan slowed down the car near Lara's house and frowned. The house was dark. He hadn't considered that she might not be there yet. He'd been waiting to confront her, and her not being home only increased his anger. He swerved into his driveway and was just getting out of his car when headlights appeared down the street. He watched as the garage next door opened, then closed behind her car. He tried to steel himself, considered letting it go until he regained his composure, and found himself at her front door.

Inside, her home system registered him. Standing at the control console at the door to the garage, Lara braced herself and let him in. She dropped her jacket on the back of a couch, then walked to the kitchen and placed her briefcase on the counter, and leaned back on it, IDSD ID at a clear view on her belt, no longer needing to hide. Then she waited.

Donovan strode in, his anger, fueled by a concern he wasn't used to, getting the best of him. "Why the hell didn't you tell me what, *who* Oracle is? Why didn't you just tell me it was you?"

"That name isn't said lightly outside the IDSD war room," she said quietly, not trying to justify, just to find a way to explain, to deal with this situation she had had no idea what to do with from the start. "And you weren't cleared to know."

"I wasn't cleared—" Donovan turned away from her, furious. "Christ!" He turned back, anger flowing from him in powerful waves. "I've been running around like crazy because of Oracle, had walls placed at my every move, and all that time this was about you?"

"No." Her own anger flared. "It's about them. The soldiers you saw today, the people out there in all those missions, the civilians who would die if we fail. It's not about me, it's never about me."

"It is for me!" He had no idea where that came from. Nor when it had become true.

She was as shocked as he was, that much he could clearly see.

He forced himself to calm down. "I sat here, just yesterday, and you let me talk about computers and human-AI links, and all that time you knew I wasn't even close. I sat here talking to Oracle about Oracle, and you said nothing."

She let out a deep sigh. "I couldn't say anything. Now that you know, don't you see that?" She wanted so much to make him understand. Needed him to understand. "Oracle has touched so many missions, untangled so many difficult situations. There are missions that would never be thought of, that get further than ever before possible, because of Oracle. There are plans of theirs, the bad guys, wasn't that what you called them, that were ruined because I got in their way. Elijahn—think about what I did to him. I ruined him. I gave our people, yours and mine, a way in, and I led to the total destruction of his entire base, and with it the future of his group. I did that. You think I don't know it? You think I don't know what I am?"

She shook her head. "If they kill Oracle, that's over. We won't have that edge anymore. Your people, mine, the entire alliance won't have that edge anymore. And it's not only that. Think about it, if they connect Oracle to me, if they expose who I am, then through me they could get to so many people. So many who were in the field the same day I was working on a mission, who were in Mission Command and in TACs and operation centers and in bases all over the world and so many who I speak to on these missions, so many I work with, whether they know who I am or not . . . all those people. All those lives."

The thought was unbearable, and she walked to her favorite couch not far from the closed patio doors, sat down and tucked her feet under her as if trying to gain some comfort from this small corner of hers, and just then Donovan had an idea of the toll this situation was taking on her. He thought about missions he'd been in, unspeakable situations where out there, in the field, alone, he had had to find a way to protect his people, the many times he'd faced death, the too many funerals he'd been to those days. Tried to imagine what it was like for her, the moment she was called to step in, all eyes on her, knowing that if she couldn't save those on the screen before her, they would, quite simply, die. Wondered how many times she'd lost, what it did to her. What it was like for her, being responsible for so many lives, in so many ways. Thought about the artificial intelligence he had thought Oracle was, safely immune to emotions such as loss and regret, and realized he couldn't even begin to grasp how extraordinarily strong this woman, so incredibly human, had to be to stand it.

She looked up at him. He was watching her, the blue in his eyes powerful and intense, and it was as if he was reading her, she thought, and was at a loss to realize that she was unable to protect herself, unable to hide under his gaze. "How many will get hurt because of me?" she asked, weary. "I don't know. Maybe Oracle should stop. Lara's disappearance can be disguised. Then we can at least protect those who were involved in past missions in which Oracle participated."

The pain in her voice hurt him. He walked over and sat on the coffee table before her. "How many will die if Oracle is not around?"

She closed her eyes.

"That's what it's all about, what's important here, isn't it? Frank and I had a little chat. He told me all about how Oracle sees what no one else can. How you save lives no one else is able to."

She opened her eyes and looked at him, and there was no vanity, no acknowledgment of those extraordinary accomplishments he'd heard assigned to her, the achievements she was so aware of. Just weariness and worry. Enough to fuel his own concern. Part of him had thought she had no idea of the danger she was in. But he now realized he was wrong, so wrong. She was very much aware of it. But she wasn't thinking about herself, and suddenly he wasn't sure she cared. It was only the others she seemed to worry about. Those who would be at risk if her existence was known, those she would not be there to bring home if Oracle was gone.

His mind went back to what he'd seen in Mission Command, and he wondered about this intriguing woman who talked about what she did as if it was, for her, the most natural thing in the world, this ability no one else could even come close to.

"How do you do it?" he asked. "I saw you, what you did there. You're a strategist and tactician and behaviorist and so many other things all rolled into one, there is no doubt about it, but there were moments there where none of it would have helped, and then you relied on something that wasn't even there, intuition, something I can't put my finger on." He tried to explain, found he couldn't. "It's like you were running, and no one, nothing, could keep up with you."

"I've never heard it described quite like that," she mused. "But I guess that's one way to describe it. And it's also . . ." She thought about it. "It's like everything around me reaches a wall and stops, but I go through it, without even realizing I have, and then I can see what's on the other side. Yes." He was watching her, absorbed, really wanting to understand, and she realized with wonder that she'd never talked to anyone about Oracle this way.

And that they weren't fighting anymore.

She smiled, a small smile. "It's nice."

He looked at her questioningly.

She shrugged. "Not having to hide."

He thought about that. About the life she had no choice but to lead. About being unable to talk about what she did, about Oracle. About herself.

"Are you afraid?" It came out of nowhere.

The question caught her off guard. "Yes. Shouldn't I be?" She closed her eyes, shook her head. "If he finds me, this could hurt so many people. And I don't know what to do, how to stop it."

He couldn't help but smile. She opened her eyes and saw his reaction, and understood that that wasn't what he was asking. Self-conscious, she turned the question back to him. "Are you?"

"What? Afraid? That I might fail to stop Elijahn before he gets to you? Yes," he said evenly.

She'd meant if he was afraid Elijahn might target him too, because of his investigation. Because he was close to her. It surprised her that he would see things that way. Worry about her, that way.

"If anyone can stop this, it's you," she said.

"I hope I can. And in time."

"You can. That's why I approved you."

He started. "You approved me?" He contemplated this. "That's why you involved yourself in the investigation at the beginning. That's why you were in that first videoconference."

She shrugged.

The anger erupted again, out of frustration, this time, at the danger all the delays in his investigation posed for her. "Why the hell didn't you just confide in me earlier?"

"Are you kidding? You kept coming at me! You made it clear at least on one occasion that all you wanted was to shoot me!"

"Yes, well, I'd love to do that right now!"

"Stand in line," she said wearily and settled back, closing her eyes. She was so tired. Of having to hide. Of being pursued. Of the possibility that someone would get hurt because of her. Even him, Donovan.

The expression on Donovan's face changed, and he shifted just that much closer. "I won't let anything happen to you."

"You're investigating, that's enough," she said, her eyes still closed. "Thanks to you we now know who he is, why he wants me. But if you get closer to this, it could put you in the line of fire. I don't want that." She didn't know what to deal with first. The idea that he might get hurt, or the fact that she even cared this way, more than she had thought possible.

"It's not your choice."

She looked at him then, and there was something new in her eyes, something sad. "I don't want you to get hurt," she said again, her voice barely a whisper.

He wanted to hold her. The realization struck him so hard he couldn't breathe. He wanted to go to her, take her in his arms, and not let go. Never let go. This was new, he never . . . He shook out of it inwardly. Forced the investigator to take over the man. For her.

"Then cooperate with me," he said. "That will reduce the likelihood of that happening."

She smiled. "Manipulation, Agent Pierce? Really?"

"Hey, whatever works," he answered, relieved at the smile.

He had her program his priority number into her phone, and programmed hers into his to allow for a call from her to come through even if he didn't care to answer his phone, which was easily the case if he was involved in an investigation. While she was here, in her home, he said, and he was next door, he was close, and all she had to do was call and he would come.

She didn't argue.

While she was sending his contact details from her phone to her home system, the phone beeped. She took a look at the message received and her eyes focused. "I've got to go." She stood up.

"You just got back. And you're tired."

She shook her head and went to pick up her briefcase, absently making sure her IDSD ID was on her belt, and grabbed her jacket on the way to the door to the garage. "It's not one of mine, but I'm on standby for it. And if they're calling me, then it's going wrong." She glanced at him, saw his brow furrow, and stopped. "This is what I do, Donovan. It's what Oracle is." She gazed at him for just a moment, then smiled, that quiet smile again. "And it's not like there's anyone else I can send instead."

"There really is no one else, is there?" He watched her as she walked to the door, understanding, he thought, just a little bit more.

She stopped again and turned back to him, gazed at him thoughtfully this time, as if sizing him up. "Could you close up? The house will lock down automatically." She gave him that resigned look again. "Frank gave you access, didn't he?" And she left.

He remembered then something that Scholes had said. That Lara wanted to live her private life outside IDSD's security hold. And here he was, with full security access to the very place she tried to call her own. There was more than one threat closing in on her—and he himself was a threat somehow, too, he'd seen it in her. That one confounded him. That was not a reaction he was used to from a woman. And it wasn't a reaction he wanted from this woman.

He heard the garage door open and her car

move out. He took out his phone and made a call. "Frank, she's on her way to you," was all he said. He then engaged the security system and left.

As much as he tried to that night, he couldn't sleep.

Something about this bothered Elijahn.

The latest part of his plan had gone smoothly. The security agent had been easy to kill. Elijahn had had someone watching him for weeks. A woman. That always worked. When the time came, she killed him—she was dead now too, of course, Elijahn no longer had use for her—and the hacker had used the dead man's access authorization to get what he was told to from IDSD. The names of the people who were at its missions building on the dates of the three attacks—the destruction of his base and the two attacks in which the name Oracle was mentioned that were included in the data the hacker had managed to get from the data center.

"So I did a quick search and download of the people who were at that specific building on the relevant dates. It was easy, with that security guy's authorization," the hacker said. He was still hunched over the computer, filtering out and printing hard copies of what Elijahn wanted. Elijahn did not like computers. He understood technology, understood it extremely well, in fact, and used it to his advantage, but that did not mean he had to like it. He preferred to buy people to deal with it.

The hacker was still talking, explaining endlessly, trying to impress—Elijahn was used to the technical people he bought trying to impress, so unlike his militants, whom he preferred—and his voice was an irritation. "Of course, knowing who was in the building at the time of the attacks is not enough, so I hacked a bit higher than his authorization to find the clearance levels they use." The hacker knew all about clearance levels, he continued bragging. He was used to using them to get what he wanted, be it knowledge or money. But these particular clearance levels he did not want to use. He only wanted to find out what they meant and who held them, which he did.

"So I found some people who were there on all those dates we have for Oracle and some other dates around them, just to establish a pattern, and whose clearance is high enough to give them access pretty much anywhere. Which I'm thinking is exactly the kind of clearance Oracle's operator would have. Yes, I'm sure. Yes," he said, pulling sheets out of the small printer beside him and handing them to Elijahn. "Couldn't get more without risking it, they've got pretty good cybersecurity in there. But don't worry," he added quickly, not wanting Elijahn to mistakenly think he'd messed up in some way, "they never even knew I was there."

"This is all you found about them?" Elijahn was looking at the information about the people the hacker had singled out.

"I . . . I had to be careful. And there were too many people, I thought the clearance levels are important, to narrow the search. And after I got them, it was too risky to go back and find more about them. I could try hacking again . . ."

"No." This was not worth the risk. Or the time. Elijahn turned his attention to what he did have. In no time, he had the list narrowed down to three. He would have preferred to kill them all, and to target, perhaps, several more of their leaders. To satisfy his anger, if for no other reason. But this was a foreign land, not his turf, and his resources were limited.

He focused on his chosen targets. The first, a man named Dr. Bernard Miles, was currently stationed at IDSD Missions although he had formally been part of IDSD's Advanced Technologies Research Division for the past eighteen years. His specialty was artificial intelligence in military command applications, and he had no military training, but according to the data about him he was authorized to join troops in the field as part of his work. As such, Elijahn thought, he would be in a unique position to help develop a missions system such as Oracle. In fact, he would be in a good position to also be Oracle's operator. Looking at the man's professional brief, he thought it was a man he himself would hire.

The second man was an IDSD army colonel, John Edwards, who had the obscure title of critical mission expert. Elijahn did not know what that was—nor did the hacker—but the man was a decorated combat soldier with experience in an impressive range of areas. However, he was sixty-three and had never worked in anything relating to computers. Still, the hacker had pointed out, quite correctly, that technology had been a major part of combat throughout this man's military career, all the more so since he was part of IDSD, which from the start focused on creating a smart, professional military force. The hacker had also explained that unlike the artificial intelligence's creator, an operator would not necessarily have to have a computer-related background. He could, instead, have expertise related to whatever attacks Oracle was used in, although even the hacker seemed skeptical there, stretching it, perhaps, to placate Elijahn. No, the first man, Miles, sounded more fitting.

Still, this one would be killed, too. Just in case.

Elijahn's problem here was that neither could explain what Oracle did. Not entirely. The hacker might have been on the mark if there were only the audio files to consider, and the transcripts taken from the data center. But Elijahn had actually seen the attack on his base, through the cameras he had there. And hearing the audios from the drone later, all he had to do was close his eyes and see the images that came with the sounds and voices he was hearing.

And even now, two years after the attack, he could not let go of the feeling that what he had seen was impossible. The attack was impossible. Oracle was impossible. It did not fit, certainly not snugly, with the image the hacker had built for it. There had to be more to it, Elijahn's gut told him. Yes, perhaps an artificial intelligence such as the hacker was sure Oracle was could have capabilities that were beyond Elijahn's knowledge, and that could explain it all. And so yes, Miles and Edwards would be killed, and perhaps the chatter Elijahn would look for later would show panic about the death of whoever it was of the two who had been the force behind Oracle. But perhaps not.

Something was still missing. And Elijahn wanted to know what.

His eyes flickered to the third photo, the third person he had decided to pick.

This one was a different story. This one he had selected out of the people whose information the hacker had given him even though she did not fit the profile. No, that was not quite accurate. Elijahn had no way of knowing if she fit the profile because there was nothing about her. No information at all. And yet, this person was at IDSD's missions building on all dates.

And her clearance was the highest of the three.

All he had were a photo, and the dates and times that had caught his eye. Not the dates of the destruction of his base and the two additional missions. No, the other dates and hours that outlined the pattern of her arriving at IDSD and leaving it, automatically recorded by its security system. It seemed to him that she was there a lot. Several days in a row, at times. She came and left at odd hours, and there was no regularity to her stay there. And then there was that title again, critical mission expert.

He could act now, complete his revenge. Kill the first two, and thus, he was almost certain, cripple Oracle.

Almost certain.

His eyes flickered to her photo. And her name.

Lara Holsworth.

Beside him, the hacker sneered. "A looker."

Elijahn punched him.

He did not heed the man's pitiful whimpers. The hacker had now outlived his usefulness. True, he was Elijahn's best. That was why he was the one Elijahn had brought with him here. But the fact was that Elijahn's plan was nearing completion, and he was not planning on leaving any loose ends behind. And since he would not take the hacker on the final part of his plan, he was just about disposable.

His eyes were glued to the photo. He wanted to think about this one a bit more. A lot of secrecy there, the kind of secrecy he himself would put in place if he wanted to hide something. Like he had hidden himself. Like they would hide Oracle. Or the person responsible for its impossibly extraordinary achievements. He decided to add her to his list.

Although he might not kill her after all.

Chapter Fourteen

The next day found Donovan at IDSD Missions once again, walking with Nathan through the war room to Frank Scholes's office.

"Donovan." Scholes motioned him in, and Nathan stayed outside with the vice admiral's aide. "I've assigned a team based on what you said you'd need. They're under your command for the duration of the investigation. Nathan will make the introductions."

Donovan nodded. He was now focused on finding Elijahn, and adding an IDSD team to the search was the best way to go. IDSD had better international resources and access, and considering the information it had about Elijahn, his group and his former affiliates, and its original involvement in stopping him two years earlier, its team had a better chance of successfully tracking his movements worldwide, while Donovan's designated SIRT team, under Ben, would be far more efficient inside the United States. To ensure seamless contact between the two teams, so that nothing would be missed, Donovan had suggested that Nathan join his people at USFID, and do what he did best, liaise. Which Nathan had readily agreed to do once he would make sure Donovan was working just as seamlessly with the IDSD team.

"How did you get on with Lara yesterday?" the vice admiral asked. "I didn't have a chance to talk to her much today, she's on a mission. A bad one to start with."

The one she'd been called to the night before. Donovan frowned. "Bad for Lara?"

Scholes's eyebrows rose. The man's first question was not to satisfy his curiosity about the mission or about Oracle. It was to worry about Lara. "I'm afraid there's a chance it will be."

"She's exhausted."

"The past days haven't been easy."

No, Donovan thought. Not in the least. "We're fine, we've straightened things out between us." He contemplated the vice admiral. "You told her you gave me security access to her house."

"Yes."

"I'm not sure that was a good idea. I get the feeling it's difficult for her to accept."

"Naturally. I gave you access to her life outside her work. And without asking her permission. As for my having told her—one rule, Donovan. Never lie to Lara." He raised his hand to stop Donovan's objection. "Somehow I don't think you would. Not even to protect her, is what I mean."

"I understand. But as it is, I've now invaded not only her work life, but also her personal life, in a manner of speaking."

Scholes looked at him slyly. "And here I thought you were doing that anyway. Or were intending to. Don't bother." He stopped Donovan before the latter could speak. "I've commanded people most of my life, and I'm a husband, a father, and a grandfather. Bullshitting me is not an option." He laughed, but the laugh was cut short when his aide stepped into the office.

"Sir," Celia said. "We have a . . ." She darted a glance at Donovan, and Scholes indicated for her to go on. "Somalia is now MC4."

"At least that one we expected." Scholes stood up. "Good luck with the hunt," he said to Donovan, then called Nathan in and ordered him again to make sure Donovan had what he needed. With that, he left.

"What's MC4?" Donovan asked Nathan as they exited the office.

"Mission Command at level four, a mission that's not under IDSD control and without its prior involvement, but that is known to it and now requires its assistance." Nathan threw a glance at Mission Command. "It must be bad. They've had this going throughout the night, but apparently now it's coming to a head. It's always more complicated when it's something IDSD was not a part of in the planning process."

Donovan stopped to look. Across the war room, Scholes was walking toward the office nearest the conference room, where a harried officer stood. They spoke briefly, but when Lara exited the office they made way for her, then followed her briskly to Mission Command. As she walked she turned and called out, "Bailey, Walsh, keep the drones away. For now I want only space eyes, zero interval, full overlap."

As the "yes, ma'am" sounded she began turning back, saw Donovan, and slowed down. She acknowledged him, with some hesitation, he noticed, then hastened her pace again and disappeared through the heavy Mission Command door that opened before her.

"So," Donovan said, now able to put what he'd just seen in context. "What happens when Lara asks for full satellite coverage?" Even with the abundance of alliance space technology, satellites were constantly at work on multiple other tasks at defined sectors. Constant coverage at full sector range, which was what she'd asked for, would be near impossible for a substantial duration, unless a complex retasking of a series of satellites was employed.

"She gets it," Nathan simply answered and led him to a workspace in the midst of the war room. Inside, a small team was discussing something near a screen where a map moved beside running data. Donovan knew what they were doing, because he was the one who'd asked that they do it. They were trying to track Elijahn's movements prior to his arrival in the United States, based on criteria he had given Scholes the day before. Over the next hours he would add criteria, eliminate others, work with them to retrace Elijahn's steps, then go back to USFID and do the same with his investigators, focusing on locating Elijahn's whereabouts inside the country.

"There." The hacker pointed. "And there, and there." He indicated three frames on the screen. Three cars. "My recognition software found them."

"It took time," Elijahn grumbled.

"I had to wait until night to place the camera, I couldn't risk anyone seeing us, and cars arriving in the morning, there are so many of them, the software needed time to identify the people you want." The hacker spoke quickly. He was very aware of how close he had come to dying. He needed to be of use, needed to find a way to stay alive. The man standing behind him clearly had no compunction about killing him despite the role he had played in his plan ever since the loss of his base.

So far everything had worked out well. Since the data stolen from IDSD did not include addresses for the three people Elijahn chose to target or details of their vehicle registrations—these required a higher authorization level—the hacker had implemented a contingency plan for tracking their movements. In the small hours of the previous night, he had traveled with two of Elijahn's militants to IDSD. They approached not from the main road that led to the huge complex's main gate, but from a narrow path that cut through the woods behind the open fields that flanked that same road. Hidden by the trees at the edge of the woods, the hacker had navigated a small remote-controlled ground device, not larger than a toy car, into some vegetation just off the road and half a mile from IDSD's main gate, far enough from the security cameras and tracker beams not to be seen. He then directed the miniature camera on the device to slide up its pole to the vegetation line, where it would provide clear visuals of the road, yet still be hidden enough not to be detected by a surveillance drone.

Hours later the hacker was back at the warehouse, while the camera was still in place, recording all vehicles passing by to and from the IDSD complex. This was potentially valuable information, the identities of all the people driving on that road, even those who were not Elijahn's immediate targets. And yes, the hacker would file it away for future leverage. But for now, his facial recognition software focused on locating the three people Elijahn had chosen as his targets.

His idea was simple. Once he would locate the targets, he would have their cars and would hack the software in them—the manufacturer software, he did not want to risk being tagged by the IDSD security software he assumed these high-ranking people had in their cars. He would then track the cars from afar, know where they were at any given moment, and this would allow Elijahn to plan his attack on the targets. Yes, he would be valuable to Elijahn yet.

So far it had worked liked a charm. He had them, their cars, and hopefully more time in this life.

"What now?" Elijahn's tone was never patient.

"Now I hack the cars. And their positions will be tracked on these screens." The hacker pointed to where three screens stood, one beside the other. "We will be able to discern travel patterns and know their positions at any given moment."

"How long will that take?"

"I will be tracking all of them by tonight. Morning the latest."

Elijahn was silent for far too long. The hacker prayed.

"Do it."

The hacker breathed in a sigh of relief and went to work.

Back at USFID, Donovan spent some time with Ben's team, IDSD's liaison now included. Satisfied with their work, and with the interagency collaboration, which was crucial in this investigation, he then decided his own work would best be served if he took the time to clear his mind, and a thorough workout at one of the gyms gave him just that. By the time he'd showered and dressed in jeans, a USFID T-shirt and a light-weight jacket the investigation was running smoothly in his mind, and he was easily observing it from every angle.

Skipping his floor, he joined White for a quick dinner at the director's office, where he could update him in private. It was also the only place White dared have the burgers and fries he so craved, which his wife had sworn him to avoid for his health. He tried, he really did, but those working dinners with Donovan at his office were his chance to happily fail.

The pressure from the agencies was down, White told Donovan. Donovan was now in the loop about Oracle, which meant he no longer had to be watched in their effort to protect it, and his insistence in the investigation was what had ended up directing them to Elijahn, and so he finally had their trust, along with the freedom to do as he wished.

Night had fallen by the time Donovan returned home. He'd hoped Lara would be back by the time he got there, but her house was dark and silent when he drove by and pulled into his driveway. He frowned. She was still at Mission Command when he had left IDSD's war room, and from the anxiety around him and Scholes's expression, he had understood something had indeed gone very wrong.

He contemplated having some coffee and sitting down to do some work, but instead walked out to his back yard. He couldn't take Lara off his mind. There was a lot he understood now, a lot he could reconcile in his mind. But not quite enough. Not for him. Not when it came to her. He needed more. Even if he no longer tried to explain to himself why, he wanted to know more.

The thought sent him to her house, to ensure it was secure. Just in case. Even though her home system would have picked up on a security breach. Maybe the fact that the data center's much more sophisticated security had failed made him reluctant to trust any security system right now, or maybe it was because he was wondering when Elijahn would figure out who she was and come after her. It didn't matter either way. He simply had to make sure.

He crossed his back yard to hers and started in surprise. She was there, sitting on the grass in the middle of the yard, only the low security lights illuminating her. She sat huddled, hugging her knees, her face hidden in her arms. He watched her. She had changed her clothes, he saw, and was dressed comfortably, it looked like, but not nearly warmly enough for this chilly night. She must be freezing, he thought. He watched her. She didn't move. Normally he would stay away. And this was her, after all. It must be nothing. She was thinking, maybe.

Except that his gut was churning. Everything about her screamed wrong to him, awakening a dormant instinct deep inside him. And that mission she'd just been in. . .

He moved before the thought had a chance to be argued in his mind, walked to her quickly, and crouched before her huddled form. "Lara?"

Nothing. He put his hands on her arms. "Lara."

She raised her head slowly, and he flinched. She

was pale, so pale, black shadows under tired, lifeless eyes. A single trace of a tear was visible on one cheek. His hands tightened on her arms.

"What's wrong? What happened?"

She said nothing, just stared at him with a hollow look that pierced through him.

"Please." His voice was soft but insistent. "I want to understand. I need to understand."

Her eyes grew distant, and he knew she went somewhere inside herself, replaying.

"I get their files." She closed her eyes as if the thought had an unbearable reality behind it. "I get their lives. All of it. Who they are, who they love, their fears, their dreams." She opened her eyes again, and the intensity in them scared him. "Their reason to live. So that I can use it if I need to. To bring them back. Motivate them. Remind them."

"Touch them," he said, understanding. Like she had done with that soldier, Finn, made him think of his son.

"Touch them," she repeated with that hollow voice that sent a stab of fear through him, fear for her. He thought about what he had seen in Mission Command. The depth of it. The intensity.

"So before a mission even starts, before you know if there's even anyone left to save, you already . . . feel them," he said slowly.

She nodded, focusing on him as if he'd hit the mark, and tears welled up in her eyes.

"And they died," he said. He got it. He had seen

many senseless deaths in his life.

She nodded again.

"All of them?"

She closed her eyes wearily and lowered her head to her arms again. Hiding. She was exhausted, and Donovan wondered when she had last slept. No way she could even begin to have the energy to deal with this. With death.

He remembered what Scholes had told him. About her opening herself up, looking beyond, feeling beyond, to bring back those she was there to save. "I wonder where she goes, how deep she really goes, to save them," he had said. Oh, God, Donovan thought. Oh my God. So that's what it's like for her. Not the wins. The losses.

He wrapped his arms around her. She was ice cold. His mouth near her ear, he whispered, "Come on, let's get you inside."

He picked her up easily, cradling her in his arms, and took her into the house. He lay her gently on the sofa, then went back and closed the patio doors. On his way back to her, he stopped at the main console, started the heating, and turned the living room lights on low. Turning from the console, he looked at her. She'd remained where he'd put her, laying on her side, her eyes vacant. He wanted her to be angry at him for butting in, for not leaving her alone, wanted her to fight him, to be herself, to be all right. Wanted her not to go through this. How many times had she already, he wondered, alone?

He returned to her, took her slippers off and covered her with the throw laying on the back of the sofa, then sat beside her. He pushed a lock of soft hair from her face, and rested his hand on her back. "Close your eyes," he said, his voice soft, his touch tender. "Let go."

He sat with her while her eyes closed, sat there while her body relaxed and her breathing calmed under his touch. Sat there for a long time afterward. Then he got up and crossed to the closest couch, and sat down to watch her.

He was still sitting there, watching over her, when she woke up.

As sleep receded, Lara felt hazy, fought to remember. Getting home, taking a hot shower that did nothing to alleviate the tension, crawling into bed, trying to sleep. But the pain she felt deep inside her had been too great and she had to escape, needed air and so she went outside. And then . . . Donovan, she remembered and opened her eyes to find herself looking straight into his. Caring, she realized with confusion. He smiled, something new in his smile, and this only confused her more.

She sat up slowly and shook sleep away. The color had returned to her face, and her eyes had her strength in them again. And the confusion, he saw that, too. His smile widened as relief surged through him, and he masked it with the attitude he knew she would be more familiar with from him.

"Truce," he said, raising his hands.

Confusion was replaced with embarrassment as memories came flooding in, and he saw it and got up before she could do or say anything.

"I'm thinking coffee," he said as he walked to the kitchen. On the way, he ordered her home system to open the shades he'd closed earlier, and the early morning sunshine flooded the living room.

She followed him with her eyes, said nothing. She had no idea how to deal with this. With him, like this, of all people. She wasn't used to anyone being with her when things got this way, seeing her this way. But also . . . this was him. And the way he was now, the way he'd been the night before . . .

She had no idea how to even begin reacting.

He brought the coffee mugs over, handed her one, her favorite reddish brown mug, and she wondered fleetingly how he knew, then remembered.

She took it hesitantly. Abruptly she said, "Thank you," and meant more than the coffee.

He looked at her for a long moment, then nodded. Returning to sit on the couch he said, "I had no idea."

She shrugged slightly, lowering her eyes to the mug. Trying to hide again, he thought. But he wasn't about to let her do that, to go back there alone. Not anymore.

"To do what you do, wouldn't it be easier to keep your feelings out of the way, think logically? It would shield you, wouldn't it?"

"The feeling part helps me lock on them, know what's happening to them, and then I can see what's around them, make connections I can use to bring them back. I do whatever it takes."

"And then what, you just come home and deal with it alone?"

"It's not always this bad. This mission . . . it was a rescue mission to try to get out people who'd been caught in hostile territory." She hesitated, although his clearance and recent events meant she could talk about it. And she knew he would understand better than most. "In Somalia, just a couple of weeks ago. But when the would-be rescuers got in, we found that they were already dead. And when the rescuers tried to get out, they were ambushed. By the same people."

"You got them out."

"But just them, and just barely. And they couldn't even take their dead friends with them."

"Are they sure . . . ?"

"Yes, we found them. All of them. What's left of them. The way they were killed . . ." She closed her eyes. Didn't want to remember. "Why didn't they involve us earlier? In the original mission? Maybe . . ."

"You didn't know about the original mission?"

"No. This was an African Independent Territory mission. They're not officially a part of the alliance yet."

He nodded slowly.

She held the mug with both hands, as she had

when he saw her that first morning he discovered she was his neighbor, and looked down at it. "I shouldn't be reacting this way, it's stupid, I knew there was a chance they were dead. I guess it was a dead-end mission to begin with."

He raised his eyebrows. "Right. First of all, you either take it to heart all the time or not at all, and I'm guessing part of what makes you so good at what you do is that you take it to heart all the time. And second, how many missions have you been involved in since we met? No, forget that. How much sleep did you get since we met?"

She shrugged again. "It's worse for them."

"You know," he said, leaning forward. "I've seen enough combat soldiers return home after a tour of duty wiped out because of the emotional burden they were subjected to. And the way I understand it, you deliberately set yourself up to feel it all when you go into your Mission Command." He shook his head. "Maybe you're not living it every day for months on end, like they do, but you are getting concentrated bits and pieces of it all the time, sometimes without warning, don't you? And they finish with the mission and come back, while you immediately go on to the next one, and continue dealing with mission after mission, living that reality every single time." He leaned back again, shook his head. "How do you deal with it?"

She smiled. "Donna, sometimes. And that should tell you a lot."

He conceded the point, smiled back, but what he really wanted to ask, and couldn't, was why she didn't come home after a mission to a man who would hold her, not let her go, why a woman like her went to bed alone at night. Couldn't, because of the realization that had finally come to him sometime in the small hours of the night as he watched her, that he wanted to be that man.

He concealed his thoughts by standing up and going to the kitchen to refill his coffee cup, and keeping his back to her for the moment it would take him to ensure he could mask his feelings.

"Did you sleep at all?" she asked.

"Some," he said and turned back to her. "Comfortable couch," he added appreciatively.

That made her smile, just Lara's smile, and his heart beat just that much faster.

He went to the refrigerator and opened it. "You don't rely much on ready food, do you? There's an awful lot of real cooking in here."

"I like real food. What are you doing?"

"Making breakfast," he announced, and proceeded to do just that, taking out what he needed. "I never would have thought you cook."

"I don't." She found her slippers neatly placed beside the sofa, put them on and joined him in the kitchen. "Rosie does. My housekeeper. She does everything around here, wouldn't have it any other way." She got some vegetables out. "She always tries to feed me. If it were up to her, I'd weigh half a ton at least."

He threw an appreciative look at her. "Doesn't look like she's succeeding."

Color rose in her cheeks, and she turned away, flustered. She wasn't used to this, to having a man in her house, or being taken care of this way. And Donovan was one hell of a man, she couldn't help but admit. And as if that wasn't enough, the way he looked at her disconcerted her, threatened places in her she'd thought safely immune by now.

"Do you cook?" she asked, to change the subject.

"Yes, as a matter of fact I do." He took the vegetables from her and his hands brushed over hers, fleetingly but it was enough. "When I have the time. The coffee is good, by the way. It's real, isn't it?" Too many things were synthetic nowadays.

"I have it flown in through our diplomatic branch in Sumatra."

"Oracle has its perks," he mused.

She smiled mysteriously, then laughed, and he wondered at that, at how good this, the two of them making breakfast together in this kitchen, felt.

He took the lead on making breakfast while she went up to her bedroom to change. The next hours were for her an unexpected reprieve, a door into another reality without missions, without someone hunting her, without memories. A new reality, here, in her house, with this man she never expected to feel this comfortable, this good with.

When Donovan left Lara later, it was only to go next door to change. He was due back at IDSD and wanted to get in touch with Ben at USFID, was anxious to get on with finding Elijahn. Lara would need to go back to IDSD, too, and he preferred that. He would feel better with her safe in the impenetrable missions building and its war room.

He thought she needed some rest, a bit of time off. There had to be a way even for Oracle to have that. But at least she'd slept, and had a good, relaxed breakfast. That thought, spending the morning with her that way, made him smile, and he wondered. That it felt that way, that he thought about it with a smile. That he wanted to do it again.

That he wanted more. He had never wanted more.

Still wondering about this, about the effect she had on him, he changed into a crisp white shirt and a dark gray suit. The man he saw in the mirror hadn't slept more than a few hours the night before, and on a couch, but was alert and energetic, adrenaline rushing through him.

He would not let anyone take her away from him.

Chapter Fifteen

The small woman looked up at him with suspicion.

Donovan flashed his most winning smile and indicated the grocery bags. "May I help you with these?"

"Who are you?"

"My name is Donovan, Donovan Pierce. I live next door." He took the bags from her and followed her to the kitchen, where he put the bags on the counter. He'd returned to Lara's house through the patio doors just as the housekeeper, who he now knew was called Rosie, came through the front door.

"What are you doing here?"

"I'm also working with Lara on a case."

"Case?"

"I'm a US federal investigator, ma'am."

"Don't you ma'am me, young man. I'm Rosie." The suspicion waned a bit. She looked him up and down openly. He had a feeling if she didn't like him or thought he was any danger to Lara she would easily proceed to try to chase him away with those fresh carrots she was holding. Luckily for him, her gaze turned approving. "You are a good-looking man. How old are you?"

"Thirty-six," he answered obediently.

"Hmmm." She assessed him. "Married?"

"No."

"Girlfriend?"

"No."

"Why?"

It took him a moment. "I, eh, haven't found the woman for me until now." He hoped he answered that one right.

To his relief, she nodded approvingly.

He half expected her to ask if he was currently sleeping with anyone, but she spared him that, at least. Just to make sure, he took over.

"I've seen you before," he said conversationally. "A few times."

"Yes, I come here two, three times a week. More, sometimes," she said, putting the groceries away, apparently deciding he was harmless. "I do everything here. Miss Lara has no time for anything, she works so much. I think when she doesn't work she should rest, maybe have fun, a young woman like that. Not worry about the house and shopping and cleaning. So I do it."

"How long have you been working for her?" He was genuinely interested.

"Five years. Since she first came to live near Miss Patty and Miss Donna." She appraised him again. "Good body. My husband, God rest his soul, had a good body too. Shorter, but good body. Very important for a woman, a good body."

He sat by the counter and listened to her, bemused. Then a thought struck him and he used a rare pause in her thorough description of her deceased husband to interject. "Rosie, how did you know I didn't just spend the night here, with Lara?"

"No, no." She shook her head emphatically. "Miss Lara never brings men home. So you can't be a man."

His eyebrows rose. He could argue the point but had a feeling he might actually lose to this small, decisive woman. So Lara doesn't bring dates home, he thought, interested. He was about to dig deeper into that revelation when Lara herself came down the stairs, striking in a sleek black suit that hugged her body, a gold-colored top that accentuated her eyes, and mid-heel black shoes. Oblivious to Donovan's admiring gaze, she smiled at Rosie as she came toward them and placed her briefcase on the counter near him, her IDSD ID on it.

"Morning, Rosie," she said, and cast an amused glance at Donovan when he took her ID and scrutinized it.

Unlike his, which also held his photo and title for easy recognition when he was out on an investigation, and unlike some of the IDs and badges he had seen at IDSD, hers only had the IDSD symbol on it, and a holochip. He chuckled and looked at her. She shrugged sheepishly.

Rosie looked at Lara with a happy smile. "Miss Lara, how about I make you something nice to eat? You look a bit thin," she added reprovingly.

"Thank you, but we've already had breakfast. And we have to go." She turned to Donovan. "Frank called, he was worried about me. And he says your IDSD assigned team has something for you."

"That's our cue," he said, and they left Rosie humming a cheery tune while she took over the house.

Donovan watched Lara's car leave, then waited a beat until he saw the other car he was expecting move out to follow a discreet distance behind her. Nodding to himself, the intense gray in his eyes drowning the warm blue, he got into his car and followed.

He wasn't escorted by a security agent inside the missions building this time. Coming from its guest parking lot, he found Lara waiting for him in the lobby. As they walked together through to the elevators, no one delayed them until the doors to the war room slid open before them.

IDSD's war room seemed calm. No missions that day, it looked like. It was still busy but the sense of efficiency, of organized concentration, lacked the tension Donovan had felt both times he'd been there. Lara barely took a step in before a young aide, whom Donovan recognized as the one who had accompanied her after the mission on the day he was told she was Oracle, intercepted them. Acknowledging Donovan with habitual formality, he proceeded to inform Lara about an assortment of materials she had waiting in her office—the Somalia mission he

mentioned was the only one Donovan recognized—
and a meeting she had later in the day. Lara nodded
at Donovan and allowed the energetic aide to whisk
her away. Before she even reached her office she was
intercepted again twice, and Donovan noted with
appreciation the smooth, practiced way her aide had
her free and continuing on her way each time, until
she finally walked in. The aide stood for a moment
at the outer door, taking a long look around him
before returning to his station, and Donovan had a
feeling not many would dare deal with him. Good.

"Agent Pierce." Intelligence Specialist Lea Gallo,
a member of the tracking team assigned to him,
motioned him from the workspace they were working in. Donovan walked over, but Gallo didn't wait.
"We found him, we found Elijahn. I mean, we don't
know where he is now, but we know he came into
the United States two months ago."

Donovan reached her. "Where?"

"Florida."

Rather far from IDSD, Donovan thought. But
then, Elijahn wasn't stupid.

Intent on the holoscreen before him, Intelligence
Specialist Cy Lehn already had the trace results ready.
He got right to the point, not taking his eyes off the
screen. By now Donovan wasn't sure the guy ever
did. Lehn was one of IDSD's best trackers, Gallo had
told him. Nothing else interested him, and his social
skills were lacking, although after seeing what Lehn
was capable of, Donovan didn't mind. The guy was

good, and Gallo was a natural at handling him—and communicating with others for him.

"He didn't even bother to change his face," Lehn mumbled. "We identified him at a remote airport in Venezuela."

"Venezuela?"

"Haven't found anything before that, not yet that is. Not yet. We know he landed there in a private plane, though, that much I can tell you. Money buys anonymity in some places. Yes. Good place to get lost in, too. From there to Bolivia, by land I bet, no air travel that I can see. So, got a first sighting of him in Bolivia a week later. Then he lay low for a while, then we have him again in Argentine, and from there he came into the United States in an organized tour group on a South American airline, right there in plain sight."

That was one way to do it if you didn't want to draw attention to yourself and if you knew no one was likely to look for you because they thought you were dead. And Elijahn was, after all, arrogant. "And that's it?" Donovan asked.

"Not a thing between Chad two years ago and Venezuela."

"So he hid well, not to mention patiently, and we know he spent that time preparing. We need to find this guy." Donovan looked at the closeup of Elijahn's face taken on his arrival in Florida. "Anything about people he would have brought here? He's got to have combat-ready people, and some damn good hackers. Money moving? Firearms?"

"Nothing yet. And I mean nothing."

Donovan knew what Lehn was saying. This was IDSD. These people's way of doing things and the contacts they had in both friendly and unfriendly territories meant that if they found nothing in the international arena, it was either well hidden, so they would need more time, or there simply wasn't anything to find. And anything that wasn't there internationally meant it likely came from inside the United States. Like firearms. It made sense that Elijahn would prefer to procure whatever he needed here instead of risking capture and exposure when crossing borders.

"Okay. Keep looking," he said.

"You want us to trace this guy's footprint in the United States?" Gallo asked.

Donovan didn't. Their experience and resources would best serve his search if they would continue to look outside the United States, try to find anything they could about Elijahn's whereabouts and actions between the raid on his base and his arrival in the country. Here, it was he who had the best. This was USFID's home turf. And his.

An internal comms beeped, and Lehn reached for it. "Vice Admiral Scholes is asking for you," he said, never taking his eyes off the screen. "The plane he used to get to Venezuela is an oldie. I wonder who you belong to," he said to the aircraft on the screen, already absorbed again in the hunt.

"Niiice," Gallo said, following his line of thought.

Donovan left them to it. These two would be busy for a while. They would use the plane as the center of a new search sphere, and dig for any clues that would lead to useful information. It's what he would have done.

As he walked to Scholes's office he could see into Lara's. It was empty. Walking on, he saw her standing, surrounded by uniforms, in one of the enclosed workspaces. He couldn't hear the discussion, but he could clearly tell it was somber.

"Donovan." Scholes waved him in. He was holding a pen, writing on a traditional paper pad. Donovan didn't know many who still did that. He himself jotted down a note here and there. He liked the feel of it, just like he still liked to read a real book, rather than use a screen for it. Sometimes there was comfortable simplicity, a quieter focus, in the tangible ways of the past, was the way he saw it.

Scholes saw him look and let out a self-conscious laugh. "Hell, I still find it easier to concentrate with the old-fashioned pen and paper. And as long as Celia, my aide, puts up with it, I intend to continue in my oh so ancient ways." He put the pen down. "So. I understand we have a confirmation it's Elijahn, no more doubts."

"Yes." Donovan sat down across from him.

"What now?"

"My investigators will focus on tracing his steps

from Florida to DC, including to identify equipment and weapons purchases and if he hired any locals. This will also help us find out if he contacted any domestic groups with anti-IDSD or anti-Internationals agendas, which would allow him to tap into their resources if he wants to bring about other forms of attack. Although I doubt it, from what I understand from the intelligence on Elijahn he is single minded and wouldn't care to further someone else's agenda, or risk his own. In any case, our main focus is on finding where he is.

"Your trackers, in the meantime, will go backward, see what they can find about his whereabouts since the raid on his base, until his arrival here. They are best positioned for that. We need to know what this guy has been doing all this time. Where he hid, who he has on his side, what kind of resources he has. This would throw a light on his current capabilities and plans, and, in the worst case, could help us track him faster if he manages to get away, leave the United States again. And while they're at it, they'll see if they can identify any of his people who he might have sent here, although, since we've got nothing about them, names, biometrics, nothing, I doubt they'll find anything within our time limits."

Scholes nodded. Donovan's plan seemed to be leading where he wanted it to. As the investigator had explained to him when he had asked for the trackers, he was after two things. The first was to make sure beyond doubt that they weren't wrong and that it was in fact Elijahn who was after Oracle, that they were profiling the right perpetrator. Until Donovan had substantial proof, it was all circumstantial as far as he was concerned—Elijahn wasn't the only one who was hit by Oracle, and if information about it leaked out once, it could have done so again. Even the dates targeted in the second data theft, from IDSD's administrative system, didn't sway him. Information about two other missions had been taken in the data center break-in, and their dates were targeted too. There was no way to know if the perpetrator might have deliberately searched for these missions. Elijahn could be working with someone connected to them, or he could have been killed in the raid on his base after all, and someone else could have taken his place. Maybe someone connected to one or both of those other two missions, who knew all about the Chad raid.

And then there was the second thing Donovan had wanted to make sure. That Elijahn wasn't planning anything else besides getting to Oracle, or, as his most recent theft from IDSD's administrative system indicated, to whoever he thought might be connected to Oracle.

"You're still assuming Elijahn would conclude that Oracle is a technology that coordinated the raid on his base," Scholes said. Technology being the key here—technology, not a person.

"Just like I did," Donovan said. "It's simple really. There is no way Elijahn, or anyone else for that matter, would think Oracle is a person. It's an impossibility. She's an impossibility. I mean, I know she is Oracle, hell, I've seen her at work, and I'm still having trouble wrapping my mind around it."

Scholes nodded. That, he could understand. He'd seen Oracle grow and develop, and even he was still at awe of what she was capable of.

"And say he does go in a different direction, and think Oracle was a group of people working together, disguised behind a uniform computerized voice, although that's a bit more cumbersome conclusion to reach, all in all. It would still leave us exactly where we are—with Elijahn targeting the same people whose names he had taken from your administrative system." Donovan's eyes were thoughtful. "But we've got to keep our minds open when it comes to this guy, we can't discount his tenacity. Look at his comeback two years after the destruction of his base, his dedication, the resources he must have put into his plan. I want to make sure he's not preparing some major firepower—arms and people. That he's not employing some militant group after all, perhaps domestic—there are enough here who object to you and to the alliance." Even in the United States, there were still those who thought every nation should focus only on itself, no matter how badly that had turned out in the past. And yes, there were those who would do anything for the right amount of money. That never changed, never would.

"What about the people you think he might have brought with him?" Scholes asked.

"We know Elijahn himself came here two months ago. He would have sent others here at about the same time. And he must have sent people before him, as far as a year ago even, at least whoever had been watching the data center, looking for a way to break in. Both my investigators and Evans' people have been looking, especially at the area closest to the data center. So far we've got nothing, no suspicious activity or surges in electronic activity or hacks, but then, we know Elijahn has to have used someone good.

"Thing is, at least with Elijahn we had some past intelligence and a face to help find him. The assumption right now is that every one of his people who you knew about had been killed in the raid on his Chad base, so that anyone he is using nowadays is a complete unknown, someone who wasn't at the base at the time or who might have joined him later. Time would bring us the type of information we want, but time is the one thing we don't have."

"Seems to me you've thought about everything," Scholes said.

"Yes, well, you have to in my job." Donovan said. "Anyhow, I'll be going back to USFID soon. Looks like between your people and mine the search for Elijahn is covered, but there are some contacts I'll be needing to talk to myself." Donovan fell silent and contemplated the man before him.

Scholes knew where this was going. "I can't."

"You have to. Especially now that we're sure it's Elijahn. He's got every reason to want to kill her."

They were continuing the discussion they had started after Scholes told Donovan who Oracle was. Donovan wanted Lara in protective custody. They had settled then for the protective detail she hadn't been told about yet, but Donovan still refused to let the matter go. Especially now.

"Elijahn could strike at any time," he said.

"I would have to make all those whose names he took from our administrative system disappear," Scholes said. That would be the only way to protect Lara without letting on that of all the names Elijahn had, and who might be mistaken as being connected to Oracle and targeted by him, she was the one he was looking for and therefore the only one being hidden. So instead, every one of them now had a protective detail like Lara's watching them. To protect them while also keeping the identity of the real person behind Oracle unknown.

"Why not? We don't know who he'll go after. They should all be protected. And you should be, too, Frank. It was under your command that Elijahn was hit."

"We can't halt IDSD Missions' work."

"How much of IDSD Missions would be left if Elijahn succeeds?"

"Be that as it may," Scholes said, "we will not, cannot give in to threats. And you know I'm right. If it were you you'd say the same thing."

"Yes," Donovan said. "But this isn't about me, is it?" He got up to leave. There was nothing else to be said.

"Donovan."

At the door, Donovan turned back.

"Can you find him?"

"Yes. The question is if it would still matter." Donovan turned his back to him and left.

He knew he wasn't being fair to Scholes. There was more than just IDSD's people at stake here. But he didn't care. Elijahn was an imminent threat, and he had to be protected against before anything else.

He headed to Lara's office. The outer office was empty, and the door of the inner one was closed. He introduced himself to her aide, although he was sure the young man, who introduced himself with the same cool formality he'd exhibited earlier, would know who he was, by association to Lara. "Is Lara in there?" he asked him.

"Ms. Holsworth is working on mission data, sir. She cannot be disturbed."

Donovan glanced thoughtfully at the closed door. "Yesterday's mission?"

Aiden said nothing, and Donovan turned to face him. They contemplated each other.

"You're loyal to her," Donovan stated.

"Sir."

"Good." Donovan reached into his inner jacket

pocket and took out his phone. He brought up the aide's IDSD number—given to him by Scholes when he'd asked Donovan to put an eye on Lara—and sent him his own number along with a code. Aiden's phone beeped on his desk and he picked it up and glanced at it, then at Donovan.

"That's my priority number. Program it in along with the code and you'll be able to get directly to me at all times. If you think anything, *anything*, is wrong, if she is in any trouble, call me." At Aiden's frown, he added, "We both have her best interest in mind." And with this, he turned away and returned to the trackers.

Aiden contemplated him as he walked away. Aides at his level were hand-picked according to strict attributes and trained from their first day at IDSD not to miss anything, to anticipate, to ensure that the people they were assigned to would have all they needed so that they would not find it neces-sary to focus on anything but their jobs. And Aiden also liked who he was assigned to. She was a good person. He saw the things she could do, saw what it did to her, saw that she went through it alone.

And now he saw this man's eyes when he talked about her. As far as he was concerned, anyone who had that look in his eyes when he talked about Ms. Holsworth was fine by him.

"Well?"

The hacker jumped up so abruptly that his chair flew backward. He scrambled to pick it up and sat down again, trying in vain to get his hands to stop shaking. The man who had come up behind him did not bother to heed him, instead watching the three screens.

"They are all at the IDSD complex. Miles first, then Holsworth, then Edwards an hour later." The hacker had barely slept. He didn't dare leave the screens that showed the locations of the targets Elijahn had chosen. The man was becoming increasingly cold, increasingly . . . scary, yes, that was it, and the hacker wanted to make sure he would still be considered useful in his eyes.

Elijahn watched the screens in silence. The hacker tried to remember a prayer. Any prayer.

After what seemed to the hacker to be an eternity later, the big man turned and walked away, and, still not daring to move, to breathe, to take his eyes off the screens he was ordered to watch, the hacker heard him open the door to the training area, where he could hear the rest of the men talking.

Satisfied that the IDSD trackers—joined by a US Global Intelligence officer and an IDSD Intelligence officer, both of whom had been involved in tracking Elijahn and his group before the raid on his Chad base—could continue on their own, Donovan was ready to leave. He went by Lara's office again. Her inner office was now open, and he walked by Aiden, who made no move to stop him.

Lara's office was spacious, and clearly designed specifically for her. A multitouch desk stood not far from the window that spanned its back wall, a high-backed chair between them. On Donovan's left, in the far corner, stood a comfortable-looking recliner. Something someone could sleep on, he noted, and wondered how many times she found herself sleeping there while working on a mission, and if that was another way for her to be alone. The upper halves of the walls on both his sides were screens, and he saw that the tinted glass in which the door he was standing at was set had the telltale signs of glass-to-screen technology. He looked at the window, saw it there, too, and imagined she could close the door and surround herself with uninterrupted data, images, whatever it was she needed when she worked. This was, in fact, a miniature Mission Command disguised as an innocent-looking office.

He turned his eyes to the woman herself. She was leaning back in her chair, watching him.

"Okay, yes, I'm curious."

This made her laugh, and he felt his heart give in. He masked it by sitting down on one of the two chairs she had on his side of the desk and settled back. He then returned his gaze back to her. "Are you okay?" His tone mirrored his eyes.

She nodded.

"Your aide out there wouldn't give out any info, but I'm assuming you were analyzing your latest mission."

She knew what he was getting at. She nodded again, reassuringly, a bit of wonder in her smile. Yes, she was fine. And he had a lot to do with it. Normally she would fight to deal with the consequences of her work herself, deal and hide, which would only take more from her and prolong the strain. But this time was different. It felt different. And as a result, she was rested, focused. Ready for whatever would come.

She watched him now, watched the eyes that watched her back.

Aiden coughed politely, and they both started and turned to look at him. "Would anyone like coffee?"

"No, thank you." Donovan got up and nodded to the aide to acknowledge the gesture. "I'm going back to USFID, need to check out some leads," he said to Lara while Aiden retreated discreetly.

Her eyes flickered outside, to where she knew the team he was working with was busy.

"I'll update you myself at home," he said, and two hearts missed a beat at how that sounded, at how natural it came. After a brief hesitation, they parted ways.

Chapter Sixteen

Donovan's floor at USFID was busy. The US side of the data center investigation, finding Elijahn's current whereabouts and any resources he might be using, was now the primary focus here. But Ben and his team were on top of things, and so Donovan spent some time with SIRT teams working on other investigations to make sure he was up to date, as was his responsibility as the agent in charge, and to assist where needed, which was rare. His people were good, and when something like this came his way, an investigation he was forced to give his entire attention to, he could count on them to do the job.

Finally turning his attention back to Elijahn, he checked if anything new had come up. Everything that could potentially lead to the man and to his possible accomplices was being looked into. New property acquisitions or leases on spaces that might be used to hide people, in the city or in the wider metropolitan area, and specifically at a limited radius around IDSD, taking into account distances, back roads, police presence at selected points, distance from the substantial US and IDSD military presence in the area—any factor that would limit Elijahn or assist him if he wanted to get to IDSD or to any of the people he was targeting, and then get away again, and that would therefore dictate where he would be hiding. Places that in the past year or so had had a surge in electronic activity or communications—because of whoever had scanned for the data center signal, something that, considering the means Elijahn's people would have had, had to be done within a certain distance from the data center. Money transfers into the country and within it. Movements and chatter involving rogue groups, with emphasis on indications that such a group, most probably militant, small, independent, and trying to remain under the radar, might have joined Elijahn or had provided him with people. Vehicle purchases and retrofitting, firearms purchases and theft.

These and more, and there were already some interesting leads, but eventually Donovan left his investigators to it. He had something else he needed to do. One thing only he could do, and that was to talk to some of his contacts from the past, the kind of people who would speak only to him, who only he could get to. And there was one he wanted to see without delay. He made the necessary arrangements, and left his office after night was well on its way, heading home. He needed to change.

Lara raged. "Frank," she said, and the phone initiated the call.

"I thought you were going home," Scholes said, answering immediately. He'd only just now updated Donovan that she'd left.

"I thought I didn't have a protective detail."

The line was silent for a long moment. "How...?"

"Like I'm going to tell you so you can hide it better next time." It was easy, really. IDSD used specific car models for their security. She'd noticed one a couple of cars behind her that morning as she approached IDSD and was searching for Donovan's car in her rear-view mirror, and had seen it again behind her when she was at the gate a moment ago, but had taken no note of it. It could well have been unconnected to her, a security car coming into the complex and leaving it for a myriad of other reasons. It might even not have been the same car.

Except that these cars had a tracking system in them that allowed the protective or security agents using them to lock on any car registered to IDSD or to its staff. And the tracking system of the security car apparently following her was locked on the transmitter IDSD had originally installed in her car. It must have lost its signal as she was going through the gate, because when it did, it beeped her car. And her car beeped back. Except that she'd long ago made sure she would know if this happened, if security was following her contrary to her agreement with Frank, and, as she'd ensured it would, the signal alert appeared on the car's media screen.

"Lara, until this is over, I've upped your security," Scholes said, his voice determined.

"Are you kidding me? Frank, we had a deal." Now, more than ever, she just wanted to be left alone.

"It's either that or protective custody."

She terminated the call without answering him. She now knew who had decided her new security arrangements.

It was now Lara's turn to walk through Donovan's patio doors into his house. She had meant to storm in but couldn't help slow down and look around her, curious. This was quite obviously a man's house, a single man who had lived here for a while, made this his home and maintained it well. It looked comfortable, tidy, its colors cozy, although the shades here were clearly more masculine than in her home.

Movement caught her eye and she looked up to see Donovan coming down the stairs, putting a black shirt on a well-built torso, she tried not to notice. He slowed down when he saw her, then continued to descend the stairs, buttoning the shirt.

"Why do I have people following me?"

"It's called a protective detail," he said mildly.

"I know what it's called."

"I got this thing, I don't know, about keeping you alive."

"I don't want them."

"I'm not asking."

Her eyes blazed with anger at him. God, she looked beautiful. She saw the way he was looking at her, he could tell. He didn't care.

"How did you know, anyway? That it's my call?" he asked her.

"Something Frank said. 'It's either that or protective custody,'" she quoted Scholes.

"Ah," was all Donovan said.

"Frank would have settled for a drone. At least I wouldn't—"

"I don't want to just watch Elijahn kill you, I want someone to actually be there to stop him."

"Fine. Then tell me the others all have the same security."

"They all have the same security."

Suddenly she felt stupid. Of course he was protecting everyone whose name Elijahn had. Which was good, it was what she wanted. It was just that she thought he . . . she didn't know what she thought, she must have been mistaken. But then just now, the way he looked at her . . . okay now that was stupid. What was she thinking? How could she be thinking about this? Where was this coming from?

He was watching her. Reading her, she knew, blue playing in dark and light hues in his eyes. "You know something, you should increase my security." She dived in to regain her footing, focused back on what should be on her mind, anything except this, except him. And she had an idea. Yes, that would work. "Think about it. Elijahn suspects the person behind Oracle is one of the names he took."

He raised his eyebrows in question. He didn't like where this was going.

"And if he doesn't know which one of us it is," she said, "if he doesn't know it's me..."

"He might go after one of the others."

She nodded, concern for those who might be harmed through no fault of their own clear in her gold-flecked eyes. "But if you increase my security, he'll know it's me."

"And what if he does?" he asked, walking to the living room safe, where he had placed his Glock.

"Well, then that's okay, he'll come after me."

He turned back and strode to her so suddenly, anger flaring in his eyes, that she had no time to react, to step back, before he grabbed her shoulders. "How? How is it okay for him to come after you?"

And now she not only saw it, but felt it, too. There, for the first time, the first time with him, the first time ever outside who she was as Oracle, she felt him, his feelings for her, the uncontrolled emotions momentarily and powerfully drowning all else. Her breath caught in surprise.

His did too. He felt it in her even as he saw it in her eyes, saw the intensity of the look, the shift in it as the realization came. Realization, and shock.

They stared at each other. Then she fought for control, focused again. Pushed it away, to be dealt with later. Maybe. Maybe never. She wasn't sure she could, for too many reasons.

"Donovan." Her tone was softer now. "I don't want someone else hurt for something they didn't do, so it has to be fine with me."

"Well it's not fine with me!" He realized he was still grabbing her and forced himself to let go, then busied himself with turning away again, walking to the safe and taking his gun out, checking it, strapping the holster on his belt.

Gun, phone, but no badge, she noticed.

When he walked back toward her, he was composed again. "In fact," he said in a conversational tone, "with that attitude, I think it would be better if I do place you in protective custody." He contemplated her. He should just do it and that's it. In fact, at this point he didn't mind locking her up right here with him standing guard if it kept her safe.

"Yeah, just try it. I'm still an International, and I'm still IDSD, remember? You have no jurisdiction over me, even if you do have some obscure agreement with Frank."

"Maybe it's time that changed. You need to be protected."

"Nevertheless," she said, "Oracle is needed. And," she continued, seeing the renewed flare in his eyes, "if Elijahn still doesn't know who is behind Oracle, and I disappear, he'll know for sure. Which you apparently don't want. So we're back to no protective custody."

He picked up a black jacket and slipped it on, his

eyes on her. Yes, that was the only reason she wasn't already locked up in a safe house with a dozen agents following her every move. Or, well, here. With him. But once this was over, once Elijahn and his band of militants were gone, he had every intention of revisiting the issue of her safety.

He straightened his cuffs thoughtfully, then passed a hand through his hair. Devastatingly handsome, wearing black, meticulously tailored black, from head to toe. No, not just handsome, Lara thought, looking at the way he assessed his own reflection coolly in the hallway mirror. Dangerous. But he wore the dangerous part of it comfortably, as if he'd slipped back into a persona that came naturally to him. She wished she'd read more of his service file.

"You're going out." It came out before she could think better of it. "Am I in the way of a date?" But that didn't fit the dangerous part. Nor what she had seen in him for her since she came in here. Although, he must have a life, had one before all this started, and she wasn't sure now. . . maybe she got it wrong after all. Feelings, this type, were long out of practice. And anything that had to do with this man was certainly too easily unsettling her.

Donovan turned his head and looked at her. Clearly read her again, which only took her further off balance. "Not a date." He tilted his head a little, contemplating her. "It seems I'm done dating."

Before she could react to that he walked out to the back of the house, then waited for her to follow.

"I'm going to see a woman about some guns," he said, shutting the patio doors behind them.

She understood. "Elijahn."

He had promised her an update, he remembered. But first, his meeting. "You're staying in?" he asked.

"With my bodyguards outside my door, I assume."

He turned to her.

She raised her hands, palms out. She wasn't up to fighting out anything with him right now. "Truce. I'll try to behave."

"Don't just try." He thought of something. "Do something for me."

This surprised her. "Okay, sure."

"Lock the house down now. Before I leave." To be safe. He wasn't going to be around for a while, and protective detail or not, he was worried.

She held his eyes for a long moment. Then she nodded.

"And . . ." He ventured ahead. "Lara, please try to get some sleep."

For a split second, just that, her eyes lowered. He frowned.

He waited until she entered her house and closed the patio doors behind her. He couldn't see inside the tinted windows, but knew she would be looking at him standing there, waiting for her to be safe.

As soon as the house locked down, he turned away. Time to focus on the meeting ahead. He made his way to his garage and opened it from the outside.

His USFID car was parked at the curb, his driveway clear. For this he would use his own car. Back when he was still in that wild, reckless seam between past and the man he was at present, he was in the field for a stretch of time. He went deep, teetering on that unseen line between the two opposing sides of the law, and made some valuable contacts. He was going back to one of them now. The woman he was meeting knew quite a bit about a lot of the guns that moved inside the United States, simply because she had her hands in it. She had had an eye for him, the man he was back then, so that night that was who he went back to being.

Lara continued to stand at the closed patio doors long after Donovan was gone, wonder in her eyes. Wonder at him. When she finally slipped into bed between soft sheets, she couldn't sleep. But this time it wasn't because of thoughts about a mission or dreams about the past. This time it was fear that kept sleep away, the kind of fear that came with the realization that she cared again. And caring was too painful. She closed her eyes, tried to will herself to sleep. The thing about the life she led was that she never knew when she would be called in, or how long it would be before she had any decent sleep again. But sleep didn't come, and the thoughts just wouldn't go away.

She had had to learn to protect herself because

of what being Oracle demanded of her. Sometimes, getting to them, to those she was charged with bringing home, meant locking on to their feelings while they were out there, trapped, not only to see them better—her way—in the context they were in, but also to be able to remind them, at just the right time, of what they had left behind, what waited for them back home. That, more than anything else, had the ability to give them the focus they needed, and that extra mental strength that enabled them to scale walls they did not think scalable.

But that meant exposing herself to just that, feelings. Making herself susceptible to theirs, and, in the process, to her own. But hers were too painful. And so she'd had to make a choice, early on. She could let Oracle go and distance herself from her own pain, her own open wounds, perhaps letting them heal with time—it might have worked, she would never know, never tried. The choice she had made back then was the other. She had weighed the cost to herself against a single instance in which she was in Brussels and had visited the alliance's military hospital there to see a man who had returned wounded from a mission she had guided, and his family got there just moments before she did. And she saw their reunion. She saw the small child jump happily on his father's hospital bed before anyone had a chance to stop him, heard the wounded man laugh. Saw his wife, herself in uniform, approach the bed and touch his cheek tenderly, heard them both cry.

She had turned then, walked away, flown back home. Went right back into Mission Command. Never considered her own protection over theirs again.

But that meant she had to learn to keep the part of her that hurt out of reach. So she shut it down. For them she had to believe in love. And she did, she used to have it, after all. But she also had to believe that love could exist unharmed, that being together, without it being cruelly taken away, was possible. And she did believe this, believed it could be for those she cared about, and for those Oracle saved. But she did not allow, did not believe it for herself. It simply could not be, this she knew without a doubt. She was taught this by life, her own, and had sworn not to risk such loss again.

There were only a rare few who were close to her since. People like Donna, or like her brother Tom and her niece, Sarah, or Frank. They all knew, because they were there with her back then. They wanted more for her, but they knew to leave it alone. That was how she wanted it. Donna was the only one who dared push, and did. She kept trying to set her up, trapped her into double dates—Lara would meet Donna and Patty, and there would be a guy there. Lara objected, tried to make Donna understand, but of all people it was Donna who simply refused to accept that there was nothing there anymore, that she didn't want there to be. It hurt too much when love died, and she'd worked hard to make sure it could never happen again.

So why was Donovan... what was Donovan?

She opened her eyes and stared at the comfortable darkness of her bedroom, her mind going back to what had happened earlier. To that split second there, in his house, when she'd felt what she had from him, had been flooded with a powerful, clear rush of his emotions. She had no idea how this could be. When she was in Mission Command, the empathic depth of what she felt in those she watched over was focused, concentrated, geared to complement the heights she took her mind to for the sole purpose of bringing them home. But it was there for Oracle, and for Oracle only, and she controlled Oracle well. And this, what happened earlier, that had never happened to her before. Was it because his feelings for her were so intense at that moment? Or was it because hers were? And still, how could it be?

It couldn't. It mustn't. She would not risk loss again.

She thought of the way he looked at her. Of the fact that he'd managed to awaken something inside her, something that wasn't supposed to ever be there again.

She closed her eyes, tried again, but no amount of fear could push her thoughts about him away.

Chapter Seventeen

When Donovan rolled his car back into its garage hours later, he had some of the answers he needed. The bullets taken out of the data center guards had already told him that Elijahn must have gotten his firearms in the United States, although in their absence he would have reached the same conclusion. It made more sense than smuggling them into the country and risking discovery, and acquiring guns here was still possible nowadays if one had the right contacts and enough money.

But thanks to his contact, and with his knowledge of when Elijahn had entered the country, he now knew for certain that Elijahn had had firearms delivered for him soon after his arrival, in two locations—southern Florida, where firearms had been delivered to four men Donovan now had the description of, and Virginia, where the delivery had been made in a way that, while its contents he now had, neither the receiver nor the current whereabouts of the firearms were known. Both would eventually be identified, but it would take time Donovan knew he might not have. He also knew that Elijahn had asked for very few selective-fire guns, the kind that could go fully-automatic and would indicate a large-scale attack. What he had wanted were mainly handguns with silencers.

As for the explosive devices used to destroy the data center, without any remnants of them left the purchase of the parts they were made of could not be traced, even though it would have been made in the United States—whoever was helping Elijahn with the technological side of his plan wouldn't have known exactly what devices would be needed to destroy the data center until after they had the details of its exact structure and built-in systems, that is after they had gotten into the monitoring station's mainframe, which gave them the access they needed to this information.

Donovan's contact not only provided him with valuable information, she would also ensure, through her widely dispersed organization, that Elijahn had not divided his purchases into additional deliveries or among additional suppliers to better conceal the quantities of firearms he was procuring, and that those, the firearms he had purchased from her dealers, were indeed the only ones he had. Although Donovan had asked her to run some checks to that effect, he didn't think earlier purchases had been made or that Elijahn had begun to set up his local cell before he himself arrived, simply because he was a hands-on man who had been burned before, and it seemed unlikely that he would trust anyone or risk in any way his chances of getting what he wanted.

Assuming that Donovan's supposition was right, and that the purchases he now knew about were all Elijahn had, he no longer had any doubt that Elijahn wasn't preparing to attack a secure complex such as IDSD, in an attempt to reach what he might think was a technology, a machine. He had a more localized attack in mind. He was going for the people. And the number of firearms he was known to have purchased showed that he planned to employ only a small number of militants here, enough to carry out his plans but not enough to be discovered.

The sun was still considering whether to wake up a short while later, but Donovan was already showered, dressed for the day, and looking at Lara's patio doors while putting on his jacket. Good, they were closed, and the house was still locked down as he'd asked. After considering for a moment, he smiled, took out his phone, and texted her. "Are you up?"

Still smiling, he sent the message.

Seconds later the doors slid open to reveal Lara, dressed a bit more informally again today. He hoped that meant no planned missions. A more relaxed day perhaps, whatever that meant for her, even under the threat she was under.

"Really? Texting?" She was clearly amused.

He shrugged, grinning.

She was still laughing when she walked to the kitchen, with him following her. "Coffee?"

"Oh, yes, please." He sat at the counter, rolling

his shoulders to get the kinks out.

She threw him an inquisitive glance. "Have you slept at all?"

He smiled a little. "I guess we both have jobs that keep us up the occasional night."

"This one was me."

"No, this one was Elijahn. You're a different story."

She raised her eyes from the coffee she was making to meet his. He held them without the least bit of hesitation.

Her heart wasn't supposed to flutter, she reminded herself. She tried to think. She knew what to do. She was experienced at this, at pushing men away. Well, not at this, not the way it was with him. Funny, with him she couldn't think of one thing she should be doing. Yes, one. Disregard.

He watched her. He knew she was aware of his advances. Knew she was turning away from them intentionally, that it wasn't because she wasn't attracted, had no interest in him. There was something else there, something hidden which he'd already had quite a few clues about, and not only from her, and he intended to understand what and why. He wasn't entirely sure what was happening here, where this was going, but he sure as hell was going to find out.

"Cheese rolls?"

He started. That one he didn't see coming.

She shrugged, a hint of mischief in the golden flecks' dance in her eyes. "I told Rosie you liked them when you and I had breakfast here yesterday, so she made about a million of them."

"She did?" He got up himself and went to the refrigerator. She wasn't kidding. There were humongous amounts of cheese rolls in there. He took out a bunch and heated them. "That's it, I'm hooked."

Lara laughed. "Good, because she is just going to keep making them for you."

"After we stop Elijahn, there must be something nice I can do for her. Any ideas?"

They were still going to be neighbors, it suddenly occurred to her. He was still going to be there when this was over. She raised her gaze to him, caught him looking at her. What she saw in his eyes sent her reeling. Anything much less than that look on a man's face always sent her turning away and never seeing him again.

With him she didn't want to turn away. When did that happen?

Donovan was the one to turn away, busying himself with placing the heated rolls on a platter. Giving her time. "Maybe I could cook her dinner." He took the rolls over to the counter. "Maybe I could cook you dinner." As he spoke his eyes fell on the screen that was sitting on the far end of the counter, the one he'd seen her work with. He immediately recognized what it was showing. He stopped, reached out. Pulled it to him, turned it around. Sat down.

"This is the intelligence file on Elijahn." His brow furrowed. He thought they'd established some trust between them, even if not as much as he wanted.

"No, it's not what you think, it's not like it was." She wanted to explain, wanted him to understand. Even if she couldn't tell him all of what was going through her mind, not yet. She tried to find the words, then remembered he knew who she was, had seen what she did. She didn't have to censor herself, not with him. "I've only ever seen the original file, before the Chad mission. I know that after it was over, the joint intelligence task force set up for the mission added to it, before they finally concluded he must have died there. I don't know, I keep thinking, maybe if I know enough, if I can put things in contemporary context, I can help. I mean, I was there, I touched everything he had built, I should be able to . . ." She fell silent.

"Is that why you didn't sleep last night?" His voice was soft.

She lowered her eyes. It wasn't the only reason, not even the main one, but that was the last thing she wanted him to know. "I slept."

He raised an eyebrow.

"A little. It's enough. And it's more than you did."

"Point taken."

Her eyes went back to the screen. "There must be something I can do, Donovan. I can't just sit and wait while he . . . we don't know who he'll go for. I mean, I'm Oracle. Isn't there anything you need me to do?"

"I need you to be safe." He surprised her by putting his hand on hers.

She looked down at it. After a silence, she raised her eyes to his. "You thought I was following your investigation again, not trusting you," she said, her voice quiet.

"The thought has crossed my mind." He let out a breath. "But at least now I know you have every right to be in on this."

"But I wasn't." She shrugged. "You said you would update me. I believed you."

He nodded. "I'll make you a deal. I'll update you right now if you eat a cheese roll."

"That's a pretty good deal." She took the roll he offered.

He updated her, and answered all her questions. An hour later found her sitting on the sofa, her second cup of coffee growing cold in her hands as she stared at it. She could feel him watching her. He does that a lot, she thought absently. But this time his gaze, when she met it, was pensive. She nodded slightly. Yes, she'd been thinking it too. Ultimately, no matter what Elijahn knew or intended to do, one thing was a certainty. She was the true target. This man was looking for her. Coming for her.

"I don't want you to leave IDSD alone tonight."

"Donovan."

"I'll come for you."

"You can't play bodyguard. You have more important things to do. And I do have a protective detail tailing me."

He said nothing, but he wouldn't take his eyes

off hers.

Finally, she nodded. "I'm still taking my own car."

"I'll drive you."

She thought of the man called Elijahn. How badly he wanted Oracle. She was on his list.

Donovan wasn't.

"I'm taking my car."

Frustration flared at her stubbornness. Just when he thought he was making headway. But her eyes were steady on his. "Fine," he said. "But keep its top up and the windows closed. I'll follow you—along with your protective detail—to IDSD this morning, and you'll wait for me at IDSD tonight."

She nodded. A fair compromise.

That wouldn't stand in her way.

"We got it," Ben said, and put alternating views of the site up on the screen. "It's a warehouse that was used as a supply center for robotic parts until eight months ago. The company had gone bankrupt, and this warehouse remained empty up to three and a half months ago. That's when it was sold through an attorney to a—get this—private start-up company that is developing some sort of a pharmaceutical product. That's the cover they used to pretty much rebuild the place, looks like, including some substantial security to keep people out. The site is kept clean, is quiet, and hardly anyone comes and goes. An SUV with the start-up's name on it arrives and leaves regularly, according to people who work in the area, I'm thinking supplies maybe, but otherwise nothing. We checked the company, it exists. Registered and all, nothing that would raise undue suspicion."

"Municipal traffic and security cameras?"

"They don't cover that corner." Ben glanced at Donovan meaningfully. "They're positioned to focus on the mall down the street. This warehouse is standing in a blind spot. All we have are street photos that are pretty current, and blueprints we sort of hacked the construction contractor for, the one who had renovated the place, we didn't want him to know we were looking just in case he would think about warning anyone. Although from what we could find, neither he nor the firm that handled the sale knew what the warehouse was really being bought and prepared for."

He brought up the post-renovation blueprints. One story, above ground, with an internal room made of soundproof walls and ceiling, which made up most of the main area of the floor. An enclosed area for vehicle parking stood on the left of the structure, connected to it. It was originally an open parking lot, Ben informed Donovan, but was built around as part of the renovation. The structure in its entirety wasn't very large, but it was big enough for what Donovan thought Elijahn would need. And with the security around it and the soundproof interior, it seemed it was indeed what they had been looking for.

As for the time frame—the warehouse having been bought and prepared only three and a half months earlier—that didn't bother Donovan. Elijahn wouldn't need this place until he and his militants, whom he must have sent here at around the same time he himself arrived, had use for it. Whoever had handled the technological side of the data center break-in didn't have to have the warehouse. In fact, the initial scanning of the security signal would have been done from a far more suitable location closer to it.

And then there was the damning evidence. Communications from the place were high starting two months earlier, coinciding with the time since Elijahn had arrived, and right up until the data center was destroyed, and then again when IDSD's administrative system was accessed from the outside. But what worried Donovan the most was the fact that on the night after that second incident communications from the warehouse increased again until some hours into the next morning. They then stopped for several hours and then increased again, far more this time, and were still at that level, even now. This would, he thought, be explained by hacking attempts.

Either that, or Elijahn was watching, tracking. The people he was after?

Donovan glanced at his watch. And made a call.

"Yes, as a matter of fact I'm right here with her, in her office," Scholes confirmed. "I will," he said when Donovan asked him to keep Lara at IDSD.

"He wanted to know that you're here, safe," he said after ending the call.

On the other side of the desk, Lara was leaning back in her chair. She looked at him questioningly.

"He thinks they've found Elijahn, his hiding place. They're going to raid it."

She sat up. "Donovan is going himself?"

"He's heading the investigation. It's what he does," Scholes said, looking at her curiously.

She turned her chair around toward the window, and sat staring outside.

"This is odd."

Elijahn approached the hacker with a measured step. There was no time for problems now. The men were already busy preparing behind him, beside the vehicles.

"The targets' cars haven't moved. Since last night. They're still at their homes."

"All of them?"

"Two, the men. The woman is at IDSD."

"Show me."

The hacker showed Elijahn the tracking data for each of the three targets.

Elijahn looked at the data carefully. This *was* odd. Although, it could be a coincidence, there could be

a perfectly reasonable explanation for this. Unless...
was it possible they knew of the threat to them and
had therefore remained in their homes? Would IDSD
know his hacker had obtained information about
them? The way to ascertain that would be to see
what the others on the list of names the hacker had
initially gotten him were doing. But there was no
longer time for that. And in any case, why was the
woman at IDSD, and not in her home? This made it
unlikely his enemies knew what he was up to.

Instinct made him look back on all he had done
so far. No. He had been careful. They would not
know about him, nor about what he was doing. Not
this time. This time, he had been so much more
vigilant. And they had every reason to think he was
dead, that was a decisive factor to consider. It was
the pillar of his plan.

As for the targets' locations, all it did was make
things simpler for him. He would send three people
each to the two in their homes. That would do it.
His men were good, and he would not even be
sending this many, but the two men had families
who might get in the way, a probable occurrence
since they were now to be killed in their homes, in
the deep of night. Elijahn did not care, the families
were of no consequence to him.

But his plan had been to hit them all at the same
time, if that was possible, certainly all at the same
night, hit and get away before anyone understood
what was going on. Which meant that the woman

would still have to be targeted at the same time as the two men. And since she was at IDSD, and with the hours she kept, that meant he would have to be ready to get her when she left. But he was prepared, he had been ready for the possibility that he would have to follow all three of them in order to hit them simultaneously on their way from IDSD to their homes. Yes, it was better this way, that he would have only her to deal with on the road, only her from among all his targets. It would make what he wanted easier.

"What do you want me to do?" the hacker asked.

Elijahn's eyes narrowed.

Chapter Eighteen

Miles away from the raid site, Donovan's phone signaled an incoming call. He pulled it out of the pocket of his bullet-proof vest.

"Communications at the warehouse just stopped. Electricity use too," Ben, two cars back, reported with unmistakable urgency. "The place just went dark, we're getting no signals. Just heat. Lots of it."

Damn, Donovan thought. Always one step behind. He got on the comms and ordered the police officers deployed in cruisers and on foot in the area to stand watch. He reiterated that anyone they might encounter would be armed and dangerous, but had a sense of foreboding that the raid was already too late. Elijahn had proven to be elusive. If Donovan would find what he thought he would when he finally reached the warehouse, this guy and his militants would be long gone by now.

He willed the operation to go faster but knew it couldn't. The deployment was tactically careful, anticipating the potential dangers ahead. The police presence comprised only the outer perimeter and the force that would shield any civilians who might

still be around, in one of the restaurants near the
mall, perhaps, this time of night. The warehouse itself would be raided by two USMC Special Reaction
Teams accompanied by USFID agents, with Donovan
in charge, and USFID-SIRT techs would be ready to
go in once the site was cleared and work the scene
as quickly as possible without overlooking anything.
But once again, Donovan's gut feeling was telling him
any findings would only be good for the aftermath
of wherever this was already going.

The comms chirped, but he didn't need to hear
what the voice was saying. He already saw it even
before the heavy military protected vehicle he was
in skidded to a halt in front of the one-story building. The raid was delayed not by resistance, but by
the black smoke that was already escaping even this
carefully sealed space, blending in with the night sky
as soon as windows and doors were broken by the
USMC teams. Which was only after the techs had
cleared the place from the outside, concluding that
whatever security had been set up in the building
to protect its contents had been rendered harmless
either by the loss of power and communications or
by the fire inside, whichever came first, and that
Elijahn did not leave any booby traps.

Nor did he use explosive devices here in his attempt to destroy all evidence of his activities, as he
had done at the data center. The robot the USMC
teams had brought with them was able to easily
move through the fire inside, find its origins and

quench it. The USMC teams then followed it in, along with the USFID agents, and tackled the rest of the fire, clearing the place as they did, although they already knew there was no one inside. No one alive, that is. Still, it paid to be careful. It was not beyond Elijahn to try to use something that would interfere with the technology they were using to identify any traps. The man had already proven that he valued technological advancements over the more traditional means.

Even before the place was cleared, Donovan canvassed it quickly. The computers and screens that filled the area immediately beyond the entrance were barely recognizable, having been at the center of the fire. The human remains beside them worried him. The body was no longer recognizable, but a quick check told him that it was a man, with what looked like a bullet hole in the back of his head. Donovan squatted down beside him, looked at his position, the position of the technology. He was willing to bet this was Elijahn's technology expert. The guy responsible for the hacking, perhaps the one he had seen in the data center break-in footage connecting to the IDSD storage unit and stealing the data.

He contemplated the converted space around him. Abruptly, he stood up and walked to what he knew to be the parking area. Empty. He crossed behind it, to the back of the warehouse. The fire didn't get a chance to destroy this area, the material of the soundproof structure that dominated the floor,

standing between it and the heart of the fire, serv-
ing as a hindrance. There were sleeping bags piled
up in one corner here, and a makeshift kitchenette.
He crossed back and entered the soundproof area.
A lot of scattered ammo on the floor, which Elijahn
hadn't bothered to destroy. It wouldn't tell him anything new, he already knew where Elijahn's firearms
came from. He squatted down and picked up a shell
casing. It was the type he expected it to be, what his
contact had told him. For a selective-fire gun. He
scanned the others quickly. Most were the same,
some were for a handgun, the same type of bullets
found in the bodies of the data center guards.

He stood up and strode out. Anything else here
his people would analyze. But he doubted it would
help. DNA would probably lead either to a dead end
or to untraceable militants in international databases.
There might be hits if Elijahn had added to the man-
power available to him for his plan by using local
hires, but Donovan figured they would all either be
found dead or disappear before this was over. What
did interest him were the cars whose traces he had
seen in the parking area. The tire tracks and what
must have been a brush with the corner of a wall indicated dark and heavy harsh terrain vehicles. Four,
maybe five, he couldn't be sure. Elijahn could have
more people, more vehicles, more of whatever he
needed for his plan stocked elsewhere, but none of
the searches Donovan had initiated had shown any
indication of that, and in any case, he didn't think

so. Elijahn wanted control. After the destruction of his base, he would have become obsessed with it. He would keep everything, everyone close. This site, Donovan was willing to wager that this was it.

And Elijahn would want to be present during the attack. Donovan's stride quickened. To be sure, just in case Elijahn was playing it smart and was somehow still listening, he waited until he was out of the warehouse before he made the call, motioning for his techs to go in and get to work. He himself was already heading to his car, which one of his junior investigators, not yet cleared for field agent duties that would have allowed him to participate in the raid, had driven over, and that was now standing with the other USFID vehicles down the street.

An empty warehouse, a dead tech guy, destroyed computers. Elijahn didn't need them anymore. We're too late, I'm too late, Donovan kept thinking.

Elijahn was already on the attack.

He knew where Lara was. So his first call was to the protective detail of another name on the list Elijahn took, Dr. Bernard Miles.

"All is quiet here, Agent Pierce," the agent who answered him said in a calm voice.

"Looks like Elijahn is getting ready to attack, so keep your eyes open. IDSD will be sending you backup, and we'll have local law enforcement assist as required."

"Sir? I don't understand." The agent sounded confused. "How would Elijahn get here?"

"What are you talking about?"

"We're not in DC, we haven't been there since last night. Our orders were to move Dr. Miles and his family to an undisclosed location." The agent was trained well enough not to specify the place, even though the call was secure and Donovan had been cleared by IDSD.

"Whose orders?"

"Head of Security Ericsson, under Vice Admiral Scholes's order, sir. We were instructed to stay away until we are contacted by either of them when it's over."

Donovan thought quickly. "Okay. Keep them indoors and keep an eye out for anything out of the ordinary. Shoot first, ask later."

Donovan made the same call to the protective details of two more of the people on Elijahn's list, with the same results. They had been moved the night before, along with their families, under Ericsson and Scholes's orders. To different locations than Miles. These agents wouldn't specify their exact locations either, but one of them did mention that all protective details had been doubled.

So these were three of the possible targets on the list of people Elijahn had information on. Donovan didn't bother calling the protective details of the remaining names on the list. He already knew what he would find—they too would be safely tucked away somewhere. Normally his first thought might have been that Elijahn had duped them again, and had found a way to move his targets to where he wanted them, but he wouldn't have scattered them this way. And anyway, this time there was no way he could have done that. IDSD had learned its lesson, and nobody could be more careful.

And then there was Lara. Donovan knew where she was. And she wasn't safely hidden far away, she was at IDSD.

Something played in his mind. Something she had said that morning.

He reached for his phone again.

Scholes picked up after one ring. "Been waiting to hear from you. Anything?"

"Did you order Elijahn's possible targets taken to safe locations outside the DC metro area?"

"What?"

"They were taken away, quite a distance away as a matter of fact. Apparently all except Lara."

Donovan heard Scholes shout, "Celia, get me Carl. Now. Hold on a sec, Donovan."

He heard the vice admiral talking on another phone. When he came back on, his voice had an edge to it. "You're right. No one on that list came in today. They got their security, so Ericsson didn't check on them, he was sure he would have been alerted by the protective details if anything was wrong. And I myself only made sure I know where Lara is."

"And?"

"Ericsson just found orders on his computer. Apparently someone entered them yesterday, remotely, while he was still in his office, but there's no record of this being done, which is why he wasn't alerted about it. There seems to be a set of orders for the protective detail of each name on the list Elijahn has, specifying where that person and his or her family should be moved, and how the agents should act, including to speak to no one about their orders, since Elijahn seems to be everywhere, and to avoid checking in with any of us so they wouldn't be located. And there's a collective order to increase the protective details of all potential targets, to allow for alternate shifts." Scholes paused. "The instructions supposedly came directly from Carl, under an order from me."

"Except that you didn't order this. And neither did he."

"No. And the protective agents wouldn't suspect anything. The orders were sent directly to the head of each protective detail as an encrypted message through a designated secure channel, something we do when there's someone we need to keep hidden, which does happen, as you can imagine. It's standard procedure for high-risk targets."

Donovan closed his eyes. "And the orders covered everyone except Lara." He thought for a moment. "Frank, does Lara have to be there today?"

"How do you mean?"

"Is there anything urgent, a mission, meetings, anything she has to be at IDSD Missions for?"

"No," Scholes said. "Nothing much is left open from the last missions. There are pending ones, but she's at the stage of getting the info on them and some of it is still being prepared. And there are no urgent meetings for today." He was thinking aloud now. "There's a diplomatic mission she's advising, but theoretically she could work from home. She's got a secure connection and a secure laptop she always has with her."

"How does she usually work?"

"You saw how crazy things can get for her. So she's got full freedom. She can come and go as she pleases. Aiden is here regularly, runs everything for her and is everyone's direct line to her. If she's not here and we need her, we call her in. Hell, we started this because she's not getting enough time off, and with the things she does—"

"And what would she do on a day like today?" Donovan tried to keep his urgency at bay.

"If not for Elijahn, and with the days she's had? Even if she decided to come in for the diplomatic mission—she'd do that if she wanted to have her office or Mission Command to work in just in case, if she thought there was a risk there—she would probably have come in sometime in the early afternoon, sat in on the mission as she did, then she might have wound down with a swim, then gone home straight from the IDSD fitness center."

"Except that instead, she arrived in the morning, at about the same time she came in yesterday. I'm betting she intends to leave at about the same time she did yesterday, too," Donovan said.

"She's creating regularity." Scholes stood up.

"Nothing like regularity to help someone who is targeting you." The hollow feeling in the pit of Donovan's stomach had no bottom. "Frank, why now? Why would she think he would attack now? How would she know?"

"It's her, for heaven's sake!" Scholes exploded, and hit his desk with a closed fist. "She plays the likelihoods in her mind in a different way than you and I do. All this time that we've talked around her, let her know everything that's happening, everything we're doing, she analyzed it, took it one level up."

"She was looking at Elijahn's file this morning," Donovan said.

"Well, I can tell you she had the Chad mission files called up yesterday. I'm looking at her access authorization right now. She did it straight from her office, viewed them all."

"I wanted to take her to IDSD this morning, then take her back home when she was done. In my car. She said she wanted to take her own car."

"She's good." Scholes's chuckle had no humor in it. "She's kept us both in the dark."

"She actually used the fact that we focused on her. While we were watching her, she was watching us. And we watched her but not what she was doing." Donovan was stumped. And mad as hell.

"Worse. She used Oracle against us. This is something Oracle would do. Christ, she must have been planning this for . . ." Scholes sighed. "It wasn't exactly difficult for her to access Carl's office system and send those orders. And I'm betting we'll find that a backing order has in fact been sent from mine. And in the right wording, too. She would have done it from her laptop, it's probably the most secure thing outside Mission Command, and it's designed to give her access anywhere without leaving any record of it if that's what she wants."

Donovan cursed under his breath. "She told me."

"What?"

"Yesterday. She came to me. She was angry that she has a protective detail. Told me she won't risk Elijahn going after the others when it's her he's looking for, that it would better if he knows it's her he wants. I got angry, told her I wouldn't stand for it. Showed her . . ." that I cared, he didn't say. That I would do anything to protect her. That she came first.

"So she did the only thing she could. She made herself available and is pointing him to herself. God, when he comes after her . . ."

"She'll let him know she is behind Oracle. So he'll know he's got the right person. Frank, where is she? I asked her to wait there until I come to escort her home. Where is she now?"

"She's not here." Scholes was already accessing

her data. "We're too late. She's left IDSD." Scholes looked up as Ericsson entered his office.

"Can you stop her at the gate?" Donovan asked.

Ericsson heard him. He approached Scholes's desk screen, used his own access authorization to check. "She's out. I can beep her car, track it."

"Do that, route the tracking data to my phone. Where's her protective detail?"

"Here." Ericsson let out a breath. "They were supposed to be alerted when she leaves the building."

"They wouldn't be." Donovan guessed what Lara had done. "She took care of that. Just like she didn't let me take her to IDSD and back. She made sure she would be alone."

Ericsson wasn't listening. "Agent Pierce, the tracking transmitter in her car isn't working. We've lost the signal."

Donovan was already driving and breaking every traffic law by now. He turned on the blue lights that would flash along the front of his car. "Could she do that?"

"No. It had to be someone on the outside. And I can tell you it wasn't us."

Donovan hit the accelerator, even though the car couldn't give him any more than it already was. "Trace her phone."

Ericsson was already doing that.

"She has an emergency distress signal she can activate, and the ability to connect directly to IDSD with the push of a button or a voice command. If she was in trouble, I'm sure she would. . ." Scholes was frantic. "I can't believe it. I can't believe she set herself up. No, what am I saying? Of course she would. She would weigh the odds, but ultimately she wouldn't allow anyone to get hurt for her even if the odds were against her."

"Shit. Oh, shit." Ericsson breathed in. "We can't trace her phone. There is no signal for her."

"So she can't get to us."

"Worse, I tried to trace her laptop too, the device we've put in it just in case. It's here. She left it in her office. She never does that, ever."

"When did she go off the grid?" Donovan's hands tightened on the steering wheel.

Ericsson checked. "Minutes."

"Last position?"

Ericsson gave him the coordinates. Donovan hit the accelerator again. "I'm on my way to her, get backup!"

But he could already hear Scholes. "This is Vice Admiral Francis A. Scholes, ID Two-Lima-Seven-One-Foxtrot-Alfa-Sierra. We are at FPCON Delta. Oracle is under attack."

Donovan terminated the call. What he had just heard, these last words, made it real, too terribly real. Fear the likes of which he had never known coursed through his veins, pushing him on.

Lara.

Chapter Nineteen

Lara had wondered what she would be thinking about right about now. After it was over and done with—the analysis, the decision, the planning—that was all that had remained for her to do. Wonder what it would be like to sit in her car, waiting. What she would think about.

She never imagined she would be thinking about Donovan. She was driving on the familiar road from IDSD to her home, the formidable gate of the complex in which she would have been safe growing smaller behind her, the likelihood of an attack on her increasing with every roll of her car tires. And yet it was Donovan she was thinking about. She wondered how angry he would be at her. If he would wish he had shot her after all—that one brought a smile to her face, even now. She remembered how caring his blue-gray eyes had been when he'd said that last time.

Caring. The way he held her after the tragedy of the Somalia mission. The way it felt, his touch. How close they had become since, how close they were that very morning. The way he looked at her, how much that look had changed since that time when he had been so angry, raging against her. What she saw in him, felt in him, for her, in his home. The smile faded. He cared. And it wasn't just his investigation, or Oracle. He cared about her. If she died tonight, what would he feel? Would he hurt? They barely knew each other, just met days before. Surely that wasn't enough to...

She knew that wasn't true. It was enough. It was certainly enough for her.

But there was no other choice. If she didn't do this, Donovan would be as much at risk as everybody else around her. More, since he was so protective of her, and would stay close.

More, if there was anything between them.

There it was again. It was crazy that she would even consider that, and now, of all times. Except, maybe that was exactly why she could allow herself to think about it, think about him. There was no fear, now. No fear of loving again.

She could not, would not allow him to be hurt because of her. Not him, not anyone. No matter the price she had to pay.

In reality, she had analyzed, had taken the leap already the day before. Or rather, Oracle had analyzed and had taken that leap. She knew she had no choice. Both Donovan and Frank were hinting at protective custody, and while there were several possibilities as to what Elijahn would do, the one thing Lara knew was that he would not stop until he believed he had destroyed Oracle. And that meant that as long as he didn't know for certain who was behind it, others in addition to her were likely to get hurt. The others whose names he had, their protective details, their families. And yes, Donovan, who was getting in Elijahn's way—the realization that he was heading the raid on Elijahn's hideout had sent a shock wave through her. Donovan hadn't chosen to get entangled with Oracle. With her. And she wasn't about to let him die for it.

All indications were that Elijahn would attack soon. Indications, and her unique view of them. So she had moved his other potential targets out of the way. All of them, although her analysis had easily shown who was more likely to be hit. She left only herself available to him. Her brow furrowed. She thought about what Donovan might find in Elijahn's hideout. If maybe, just maybe, Elijahn had already been caught. If she would make it home that night after all.

She wondered if she would see her family again. And Donna and Patty and baby Greg. They had been on her mind the entire day, but she didn't call, wouldn't know what to say. Wondered if she would see Frank again. Would he be all right, would he blame himself for this? Would he remember enough of who she was to know that it was simply something she who had become Oracle all those years ago would do? She wondered what would happen when Oracle was not there the next time alliance soldiers needed her, if they would have a chance of surviving without her, how many would have to go through the same loss she herself carried with her just because Oracle was not there to save their loved ones. Wondered what the future, Oracle's, hers, could have looked like.

Wondered what could have been with him.

That was all she could do now, let these thoughts chase through her mind. She had already made her decision, and all that remained was to carry it out. Bring it to this moment, in this night, to her here, in her car, on this empty road.

Waiting for Elijahn to attack. Now there was nothing more to think about, except those who mattered. There was nothing else she could do. She was all planned out, thought out. Feared out. Yes, that too.

She was still deep in thought when the black giant of a car hit her from behind. New fear surged, but she reacted as she'd planned.

If she was the decoy, had set the trap, someone had to be there to close it. She pressed the emergency button on her phone, ready in her hand. It would bring her directly to an emergency line, and she would be automatically identified. Being Oracle, she figured half of IDSD's combat forces stationed in the complex she had just left would be on Elijahn before he knew what was happening. Yes, she had planned this carefully.

Oracle was not about to go down easily.

She waited, pressed the button again. Nothing. She said Frank's name, which should have prompted a call to him. Nothing. And suddenly she knew. She activated the media screen in her car, touched the GPS. Nothing.

All outgoing signals were being jammed. Elijahn was doing to her what he had done to the data center.

She focused. She needed him stopped. She had to—

The black car struck her again, and another appeared on her left. She couldn't let them stop her, had to gain time. If they killed her and disappeared, Elijahn would have what he wanted. The clout, the freedom to do as he pleased. To hurt God knew how many others.

She accelerated the powerful car and swerved across the road and into the stretch of wild-growing vegetation that flanked it on the other side. It wasn't the cover of vegetation she was after, it was the clear ground it gave way to, as opposed to the other side, on which the vegetation continued too far toward the woods. Her car wouldn't make it through it, it wasn't an all-terrain vehicle. It was built for speed and agility on a paved road, and was nothing like the harsh terrain monsters that were following her, one still immediately behind her, having swerved across the road along with her, and the other taking more time to turn but another one joined them from the same side of the road she was now on and was preparing to push her off it, it seemed. She couldn't allow that, had to be in control of where she was going, for a while longer at least.

She reached the downward slope that she knew would be there. That was the thing about being her, she could call up current aerial photos of the area around IDSD without anyone knowing. She knew every stretch of the place, from fields and woods to paths and roads. She knew where to go so that her pursuers would be easy to see, a location where they could be caught but where there would be no one else around who might get in the way, get hurt. But she still had to contact those who could catch them. Otherwise, it would all be for nothing.

She held her breath, then let it out in relief when her car didn't flip over as she descended the steep slope. But as she straightened the car, sped forward again, her pursuers were too close. Their vehicles were far most suitable for this than hers.

She didn't hear the shots, but she felt them hit the car. The wheels went, she had no idea how many. She skidded, swerved and came to a stop on soft ground.

Okay. Okay. She breathed in, tried to force her heartbeat to slow, failed. Okay. That was to be expected too. Fear was to be expected. This was her, here, alone, about to face her killers. All she had was her plan, her mind. She was no soldier, had never been in combat, never held a gun.

Never sat in her car in the dark of night, in an

empty field, alone, surrounded by a group of militants sent to kill her.

Another shot to the car. A shout.

No more shots. She turned to look. The SUVs had come to a stop some distance behind her, their headlights on her. No one was coming out.

In the SUV closest to the car, Elijahn sat beside the driver. He sneered. The men were awaiting his order but he didn't give it yet. He had her now. This had gone better than he expected. She was alone. And she had no way of contacting anyone. No way of moving. An order from him and his men would flow out of the cars and surround her.

His phone rang. He listened, and the sneer disappeared, replaced by an expression of dark rage. "Meet us," he snapped, and disconnected. Without taking his eyes off the woman, sitting in her now useless car, he made a call of his own. As he listened to the report, his hand tightened around the phone, knuckles white. He repeated the order, then terminated the call. If the hacker was alive, he would kill him all over again. The stupid man had missed it, and had allowed the two others Elijahn had wanted killed that night to get away. When his men had gotten to their homes, these were empty, they and their families long gone. But that meant that IDSD had somehow discovered someone had been inside its computers and had taken their names, which, under the circumstances he himself had caused, would have led to their being taken away. It really was a pity he had killed that incompetent fool so painlessly.

Elijahn's eyes narrowed. No matter.

He still had her.

Her phone rang.

Lara stared at it, laying on the passenger seat beside her. Picked it up slowly. Answered.

The low laugh on the other end of the line made her blood freeze. "Interesting, I think, that you are all that remains." His tone of voice was mild, the accent clear, the foreign trace almost imperceptible.

"That's the way it should be." She struggled to keep her voice calm even as her heart beat fast. She thought hard. He must have released the signal interference. She pressed the emergency dial again, tried to open another call in parallel.

"No. No, that will not work."

She froze.

"Yes, I can see all your dialing attempts. I have blocked all signals to anyone who might help you. There is no one coming. No help. You are mine."

Blocked all signals to anyone who might help me, Oracle thought. That's what you think.

She terminated the call and quickly pressed a button on the small device she had laying on her knees. The signal jammer activated a pulse, a brief, powerful one, canceling his interference and clearing the single frequency she had selected in advance for the fraction of a second it took Elijahn's signal jammer to recalibrate and jam that frequency again. Which was exactly what she had assumed it would do. She had known if he would decide to use one, it would be so much more sophisticated than what she could obtain in the limited time she'd had and without alerting anyone to what she was doing, certainly not when she was being watched as she had been.

But that one frequency, that split second, was all she needed. Her analysis of his possible courses of action had shown he would jam all her outgoing signals, and likely take special care to block certain call destinations he would think she would attempt to reach. So when she jammed him back, she also sent out a preset message to the one person he would never think of. Herself.

The code she sent activated her home system and, unbeknownst to Elijahn and far enough from his reach, it now made a secure call. When the call was answered, and it was answered immediately, the system automatically initiated a call back to her. An incoming call.

She barely managed to speak when it was cut off again. Her phone went dead, and then the signal returned. It rang. She answered.

"Well. You are a feisty one, aren't you? Nice try. But now your phone is entirely controlled by me. You will either speak to me, or to no one."

"No one sounds rather nice right now." She was breathing more easily. She'd gotten through. Elijahn could kill her, would, she knew. But what she had just done would be enough for the right people to locate her. They would get him.

"And yet, I would like to continue this little chat."

He was enjoying himself, she could hear it in his voice. Still, it suited her. As long as his arrogance drove him to speak he would remain here, increasing the odds that he would be caught by those she knew would come. And it wasn't as if she had any other choice.

"So tell me, what is that title of yours, critical mission expert? And why do you have all that clearance? Why are you so important? Yet, here you are, of all my targets, left behind while the others are gone, disappeared."

"Safe from you."

"You think so?" His laugh was harsh. Cruel. "No, I will still get them. Oracle will be destroyed no matter how many I have to kill to get to it."

Her eyes went cold. She calmed, the fear forgotten. No, you won't, she thought. You won't go after them. She had known she might have to do this, had known it was the most likely outcome, and yet now that the time came it was more difficult than she had thought it would be. But there was, simply, no other choice.

"There is no need for that. You have who you are looking for." Her eyes closed as she gave herself up. "There is no Oracle without me." The words, their true meaning, reverberated throughout her, throughout all that she was.

In the SUV, Elijahn leaned forward in surprise. "What? That machine, that artificial intelligence? You are the one behind it?"

So that really is what he thinks, she thought. An AI. But then it had made the most sense from the start. It was what those who didn't know the truth usually thought. Even Donovan had.

"Yes," she said.

"You are the one who created it, or the one who uses it?"

"Both."

"No. That cannot be. The others have the background."

"You checked theirs, so you checked mine." Her voice was calm. She was focused. "Yet what have you found about me?"

"Nothing."

"You are smart enough to put two and two together, Elijahn."

As she said his name it was his turn to start. "So you know who I am."

"Who else would want Oracle destroyed as much as you do? After all, we destroyed you, Oracle and I." She had to convince him, and letting him know what she knew was her best bet. "I know who you are, and I know about the data center and about the names you took from IDSD. I've known about it all for a while now."

"Well." He leaned back. So she knew. Which meant that blasted IDSD knew.

He didn't care. It didn't matter to him anymore. He had the person behind Oracle. She had to be, it explained so much. The mystery woman with the high clearance and the impenetrable secrecy surrounding her.

"Why don't you just kill me?" This was getting to be a bit odd. This conversation, his people doing nothing. His behavior. The risk he was taking by not getting this over with and running.

"If I was going to kill you, I would have done it by now. Do you really think I need all these people to do that?"

She threw a look back at the black SUVs. Men were pouring out.

"No, I think I am going to take you. We will spend some time together, you and I. See what you know. See what you can give me. Perhaps you and I can create another Oracle together. And perhaps... who knows." He let out a low laugh, not bothering to hide its meaning. "You will, I believe, like my headquarters. Perhaps you might even learn to like my home. You look better than your photo, by the way."

Oh, God. Oh my God. He wasn't going to kill her. The implications, all of them, were too unbearable for her to wrap her mind around.

She snapped out of it. Reached slowly under the steering wheel. Opened a small, hidden touch panel. Pressed it with the tip of a finger, heard the biometric identifier beep once.

A small light started blinking, one only the driver, she, would know was there.

Come on. Come on already.

"You know what, I will be gracious. You have one minute. One. To think about it. Come to me, before I come for you myself."

The call disconnected.

She turned around in her seat. Behind her and to the left, Elijahn's men stood, scattered. The passenger side door of one of the SUVs opened and a man came out. He walked several steps toward her, then stopped, clearly illuminated by the vehicles' headlights. She could see Elijahn clearly now. His face. Those eyes, on her.

She took a good look at him. Then turned away. Strangely calm now that she'd made her final move, that it was her move, that it was she who initiated the sequence that would blow up her car in thirty seconds. She closed her eyes. This would work. Even Elijahn's technological ploys couldn't stop this. And he had no idea what she'd done. Even if he and his men tried to get close, get her out of the car, there would be no time, the self-destruct device installed in the car's main power supply could not be stopped, and it would go off no matter what, taking them with her.

It wasn't as if she hadn't known she would likely die here today. So what if it was like this? Hadn't she thought this through, weighed all the costs? And what did it matter, hadn't she stopped caring about living all those years ago, hadn't she given up hope that the pain could ever be healed? How easy it would be to stay here, she thought, let this happen. The memories would stop. The pain would go with it. So simple. Easy. Except...

The light blinked. And blinked. She didn't need to look at it, or at the small numbers moving on the tiny panel beside it. In her head, the count was reaching its end.

She wondered what had changed to make it less easy to do this. It would have been easier just a few short weeks earlier, so much easier.

No, she knew what had changed. This is crazy, I must be out of my mind, she thought. I can't believe I'm about to do this.

And she jumped out of the passenger side of the car.

"Trying to run, are you?" Elijahn called out. "If you think—"

Lara's beautiful, elegant, custom-made convertible blew up.

Elijahn lay on the ground, stunned. So did most of his men, he saw, looking dazed around him. Some were injured. One of the others pulled him away as a burning piece of the woman's car fell too close.

"Get her," Elijahn snarled. "I want her. Alive."

"Donovan!"

The urgency in her voice made Donovan brake so hard that the car skidded several feet.

"Donovan, he's here. Send—"

"Hold on, I'm on my way. You hear me? I'm coming for you." But the line was already dead and Donovan cursed, fear for Lara surging through him. The locator he had working for her in his phone had automatically activated as soon as it registered her incoming call—tracing her first to her home, which had him frowning, then to her actual location, which had him shaking his head in wonder—and he now had her approximate whereabouts. Just miles away from IDSD, a few miles from where Ericsson had her last position. He was pushing the car to its limit as he made the call and gave her coordinates to those who were waiting for them.

He approached the area with the headlights off, the car sliding into a sparse spot in the vegetation that separated the road from the open fields in places. It would be hidden here. Black in the dark of night, it had little chance of being seen. He took out a silencer from a hidden box inside the glove compartment and attached it to his gun. He then got out of the car, ripped off the bulletproof vest he was still wearing and threw it in, not wanting it to limit his movement, tucked the gun into his belt, and, looking up to judge where the moon was sending its light and might expose him, set out at a smooth run to the last coordinates he had for her.

In the distance, an explosion pierced the night and a pillar of smoke rising into the sky prodded him to increase his pace.

Lara, was his only thought.

He came, low, to a rise beyond which the ground dropped at an uncomfortable slope to mostly barren soil that gave way to vast woods a distance away. His heart missed a beat. Three massive SUVs stood at the bottom of the slope. To their right, what used to be a smaller car burnt, angry flames reaching for black skies. Grief flared as the burning car filled his vision, searing the new beginnings that had only recently began filling his heart, and he let it, as he prepared to destroy those who destroyed him.

Movement caught his eye, stopped him from taking his gun out. There were men there, standing not far from the SUVs, some moved slowly toward the burning car. But beyond them, closer to the woods, he saw others, running.

Chasing.

His eyes lost their rage, turned to ice as training took over. His body braced, his entire being focused, as his mission changed from revenge to defense, his grief to fueling hope. He moved quickly to his right, judging from the men's movements where he should go and staying out of sight. He knew they were trained killers, but then so was he.

He entered the woods downhill from them and moved stealthily deeper in. The foliage of the trees was thick enough here not to let in the light of the moon above, and the night around him darkened. He stood still and listened, let his eyes get used to the dark. To his left, in the distance, he heard a single shout, a clipped order by the tone of it. He moved toward it, concealing himself among the trees.

A rustle on his one o'clock, another farther away. By the sounds, the way they moved, they were trying to flank her. He dropped to one knee, still, waiting.

When the first man was close enough, Donovan pounced, moving with practiced agility to place an arm around his neck. Iron muscles tightened and the man's handgun fell. He lowered the dead man to the ground, then crouched beside him. He took his Glock out and waited. When the other appeared, he judged, aimed, pulled the trigger twice. The man fell with barely a groan.

Donovan pressed on.

Lara ran. She had used the explosion, knowing she was the only one who would not be surprised by it, and began moving a brief second before the count-down in her head ended. The powerful blast threw her a distance, and she'd been hit by shards. But she got up and continued running toward the woods. Something from the car hit her on her left side, her lower ribs, it felt like, and the searing pain made her lose her balance again, but she quickly regained it and pressed on, running as fast as she could. She was in good shape, swimming kept her muscles toned and endurance was not a problem, but her pursuers were relentless and the explosion had hit her hard, and that pain wasn't helping either. For a while she couldn't hear anyone behind her and thought she'd lost them, but then she heard a shout not far enough away. And then another. She was being hunted. They were surrounding her, getting closer. She picked up speed, ran through the trees, ran for her life, hers and so many others'. Focused on one thing, one hope—

And gasped in surprise as strong arms caught her, clamping around her, and only the hand that reached up to cover her mouth stifled her startled scream. She struggled, but the arms gripping her didn't budge.

"It's me," he said near her ear, and she stopped struggling, almost falling down with relief.

"Shhh," Donovan whispered and pulled her with him back into heavy brush. "Stay down."

He kept one arm around her and took his gun out again with the other. Her pursuers were now coming from two directions, to their west just outside the woods and to their north, the direction she had come from. He calculated, considered continuing toward them and sending her southeast, to a path that cut through the woods and rounded back west to the main road a safe enough distance away.

And then he heard it, the smooth whisper of rotors swooping low in the air, saw in the distance to the west the searchlight beam the stealth helicopter sent down, heard the shouts, rapid gunfire, then the sounds of heavy vehicles. Subconsciously he moved, shielded Lara, as a swarm of people swept the woods from multiple directions, and as the sounds of gunfire came closer.

Branches crunched under heavy shoes as black shadows ran toward them. Recognizing their gear as they approached, he stood up slowly, keeping Lara behind him, his gun in the air, knowing they were on a mission of their own and would shoot first any man they saw, ask later. Five of them came to a halt before him, assault rifles drawn, while those behind them continued around him, to the south.

"You Pierce?" The first figure took him in, the fact that this man was obviously shielding the woman behind him already prompting him to lower his weapon, although those behind him kept theirs aimed at Donovan. He peered behind Donovan and stepped forward. "You okay? Are you hurt?"

"I'm fine."

Her voice was steady, but the shocked undertone he recognized in it made Donovan turn his back on the soldiers and put an arm around her again. "We need to get her out of here," he said, turning his eyes to the soldier who'd spoken.

The man nodded and motioned to the others. "We've secured most of the area, got helos and a hell of a lot of our guys clearing the place. It's safe out there now," he said and fell to beside Lara and Donovan as his people surrounded them.

As they came out of the woods, Donovan saw that the three SUVs and the smoldering wreckage of Lara's car were surrounded by a mix of IDSD and US military vehicles and uniforms. Above them, a helicopter swooped down, its searchlight focused on them for a moment, then moved on.

More soldiers ran toward them, assault rifles at the ready, behind them medics. Lara stopped and looked on in astonishment. There were so many of them, she could see different uniforms, designations. So many.

Donovan saw the astonishment in her eyes and mused, "Looks like you're as important to them as they are to you."

Beside them, the soldier, a lieutenant colonel who introduced himself as US Marine Raider Battalion commanding officer Gabriel Martinez, said, "Hell, yeah. You save us, you think we don't know that? You think we don't know who you are? Damn if we're going to let anyone get to you."

Lara looked at him.

"Yes ma'am, all of us here, we've all been out there at one time or another with Oracle on the other end of the comms, probably will again," he said to her in a low voice. "We'll do what it takes to protect you."

"There's a small military here," Donovan noted and urged Lara forward. His arm was still around her, and he was holding her close to him. He could feel how cold her body was, and now that they were surrounded by more light he saw that her fist was clenched. She was in pain.

"We were at the IDSD simulation training range in a joint exercise, us marine raiders and our IDSD counterparts. IDSD called their people out, and everyone else tagged along. Good thing, too," Martinez said. "We got eleven so far, still chasing a few, and we intercepted another SUV on the way here, they gave one hell of a fight. They really wanted you gone." He laughed. "You keeping us alive bugs them, does it?"

One of the medics approached, pushed his way through the circle of soldiers, and held his hand out for Lara. She looked at Donovan.

Reluctant to let her go, he let his arm drop. "Go with them," he said gently. "I'll be there in a bit."

He stayed with Martinez, watching Lara walk away with the medic, surrounded by a ring of soldiers so thick he could barely see her. He needed to know more about her attackers, and the man beside him had just the kind of training that could give him that—he could judge the capabilities of those he and his people had just fought against. And the lieutenant colonel did just that. And he also told Donovan that the attackers did not let themselves get caught alive, which was worrying in itself, the zealousness that would take.

Worse, Martinez couldn't be sure that no one had gotten away.

Donovan approached the medevac ambulance, breaking into a run when he saw Lara clearly in its harsh light. She had cuts on her forehead and the left side of her face, and the medic had raised the left side of her torn shirt and was checking her lower ribs, which was obviously causing her pain.

Donovan indicated it and the medic said, "Doesn't look like anything is broken. Nasty hit, but it'll heal. The rest is the explosion of the car, she was too close. Some scratches from shards and branches, I think." He took a step back while his friend wiped the blood off Lara's face and cleaned the cuts. "This will do until we get to the IDSD medical center, they'll need to run an internal scan. There will be some bruising, I expect, and shock to her body from the explosion."

Lara shook her head. The last thing she wanted was to go to a hospital. What she wanted was to go home. Now that this was over, she just wanted to go home. She couldn't think clearly, needed to get a handle on things. She had refused both a painkiller and a sedative to keep alert, and this was difficult. Painful too, the adrenaline was down and she was really feeling the pain.

Her eyes were lowered, looking behind Donovan, and he turned around to see what she was looking at, then moved to block her line of sight. Her pursuers' bodies lay not far away, guarded. She raised her eyes to his, and he held them.

"She'll go with you," he said with finality, his

eyes still on hers. He crouched before her and took her hand, not caring who was there to see.

"Please go with them. You'll be well guarded." He indicated the stern combat soldiers surrounding the ambulance. The rest of them were still securing the area all the way to IDSD. They already had a lead on another car that had been on its way there with Elijahn's people, and had made a run for it. Donovan wanted to stay with them for a while longer, to understand what the situation was, where her safety stood.

Lara's eyes remained on his, and he felt his chest tighten. He could have lost her that night. "I'll be there soon, I promise," he said.

Elijahn wanted to turn back. He wanted to take his gun and go back and shoot all those soldiers in his way, every one of them, then walk up to the woman and strangle her with his bare hands. Wanted to stand there with his hands around her neck and watch the life seep out of her.

He fisted his hand, his fingernails digging into his palm, drawing blood. Rage controlled him, would not let go. He could not believe it.

He could not believe she had done it to him again.

Chapter Twenty

Lara didn't move as the car slowed down before her house, pulled into the driveway, and stopped outside the garage her own car would normally be in. Beside her, Donovan turned off his car and turned to look at her. She was pale. There was a dark bruise down her jawline, a bandaged cut on her forehead, and several shallower cuts and scratches on her face and neck. There were others, too, cuts and bruises on her body, and her right arm hugged her left side where she'd been hit during the explosion.

She had stubbornly refused to stay at the IDSD medical center. The internal scans had come back clear and even the already apparent bruise on her lower ribs presented no danger, but they had wanted her to stay overnight. For observation, they said, because of her proximity to the explosion. The shock of what had happened, being attacked, chased that way, was another reason they had argued. Donovan remembered how cold she had been when he held her, and had agreed with them.

But she wanted to go home, and the head physician had finally relented, gave Donovan her personal phone number, and told him to call if Lara needed anything. And perhaps, Dr. Mallory had said, it was better this way. Lara would be more comfortable in her home, and was more likely to recuperate faster there.

So Donovan had taken her home. He would have liked her to stay inside the protected IDSD complex for safety reasons, too, but he could keep a close eye on her here. And it wasn't as if he would do so alone. Wherever he turned to in the medical center or on the way to Lara's home, there was security presence. And the house was now substantially more protected, too. In addition to the usual stationary drone watching from high above, another surveillance drone was now scouring the area, and somber IDSD protective agents were guarding the house. Donovan had opened his own house to them, for their use. He wanted Lara's place to remain quiet, wanted her to have a chance to rest. As it was, an IDSD specialist team would be coming in later in the morning to overhaul the entire security system, which for Lara would be an intrusion.

Lara's status, her life, Donovan knew, would now change in many ways. Recent events, and this latest incident in particular, had shown to everyone just how much impact Oracle was having and the extent to which this had the potential to expose her to attacks. It also showed them how far those Oracle was standing in the way of would be willing to go to destroy her. Oracle could have died that night. No one was about to let danger come this close to her again. And there was, of course, the more immediate issue.

Elijahn had escaped.

Donovan got out of the car and looked around him. The vehicles that had flanked them on the way were now positioned up and down the street. The security threat level would not be lowered until Elijahn was caught and until they had a clearer picture of how many of his men were still out there. Donovan was glad Lara was hazy from the meds she had finally agreed to take at the medical center, which would dull the pain and, in the state she was in, would also jumble things somewhat in her mind. She didn't seem to realize what was happening around her, the extent of the security surrounding her. She hadn't been told that Elijahn was not among the dead militants. Donovan didn't want her to know yet, he wanted her to recuperate a little first.

He walked around the car, opened the passenger side door, and helped her out, carefully. She had his jacket on her shoulders. Her clothes had been ruined, and she was wearing maroon medical scrubs. She looked dazed and exhausted. It had been a long night, and the sun had yet to have come up.

"What day is it?" she asked, glancing at the silent street, at the darkness beyond the lights that surrounded her home.

"It's still tonight, the same night," Donovan said,

gently putting his arm around her. He expected her to be confused. It was hard to believe it all happened that same night—Elijahn's attack, the rescue, the commotion around her at the medical center.

"Home," she said. "We're home."

"Yes, we're home," he said, and guided her to the front door. She didn't seem to notice the agents on her front lawn.

The agent standing before the door opened it for them and let them through. "Sir, we've taken control of the house's security system, but you'll still be able to follow security from the consoles inside," he said to Donovan as he and Lara entered the house. "I'll lock down the place after you go in."

Donovan acknowledged him and guided Lara in as the door closed behind them. The house was quiet, undisturbed. Lara came to a stop in the middle of the living room and looked at her couch, at the patio doors she would normally have open. She took a step toward them, then stopped, hesitating, her brow furrowed. "It's not day yet."

"You need to sleep," Donovan said softly. He left her there, walked to the kitchen and brought her a half a glass of water.

She shook her head.

"Drink," he prodded gently. "You're still in shock." And he wanted her to have the sedative he'd put inside, given to him by Dr. Mallory when she had released Lara to his care.

Holding the glass with both hands, she drank

slowly, in concentration, as if this was a difficult task she had to put her mind to. Donovan took the empty glass from her and put it down on the coffee table nearby, not leaving her side this time. And he was right not to. Her knees buckled, but she didn't have a chance to even begin to fall before he caught her. He picked her up and carried her upstairs, holding her close, keeping her safe.

"You keep doing that," she said in hazy wonder.

"I guess I do," he murmured against her head, which was comfortably cradled on his shoulder.

He entered her bedroom and sat her gently on the bed. He took his jacket off her shoulders and put it aside, then removed the hospital slippers and lay her down gently, careful not to hurt her. Tucked her in. Sat on the bed beside her.

"I was actually hunted," she said with a blurry thoughtfulness that made him smile. It was easy to smile now, with her safe here, in her own bedroom.

"Yes, you were," he said, and dimmed the bedroom lights.

"My car blew up," she observed groggily.

"Yes, it most certainly did," he agreed, making sure the blanket was tucked warmly around her.

"And my phone too." She noted, barely coherent.

"Well, it was in the car," he said.

"You came for me." She made an effort to look at him but failed, her head heavy on the soft pillow. The sedative was meant to work quickly.

"Always," he said and kissed her temple, lingering.

"You kissed me," she mumbled and fell asleep.

"Yes, I did," he said softly, still close to her, and touched his lips to her temple again.

He sat up, and watched her until her body relaxed and her breathing calmed. Then he waited a while longer, until he was sure the meds took over and she would not wake up to find herself alone. Only then did he get up and, leaving the door open behind him, left the room.

As soon as he did, ice crept into his eyes and he allowed the anger he kept controlled inside him to surge. How the hell could this happen? She could've died.

I could have lost her, the thought tore through him viciously.

IDSD's head of security answered the call immediately, fidgeting nervously on-screen. When he saw the eyes of the man who stood before the screen in Lara's living room he cringed visibly. The fact that Donovan was saying nothing only seemed to disconcert him more.

"The drones above you and satellite feed show that all is quiet. Until we're sure there isn't anyone left who is after Lara, the agents I've got covering the house will remain there, in shifts."

Donovan remained silent, and Ericsson continued hurriedly. "The new security measures I'm having installed in the house later in the morning are the best there are. My techs will walk you through them, and you can do the same for Lara as soon as she is able to—"

"What the hell happened? Why wasn't she able to reach you?"

"He jammed all outgoing signals at a radius around her, at all frequencies. Debilitated all communications from her phone and her car in a way that prevented us from locating her and her from sending her emergency distress signal to us or calling anyone."

"You knew Elijahn's capabilities. He broke into the data center, he got into the IDSD administrative system just a couple of days ago, for Christ's sake. How could he get through your defenses again? How did he get to her? To her ability to get help? To your ability to track her? And while we're at it, how the hell did Lara leave IDSD without her protective detail? Without any of you knowing?"

The other man looked tired. Frustration was evident in his voice when he answered. "This shouldn't have happened. Couldn't have happened. But it did." He collected himself, and the eyes that looked back at Donovan were focused again. "We haven't finished implementing all our new security measures. Some things, like technological capabilities, take longer. And yes, we still should have implemented some sort of contingency defenses, certainly for Lara, you don't have to tell me that. I should have expected this. As for how Lara left here without us knowing, well, apparently she sent her protective detail away and told them she would call them when she left to go home. Simple as that. You know who she is. They did what she told them to do. Hell, she even told them she would update me herself." He sighed. "At least that one I could solve immediately. I've moved her to level five security, that's our narrowest need to know circle and our highest security and tracking level. It cannot be interfered with. Hopefully not even by her."

"Why wasn't she in this security level in the first place?"

The laugh was bitter. "We didn't think anyone would find out who she is. What she is. We never thought. . . I never thought she would be so specifically targeted. We have her hidden behind a code name, so I thought. . ." He shook his head. "I should have seen it. Look at what she's become. She's hurting them now, getting in the way of their plans too many times. I should've—"

"How compromised is her code name?" Donovan interjected. He didn't care about regrets, and wasn't about to forgive screw-ups that almost got those he cared about killed.

"None of the intelligence agencies are seeing it mentioned anywhere. Which seems to confirm that Elijahn was indeed working alone and planned to go after what he finds behind that code name first, rather than immediately exposing it, and this is working to our advantage. Either way, we're all prepared to block any mention of that name and will continue doing so from now on. Everyone is scrambling to fix this, Agent Pierce. We have all learned our lesson."

Donovan might have replied to that with the harshness he felt but he stopped himself. The IDSD head of security's oversight was already taking its toll, and he imagined there would be hell to pay after what had happened that night.

"From now on, her security goes through me," he said instead. The day he found out who Lara was he had agreed to Scholes's request that he help protect her, but that had been just between them. So far, formally he had only operated in his capacity as the agent in charge of the investigation into the data center break-in. This wasn't enough anymore.

"You're not approved for IDSD..." Ericsson's voice trailed off, and he sighed. "Yes, well, under the circumstances that might just be what happens. If, that is"—he scrutinized Donovan—"you intend to stay close to her."

Donovan nodded once.

"I'll start the process. We'll need to coordinate it with USFID. I'll need your formal permission and your director's to transfer your service file to our central security in Brussels and you'll have to come in for all the formalities protocol dictates."

"I'll do what it takes. And in the meantime?"

"In the meantime, I'll give an interim order for all security procedures related to Lara to go through you. I've no doubt Frank will sign off on it."

Donovan ended the call, and sighed, rubbing his tired eyes. He went to the kitchen and made himself some coffee, the blend Lara liked so much. He stood staring at it, reflecting on how different the night could have turned out, how different this moment might have been. Instead of standing here, making coffee in her kitchen, with her safely asleep upstairs, within his reach, he could have been mourning her. Crushed after she was taken from him, he realized with some astonishment. Somehow, the brief time he'd known her had been enough. He had no idea how it could have happened, but after that night, he wasn't sure it mattered.

Yes, he was here to stay.

An hour later he had finished with Scholes, White, and Lieutenant Colonel Martinez, who had formally been placed in charge of the IDSD and US forces searching for Elijahn, while his IDSD counterpart coordinated from IDSD Missions. Normally Donovan would have been with them, but his understanding of just how dangerous Elijahn was to Lara made him more valuable here, and the way he had intervened to protect her had convinced everyone he was the right person to be beside her. And so Scholes had asked him to stay with her. But then, Donovan wouldn't have it any other way.

He went back upstairs. The problem was that with nothing more to do, nothing except wait, he was alone with only his thoughts. And they returned immediately, mercilessly, to the events of that night. Lara had already been debriefed after her preliminary checkup at the medical center, and he was there so he knew what happened. Or most of it. He still had some questions for her. Things he needed to know, to understand. Things he didn't think she'd told them, that he read in her eyes. And he'd seen enough in his life to know this wasn't over yet, not for her. What she'd been through would stay with her.

It would stay with him, too.

He reached her bedroom and leaned on the doorway, his eyes on her. He wasn't used to this, to the way it was with her. He was used to, when he was interested in a woman, knowing it would end even before it began, not letting it go beyond a point, not letting it affect him. But then, he had never been emotionally involved before. Not like this. Never like this. Nor was he used to women resisting him this way, not when the attraction was so evidently mutual. And this one did, from that very first look. Even now. Even as they grew closer, even as what was inevitable was already happening, she seemed to be resisting it, struggling with herself to keep him away.

He wasn't going to push. This situation she had found herself in was complex, to say the least. But when it was over, he wanted to know more, to understand more about this woman he could not seem to think beyond. Or maybe, he thought, he should, when this was over, simply seduce her. One night, that's all. One night only. Maybe that would free him. Maybe it would be enough.

Even as the thought crossed his mind, he knew better.

He walked into the bedroom, meaning to go to the window, but stopped at the foot of the bed and looked at her. The sedative had worked well, and her sleep was undisturbed, even as the first light of the day seeped through the window. But there was no peace in her face, not even when she slept. As he watched her she turned to her left side, the side that was most badly hurt, and sighed softly. He tensed, thinking her injuries might be hurting her, but she relaxed, and her breathing eased again. He realized he was holding his breath. He shook his head, astonished at himself, and walked to the window, looked out to the back yard. An agent stood with his back to the house, looking around him. Another walked toward him from the direction of Donovan's house, but his gait was calm, unhurried. Donovan nodded to himself. He closed the curtains, sending the room into shadows. Then he walked over to the couch in the corner and settled down to watch over her.

Chapter Twenty-One

Lara sat comfortably huddled on the living room sofa, a mug of hot soup in her hands. Chicken soup, the ever-reigning healing broth, she thought with some amusement. Rosie, cheerfully humming to herself in the kitchen, had made it for her when she came in that morning. Lara had wanted another cup of coffee, but Donovan had sided with Rosie. And she had to admit the soup was making her feel better. In fact, the aches in her body were dull again. She wondered if Donovan had slipped anything into the soup. Probably did. She didn't want to be taken care of, didn't want to let go even for a moment of the stubborn strength that kept her from falling, but he wasn't asking.

She watched him now with the security techs at the patio doors. He'd been through the entire house with them, bringing security up to the level he wanted it to be. He'd changed his clothes and was dressed somewhat more casually, with trousers and a T-shirt, although they were both black, which she supposed fit the combative mood he'd displayed when he was briefed by the head of her new IDSD protective detail earlier that morning. He was relentless with the guy, still angry, she knew. She might have been angry too, about the fact that Elijahn had gotten to her phone, to her car, so easily, but after all it was she who had purposefully evaded the protective detail in the first place.

She contemplated Donovan. Despite the more casual clothes, he was wearing his gun holster on his belt. She hadn't seen him without it since he'd come for her the night before. Not even when she woke up that morning and found him asleep on the couch in her bedroom, the only place he would allow himself to catch a couple of hours' rest, even with the security in place around her. He was watching over her. Keeping her safe.

She wondered if he was also angry at her, at what she'd done. He hadn't shown anything so far. Nothing but protectiveness toward her. That, and the tenderness, the way he took care of her the night before. And that morning. He'd waited downstairs while she showered, carefully. Her entire body hurt. She had managed to dress in comfortable slacks, and a sleeveless undershirt she had to put on slowly. She was sitting on the bed, her eyes closed, waiting for a thousand aches to subside, and had opened them to see him standing at the open bedroom door, watching her, the blue in his eyes easily readable. He had come in and sat beside her on the bed, and his eyes had flickered to each and every one of the signs so easily visible on her body that told the tale of the night before. The medical care she had received had been good, and many of the cuts and bruises would disappear in a few days, but at least one of her injuries would take a bit longer. His touch was gentle as he examined her bruised ribs. As he helped her put on a soft cardigan. As his hand lingered on her for a moment longer.

She couldn't remember the last time a man's touch felt that way to her.

The day shift of the protective detail assigned to her was already on its way then, and he had arranged for Rosie to come in too, a little later than usual, wanting her to sleep. He didn't leave her side until the new detail was in position and Rosie was there, and then only to go to his house next door, to change and make sure the protective agents who had made their temporary headquarters there had what they needed.

She hoped he wasn't angry, knew he should be. Hoped he would understand, that he still trusted her, needed him to know that she trusted him. Knew now, finally, just how much she cared.

And was entirely, completely, and absolutely confused about how that happened.

Donovan glanced her way and saw her watching. He walked over and sat beside her. She looked better. He'd tried to convince her to take a painkiller again earlier, but she refused, even though the bruise hidden under the sweater she wore must have been causing her some pain, as did the other injuries he'd seen when he helped her put it on. She wanted to be alert, she said, in case she was needed to help find those who were after her. But he knew that wasn't it. Meds could be countered if needed, and the painkiller Dr. Mallory had given him for her would not affect her that way. Which was why he still slipped a dose into her soup.

The simple truth of it, he knew, was that the pain was easier to deal with than the fact that the events of the night before were not quite over. He had finally told her that morning that Elijahn had gotten away, and she wanted to stay alert in case he came after her again. Donovan thought about it, about her being alone out there, with Elijahn and his men so close. About the courage it took to do what she did, how hard it must have been. About her leaving him out of it.

About how quiet she'd been since it happened, withdrawn. She had responded to no one except him and Rosie.

"They seem to be very thorough." Her voice was quiet.

"They're good," he said, throwing a look in the direction she was looking. "And they're your people, ordered to give the best to their best."

The wordplay raised an absentminded smile on her face. She kept her eyes on the techs, avoiding his. What happened wasn't the only thing on her mind. If he'd have touched her just now, he might have felt her heart beat faster. Now that he was here beside her, when around her all was calm, safe for now, and because she was trying hard not to think about Elijahn or the night before, her mind kept returning to something else entirely. She wanted to ask but found she wasn't sure how, the question was difficult to utter. There were things about the past hours that were hazy, and she wasn't sure how much of what she remembered was real and how much med-induced. But she needed to know. Wanted to know. Realized that she hoped it was as she remembered. Which was just as disconcerting.

"Lara?"

She turned her eyes to him and then away again, as if magnetized by the work the techs were doing.

He was worried, wanted her to talk to him, not to keep any of it inside. But he got it as soon as she began talking, and smiled. It wasn't Elijahn on her mind. It was him.

"When you brought me here last night. . ." she said in a hesitant voice.

He nodded. He had wondered how much she remembered.

"I can't recall clearly, I'm not sure, but. . ."

"I kissed you. Your temple, to be more accurate. Twice, actually. I think you were already asleep the second time."

She forced herself to control that feeling deep inside her. She needed something it would be easier to deal with. Something . . . friends. Kissing someone on the temple that way showed friendship. Right? Except, what she'd felt from him at his place, the way he was with her, the interest in her he wasn't really hiding . . . No, she must be wrong. She'd been attacked, injured, of course he would kiss her like that. Okay, no, she wasn't succeeding in convincing herself. The fact that she was so desperately trying to was indicating something else entirely. That he cared. And that she did, too. God, she wasn't thinking clearly.

She leaned her head on the back of the sofa and tucked her legs under her. But there was no discomfort in her movement, no careful hiding from him. She looked, he thought, as if she was trying to figure him out. And herself. And them. Mostly though, it seemed to him, herself. He recognized the reaction, he'd seen it in her before. This was complicated for her, and he still had no idea why. But he hadn't changed his mind, not even close. He intended to break through whatever walls were surrounding her. That, he knew already the night before, in that moment of relief he'd felt as he held her, so alive, when he'd found her as she was being chased by her would-be killers.

"Donovan?"

He tilted his head slightly.

"Aren't you angry with me?"

"Yes. Very much so. But it can wait."

"I'm sorry," she said.

"For what? Not trusting me?" He hadn't intended

to do this now, but apparently that was exactly what was going to happen.

"I trust you. And I trust you to keep me safe. But that's just it. You never would have gone along with what I did."

"You're damn right I wouldn't."

She shook her head. "This wasn't supposed to happen. You did what you were brought in to do. You found out it was Elijahn, figured out what he was going to do. Found where he was hiding. You weren't supposed to be here for me. It wasn't your job to protect Oracle. Or me." She sighed. "And you weren't supposed to care. To get involved."

"Didn't work out that way." The anger in the quiet voice was unmistakable.

"I didn't know. . ." The words flew out. "When I started setting it up I still thought you were just doing your job, that it wouldn't matter. And my plan had Elijahn going only after me, and his being stopped, I thought that's what mattered. Don't you see? When I realized he wasn't going to stop, that he was going to get to those around me, I had to do something. And no one was supposed to . . ." She wasn't doing this right. Oracle was so much easier compared to Lara.

"No one was supposed to what, care? Forget me for a moment. What the hell's going on inside you that you don't know how much you mean to people around you? And I'm not talking about what you do as Oracle, Lara. What about Frank? Do you have any idea how much he worries about you? And Donna? She loves you, for Christ's sake. You should have seen her work on this house, how she thought of everything, how happy she was about it. Do you know how she talks about you? You're her best friend, she talks about you like you're her sister! And yes, you know what, there's me. And don't tell me you don't know, because by now you do. And you saw it before last night."

"Only in your house, that's when I realized—"

"Then you still had time to reconsider. You should have at least had me there in the car with you."

"No."

The way she said it made him stop. His anger dissipated without warning.

She lowered her eyes, concentrated on her hands. "If you would have been in the car with me, most likely Elijahn would have had you shot before he began talking to me. I went through it in my mind a thousand times before I did it. He decides what he wants and goes for it. Everything, everyone else is expendable. You would have been expendable."

"So you did consider it."

Yes, she thought. Of course I did. I would have felt safe with you. But she said nothing.

"You should have done it anyway. It's what I do, Lara, it's my job. And I can take care of myself, I'm not that easy to kill. You should have let me make the choice."

"I couldn't. I can't. Not again. You would have... he could have killed you." It came out quietly, barely more than a whisper.

He understood now the call she made to him. "When you called me, you didn't want me to come. I was a way for you to call the IDSD forces."

She shook her head. "I wanted you to come. I just didn't want you to..."

Die, he understood. So you do care. He watched her. Here she was, admitting that she cared about him, and yet the way she was doing it... what was going on here? Not again. That was what she said. Not again. Not again what? What aren't you telling me, Lara? What happened to you? He was on the verge of asking, even now, even though he had told himself this thing with Elijahn needed to be over before he pushed to know more about her. But then she spoke again.

"But you still came. And if you hadn't, I would have been—"

"Don't." He took her hand in his. He didn't want her to say it. Himself, to hear it.

She looked at their hands, together. "Does that mean you don't trust me now?"

"I trust you. Except with keeping yourself safe. Unfortunately, that part seems to be important to me." He got up and started walking back to the techs.

She watched him walk away, unsure what to say, what to think.

"Come to think of it, while we're at it." He came back and squatted down before her, placing himself squarely in her line of sight.

Making sure she would look at him.

"You with me?" He locked his eyes on hers.

She nodded.

"If you ever pull something like this again, I'll shoot you myself." Although he was using this particular statement he'd said to her before, knowing she would know what he really meant, there was nothing mild or joking about the way he said it, or about the way he looked at her. "Are we clear?"

She said nothing.

His eyes bore into hers. "Are we clear?"

She nodded.

"Good. Now, that was a generalized statement. Which means that there's a whole lot of things I can shoot you for."

"Like what?" Her own unexpected giddiness took her by surprise. Where did that come from?

The dark blue she knew so well by now and that now ruled in his eyes told her she was playing with fire. "We'll figure them out as we go along. Although we might not have to. I'm thinking I just might shoot you before this is over after all." He stood up again.

She spoke before she thought better of it. "Ever."

He looked back at her.

"You said ever. This will be over soon."

"This is. We're not." He turned and walked over

to the techs who were beckoning him. Time to test the new security system. He was being direct, he knew. But he didn't care. He had spent most of his life on the edge, and too much of it without something he never missed because he never thought it existed for him. He knew now what that was, what it was like, what it could be, and he'd almost lost it. He wasn't about to let it go. To lose her.

She watched him, the mug still in her hands, forgotten, her heart caught in a whirlwind of conflicting emotions surging inside her.

Chapter Twenty-Two

Several hours later the house was finally quiet again. It was just them now, just Lara and Donovan, and the protective detail outside.

And Scholes, Evans, and Martinez on the screen in Lara's living room.

"So this is what we know." Martinez hadn't been the bearer of good news.

"Let me get that straight," Donovan said. "So far we're aware of the three who had been at Edwards's home and Elijahn himself." These were the four unaccounted for following the attack. Security cameras installed by the protective detail outside Edwards's home had shown the three who had come to kill him, and their angry departure when they found the house empty. It also showed the SUV they had used, which was later found abandoned, burned, in a location that indicated that they had been on the way to where the attack on Lara had taken place. They themselves were gone. Other than Edwards, Elijahn had only sent people to the home of one more name on the list, Dr. Miles. But those three militants had been intercepted and killed by the forces who bore down on Elijahn.

"The good thing," Evans said, "is that according to the DNA supplied by your people, Donovan, the samples they collected in the warehouse that we were able to compare to the bodies we have, we suspect these four are all that's left. Unless Elijahn has more people stashed somewhere."

"His headquarters," Scholes said, remembering what Lara had told them about her encounter with Elijahn. "He's got his headquarters."

"Which we have no idea the whereabouts of," Evans added.

"How are we doing on tracking these people?" Donovan asked.

"Not as well as we'd like," Martinez said. "Someone shot a motorcyclist about a mile down the path crossing the woods where the attack took place. We can assume it was Elijahn who did it, the bullets are similar to those found in the warehouse. We have no idea about the other three, the burned SUV was all we found. We do know that they were warned by the ones who had been at Miles's place and who'd been met by our guys on their way to the attack site—since we'd intercepted them we could check the phones they had on them. We have profilers on it, to see if we can anticipate their moves, but it'll take time."

"We're trying to cover all transportation modes, but if they've got some private transport or go into hiding. . ." Evans didn't finish the thought.

"We're all on the lookout, and we've tightened the grid and will hold it for as long as it takes. Eventually we'll find a trail," Martinez said. "Especially for the three who'd been to Edwards's house, if they've separated from Elijahn. He's the brain and drive behind this, not them. There will be a trail of theft or bodies they'll leave behind them, and we'll find it."

"The problem is time." Evans rubbed his eyes in frustration. "We need to finish this before Elijahn gets the idea to release the information about Oracle or before his people at that headquarters of his catch on and run, and then it'll all be futile."

So far Lara had said nothing, just listened, her head lowered. She now raised her head, her eyes narrowed. She looked at Scholes. Scholes looked back at her. He knew that look.

"I agree," he said to her. "We have to get him. Not only did you get in the way of his plan, you also got away from him, and his people were killed in the process. You basically pulled another Chad on him. And he knows now to come after you, and he will, no matter what, and no matter who he hurts on the way." Scholes wasn't talking to anyone else now. Only Lara.

She nodded.

"What do you need?" he asked.

"My office, for one. Eyes—space, ours, flexible zero-delay access. Intelligence—mixed, chatter, cyber, live undercover." She looked at Evans. "Can I assume there has been no chatter about the attack?"

Evans nodded. "Not a word. In a nutshell, you had to be there to know it happened, or hear about it from someone who was there. We also had the police keep silent about the warehouse, and we spread some story about what happened there to civilians around. Just in case he's got someone listening."

"Good. I want no mention of my name or code name. The same goes for Elijahn's name. I want everyone who has anything to do with this guy guessing." That would keep them off balance for a while longer, she hoped. She had lost precious time here already, it had been only hours short of a day since Elijahn had escaped.

Martinez looked confused for a moment, then caught on. "Hey, are we saying what I think we're saying? You're coming in?"

"I believe that's exactly what we're saying," Evans said. It was, after all, the best, the only way. They were constantly a step behind Elijahn, it was time to reverse the odds.

"Gentlemen, we'll continue this conversation ourselves. Donovan, Lara will update you. Security is your call," Scholes said, and terminated Lara's end of the call.

Donovan was looking at her.

"It's the only way," she said quietly, her eyes still on the blank screen.

"Oracle," he said, his voice low, its undertone

unmistakable. "How was that just decided? After all that's happened, how was it just decided that Oracle is going in?"

"Frank knows that I have the missing piece. I can find Elijahn."

"We're looking for a man who has succeeded in evading us for days now and for his headquarters that could be anywhere in the world and that no one even knew about for the past two years. And after everything, we still have no viable intelligence on him. What's changed?"

"I talked to him." She shrugged. "That was the missing piece."

"I don't understand."

"Before, I had whatever intelligence was previously collected about him, and I went against him myself once, and even then not against him personally, but against everything that he had built, that came from his aspirations, his mind, had his distinct fingerprint on it. And it still wasn't enough. But now I've talked to him. I saw him. Related to him. And he attacked me, directly."

It took him a moment to get it. "You're going to use yourself as the anchor, the focal point, to go against him." He tried to translate what little he knew so far about the way her mind worked, into how she meant to deal with this situation she was in.

"In a way." It was a bit more complicated than that. Actually, a lot more.

She had changed during the videoconference, Donovan realized. Right before his eyes. After the attack she'd been dazed, injured. Then she was quiet, a pensiveness about her. He understood that. After a long time during which she'd been protected, kept safely away from those whose path she crossed as Oracle, those in whose way she got, she ended up being targeted right here on her own turf, where she should have been safe. True, when it came down to it, she had stood up to Elijahn and had escaped him. But that didn't change the fact that she'd been through an assault. And that after all that had happened, she was still not safe, still a target, still being hunted.

But now there was strength in her eyes. Calm determination. Like cornered prey, she was turning to face her hunter. It was her turn to strike, with everything that she was. Except that she just happened to be Oracle.

She turned to face him. "I need to do this, Donovan. And I'm the only one who can." She said it as a matter of fact. It was, simply, the way it was.

She needed to find her footing, and she needed to fight back. Donovan could understand that. But he wanted her alive. "It won't help anyone if you die. Did you consider that? This man is out there, and we have no idea where he is, what he's planning for you now." His eyes flared. "Right now my job is to protect you. I need to protect you."

"Protect me? While everybody is out there, trying

to find him? You were there, you heard Martinez. They know who I am and they will do all it takes to protect me. I won't have them get hurt for me. That's not what I am about. And what happens if he runs, if he goes back to unfriendly territory, some place where we have no reach? What would that mean? More missions? Soldiers and agents dying trying to get to him there? Will he take vengeance by targeting IDSD elsewhere in the world? Internationals like me? How about US citizens, because US soldiers came to help me? And what if he comes back in a year, ten years, after he's had time to regroup, to plan better based on what happened this time around?

"This is the guy who built the most sophisticated terrorist base ever and planned to attack the alliance headquarters in Brussels, the guy who destroyed an alliance data center, something that was thought impossible. And this is a guy who is still unable to let go two years after Chad. He's deadly, he's tenacious, and he's good, too good. I will not stay here, protected, while he's still out there, killing people. If someone dies because I don't find him now, or if I go into hiding and they die because I wasn't there to do my job, looking out for myself instead of them, it's not worth it, nothing is! These people are out there risking their lives, and they've got families too, moms and dads and husbands and wives and children and others who love them and want them to come home. They pay enough as it is, they all do. I've got to be there with them, I've got to bring them home!"

She took a step toward Donovan, and he found himself mesmerized by the passion in her eyes. Despite what happened to her, Oracle was not done. And she wasn't just talking about Elijahn, about herself, about this thing they were in the midst of, not anymore. She was talking about them all, every person who relied, who would rely on Oracle. And there was something else there, something painful, something personal.

He realized with shock that her eyes were brimming with tears. He instinctively moved toward her, but she raised a hand to stop him, keep him at a distance, and took a step back.

"No," she said. Not now. She needed to find the strength inside her that would let her get through this—and win. She closed her eyes, calmed down. When she opened her eyes again and met his, she was in control of herself.

He wasn't. And she saw his concern, his fear, what she meant to him.

She sighed. "How long are you going to protect me, Donovan? For how long are you and I going to stop our lives and stay here, waiting? And when Elijahn does come, what then? He kills you to get to me?" She shook her head. "If he gets away now, he can disappear for as long as he wants and choose when to return. Just like he did last time. And he will come back. He is not going to stop, Donovan.

He knows who I am now. And even before that, something about me must have awoken either his interest or his instinct, otherwise he wouldn't have sent most of his men after me, and he wouldn't have come after me himself. And he will come after me again. He will kill me, if he can't—" She fell silent.

Donovan took a step forward. "If he can't what?"

She braced herself. "'You will like my headquarters. Perhaps you might even learn to like my home. You look better than your photo, by the way.'" She quoted word for word the one thing Elijahn had said to her that she would never forget. The one thing she had not told anyone until now.

Donovan froze, realizing just how much worse than he had thought the situation had been for her the night before, what she had almost lost.

"Donovan, I have to do this. Last night I chose to run. To risk it, to run, to live. And now I have to fight back. I want to fight back. You did your thing. You found him. And you prevented him from getting me, you saved my life, and now you know just how bad it could have been. Now it's my turn. I'm the best bet for this. Nobody can do what I do. Nobody." She shook her head as she remembered. "I saw his face. I spoke to him. Heard his feelings, his anger, his need for revenge. His hate. His arrogance. He was sure he was going to take me, so he opened up, showed me enough of what's inside him. And that was his mistake. It was all that was missing, all I needed."

She met his eyes again with the simple truth, a smile playing at her lips. "I'm Oracle. I can find him. I can find them all."

He figured she probably could. And he now knew she had to. "I won't let him get to you," he said.

For the first time, it was she who took a step toward him. "He won't. I've got you."

He put his brow against hers, felt her soft hand in his. His thumb stroked her fingers. The last time he had her this close to him, her hunters were just yards behind her. So close. If he hadn't gotten there when he had . . .

He made his decision, as she'd made hers. He straightened up, nodded. "Are you up to it? I mean, physically."

"You made sure I would be." She held his eyes then, hers finally letting on what her heart already knew and her mind, her past were just beginning to accept.

He saw it and couldn't even begin to steel himself against a reaction he had never had before. Oh my God, he thought. I'm in love with her.

He focused. Right. Let's do this. Let's get this guy out of our way. "You do as I say," he said. "Stray once and I'll . . ."

"Shoot me," she finished the thought mildly.

His hand closed around hers. He wasn't in the mood to joke. "I'll have you in protective custody for the rest of our lives, and you won't have a say in it."

She nodded, somber.

"Okay. You need IDSD Missions."

"Yes."

"So we get you there. Safe. And you stay there. Safe. You do not leave the war room. I'm going to be with you at all times. If for any reason I'm not near you, you do not go with anyone else unless I say so."

"I'm supposed to be safe at IDSD, certainly in the war room."

"You are. But at this point, I don't want to err by guessing wrong how far Elijahn would go, Lara. I don't know if he would be able to get someone in, or if he's got some contingency suicide thing going and would try to attack IDSD after all. He already got to a security agent, remember? Despite all we think we know, this guy is smart. Which is why I'll leave agents here too, as a diversion, as if you're still here." He was already planning this in his head. "Right. I need to set this up."

Lara remained standing where she was, watched him walk away, take out his phone, start making the necessary calls. After a while, she went upstairs to change.

Donovan put his jacket on. "Lara," he called out, standing at the bottom of the staircase. She came out of the bedroom and descended the stairs toward him. "Frank called. They've set everything in motion. We're ready to go, so it's your call."

She came to a stop two steps above him. She looked at ease in slim-fit blue jeans and black boots, and a black top. She held a black blazer in her right hand.

"You managed with the shirt." He smiled.

"That painkiller you got into me helped."

So she guessed. He shrugged.

"I mean the second one. Not with the soup. With the coffee, just before the videoconference."

So she knew about both of them. He passed his hand through his hair, cleared his throat. "Yes, well, you should still be careful. The meds are masking the pain, but those bruised ribs of yours still need to heal. Quite a lot of you needs to heal, as a matter of fact."

"After we get him."

He sighed. "Are you always that stubborn?"

"Pretty much, yes."

He laughed. "You ready?"

She hesitated. "I don't have . . . my IDSD ID was in the car."

Everything had been there. Her phone, too, and her briefcase. Everything but the secure laptop she had left in her office, not wanting to risk Elijahn getting it.

"I've got everything covered. Don't worry about it." He reached out his hand.

She hesitated for only a short moment before she took it and descended the rest of the stairs.

Instead of going outside, they went directly into the garage where Donovan's USFID car now stood. When Lara faltered at the entrance, half expecting her car to be there and getting hit all over again by why it wasn't, he said, "I know. But I didn't want you in plain sight. And the windows are tinted, so no one can be sure you're in the car if you get in here."

"It's okay, it was just . . . a moment there." She walked to the car resolutely, determined not to let memories stop her.

When the garage door opened to the darkness outside, the two agents before it moved aside, looking around them. They remained where they were, but as Donovan drove down the street two cars slid into place before and after them.

Lara saw the car before them, then turned and looked behind them. "This is crazy. As if having a protective detail isn't enough, there are now more agents than before. How many are there?"

"Enough so you won't ditch them. Those you can see, that is. This time you won't be able to ditch either your protective agents or me."

At that, she looked at him. He was still angry. Out of fear for her, which she still couldn't wrap her mind around. Not because of Oracle. Her.

"They were there to protect you," he said, meaning the agents she'd avoided when she'd left IDSD the night before.

"No, I protect them. I don't do that so they'll

die for me."

He knew by now it was the switch of roles she was having trouble with. He sighed. "We've got a problem here, Lara. You're going to have to accept that from now on you will sometimes be assigned people to protect you. It will happen. Technology is good, but it's the people who make a difference. You of all people know that."

She looked at him miserably.

"I'm not saying there will be other attacks. But your status has changed. And the fact that who you are had already leaked out once, leading to your almost getting killed, means your security status will not be reduced again. Ever. So there are times, and places you will go to, where you will be assigned a protective detail."

She looked at him a little more miserably.

He sighed again. "We'll take it one day at a time."

"Firsts," she said after a while, looking pensively out of the side window.

"Sorry?"

"The first time I was in danger, the first time I was attacked, the first time I have a protective detail. A lot of firsts here. Things are changing."

He glanced at her. "Some things are changing for the better."

This time, nothing in her tried to argue. "Yes, I guess they are," she said, her voice soft.

When they reached the open road that would take them out of the city and to IDSD, the same road she was attacked on, Lara tensed. She tried to force herself to relax, couldn't.

"There's a stealth helicopter above us," Donovan said quietly, not needing to look at her to know how she felt. "We're being watched every step of the way. And you really do have more of an escort than you see."

She settled back in her seat and took a deep breath.

When they approached the IDSD gate, despite the evident heightened security level the car before them went through without being stopped, and Lara was surprised when Donovan's car did, too.

"Like I said, we've got everything covered," he said.

He followed the lead car of the protective detail straight through to the missions building, where the green light flashing in one of the special purpose parking spaces immediately in front of the main entrance signaled him where to park. As he did, the cars escorting them stopped, each letting one agent out and leaving with the rest.

As Lara and Donovan got out of the car and walked to the building she remarked, looking at the two somber agents following them at a discrete distance, "I said I won't leave here without you. And anyway, I'll be busy here for a while."

"I know. Let's assume for a moment that I trust you not to go running off if you think you're endangering anyone again. They're also here to make sure no one gets to you." He halted and turned to her, standing in her way, wanting her to look at him so that she would understand the implications of what he was saying. "Also, any order that has to do with your security now goes through me before it's implemented. So you won't be able to pull another stunt like those orders you sent to the protective details of Elijahn's other assumed targets."

"You're using me against me," she said, her eyes narrowing.

"Only until I know you well enough to use my-self against you." And with this, he led her into the building.

Lara was quiet as they walked into the elevator, quiet as they disembarked. They walked up to the reinforced glass wall that divided the upper floor of IDSD Missions, and as the doors opened before them she stepped forward and stood at the entrance to the war room while the two protective agents continued inside and positioned themselves, one not far from her and the other at the entrance to her office, near Aiden, who stood waiting. Beside her, Donovan waited in silence, gave her the time she needed.

Lara stood in this place she had spent the past five years working in. Here she had done things she knew no one else could, broke through barriers no one else had even come close to. Did, she knew, the impossible. She sometimes wondered how far she could go, and she often wondered about the difference she made, the difference she could make, in whatever future was hers.

But she had never imagined that this, what she was doing, might put her in danger. For the first time since she started this, Oracle herself was under attack. Here, in her own home, where she thought she was safe. Since the very beginning she had again and again stood up to those intent on wreaking havoc, and she had never stepped back, never relented, never let them take what they wanted, placing herself between them and those they would harm. But she had always done so with them far away. Now it was she herself they were after, and they had managed to find her, succeeded in reaching her. In hurting her. The events of the night before, the attack on her, the hunt for her, had been a shock.

But she had had time to digest, to think. To realize only she could end this.

And to understand she'd been wrong. The night before she had purposefully placed herself between Elijahn and those she knew he would hurt if she failed to stop him, and she had done so certain that she would face him alone. But instead she saw those Oracle had been so intent on protecting rush to protect her without hesitation. She had always watched over them, and it never occurred to her that if the time ever came, they would do the same for her. Be ready to die, for her.

And they weren't the only ones she mattered

to. Here, in the war room before her, people now stopped where they were and turned to look at her, seeing, she knew, the signs of the attack on her. A lot of what was here had been created because Oracle had changed things. Mission Command itself had been rebuilt for her. The teams who were stationed on this floor spent much of their time supporting, or being supported by, her. Everyone here knew someone who had somehow been affected by a hopeless situation Oracle had untangled. And no one here had ever expected Oracle to be gone. As she stood there, she met their eyes, all of them. And she saw relief.

In her mind she saw the soldiers who had rushed to protect her the night before. With her eyes she saw those who had worked with her in this war room through countless missions.

She had underestimated what Oracle, what *she*, meant to them.

Her eyes narrowed, her mind focused.

Oracle was ready to fight back.

Chapter Twenty-Three

Oracle stepped into the war room, Donovan a step behind her. She skirted the workspaces and headed to her office, on the way stopping to speak to the teams she'd asked be available, Donovan understood now, in that earlier videoconference Scholes had asked her what she needed on. He recognized the trackers, Gallo and Lehn, and the "eyes" team he'd already seen her work with. The others he didn't know. She slowed down near each team, and issued calm requests. At times she just said an informal word to those who needed her to, either the teams she'd asked for or those working on other operations on this busy floor. They each in turn acknowledged her words, then returned to their work, and by the time she reached her office the war room was humming with efficient activity. Nicely done, Donovan thought.

As Lara approached him, Aiden greeted her with his habitual "ma'am", but didn't proceed with an update as he'd done the last time. Donovan wasn't at all surprised that he would know exactly what to do. Lara walked into her inner office and slowed down before her desk. On it sat, side by side, a new IDSD ID, a new phone, and a briefcase identical to the one she had lost, open to show a number of varied items organized inside it. In the corner of her desk, her laptop sat idle. She stared.

"Activate the phone biorecognition and it will load with the content of your old phone, ma'am," Aiden said, standing at the doorway. "Tech already set it up and is standing by if you want any changes. It's not a commercial model this time, and it's the same security grade as the laptop."

She nodded, her eyes still on the items on her desk. "I... Thank you, Aiden."

"Of course, ma'am." He hesitated, then rushed on. "It's good to have you here, ma'am. I'll get you coffee." He turned and left, his normally stern step almost springy.

"He duplicated what I lost when my car blew up." Lara's voice was quiet, appreciative. "Everything just as it was."

Beside her, Donovan put a gentle hand on her lower back. She breathed in. "I'm fine. It's okay." She stepped behind her desk, slipped her IDSD ID on her belt with a practiced move, then touched the phone, which began synchronizing, and her laptop, which activated. She touched her desk, too, absently, and on it and around them the screens came on, silently flashing the IDSD Missions symbol.

She sat down behind her desk, somewhat gingerly, favoring her left side, and took a long look around her. A swipe of her hand over the desk, and all the screens turned black. A few touches, and a digital count up appeared in its center. It took Donovan a moment to realize what it was. The time elapsed from the attack. He was about to ask, but Lara was moving again. He saw the flash from the corner of his eye and turned. A section of the tinted glass behind him, near the door and in her direct line of sight, had morphed into a holoscreen, on which she had put up a three-dimensional globe. It rotated slowly, not highlighting any particular point in the world. Donovan looked from it to her curiously. She was now sitting back in her chair, contemplating the globe as if mesmerized by it. Except that Donovan could almost see the wheels turning.

Still watching the globe Lara reached under the desk, took out an earpiece connected to a nearly transparent mic, and put it on. "Okay." She turned to look at him. "Let's get this started."

"I kind of get the feeling you already have," Donovan said.

She nodded, settled back again.

"What's the count up for?"

"I need to start following him in my mind, lock on to him, so I need to pinpoint what he might be doing right now, put myself where he is. And that would depend to a large extent on how long it's been since he started running." She indicated the count. "Now this time, his time, is counting up in my mind too."

The woman who sees beyond, was how Scholes had described it. Donovan had to remind himself that nothing was impossible, not with her. "And the globe, you're looking for his headquarters, too, aren't you, at the same time? But we've got nothing, only his admission that he has one."

She said nothing. Her eyes went back to the globe. Thinking. Analyzing.

Aiden came in and handed Donovan a cup of coffee, then placed another on the desk before Lara. "Ma'am," he said, "I've sent to your system an updated breakdown of all operations and unrests."

Lara turned her attention to him. "Are the pending missions updated?"

"Yes, already in your system. Some updates since yesterday but no change in priorities. A new one has been added, but it looks like you've got a bit of time to do only this one."

Lara nodded, and as Aiden left Donovan saw the focus in her eyes shift as someone, he understood, spoke in her ear. When she was back with him, he indicated the headset. "I saw you use this in Mission Command."

"It's our design, specifically configured for me, to improve relay speed and efficiency at critical points. It has highly advanced comms capabilities and has Oracle's clearance already built in, so that I can use it with people and systems alike both in and out of Mission Command. Pretty much anyone, anything, anywhere. But right now I'm just hearing and communicating with the teams outside."

"What you told Frank you needed, it was them."

"Yes." She tilted her head slightly, assessed him. "I asked to use our own satellite monitoring station, rather than any one country's or military's. It would give me immediate access to all stations worldwide with their satellites when I want it, so as not to delay my own thought processes in the search. The best flexibility with the least likelihood of getting in someone's way or someone getting in mine."

She stopped, listened to someone on her headset again, then continued. "And the intelligence selection meant I want everyone, everywhere to see if anything relevant comes up after the attack in chatter or deep underground through cyber and undercover sources, with me getting direct real time updates. I basically want to see if his headquarters is calling out, see if they're looking for him, or if he or any of the people he still has attempt to contact anyone inside or outside the United States. And I want to see if there's any mention of the attack or my name or code name by anyone on their end, anyone outside the United States. I'm hoping there won't be any such mention for a while, or anything else for that matter. That nobody is contacting anybody, that no one knows anything. And that his headquarters is waiting for confirmation from him, which buys us some more time to find them without them doing anything in the meantime."

"Every agency is already working on this, and I

thought IDSD had access to all their intelligence."

"We do. I've simply placed this war room as top priority for any findings. Since right now we are the most likely to find Elijahn and his headquarters the fastest, and the wrong chatter will have an immediate effect on what we do and how we do it, our getting intelligence is a priority. Anyway, that's why I also asked for mixed intelligence. That means that in this war room there is also a joint intelligence team, comprising global agency representatives stationed in the United States. It's the basics really."

"For you."

"These are the kinds of resources everyone calls on in missions," she said, somewhat self-consciously, it seemed to him.

"Except it's not at all the same, is it?" he said. "And when you say 'We are the most likely to find them fastest' you mean Oracle alone, don't you?"

She frowned. "I'm just tracking him based on what I have, and a lot of that is the work of good people. And anything new they find could potentially change the direction and method of my tracking, so it needs to be known immediately. Otherwise, the entire process could be extended, which we don't want. The more time this goes on, the greater the uncertainties, the greater the chance he would disappear, and of course the higher the likelihood someone will start talking about things they're not supposed to."

He was seeing her at work up close, and he

found it intriguing. He wasn't like anyone else who might have been there now, watching Oracle. He was looking at Oracle through his own unique perspective, with the Lara he was getting to know also in his mind. He was no longer asking himself if this was purely the investigator in him observing her, he knew it was the man. But that didn't mean his professional instincts weren't alert, making him watch, study, so that he could understand better. Be there, better. This woman he wanted wasn't like any other he had ever been with.

Now that's an understatement, he thought. And then something occurred to him. When this would be over, he would still know more about Oracle than about the woman she was. If he wanted to change that, he had to do so, not wait. There would always be Oracle, always more missions. Just like for him there would always be investigations that would consume much of his own attention. There would never be a right time to start pushing for something beyond that. Something that would be theirs, that would be there no matter what, that would give them both a source of strength, as he had already seen for her, seen himself make a difference when he had been with her throughout this impossible situation she had found herself in.

He sat down on one of the two chairs on the side of the desk opposite hers, and settled back, his eyes on her.

Here, now, it was so much easier to focus, to push away the night before, easy to slip into Oracle, whom she was so comfortable being. Her mind was waking, working, accelerating. It was the way it was supposed to be.

She had turned her gaze away from Donovan to her desk console, and was setting things up to run the data Aiden had sent to her system alongside updates from the field teams searching for the escaped attackers. At the same time, deep in her mind, she was multiprocessing Elijahn.

She raised her head again to look at Donovan. "I need to know which of the DNA samples your techs found at the warehouse Elijahn used didn't belong to any of the bodies of his men, and the identities they matched them to, if at all."

"Are you asking for my help, Lara Holsworth, Oracle?"

She stared at him in surprise. Then her gaze turned contemplative. He had just the slightest smile on his face, and something she couldn't quite read in his eyes. He was watching her, waiting for her reaction.

Reading her every move. It irritated her. Her eyes narrowed. "A part of me really wants to give you an order right now, Agent Pierce."

"What part?" he asked conversationally, unfazed.

"A huge, huge part." How on earth did he manage to evoke these reactions from her? Even now, here, where Oracle had always protected her.

"That just might make cooperation between us more complex, you know."

"And here I thought you wanted to keep me alive."

"Oh, I want to keep you all right. Which is why I will negotiate this."

The slight change in wording wasn't lost on her, but there was no way she was going to give him the satisfaction of knowing that. "Negotiate?"

"Yes. You get my techs' help in return for a date."

She sat back and looked at him incredulously. "We're in the middle of a hunt for a dangerous militant who attacked the allies, including your country, and then IDSD—and me—on US soil. And you're negotiating for a date."

"That's right."

She contemplated him some more. Tried to fight it, but curiosity got the better of her. "And what would that date consist of?"

"My choice."

She laughed. "You expect me to agree to a date without knowing what you're planning?"

"Yes."

"That's . . ."

"You afraid?"

Her eyes narrowed. Donovan knew she would go for the challenge. Because of who she was. And because it was him. He was counting on it.

"Done."

"Good. I already had Agent Ben Lawson, my lead investigator on this—but you probably already know that—and my techs prepare for you everything they found every step of the way, DNA results included. They're still running a search to see if they can get an identification on any of the DNA samples, both those that belong to the men who were killed and those of the men still at large. Contact Ben whenever you want, he'll give you everything."

She sat up. "You already had your people prepare for me..."

"Of course. What, you think I'd do anything to endanger you? Or hinder the search for Elijahn?"

She settled back again. "Damn. I really should have known that."

"Lucky for me, it seems you have a blind spot when it comes to me. It comes from trying to resist what's happening between us." He pointed at her. "See? That look right there in your eyes, that's exactly what I mean."

He was reading her like an open book. This was infuriating. And disconcerting. She absolutely did not know what to do about him.

"It's okay, focus on what you need to do now. You can deal with me later."

How on earth did he know what she was thinking? "That's it. Go away!"

He was still grinning when he walked out of her office.

He motioned the agent standing by the outer

door to keep watch over her and stopped beside Aiden's workstation. "So what's operations and unrests?"

"Ms. Holsworth is involved in several standby missions she could be called to with little warning," Aidan explained with unhidden pride. "And with the ongoing search for the man who attacked her and her role in this search, this time IDSD too could be the one breaking in with an unplanned mission. So she needs to have information about all operations currently in progress under allied control. To ensure that she won't be disturbing an existing operation— whether she's working on one of the standbys or her own—since she is authorized to override orders, retask satellites, ships, airplanes. Any security and defense measure, in fact. She wouldn't want to interrupt a mission, or to impede the one she's working on because something she needs retasked is unable to respond immediately. Too often there are time-critical points—if a pilot or a drone can't fire a missile at the precise moment and location she indicates, someone on the ground could die, or if she can't retask the right satellite at the right moment, she won't have eyes when she needs them."

The aide was obviously well versed in anything Oracle. Donovan was impressed. "And unrests?"

"Hot spots that could affect a mission. Both update types are standard. Ms. Holsworth is constantly provided information on a variety of matters, and among these, operations and unrests are updated regularly as well as immediately before a mission and during it, if anything new comes up. The thing about what we do here at IDSD Missions is, you never know when an incident might break in. And the thing about Oracle is, you never know when it will be needed. And when something comes up that requires immediate intervention, Ms. Holsworth needs to be free to focus on priority mission-pertinent information. Hence the regular updates."

Donovan turned to go, then turned back. "Does she ever let her guard down?"

Aiden considered him. "Do you, Agent Pierce?" he finally replied.

Donovan smiled. "Good answer."

Chapter Twenty-Four

Lara watched Donovan walk out of her office. She saw him motion to the agent and her lips curved up, saw him stop to speak to Aiden and looked on curiously. He was at her home, and he was here. He was making himself part of everything that was her, coming to stand beside her in everything she was and did. Taking her as she was.

Taking her. She thought about that. Here, in her office, where Oracle carried far more weight than Lara, the woman she was, it should have been easier to look at what was happening between them in a more dispassionate way. Analyze, conclude, decide, the way she always did, the way she wanted it. Her decision only. Not his. But it wasn't working this time. There were no logical processes involved, those she normally used so efficiently to push men away, no detached analysis, no final, unwavering conclusions. Only more reactions, despite herself. And this man, he wasn't about to let anyone decide anything for him. He read her as easily as she read him, and he had a mind of his own about what was happening between them.

Watching him now, she knew he couldn't see her through what he would see as the tinted glass divide of her inner office, so she let her gaze linger. It flickered over his handsome face, the intense eyes, dark gray in this light, in this situation where he was assessing everyone and everything. He was dressed in black again, and his entire demeanor gave him that dangerous air she'd seen in him before. It occurred to her that he hadn't been anything but dangerous since the attack, except in those rare moments with her, the looks, the touches. She felt that flutter again. But then that was the problem, wasn't it? She supposed she could have expected her body to react. But not her heart.

She followed him with her eyes until he disappeared from her sight, then swiveled her chair toward the wall-wide window behind her, her eyes thoughtful again. Throughout her contemplation of him the part of her mind that was Oracle never stopped analyzing, and she now brought it to the forefront again. Soon a day would have passed since Elijahn and his men had gone on the run, and the search for them wasn't any closer to being over. It was, quite simply, like looking for four needles in an ever-expanding haystack. Elijahn had apparently reacted quickly, running while his people were still engaged in battle with the forces that had come to her help. That stroke of luck that had him intercept a motorcyclist sealed the search's fate, giving him too much of a head start and allowing him to all but vanish. His three missing men who had been on their way from Edwards's home had been far enough from the site of the attack on her when they had gotten the warning from their peers who had been on the way from Miles's home, and who had died together with the rest of Elijahn's men. They had easily gotten away, and they too were now always a step ahead of the searchers.

A search was being carried out for possible ways for Elijahn to get out of the country once he got what he wanted. Donovan had updated Evans with what she had finally told him, and with what they now knew had been Elijahn's intention, an abduction that would force him to disappear with an unwilling victim, US Global Intelligence was looking for a private jet or a boat, a yacht perhaps. Something Elijahn could use to disappear with his remaining militants. And with her.

She pushed that unwelcome thought away. Then reconsidered and turned mentally to face it. Use it. That, precisely that, was the very heart of what she needed.

In her mind, Oracle had everything she knew about Elijahn. Everything she had read, seen, done, and felt from the moment the first data batch on him and his group was given to her two years earlier. She now closed her eyes and gradually blocked out everything around her. Her breathing slowed, steadied, and her cerebral dynamics shifted as that part of her mind that she needed synchronized with the still raw reality of the attack on her, focused, and erupted in a powerful pulse.

Inward.

If normally when imminent danger loomed she would lock on the people on the screen before her who needed her help, use them to see the surrounding dangers, assess the situation, reach the conclusions she needed in order to act, this time she focused on herself, on the connection she'd created to Elijahn during the attack, and used it to find her own hunter. She saw herself that night, her fear, her decision, her escape, felt it as it had been, every all too real second of it. In his attack on Oracle, Elijahn had made it a target like any other she had protected in the past.

But when he had threated not to kill her but to take her instead, he had also made Oracle itself, the possibility that it would be used in the wrong hands, an unprecedented danger to everyone and everything she valued. And what he had then implied he had in mind for her, that made it personal, unthinkable on a whole new level. Which gave her exactly what she needed to work this unusual situation. It allowed her to use the emotional to focus and strengthen the logical. She had never done this before with herself as the focal point, but then what was it she had told Donovan? There were many firsts here.

She focused.

And took the leap.

The feeling that erupted within her, drowning everything else, was something she would never be able to explain to anyone, not even to those who saw Oracle at work. So she never tried to. They had to feel it to understand, and no one could. Her very being changed in that moment, as those functions that defined human capabilities were exceeded in a fraction of a second, giving her the freedom to go further, faster.

Time ticked by, unheeded.

Finally, Oracle opened her eyes, swiveled back in her chair, looked at the globe rotating slowly on the screen.

And smiled.

Donovan came to stand just inside Scholes's office in a way that allowed him to look out toward Lara's. He leaned back on the wall, his arms folded across his chest. Alert.

"I saw the two of you come in. Thought I'd let Lara settle in." Scholes had come to the IDSD medical center himself the night before, after Lara had been brought in, and had been updated. Donovan had arrived shortly after him, and Scholes had seen the way he had walked in and simply gone through everyone there to get to her. He had blood on his shirt then. Lara's.

"She did. She needs to be here, do this. Fight him her way."

Scholes marveled at his acceptance. Over the years it had occurred to him that it would take a special man to get through to Lara. And to accept Oracle. By now he'd learned enough about Donovan to know that man was standing before him. He smiled, allowing himself a moment of respite in this as yet too complex a situation. "I bet you had no idea what you were getting into when you were handed this investigation."

"I'll say."

"So how's she doing?"

"We'll see after this is over. Right now she's pushing it away to help get Elijahn, and that's certain to have implications for her later. But she's a strong woman."

"Yes, she is," Scholes said softly. Donovan didn't know the half of it. "I'm still worried about her, though. She's been through too much these past days. It's going to catch up with her eventually, in a bad way."

Donovan's eyes flickered back out, to where he knew Lara was sitting. The agents were now both standing with their backs to the outer door, their eyes looking everywhere. Good.

"I'll take care of it," he said. The finality of the statement resonated between them. "However, we do have another problem."

"Oh?"

"She objects to any notion of manned security. Next time we want to put a protective detail on her again she'll fight it. And I have no intention of letting her pull another runaway move like she did this time."

Scholes nodded slyly. "Next time."

"Next time you've got a security breach, next time you send her off to wherever."

"That's not quite what I meant." Scholes nodded. "I've already approved Carl's request to run her security through you for this incident, and until the long-term arrangements are finalized, at which time you'll have a say in her security along with him. This needs to be cleared with IDSD HQ in Brussels, of course, considering who Lara is. Shouldn't be any problem, with your involvement in this incident and your job and training." Donovan, he knew, was well versed in the security of high-profile ranks, and had the background, the training, to back that up with actual protection. "You'll also have to go through our security clearance vetting process. If you're with Lara, you'll need clearance for what she does and, well, says." He contemplated Donovan. "We'll start with that, see where we go from there. I'm thinking eventually you'll have a say in her IDSD security and authority over her security outside IDSD. It'll be continuing our little security arrangement." He sighed. "She's going to love that."

"I'll deal with it."

Yes, I believe you would. I believe you, finally, can, Scholes thought. "One thing I remind you," he said aloud, "is that Lara isn't supposed to be living where she is. She is supposed to live in a secure complex, but she refuses. IDSD security has had to approve where she lives now."

"Good. Then it's either my security decisions or a secure complex. I'll remember that, it'll help. In the meantime, once this thing with Elijahn is over we'll return—for now—to strictly technological security. Besides me, that is."

Scholes concurred. "No one can interfere with her new phone. And the newly-installed security system in her house is, frankly, identical to mine."

"Car? She'll want to replace hers."

"Yes, that's going to be tricky."

Donovan looked at him questioningly.

"She can't have the convertible again. It's not secure enough. I've let it pass until now because she didn't really give me a choice and she loved that car, but now she's going to get an IDSD one. Once this is over she'll be asked to choose out of the models approved for high clearance ranks."

Donovan knew what that meant. The car she would choose, or that would be chosen for her if she refused to do so herself, would be retrofitted to IDSD's security specs. He approved.

"In the meantime, she'll be given a car and a driver—" Scholes stopped and sighed. "No, that's never going to work. It'll limit her. We keep secure cars for high-ranking visitors, I'll assign one to her until she gets her own. She's still going to hate that, though." He shook his head. "She is going to hate all of it. Things will be different. It's not what she wanted, not what we had agreed on."

"Not what you agreed on?"

"Long, long story. Short version, when I recruited her she asked for very few things. Two of them were to be left alone and have her freedom to do as she pleased, and not to be ordered around. Otherwise, she can quit when she wants. Except she can't, anymore, can she? She can't quit and she knows it. I'm worried she would feel trapped. It's not good for her, it will be impossible for her to deal with."

Donovan had already had more than a glimpse of that. "We'll take it one change at a time. She won't feel the status change all at once, certainly not until something warrants heightened protection again, and some things will stay the same."

"For now. The difference between five years ago when she started and now is staggering. What's it going to be like in another five years? It's not going to be easy for her."

"I'll make sure she has what she needs."

"Donovan . . ." Scholes hesitated. He wasn't sure how much he could tell him. It wasn't his to say.

"I know, Frank." Donovan's tone was calm, quiet. "I've seen the walls. I know she's hiding something. Something that hurts her, that she's struggling with. I don't want you to tell me, it's something she will do when she feels she can. But don't expect me to just sit and do nothing while she goes through it alone."

"You love her." Scholes simply stated the truth he saw in the man before him.

"Yes." Donovan looked outside again. It was easier to say than he ever thought it would be.

"Do something for me then. Please. Don't let go of her."

The heartfelt words took Donovan by surprise, made him wonder again what Scholes knew that he himself had yet to find out.

And no, he had no intention of letting go of Lara.

With Donovan there, Scholes took the opportunity to call Ericsson and get Donovan's side in the process that would add him to Lara's security protocol started. By the time they were done and had received an update about the search for Elijahn and his men, the inner door to Lara's office was open again. When Donovan walked in she was standing, leaning back on her desk, looking at the results of the DNA samples collected at the warehouse being displayed on one of the screens beside the people they belonged to. Unfortunately, these were all photos of their faces post mortem. Donovan cursed under his breath. He didn't want her to see them, her dead pursuers.

Ben was on the adjacent screen. "We're running the DNA and the photos in the global databases and in ours, but it's taking time. Nathan has gone back to IDSD, since the focus of the investigation has shifted, but I'm thinking I'll contact him again, see if he can get us better access to what we need." He acknowledged Donovan, and Lara turned to see him standing at the doorway.

She nodded once, then turned back to Ben. "My aide will transfer this call to him, he'll put you in touch with a team here that can check them against what we have from Elijahn's past connections." She touched her desk and updated Aiden, who took the call.

Donovan came over and stood beside her, leaning back, as she was, on the desk. "I'm sorry you had to see them."

"They're dead. It's the live ones I need to think about now."

That tore into him. One of those DNA samples was of the man who would stop at nothing to get to her. He took an angry breath in. "I should have gone after the bastard myself." He wanted nothing more than to kill Elijahn. To Know that he was dead. To see for himself that he was dead, that he would never come after her again.

Lara heard his anger, his need to protect her. Thought about what he had done. Everything that he had done. He was, she realized, as affected by all this as she was. "You were," she said slowly, her voice soft, "where you were supposed to be. Where you were needed most."

Surprised, he turned his gaze to her. She met his

eyes. "I never could have gone through the hours . . . after, without you. I felt safe with you there. You made me feel safe. And you were so—" She tried to find the words. Couldn't. Which, for her, new. "I'll be fine, and I'm able to do this now, because of you."

His arm came up around her waist. He held her lightly to him and kissed her on her temple again. She didn't resist him, and she wasn't hazy this time. "There's that kiss again," she said quietly, flustered in a whole different way this time.

"When this is over," he murmured in her ear, "when you can focus on me and on what I'm doing, I'm going to kiss you properly. That's a promise."

His phone beeped. He took it off his belt and glanced at it. "It's Scholes. They're ready for you in Mission Command," he told Lara. She nodded and pointed to her earpiece. She already knew.

Chapter Twenty-Five

A swipe of Lara's hand, and her entire office showed IDSD Missions' symbol again, securing all information. She followed Donovan out and frowned as the two agents stationed at her office door moved to follow her.

"I'll take it from here," Donovan said, stopping them. "But if she comes out of that door"—he indicated Mission Command—"without me, stop her."

Lara's eyes narrowed. "You're impossible."

"Get used to it," he said mildly.

"I'll deal with you later."

"I'm counting on it."

Saved by Oracle, she thought as the heavy door to Mission Command opened and she walked inside, where Oracle was all that counted. Once again, all was as should be. She took it all in, felt herself focus. This was her turf.

She approached the spanning wall screen, joining Scholes, who was standing on the operations platform before it, and acknowledged the people displayed on the screen. Martinez was there, as were Evans and his agency's supervisory agent in charge of the search operations alongside Martinez, who introduced herself as Angela Bates, and Major General Oliver Grant, the joint operations commander of IDSD's Air Force Global Strike and Defense Command that would be coordinating the attack on Elijahn's headquarters, once it was found. Besides Lara, Scholes and Donovan, only the system operator coordinating the videoconference was physically present in Mission Command, sitting at her station on the far left of the screen.

Bates began. "We found Elijahn's transport. A private jet at a private-use airport southwest of DC. We're still checking its registration. We also still need to check how they intended to leave US airspace, that airport is not a point of entry and they haven't filed a flight plan, at least not yet. The pilots cracked easily, by the way. They had no interest in this, it was all money for them. The plane was heading for—get this—"

"Lake Chad," Lara said.

"How did you know?" Bates had never worked with Lara and was not privy to Oracle's existence.

"Symbolic." The plane itself was no surprise to Lara, it was a quick getaway. And once Elijahn had made the decision to abduct her, it would also have been the most convenient one—all he needed to do was land at the former site of his base, where he could have someone waiting to pick him up. Ironically, had he succeeded he would have brought to his base the very person behind its destruction.

"Why wouldn't he do what he did when he came here, head for an intermediate destination first, maybe switch transport? Didn't he think we might get to the plane or the pilots, or be able to track its route even after it left?" Evans wasn't entirely convinced.

"The plane and the pilots were expendable. It was a one-way ticket for them, which is why Elijahn wouldn't care what they saw. As for the route, this is Elijahn," Lara said. She turned back to Bates. "Better make sure that plane isn't moved before it's manually checked. And not just electronically, he has people who know how to get around our technologies. You should find a signal jammer and a self-destruct device on it. Elijahn was going to prevent tracking and destroy the plane—get rid of the pilots too—once it reached its destination."

Bates stared at her. "I don't know who you are, but I get the feeling I should be glad you're on our side." She signed off.

"There wasn't going to be a flight plan, was there?" Evans said.

"No. No one was ever supposed to know he's in the air. All he would need to worry about are other aircraft, and your agents will find an air traffic surveillance display on board. He would've disappeared. Not even satellites could have tracked him, not with the jammer he would have. And anyway, no one was supposed to be looking for him as we are, so disappearing would have been easier than it is now that we know who he is, and that he is being chased rather than leaving at his leisure." She thought about it a bit. "Something should be done about that aircraft signal jamming, by the way."

They all agreed. Those jammers could pose a risk if they fell into the wrong hands, if they hadn't already. Clearly technology would have to be developed that would render them useless.

"You wouldn't by any chance know where his headquarters is?" General Grant asked. He'd worked with Oracle many times before.

"Yes," she said, but first she turned her attention to Martinez. "Colonel, the three you're looking for."

"We're canvassing the area inch by inch. The way they disappeared, we're worried they may be holed up somewhere. They might even be holding hostages, in a private residence, maybe, where they can hide. If they haven't yet, they might hurt someone on the way."

"No. Elijahn thinks too much of himself, of his goals. He sees himself as being above the other militant groups and the old ways of terrorism. He would never risk being associated with their type of actions. And you won't find them. Either they're with Elijahn or two are dead, in which case you'll find their bodies, and the remaining militant would be with Elijahn."

"Two are dead...?" Donovan, who was standing beside the operations platform, was as confused as the rest of them.

She turned to him, speaking confidently, not a

hint of hesitation in her voice. "He already had his headquarters back when we attacked his base. That's where he must have been during the base destruction, it's where he would have brought the drone, where he was hidden all this time so that there wasn't even a trace of him. And to keep the headquarters after his failure to carry out his plans, and to be able to plan his hunt for Oracle, do only this for so long, undisturbed and undetected, he had to still have had loyal followers. He would have killed those who doubted him, kept close to him those who would remain loyal, who would obey blindly. But keeping many militants quiet all this time isn't easy, so he couldn't have kept that many. Didn't need many, either, at that point he would need mainly brains.

"And coming here, he would have had to leave some of his militants behind, to watch over what's really important to him, his only remaining stronghold, the headquarters. So the people he had here, either all of them were his or he handpicked additional hired guns with no previous loyalties that could stand in his way. But that type of hired guns goes with the promise of money and a strong hand to control them, not ideology, certainly not loyalty. And once the attack last night failed..."

"Elijahn would need to get rid of the hired guns before they ran with his secrets or turned on him, and either way they would tell others that he failed." Donovan said.

Lara nodded. "Let's assume some of his people here were, in fact, hired guns. Stands to reason that he would send to those he meant to kill in their homes, the easier jobs, if you will, Edwards and Miles, his more expendable people. If all the people he had here were his, then all those he sent to Edwards and Miles were his, and the three who had escaped would be at his side by now. But if he did bring with him a limited number of loyals and used hired guns, two of the three sent to Edwards and Miles each would have been a hired gun. The third would still have to have been a loyal, to ensure the job is done." This was no assumption. She knew beyond doubt there were hired guns. She also knew it was two out of three in each group sent to the targets' homes. But she had long ago learned that sometimes conventional logic was easier for those she spoke to, even if they knew her, even if they could, to an extent, accept that her mind was capable of going different places than theirs.

Martinez was quiet for a moment. "And if there are bodies, where would they be?"

Lara tilted her head slightly. "In the immediate area where you found their SUV."

"We've searched."

"They're there. Look again. Elijahn would need his loyal back, so if the others were hired guns, the loyal would have killed them as soon as he realized what happened and joined Elijahn, which only a loyal would know how to do."

"Got it. I'll let you know what we find." Martinez signed off.

Donovan looked at Lara. "When the hell did you do that?"

"Do what?"

"Find all the answers."

"I don't have all the answers. Yet."

Someone cleared his throat. "Excuse me. Oracle?"

She turned to the general.

"You said something about headquarters?"

"It's in the Sahara."

Grant shook his head. "We've got eyes on Africa all the time, you of all people know that. We're seeing nothing in the Sahara."

"Under," she said.

His jaw dropped.

"Go back two years, to the Chad base. Look at the communication frequencies the pre-raid analysis showed. The unique signals Elijahn used in an attempt to avoid detection. The ones in the Sahara today are similar or somewhere around them. Think about it." A contemplative frown crossed her brow. "But you would need to take into account frequency cancellations, he's smarter now and wouldn't risk being discovered. And he would also need to mask the signature of the holographic spot that is the access way to and from this underground place of his, something that can be accessed by either ground or aerial transport. Between these two, any signal would be less specific and far more dispersed."

Evans reached for his phone, but Lara said, "I've got our comms and joint intelligence teams on it already. They'll try to find its whereabouts."

"One step ahead of us again, aren't you?" Scholes said, shaking his head.

"I'll get the airstrike teams ready," Grant said. "But we need Oracle to give us the exact coordinates. And fast. We have to assume that this is a time-sensitive mission. They already have too much information in that headquarters. And we can't know if Elijahn has a way of passing them what he knows about you, or if he already did that, and if he gets to them and tells them to release it, or if they don't hear from him and decide to expose the existence of Oracle themselves, the consequences will be the same. We need to erase that place."

She nodded. "Who's doing this?"

"We all are. It's an alliance joint operation," Scholes said beside her.

On the screen, the general nodded in agreement. "We'll all end this, protect Oracle together. It was our oversight that allowed Elijahn to survive these two years and get to you. Frank, I'll let you know as soon as we have everything in place. I assume you would both like to see this through in person, of course."

"And we still need to find Elijahn," Evans said, but Lara wasn't listening to him or to Grant anymore. She was getting the information she requested from the comms team outside, in her earpiece.

Forgetting those around her, she issued a series of commands to the mainframe, and the rotating globe from her office appeared at the rightmost section of the screen. But even as she walked toward it, she spoke again, and the view changed, zoomed in on Africa, bringing the entire continent into view, then zoomed farther in on Lake Chad and north of it, encompassing Sahel and the Sahara Desert. On the screen, frequencies began to flash—the fluctuating communication frequencies she had the teams outside identify. But they were too scattered, with too much interference, which she'd expected from Elijahn, and were rerouted too many times to global locations in an attempt to mask them, so that it was impossible to focus them, even with the probabilities the experienced minds just outside Mission Command had run. The area they tagged was too big, encompassing too much of the great desert, and since this was an underground base, an attack would have to be focused, powerful, to succeed. Worse, this was unfriendly territory, and so an attack would have to begin and end before local foes of the allies would be alerted.

More quiet commands to the mainframe, and data appeared beside the image, running in multiple parallel columns. It came faster, denser, switching as she asked for more input. The only thing those in Mission Command with her could understand was that these were dates and coordinates, interspersed with other figures they couldn't identify. But for her this data was so much more—it was the Chad base data from two years earlier, current pertinent data, and satellite and drone remote sensing data regularly stored in IDSD Missions' mainframe.

As Donovan and Scholes watched the data accelerated, moving fast, faster, a staggering amount of information running, reorganizing, changing at her command. And then, abruptly, it all went blank, all of it, the data and the map, as Oracle shut it all down. She just stood there, her eyes on the blank screen, her arms folded across her chest, her head tilted slightly, as if it was all still there. As if something was still there.

And then she closed her eyes. In her mind, all that existed were images and numbers. Aerial, space. Layered, topographies. Depths, textures, geological data. That and more, information she had pulled from her available sources. Before, in her office, and now, to complement it. Memories of the Chad mission. Elijahn. His aspirations. His words to her. What she knew, what she still didn't. She focused on the gaps, on what she didn't know. Pushed the probabilities aside. Came up with her own. Took a mental step in a specific direction. Then another. Leaped. Opened her eyes. Gave a command.

On the screen, the Sahara shone once again, empty, forlorn. A mark appeared on it. Beside it, a set of numbers. Coordinates. Depths. Tolerances. All changing fast, the small mark not resting for a moment as the tracking system marked every point in the great desert. Not a search. Just for her. She wanted to see them, the numbers, the points that, somewhere in the world, were real. Wanted to see the possibilities of where it could be. Of where what she wanted destroyed could be.

She continued, her eyes not leaving the mark. Took one more step, another leap. It was there, it existed, had tangible spatial coordinates in this same reality where both she and it existed. It was there two years ago, when she had annihilated his base while he had looked on, hidden in it. It was there at the time of his attack on her, when it and her had been the center of his plan. It was where she was supposed to be taken by him, where she would have been right now, lost forever. It was right there, one of the locations being marked on the screen. All she had to do was go to it, be there, then. Exist where and when it existed. She could do it. Had to do it. Boundaries were there to be moved.

The mark disappeared. Then reappeared immediately at a location hundreds of miles away, a set of numbers beside it. Longitude, latitude, depth.

Elijahn's headquarters was marked.

On the screen to her left, Grant and Evans were watching this in their respective offices. As Oracle turned her eyes to them, they both nodded.

"Got it, Oracle," the general said with unhidden astonishment, even though he had seen her do so much, so many times before. Both he and Evans signed off.

In Mission Command, now alone with those she allowed to care, Lara let go, took two stumbling steps forward and leaned her hand on the screen that rippled under her touch like an angry black sea. But she didn't feel it, didn't see it. Her mind was screaming in protest with the strain, her bruised ribs sent waves of pain through her, her entire body felt like she was back immediately after the explosion, as if the restful hours since then had never happened. She had known it would be too soon to come back, but there really had been no choice. There never was.

Donovan was already beside her. He turned her to him and enveloped her in his arms. She was trembling with the strain and held on to him, fighting to stay standing.

Scholes sat down on a seat behind them, stunned. "You've never done anything like this before," he said, but knew better than to ask how.

"You need to rest," Donovan said softly.

Lara shook her head and straightened up slowly. "I need to finish this."

He started to object, and her hand, on his waist, tightened a little, her eyes never leaving his. He nodded.

She breathed in steadily, found what she needed within her. Stronger now, she turned her head and looked at Scholes. She didn't notice that she didn't move away from the man beside her, that he was still holding her. As she began to speak, her attention pulled away once again from the physical sensations, from the pain, the exhaustion, and back to where she needed it to be. Donovan felt the change in her, knew to move slightly away, knew to let her do what she needed to.

Scholes watched, fascinated.

Oblivious, Lara said, "He's not running."

Both men focused.

"He's coming here."

Donovan took a step toward her again. But she wasn't looking at him. Her eyes were distant now as the final pieces that had been organizing themselves in her mind fell into place one by one and the dynamics of it shifted again. "He is coming to IDSD."

Scholes called out to the operator, "Get Ericsson in here." Then he turned back to Lara.

"He has to," she said. "He won't try to get to the plane he chartered—he's seen the forces we sent after him, he won't underestimate our determination and our ability to find it. And he knows we know who he is." They knew she had made the choice to tell Elijahn this when she baited him to keep him from going after his other targets again. "And running, hiding, won't be easy. He's not a ghost anymore. Everyone knows he's alive.

"There are other ways he could leave, return to his headquarters. But then what?" she continued. "He's lost all the men he brought with him here, has three left at the most, most likely one. He's been discovered, and he's failed to destroy Oracle. A second failure, and after all his preparations. How do you think his people will react? Even the most loyal ones.

"Worse, it's likely he doesn't know if he succeeded or not. He meant to keep me, but if he couldn't, he would never allow me to live. And if he sent his people after me after my car exploded but didn't follow me himself—and it stands to reason that that's what he would do, he's the boss, the brains, they're only the muscle—then he doesn't know about you, Donovan. He doesn't know you came for me, and the military intervened before he could at least make sure I was dead. He ran. He doesn't know if I died or not, if his people killed me before they themselves were killed or if I died in the battle. He needs to know, to make sure. And he needs proof. Even if he succeeded, he has failed unless he can provide proof. We haven't given him chatter, I made sure everyone remains silent on the attack, and that the name Oracle is not mentioned, nor mine, remember? He doesn't know what happened to me, and his people at his headquarters won't know either, even if they are trying to listen to our intelligence."

Donovan frowned. "You're right. He wouldn't know if you're still alive or not." He hadn't considered the possibility. They all assumed Elijahn would know she was alive.

"He could lay low. Wait in the United States,

even here in DC." Scholes said.

"For how long? If he doesn't contact his people soon, he will be assumed dead and will lose them. If he doesn't go back, they will eventually leave him or someone else will take over, and he will lose his headquarters and that's too important to him. No, he needs to show them he's alive. And he can't do that without proving to them that he destroyed Oracle, or they might turn against him anyway. Right now, he stands too much of a chance of losing everything." Her eyes were on the blank screen, contemplating. She shook her head. "He's done so much to find Oracle, to come here, to get to it. So much effort, so much time. This guy doesn't stop until he gets what he wants. He's tenacious."

"And he hates you," Donovan remarked.

"Yes, there's that." She thought back to her conversation with Elijahn. The way he sounded. The way he looked. "There is that."

Donovan's phone chirped, and he glanced at it and answered. "That was Ben," he said when he'd ended the call. "Of the four DNA samples with no bodies to match, there is no identification for two, but the other two belong to hired guns. Brothers, former bodyguards for the Niger president, back when Niger was still independent. They came here with him when he was granted asylum, but apparently went off the grid two months ago." He looked at Lara with a frown. She shrugged. There were, of course, no matches for the other two samples because they belonged to Elijahn and one of the loyals he had brought with him.

The system operator sitting on the other end of Mission Command called Scholes over, and Lara and Donovan waited, Lara watching Scholes, and Donovan watching Lara.

"And that was Martinez," Scholes said when he returned. "They found two bodies crammed in an old well, buried under some rocks. Not far from the burned SUV."

"Damn," Donovan said. That was two out of two.

Oracle shrugged again.

"I told Martinez to get his people back to watch the IDSD complex," Scholes said.

"Don't." Lara frowned. "At least, not so that they are seen."

And before Donovan could react she turned to him. "And no, I'm not doing anything to endanger myself."

His eyes narrowed.

"Irritating, isn't it? When somebody reads you like that?" she asked him with raised eyebrows. She turned back to Scholes and missed the fleeting grin on Donovan's face. "One thing Elijahn has learned from the allies' intelligence is that they don't see the obvious. They thought he was dead, and he ended up landing in the United States in an airliner, in plain sight, walking right into one of the most pro-tected, high-profile cities in the free world that is home to IDSD and US military forces, then spent two months here, preparing his people, in a nice little warehouse near a mall, of all places. Now he'll figure they think he is running scared, being hunted, so they won't expect him to double back to IDSD.

"Except we know otherwise—he is incapable of being the prey. He needs to be the hunter. And he cannot afford to lose. Even if he has to die, if there's no other way for him but to die, he will die destroying Oracle and leave his people to let everyone know that. His prestige has to be restored even if it outlives him. It wasn't that way before, what he wanted then was to live to build on his success, and he still does. But now he simply has no choice but to risk it all."

"And in his fanatic mind there's only one way he can win. Christ." Donovan chuckled mirthlessly. "We need to eliminate this guy."

"No question about that," Scholes said in a low voice.

Oracle wasn't listening again. When she spoke her voice was quiet, thoughtful. "He needs to come here, and he thinks he can. He's safe again, everyone is looking elsewhere. He'll want to see it, see Oracle with his own eyes. Try to destroy it. He asked me if I was the creator or the operator. I told him I was both. So he still thinks I'm the person behind a machine, the artificial intelligence that is Oracle. If I'm still alive and with the machine, he'll use the opportunity to kill me. But he won't look for me now. Not deliberately. Because he doesn't know if I'm dead, alive, injured. He'll look for Oracle. And only then he'll look for Lara Holsworth. And in the meantime, he'll kill anyone he encounters around the machine on his way to damage it."

"God." Ericsson had entered Mission Command in time to hear what she'd said. "Would he do that?"

"He's smart enough and he has nothing to lose. We know that two years ago he had a plan to break into the alliance's headquarters in Brussels. He still has that plan in his mind, he just needs to adapt it. Think about it. He goes to where he thinks our artificial intelligence center is, quietly. Has one man to help him. There is no one else. So that's two men alone. Fast and clean. All he has to do is get in, go through the people, find Oracle. Done." She could see it. Saw it, in her mind. Shook her head. "Here he won't mind hurting anyone he sees, these are IDSD's people, his enemies. Internationals and their allies. So we need to be careful."

"What exactly are you thinking?" Scholes asked. He didn't like where this was going.

"I want to let him in. Bring him to us."

"I'm sorry, what?" Ericsson looked stricken.

Lara was looking at Scholes. "Right now IDSD is secured like it's a fort. It's been a day. Elijahn's people are dead. If you thought he was running, all alone, that he won't dare come here, that Oracle is safe here, and its creator-operator is either safe here or dead, you would reduce security back to normal. Or near normal. So it's time to reduce security."

"How will he know where to go?"

"The Advanced Technologies Research building."

"He doesn't know where that is." Ericsson still looked stricken.

"You want to bet?"

"Right." Scholes sighed. Elijahn had made it his mission in life to get Oracle. He would know where what he believed was artificial intelligence would be.

"Hey, wait a minute." Ericsson looked from Lara to Scholes and back. "The Advanced Technologies Research building he would know about..."

Lara smiled, nodded.

"Say we do this. Do you know how he'll come into IDSD?" Ericsson asked, looking a lot less stricken now.

Lara tilted her head slightly. That one was obvious. They realized it too, once she told them.

Scholes turned to Ericsson. "How quickly can we do this?"

Ericsson went to work.

Chapter Twenty-Six

Elijahn knew he would be right. They were predictable. True, they had blindsided him before, and they had obviously found out who he was, that he was behind the data center destruction, that he had stolen information belonging to IDSD, that he was after their Oracle. That was what the woman had said.

Thinking about her made his control waver, and he had to make a conscious effort to stifle the rage that burned in him. He had no idea what had happened to her. His people had no time to report to him before those damn soldiers attacked them, and he had had to run. Did they get her? Was she with them when they were attacked? Would they remember that if there was no other way he would want them to kill her, not risk letting her be rescued?

Not knowing was excruciating, and it was what had brought him here. He no longer had any other choice but to go directly to the computer itself. Oracle was far more important. If the woman was dead, destroying the computer would be an added bonus. If she was still alive, it would be a necessity.

At least one of the two had to be gone for his plan to succeed. And perhaps she would be there, with her blasted creation, and he would have his revenge. His plans of taking her were ruined, which was most unfortunate indeed, but even her death would be not only necessary, but also extremely satisfying.

And if after that day he still did not know what happened to her, he would look for her later, find out if she was alive. With the power he would have once he exposed the existence of Oracle to all those who had abandoned him, and proved that he had singlehandedly destroyed it—without telling them of the failures on the way, of course—and with the patience he had disciplined himself to have, he would find her. And he would, eventually, kill her. Not only because if she was alive she could create another Oracle. Yes, that too. But mostly because he wanted so very much to kill her.

He was having no luck controlling his hatred. That was bad. He felt his man's eyes on him and forced himself under control. He was lucky the man was still loyal, even after this last staggering failure. He could not allow him to think something might be disturbing the completion of the plan. Another failure, another weakness, would not be forgiven.

They were walking inside the IDSD complex. Right there in the open. Elijahn sneered. It had been so easy getting into this so-called secure place. He had chosen the one role that would allow them to do as they pleased without anyone questioning their presence there. Security agents. The clothes both he and his man wore and the handgun Elijahn held were courtesy of the security agent he had killed. Ransacking the dead man's house had been meant to hide the theft, and it obviously worked. The man had, of course, only one handgun, but the jackets Elijahn and his man wore on this cool night helped hide the fact that one of their weapons was not standard issue. True, there were more elegant ways to do this, but since he had killed the hacker, and as all of his men but one were dead and he was out of time, he had no choice but to settle for some footwork.

His luck, it seemed, had finally changed. He had gotten away and had rendezvoused with his man at the extra car, a sedan disguised as an IDSD vehicle he had made sure was safely hidden, which had all they needed in it. He had not planned to use it this way. It had originally been there to allow him to transfer the woman to it and disguise himself and his men as he had now, in case they were stopped on the way to the plane. But this was as good a use for it as any.

They had waited for some hours, he and his last remaining man. The best time to enter IDSD was at shift change, and he had worried that because only some twenty-four hours had passed since his failed attacks, there would be too much security at the gates. But the substantial forces that had been there these past days were already gone. Which did make sense. After what had transpired only miles outside this place, they would expect him to be far away by now, trying to run, to disappear. And who knows, it occurred to him, perhaps they even thought he was among the dead.

They had entered on foot from the secondary IDSD gate adjacent to the residential part of this huge complex, where shift change, in fact the end of the second shift, meant the gate had quite a few people on foot walking through it. They had followed closely behind incoming security agents dressed like them, conversing animatedly, and the guards at the gate, a sleepy lot this time of night in this obviously lower security entrance, had given their IDs only a cursory glance and did not even ask them, did not ask any of the new shift's staff, in fact, to let the automated system scan their IDs. The IDs were perfect forgeries, down to a chip assigned an identical coded signal to that which the dead security agent's ID had in it, for Elijahn, a risk, of course, if it was no longer valid, and no signal for that of his man, which he could cite as a malfunction, if need be. It was fortunate that they were not scanned. Or, perhaps, it was a sign of his impending success.

Elijahn might have been worried about venturing into IDSD this way. But the fact that even after he had broken into and destroyed the data center, which led to increased security everywhere, he still managed so easily to kill an IDSD senior security agent and use his ID and access authorizations to steal the information he wanted, had taught him that despite its obviously substantial security, IDSD was not very good at protecting itself. He was, he knew, so very unpredictable for them, and so much smarter. It was all a bit too obvious perhaps, but then he had managed to get into the United States so easily because nobody saw the obvious. So why not just walk into IDSD? They would not be looking for him here. True, it was a risk. But he had to take it. After all that had happened, he had to.

Now that he and his man were in, they walked quickly to their destination through the darkness, meeting no one on their way. The three-story building was silent, dormant this time of night. The only signs of life were the lighted front entrance and the lobby beyond it, and sporadic lights that shone in the upper-floor windows. Elijahn stood looking at the name on the building. Advanced Technology Research. He felt his excitement rise.

They skirted the building and approached it from the small parking lot adjacent to it, on its right, and found the side door they were looking for. Elijahn expected the front doors to have biometric identification and perhaps also security agents—this was after all an important building for IDSD—but side doors tended to be overlooked. It was closed, though, and Elijahn told his man to cover him and attached a small device to the lock. The device interfered with the lock's local signal, and the red light on it began switching between red and green. Then it turned off. Elijahn opened the door, motioned his man in, and followed him, detaching the device and shutting the door. The lock resumed working.

The corridor they were in was empty, but neither of them drew their guns. If there were cameras there, Elijahn wanted them to see two harmless security agents. With their caps low on their heads, they would not be suspected. They walked silently through the floor, avoiding the lobby, until finally Elijahn found the door to the stairwell. He opened it and went in, his man following him. He was right. This was an obvious place to have a guidance screen that would tell anyone using the stairs what was on the floor they were on.

The artificial intelligence was not on this floor, only conference rooms and administrative offices. Both the underground floor and the upper floor had research labs. Elijahn thought for a moment, recalling what his unfortunately dead hacker had told him about the conditions that type of a computer would need. He then descended the stairs, his man following him.

It was colder down here, and the hum of the massive cooling systems reverberated in the air. This had to be it. They inched forward. This corridor was so much wider, white, flawless. They passed a transparent door to their left, then another. The first room was empty. The second had some people in it, scientists in white lab coats and masks who did not turn around, did not see them, too intent on their work. This was not it. He proceeded to the next door —some more people here—then to another, and then he halted. Ahead, the corridor ended in a wall with a large sliding door in it. A screen to the left of the door flashed a name. O.R.A.C.L.E. Command. He knew the symbol under it. High clearance access only. The active biometric system under the screen told him there was no way he could get in.

He raised his gun and shot it.

The biometric system went dead and the door began to open but Elijahn wasn't looking at it any longer, he had already turned to look behind him. No alarm was sounding. He had shot the biometric system protecting the room Oracle was in and yet there was no alarm. And they had met no people on the streets of this major complex. And this place was silent. Too silent, even for a research building, and even at this time of night. And where were all the people who should have been beside the artificial intelligence? The door to where it was housed was opening, so where were the voices of those who should have been inside with it? Not bothering to look back at what lay beyond the opening door, he walked quickly to the last room he had seen those scientists in. He peeked inside. No one.

He swerved back at his man's shout, an edge of panic to his words. "It's empty. There is nothing here."

He was in a basement. Trapped. He ran toward the stairs, aimed and shot at the first of the soldiers who were running down them, futile shots that could not penetrate body armor, and did not turn at the shots behind him, then the silence, as more soldiers, some still clad in lab coats, broke through the rooms along the corridor and shot his man who had shot at them.

Disbelief came first, and rage followed, overtook him, blinded him. But that exactly had been his mistake, he now realized. He should have run, regrouped like last time. Instead, his mind had been on a single track since the failure of the night before, when his targets—*all* of them—had gotten away from him, and the woman, the one true target, had gotten the better of him, preventing the completion of his plan and getting his men, his best men, killed. A woman, of all things.

The rage threatened to take over again but there was no time, he had to think fast. He thought about what he wanted, what was important to him. He would not, could not let himself be paraded out of here like a lowly terrorist. Already they were shouting at him to put it down, put the gun down, lie on the floor and put his hands behind his head.

Never.

He emptied his gun into them and felt shots hit him, waited for it to end.

But it didn't, they had purposely avoided fatal injury. His rage masked the pain and he lunged at his captors, but they caught him from behind, held him. He struggled but to no avail.

Around him the clear shouts reverberated, all the way to the top of the stairwell above him. The civilian clad in black who came down the stairs had him begin to lower his eyes in disinterest. The woman who descended the stairs behind him had him struggling to stand up.

"You!"

"Hello, Elijahn," she said.

"You set me up. It was all a setup." He understood now. His eyes filled with hate. "Again."

"Yes. But this one is the end. For you." This was the first time Donovan heard ice in Lara's voice.

"We've been watching you since before you approached the gate. Contrary to what you seem to think, we're rather particular about who comes into IDSD." Ericsson had followed behind Lara, more of his security agents, mixed in with Martinez's joint force soldiers, behind him.

"But the security agents, they didn't even look," Elijahn said, trying to figure this out.

Ericsson laughed. "It's the security you don't see that keeps this place safe. Oh, and this building? Nice catch. Except that it's been empty for a week now, they've just finished moving into their nice new building. It's bigger, too. Hey, we thought they deserve it, you know."

Elijahn turned his gaze to Lara, his eyes blazing with hatred. "I will kill you. If it's the last thing I do, I will kill you!"

"The only thing you're going to do is stare at

blank walls in a very, very solitary cell for the rest of your miserable life," Martinez said behind him.

But Elijahn wasn't interested in anyone except this devil of a woman who had destroyed him. "I will still have my revenge. When I do not return, my people will release everything we have about Oracle. The audios from my base that you and your Oracle destroyed, the data I stole from that data center, all of it. Everything we have, and the details we stole about your people, all those names, the photos. You. *Your* photo. You think I have not sent it all to my headquarters? You think this was a problem for me?" He laughed, that cruel laugh Lara remembered from the night before. "They will tell everyone, all those we have ever worked with, all the others, what Oracle is doing to them. Everyone will know and they will come after all those names my people now have, you among them. You will never be able to hide, you will never be safe. Imagine it, the world's terrorists coming after Oracle. It will be destroyed. IDSD, the Internationals' dream, will be destroyed. The allies will be ridiculed. And I will be remembered as the man who exposed Oracle, who made its destruction possible." He laughed, then coughed, blood trickling from the side of his mouth. And then his expression changed and the laugh ebbed.

Donovan followed his gaze, turned and saw the glimmer in Lara's eyes, her lips curve up a little.

"Would those be your people in your headquarters under the Sahara?" she said quietly.

Elijahn struggled feebly against his holders. "No. No, that's impossible!"

She tilted her head slightly, her eyes intense. "Your headquarters and everything, everyone in it will be destroyed before the night is over. I did that too, just so you know. You, Elijahn, will be forgotten." And she turned and walked away.

"I found out about Oracle, about you. Others will too," Elijahn shouted after her, livid.

"Maybe," Donovan said to him, his voice low. "But thanks to you, we now know that's a possibility. We'll be ready."

With a raging, desperate snarl, Elijahn broke free, snatched a gun out of the thigh holster of the soldier standing over him, and aimed it at Lara's back.

Donovan shot him.

The satellite feed on the spanning wall screen of Mission Command looked almost serene. The great desert was beautiful, majestic. Innocent.

If one didn't know the secret it concealed under it.

Above endless golden dunes, stealth fighters uncloaked, hovering silently in the sky. As the onboard sensors tracked remotely and confirmed, missiles shot out, drilling into the sand, their momentum enhanced by powerful internal motors. Silence ensued, no sound but the shifting mounds of sand.

And then the very ground exploded. Unmoving,

cloaked again, the fighters waited, unaffected by the powerful shock waves around them. Only when they confirmed that there were no life signs, no signals, that nothing at all remained, did they leave. Once they were far enough away, a single bomb still laying in wait in the destruction below was sent a detonation signal, and moments later only a crater was left.

Oracle was safe once again.

As the IDSD gate grew distant behind them, Lara became increasingly restless. Now and again Donovan glanced at her, knowing that in her mind she was back in the previous night, driving down this same road, fully aware that she was about to be attacked. She was reliving the events of that night, the standoff with Elijahn, the hunt for her. Her rescue, almost too late. Too close to being too late.

As they reached the place where she had gone off the road he slowed the car down and crossed to its opposite side, then stopped on a small rise. The road was empty, their only companion the light of a new day rising above the sprawling woods where she was so relentlessly chased, where he had come for her.

She had turned in her seat and was looking in his direction, not at him but beyond him, at the open stretch of ground she could clearly see from where he had stopped the car, at the spot where the wreckage of her convertible, now marked only by charred earth, had stood. The memory was clear in her eyes, in the furrow of her brow, in the tension in her body.

She didn't notice that he had turned to face her, moving close, didn't notice his hand rise to settle on her waist, didn't feel it until his other hand caressed her cheek, and as her eyes shifted to him she saw him, saw *him*, as he pulled her close and touched his lips to hers in a soft kiss.

The shock to both of them was unexpected. How could such a simple touch be so much, he thought, how could it feel like this, she couldn't begin to understand, even as her lips parted against his, accepted.

"This is what I want you to remember, to think about when you drive by here from now on," he murmured, and kissed her again, the promise of love, the recklessness of passion, and a hint of surrender resonating in them both.

Donovan drove, his hand holding Lara's between them. His eyes flickered to her. Her head rested on the headrest, her thoughts deep within herself. He'd seen the weariness in her eyes already earlier, when they'd left Mission Command after the destruction of Elijahn's headquarters. He'd insisted they go to the medical center then, so that Dr. Mallory would have a look at her injuries again. But he knew that this wouldn't help where it really mattered.

Now that they were almost home, that stretch of road that would no longer be her focus behind her, it was finally over. Elijahn was no longer a danger, there was no longer an imminent threat to her, and even Oracle could take a moment, think. All she could do now, all it made sense that she would do, was look back at it all, play it over in her mind. Events and actions, too, but mostly the implications for those around her. For herself.

For him. He knew that by now. In her mind, she'd been the one under attack, and any casualties were about her, as she couldn't help but see it, being the woman she was. And he could have been one of them. And this, what had awakened between them, her acceptance of it finally, was putting what could have happened to him in a whole new light.

He felt it himself, for her. This investigation had brought him face to face with the one thing that had never interfered with his work in the past. The one thing that had never interfered with his life, in the past. Love. He thought of that moment when he had thought she had been in the car that blew up, a moment he was never likely to forget. The grief that had seared him.

And then that split second when he'd realized that she was still alive. What it felt like when he wrapped his arms around her, pulled her to him, to safety.

The implications would follow them both for a. while.

Arriving home, he pulled into her driveway, and turned to her. "Lara?" he said quietly.

She didn't answer, didn't move.

"Lara." His voice was insistent, wanting, needing to push through.

"I called you."

He frowned. "Good. That's what I wanted you to do."

"I put you in danger. You could have been hurt."

"Don't."

She finally looked at him, and he was taken aback by what he saw in her eyes. "You didn't ask to be a part of this," she said. "That was my doing, this entire investigation was about me, and I . . . I was the one to call you, I put you in danger." I could have lost you, she thought, but didn't say. She closed her eyes and leaned her head back again. This was one thing she couldn't bear, couldn't even begin to deal with. Losing him. It sent echoes into places inside her that had been raw with pain for so long now that she had gotten used to having them in the background, and was accentuating them, feeding on them. This one, this man beside her, was still here, now, alive. She still felt his kiss on her lips, in her heart. And the reality that he could have been killed was unbearable.

This precisely was what scared him the most. This. Not that she would push him away again, he was beyond letting that happen. But the reality that she just might one day do this again, hide what she was doing from him and stand in harm's way so that he himself wouldn't be hurt, was unthinkable. "Look at me."

She didn't move.

"Lara, look at me."

Surprised at the fierce edge in his voice, she opened her eyes and turned to look at him.

"Don't you ever not tell me that you need me, that you're in trouble, don't you ever try to protect me by exposing yourself to danger again." He held her eyes, the stormy blue in his unrelenting, the overpowering fear in him that he might not be there when she needed him ambushing him into losing control. For him, too, the events of the night before were still too vivid.

She saw it with clarity, felt him, the force of his emotions. She nodded.

"That's settled then," he said, his heart still raging, this thing that now had hold of him never again intending to let go.

He got out of the car and walked over to the passenger side, met her as she got out and offered her his hand.

She took it.

Please turn the page for an extract from
the next book in the Oracle series

ORACLE'S DIPLOMACY

Chapter One

"Thank you," Ambassador George Sendor said in a distracted tone as the steward placed a cup of Earl Grey with a touch of orange flavor before him. He didn't look at the young man, instead keeping his eyes on the endless sky outside the window.

The steward was not offended. The ambassador was not a rude man, nor one to disregard those who worked for him. He was kind and caring, and took to heart any offense he might have caused. And the steward, the entire crew of the official executive jet, in fact, had been with the ambassador for the past two and a half years in his extensive travels. They knew he appreciated them. No, the distinguished man was not rude or uncaring. He was simply preoccupied, and for a good reason.

The assistant sitting across from Sendor acknowledged the steward with a smile as the young man placed a cup of coffee before him. "How're we doing today, Cyril?"

"Very well, sir. Clear sky, no turbulence. Looks like a quiet flight all the way." The steward's tone was calm, practiced.

They were flying home to Belgium—Brussels, to be exact—after four days at the negotiating table, long days that were the final milestone in an endless line of negotiations. The main terms and covenants had now been finalized, and all that remained was for the two sides to confirm their respective governments' acceptance of them. If all went well, within days, weeks at the most, they would be on their way back on this very jet, not for further negotiations but for a festive treaty-signing ceremony.

The assistant waited until the steward left, then resumed watching the man he had served for many years now, long before Sendor became an ambassador, before the assistant himself knew the kind of difference the older man could make in the lives of so many, that he would succeed where no one else had.

"Your tea, Ambassador," he prodded.

"Yes. Yes, of course." Sendor turned to him with a sigh.

"What are you thinking about, sir?"

"Hoping, more than thinking, I suppose, Lucas."

"It seems to have gone well." In fact, no one had ever gotten this far in mellowing the tense relations between the sworn enemies.

"Indeed." Sendor sipped the exquisite blend, let its warmth, its aroma, wash over him, tried hard to surrender to its calming effect. "Indeed," he repeated. Nothing he had done in his long decades in diplomatic service had been as important to him, had touched him as much as this, the negotiations that had been going on for more than two years and had now finally matured into what really did look like a viable peace accord. Bitter years of hatred and fighting, unspeakable suffering, were finally about to end. Still, Sendor couldn't help considering it all—the situation, the negotiations, the peace accord itself, the prospects for the future—again and again, worried he might have missed something, concerned that what had been so painstakingly achieved would not stand up to the test. Fearful there would be more deaths.

"Are you considering their request?"

Sendor's brow furrowed. The previous evening he had been asked to remain in the region after the peace accord was signed, as the ambassador to both countries. Rather unusual, true, but in this unique case it was most likely the best way to keep what would undoubtedly be a fragile peace alive. Except that at sixty-eight he had been looking forward to retiring, finally spending much needed time with his family. His sons had both settled in the Ardennes, their birthplace, with their families, and he would have liked to settle there himself, move back to the house he had brought them up in, spend more time with them and his grandchildren.

But that might have to wait. How could he live the rest of his life enjoying his grandchildren, watching them grow up safe and protected, when so many other children were dying because he wasn't there to secure their safety? Both sides in the negotiations finally trusted him, his motives, his ability to stand behind his words. This would not be an easy peace, and someone had to be there to take it through its first steps, make sure it did not fall apart. After so many years of dispute, too much had happened, there were so much anger and bitterness, terrible pain to deal with. The two nations, the people behind this peace accord, needed to heal, rebuild, make it to a day when they could meet on a peaceful city street without instantly feeling animosity, without resorting to raging violence.

So much work to do, and only he could do it, he was all too aware. No one knew them as he did after all he had been through with them during these difficult years.

He took in a deep breath. "Yes, I do believe I will have no choice but to—"

A barely perceptible shudder passed through the aircraft. The ambassador and his assistant both sat up, startled. In the galley, the steward stabilized himself against the countertop and sent a bewildered look at the closed cockpit door.

In the cockpit, Captain Laura Yates frowned at the autopilot. Beside her, her copilot turned to look at her, perplexed.

"What the hell was that?" he asked.

"I have no idea." Yates's eyes were on the flight

instruments before her. "Whatever it was, it didn't show on our instruments."

"The autopilot is working properly."

"It wasn't an internal—"

The plane shuddered again, more violently this time.

"What on . . . ?" Yates's hand hovered over the instruments panel, and both she and her copilot stared in astonishment as the autopilot disengaged, relinquishing control to some hidden hand. The jet kept going, level. Yates touched the panel once, then again. Nothing.

Moments later, the altitude indicator showed the altitude changing, even as the pilots themselves felt the aircraft turn, then begin to descend.

"Who the hell is flying this plane?" The copilot looked out, then realized the absurdity of the act at forty-one thousand feet.

Yates flipped switches, operated touchscreens, went through every procedure she could think of that could do something, anything, to give her back control of the jet. Beside her, the copilot followed suit. But the aircraft didn't respond. This is no malfunction, Yates thought as the altitude indicated on the screen before her kept decreasing, the aircraft steady in its descent. Someone is controlling this jet, and it isn't me.

Her precious cargo in mind, she wasn't about to take any chances. "Mayday, Mayday, Mayday," she repeated, her tone urgent, then relayed the aircraft's identification and position and hoped to God someone was listening, would come to their help. But she already knew no one would, and could only watch helplessly as even as she spoke the radio was shut off. Next to go was the ACARS, and a quick check found that the transponder and the ADS-B had been disabled. She no longer had any way to communicate with anyone on the ground, nor were there any remaining means on board the jet that would have allowed it to be tracked. Still, she recounted what was happening in detail, hoping that the cockpit voice recorder would, together with the flight data recorder, at least give those she hoped might eventually find them what they would need to make sense of this.

The last thing she did as the cabin pressure dropped was pray that she would see her daughter again.

At the headquarters of International Diplomacy, Security and Defense in Brussels, the Internationals' High Council was meeting with the heads of IDSD's branches worldwide to review strategies past and future and their implications for the present. Everyone sitting in the vast upper-floor conference room was pleased. It had been a good year. A new member had joined the alliance of peaceful nations, and another had requested to join it just days earlier, in thanks for the alliance's help in a recent incident, assistance it gave without asking for anything in return. The African Independent Territory was in one of the more precarious spots in the world, and its acceptance into the alliance would be the first successful diplomatic footprint it made in the region. Granted, there was still a lot of work to be done there, but as the pillar of the alliance IDSD was more than ready to do what it took. It always was.

And then there was the promising news from the one place in Europe that had been rapidly going from bad to worse these past years, where the political divide between Eastern and Western Europe had once been. Two small countries that could have been a symbol of unity, cultural safe havens that would have set an example for so many, had instead been entangled in an endless feud that some years earlier had finally spiraled out of control, sending the two neighbors into a destructive war and sparking mutual atrocities that had not been seen in that part of the world for more than half a century. No one had been able to make the two nations talk, try to stop what was happening. No one until the Internationals' own Ambassador George Sendor had stepped in and, refusing to give up, had stuck with them through flare after flare of renewed distrust and violence, until he managed to get them to listen to him and had helped them see another future for themselves and for their children. And now, after all the time and effort, the High Council could finally welcome news of an imminent peace treaty.

Ambassador Sendor was on his way to the High Council's meeting now, and would be joining it sometime during its second half. The Council was hoping he would accept their offer to remain in the region and watch over the implementation of the new treaty as the ambassador to both countries. The remarkable man was worthy of their trust, their respect, their support.

Council Head Ines Stevenssen was about to proceed with the next item on the agenda when the conference room door burst open and a pale aide rushed in, followed by the deputy head of security of this branch of IDSD, Julian Bern.

"Ma'am." The aide deferred to the council head.

Stevenssen motioned him and Bern in. Through the open door behind them, she saw people gathering, their agitation evident.

Bern approached the conference table. "I've just received a call from Brussels Air Control Center," he said. "They've lost contact with Ambassador Sendor's jet. The last they have is a distress call from the pilot on the emergency frequency, which was cut off almost immediately but was without doubt relayed while the plane was still in the air. They've informed IDSD Global Flights Monitoring Station, which has initiated a search protocol." He paused. "So far, they've had no success making contact with the jet. It has vanished."

The trailer was silent.

From the outside, it and the tractor unit it was connected to could be mistaken for an old semitrailer not worth the trouble of a second look, parked carelessly off the road, its driver probably having sought a quiet place to catch some rest. And there was in fact someone in the driver's seat, a man who was seemingly asleep, a black cap down over his eyes. Even with the windows up and the heater running, he had a short coat on, and his hands were crossed on his chest. To hide the gun.

The other guards—and there were quite a few of them—were deployed at varying distances around the trailer, all hidden from sight. Not that they had to be hidden, or would even be needed at all. There was no one for miles around, and no one knew anyone was there. And even if someone happened to stray into the area, perhaps stumble upon any of the hidden men, no one had even a remote chance of guessing what their mission was, what they were protecting.

Still, it didn't hurt to be cautious, considering the stakes involved.

Inside, the trailer was far from simple, nothing innocent about it. It had been converted to house, power and protect a system unlike any other in the world. Few knew this system existed, and fewer yet knew it was already operational. In fact, it was fully active now, working to the limit of its capacity in this, its maiden task.

The two men overseeing the system's activity were silent. They worked with precise efficiency, noting every single datum on the screens before them, knowing they must miss nothing. There was no time for words.

They were too busy controlling the jet flying high above them.

The initial shock had worn off, and the mood in the upper-floor conference room of IDSD's headquarters was somber. Council Head Stevenssen had adjourned the meeting for an extended break immediately after hearing the news, to give everyone time to settle, to adjust to what was thought to be a tragedy that had befallen one of IDSD's most revered diplomats, a friend to many of them. The break was also intended to give Bern a chance to collect more information and, perhaps most important at that point, to give Stevenssen herself the time she needed to make sure the news would not get out. Until more was known about what had happened, she had to do her best to ensure that the two nations whose future was on the line would not find out prematurely that their best, perhaps only, chance for a lasting peace was gone. If they would blame each other—and they would, their history had shown—there would be no stopping the tragic consequences, ever again.

Having reconvened the meeting, and with a pang of regret as she realized Sendor would by now have been here with them, Stevenssen took a long look at her peers sitting around the table, their eyes expectant on her.

"I have been given additional information," she said, coming straight to the point. "However, I suggest Julian impart it himself, since he has been in direct contact with IDSD Global Flights Monitoring Station."

Bern stepped forward. "They don't think the jet crashed."

He had everyone's attention.

"Signals from all systems on board designed to communicate the jet's location disappeared more or less simultaneously. So together with the pilot's emergency call the first thought was catastrophic failure. However, the emergency locator transmitters on board whose activation would have been triggered by a crash were not activated. Also, the jet was over land when it disappeared and our satellites would have found a crash site by now around its last recorded position, or we would have had reports from witnesses. There's nothing.

"The monitoring station has attempted to access the flight data recorder remotely—I don't know if you're aware of it, but this capability was developed to avoid the delay, proven critical too often, in having to search for the recorder in the event of an air accident or an attack, and the risk of being unable to find it if the search takes too long and the recorder ceases to communicate its location because its batteries run out." He paused. "However, the recorder cannot be accessed. We are being actively locked out."

"Could a signal jammer have been used?" The man asking was Admiral Helios, head of IDSD in the United States. It was the recent Oracle incident involving his IDSD branch that had brought to their attention the existence, in the hands of the wrong people, of a sophisticated type of jammers one of the applications of which was to conceal the flight path of an aircraft.

"No, sir, we don't believe so. We don't know much yet about that jammer I'm assuming you're referring to, how it works, but I believe a jammer would have caused a different type of interference, not what we're seeing here."

Helios nodded, although he clearly wasn't entirely convinced.

"Couldn't the emergency locator...what was it, transmitters? Couldn't they have malfunctioned?" the High Council's deputy head asked.

"There are two of them installed on the jet, sir, as a safety measure, given its designation, and it is unlikely both would have malfunctioned simultaneously," Bern answered.

"Could something have happened on board, incapacitating everyone? In which case, wouldn't the aircraft still have continued to fly on autopilot?" The speaker, Council Member Sloan, had been a military officer in her past, a combat fighter pilot. She would know her stuff, Bern knew.

"Theoretically, yes, ma'am, and the aircraft certainly had enough fuel. However, if that were the case, we would have been able to access the autopilot and take control of the aircraft. We can't. We have ascertained that the autopilot has been turned off. And no, the one thing we already know is that the aircraft did not continue on its predesignated route. He cleared his throat. "Also, once the monitoring station realized it is unable to contact the jet, it calculated possible routes for it beginning with its last known position. So far, satellites have found nothing along any of these routes." He hesitated. "I think at this point we can safely assume that the jet is no longer in the air."

Silence fell as the implications sank in.

"Are you telling us that the plane was somehow taken?" the head of Australia IDSD asked.

"That seems to be the most likely possibility. The question is by whom and how. The aircraft went through the automated pre-flight scan. Other than the ambassador and his executive assistant only the regular crew and the protective detail were on board, and I can tell you we can vouch for every one of them."

"So what the hell happened to it?" Council Member Richmond, an old friend of Ambassador Sendor, was understandably upset.

Before Bern could answer, his phone rang. He glanced at it, then excused himself and took the call. Everyone in the room remained silent, waiting expectantly.

Bern muted the call and looked at them. "The monitoring station has located the jet. It seems to have landed on the artificial extension of Cres, the Croatian island. From the air it looks intact. The alliance naval base at Split has dispatched helicopters to the area."

The room was hushed as they waited. No one dared think of the possibilities. Everyone hoped.

Bern, too, waited, the phone at his ear. He was patched through, heard it all. After endless minutes, he finally lowered the phone, stared at it. "I'm sorry. The jet's crew, the ambassador's assistant, the protective detail, they're dead. They're all dead."

He raised his eyes to the stricken leaders before him. "Ambassador Sendor is gone."

Chapter Two

While Ambassador George Sendor was still sipping his orange-flavored Earl Grey tea forty-one thousand feet above Europe, contemplating the fate of nations and mercifully oblivious to his own, Lara Holsworth was just waking up in Washington, DC. She had left the blinds open so that the sun would shine into the bedroom in the morning, and it did, another clear autumn day. Winter would be here soon enough, but she was glad it hadn't arrived just yet. She got out of bed and put a robe on, then went to the window and looked out at the house's peaceful back yard. Delaying, she realized. It was simple, really. She was delaying starting the day.

Donovan wasn't here.

This is crazy, she thought. How can I miss him? How can I miss him already? Shaking her head, surprised at herself but not entirely displeased with this new feeling, she descended the stairs to the quiet of the first floor, the late morning sun greeting her here, too, in a renewed attempt to distract her. The main security console was silently active, and for the first time in days she had no reason to give it even a cursory glance. The coffee-maker purred in the kitchen, and she contemplated it, then reconsidered and turned to go back upstairs to shower and dress when her phone chirped upstairs, then automatically sent the arriving message to the media screen closest to her. The text message made her smile.

"Have breakfast. The kind I would make you."

So he wasn't asleep. And he wasn't at his place, otherwise he would already be here with her. He had brought her back home that morning just as the sun peeked over the horizon, after first insisting on another detour to the IDSD medical center. The agents guarding her and her home were, to her relief, gone by then, all except the two who had stayed behind to formally pass the house security back to Donovan. After making sure she would go straight to bed, he had gone back to his own house next door, to get some sleep. Apparently that hadn't worked so well. But then, being a United States Federal Investigative Division senior investigator was no less demanding than her own job.

The smile wouldn't go away. "Where are you?" she dictated back.

"On a case," was his answer. "I'll come by as soon as I get back. How're you doing?"

She sent him a smile.

This is crazy, she thought again as she made herself breakfast. But the smile was still on her face.

Join our mailing list on www.authorandsister.net
for updates about additional books by
A. Claire Everward

Lightning Source UK Ltd.
Milton Keynes UK
UKHW011100170520
363415UK00001B/1